The Best
AMERICAN SHORT STORIES 2008

GUEST EDITORS OF
THE BEST AMERICAN SHORT STORIES

1978 TED SOLOTAROFF
1979 JOYCE CAROL OATES
1980 STANLEY ELKIN
1981 HORTENSE CALISHER
1982 JOHN GARDNER
1983 ANNE TYLER
1984 JOHN UPDIKE
1985 GAIL GODWIN
1986 RAYMOND CARVER
1987 ANN BEATTIE
1988 MARK HELPRIN
1989 MARGARET ATWOOD
1990 RICHARD FORD
1991 ALICE ADAMS
1992 ROBERT STONE
1993 LOUISE ERDRICH
1994 TOBIAS WOLFF
1995 JANE SMILEY
1996 JOHN EDGAR WIDEMAN
1997 E. ANNIE PROULX
1998 GARRISON KEILLOR
1999 AMY TAN
2000 E. L. DOCTOROW
2001 BARBARA KINGSOLVER
2002 SUE MILLER
2003 WALTER MOSLEY
2004 LORRIE MOORE
2005 MICHAEL CHABON
2006 ANN PATCHETT
2007 STEPHEN KING
2008 SALMAN RUSHDIE

The Best
AMERICAN SHORT STORIES® 2008

Selected from
U.S. and Canadian Magazines
by SALMAN RUSHDIE
with HEIDI PITLOR

With an Introduction by Salman Rushdie

HOUGHTON MIFFLIN COMPANY
BOSTON • NEW YORK 2008

www.houghtonmifflinbooks.com

ISSN 0067-6233
ISBN 978-0-618-78876-7
ISBN 978-0-618-78877-4 (pbk.)

Printed in the United States of America

VB 10 9 8 7 6 5 4 3 2 1

Contents

Foreword

SOME DAYS, the title of this book weighs on me. Nearly every word is slippery. *Best,* for starters. Whose definition of *best*? I read thousands of stories a year, and even on the ninth straight day of freezing rain, when my whole family has the flu, when every piece of technology upon which I foolishly rely has broken, when a stranger cuts me off in traffic and then gives me the finger — even on this day, I am to remain open and objective and decide which stories are the best? Even if the story I happen to be reading is told from the viewpoint of an enraged IT worker who is prone to cutting off women in traffic in the rain?

What about *American*? Salman Rushdie and I clung to the criteria listed at the end of my foreword, the same criteria that have appeared in this book for twenty-five years. But these broad outlines don't address the gray area — one wants adjectives, subjectivity. American short stories are bloody or prudish, they are sexy, they are flashy — aren't they? Or do these words describe something else? American TV and movies, perhaps, or a non-American's view of American TV and film? I'm sometimes asked to comment on what makes a short story American or the state of the American short story landscape, and my first instinct is to say, "Please don't ask me these questions." Because no single answer comes to mind. How can you unite naturalism with surrealism with minimalism with maximalism (all in vogue these days) in merely a sentence or two? It's a bit like trying to describe the country's political landscape. More than ever, we are a messy nation of opposites, a rumbling extended family full of warring aunts and uncles, nieces holding grudges, stepsisters and half brothers, brothers and sisters who are inseparable and others who don't speak. In this election year, it seems that stark contrasts are the norm.

All right, surely the term *short story* can be quantified. But after searching far and wide, I've yet to discover a standard word length, or even a standard neighborhood. And what about short shorts? Flash fiction? Prose poems? My personal favorite, "long short stories"? In some magazines (you know who you are), fiction and nonfiction aren't even differentiated — sometimes they're all unhelpfully labeled "prose."

Lest you think the good people of Houghton Mifflin Harcourt hired a timid, wishy-washy series editor, I will say that in my second year on the job, I've taught myself to be a lot more decisive. *Best* and *American* and *Short* and *Story* may change in some senses from day to day, but there are those fixed criteria. For at the end of the day, no person has the time or, let's be honest, the wherewithal to read every piece of potentially American, verging-on-novella-length-fiction-that-could-be-nonfiction-or-poetry. I need the criteria listed below because I am human and must, like all of us, limit what I read, or I will find myself doing nothing but eating, drinking, sleeping, and breathing short (or shortish) fiction.

This year's guest editor has the unique vantage point of a native non-American living part-time in the United States. What a treat to work with such an imaginative, rigorous writer and reader. It was fascinating to watch him try to understand the lay of this part of the land. More than anything, Rushdie proved to be a fan of surprise, of those who dare to rethink our world (as do Kevin Brockmeier in "The Year of Silence" and Karen Russell in "Vampires in the Lemon Grove" and Katie Chase in "Man and Wife"), and of humor (see Jonathan Lethem's "The King of Sentences" and T. C. Boyle's "Admiral"). He was drawn to stories that crackled with energy and life (see Danielle Evans's "Virgins" and Karen Brown's "Galatea"). Are surprise and humor and energy particularly South Asian qualities? Who knows, but I will say that every story between these two covers, thankfully, sits squarely within at least my and Salman's and the series' definitions of *Best* and *American* and *Short.*

And so, happily, I give you the criteria for inclusion in *The Best American Short Stories,* with a new addition for electronic publications. The stories chosen for this anthology were originally published between January 2007 and January 2008. The qualifications for selection are (1) original publication in nationally distributed American or Canadian periodicals; (2) publication in English by writers who are American or Canadian, or who have made the United States their home; (3) original publication as short stories (excerpts of novels are not knowingly considered). A list of magazines consulted for this volume appears at the back of the book. Editors who wish their short fiction to be considered for next year's edition should send their publications or hard copies of online publications to Heidi Pitlor, c/o *The Best American Short Stories,* Houghton Mifflin Harcourt, 222 Berkeley Street, Boston, MA 02116.

HEIDI PITLOR

Introduction

OKAY: SO I'M NOT an American, let's acknowledge that right away, and I am therefore unusually conscious of what a privilege it is to be guest editor of this year's *Best American Short Stories,* an anthology series with a long, distinguished American pedigree, celebrating a form as American as baseball, hot dogs, apple pie, and Chevrolet. I am, however, a New Yorker, or am beginning to be one, and one of the best things about this great city is that everyone who brings their story here finds that it, too, at once becomes a New York story, one among the great crowd of stories that have arrived on these shores from elsewhere — from so very many elsewheres. True, America has become fearful of late, its doors have not been open to the world's huddled masses in the old, generous way, but still the world's stories somehow continue to make their journeys to America, and metamorphose, with remarkable ease, into new American tales.

An old question — *what is an American story?* — is given a new lease on life in our interconnected, migratory, suspicious, troubled age. What is an American short story? Is it, at its purest and best — like, say, the stories of Damon Runyon and Raymond Carver — a story by an American, about Americans, set in America? Or does any story set in the United States, even though its author is not American, qualify? (In which case P. G. Wodehouse, who often brought the immortal Jeeves and Bertie Wooster to New York, and the Kafka of *Amerika,* would both be eligible.) Are stories written by Americans about places other than America still American stories? (If not, how impoverished American literature would be, deprived of so much of Hemingway, Fitzgerald, et al.) Should the rule be that the story should be first published in America, whoever wrote it? (That would have excluded at least one story in this selection, the shockingly brilliant "May We Be Forgiven" by A. M. Homes, an American whose story was first published in the British magazine *Granta*.)

Who exactly is an American these days, by the way? Canadians, for example? Are they, for our purposes, to be considered Americans too? (Yes, otherwise we would have to exclude Alice Munro, and what a foolish decision *that* would be.) What about, for example, a writer of Pakistani origin who has spent a fair bit of time in the United States but has since returned to Pakistan? (Heidi Pitlor, the series' gently redoubtable editor, and I had to scratch our heads a bit about that one.) What about Latin Americans, who have always objected to the United States' assumption that it alone is "America"? The ethnic mix of this astonishingly diverse country, from Junot Díaz to Yiyun Li, has never seemed as rich as it does now, nor has its literature ever reached as far, into as many different worlds. Who today is *not* an American, one might almost inquire.

The following is the official formulation: the writers in this anthology must be American, *or,* they must make the United States their home, *or,* they must have done so for the most part. There's a world of elasticity in that "for the most part" — it stretched enough to let in Daniyal Mueenuddin, the superb Pakistani writer referred to above — and the stories I read took me from the menaces to be found in small Midwestern towns and the familiar alienation of the suburbs to Japan, India, Latin America, outer space, and Zanzibar.

I read 120 stories submitted to me by Heidi Pitlor, and more that I found by myself. Heidi probably read a hundred times as many, in an annual rite of meticulous determination for which she deserves the profound gratitude not only of story writers and little magazines everywhere but also, perhaps above all, of readers. Certainly this reader was made happily aware of many excellent authors and wonderfully committed shoestring publications that he might never otherwise have encountered.

Miroslav Penkov, Christine Sneed, Danielle Evans, Rebecca Makkai, Allegra Goodman, and Karen Brown are among the names new to me whose contributions to this volume rebuke my previous ignorance of their talents, and ensure that I will look out for their future work. And as for writers, so also for magazines. *Shenandoah, Ecotone, Ploughshares, Missouri Review, Antioch Review, Southern Review,* and *Tin House* don't reach my desk as often as, say, *The New Yorker, The Atlantic, Harper's Magazine, Granta, Zoetrope: All-Story, McSweeney's,* or *The Paris Review,* but it's clear that the health of the American short story depends on them as much as on their more glamorous brethren.

By no means did all the stories I preferred emerge from the country's old and new multiracial horns of plenty. The majority of this year's long list, in fact, gave evidence of a return to small, domestic, private concerns, stories of broken marriages, parent-child conflicts, and deaths in the family — events which that great and much-missed story artist Grace Paley called "the little disturbances of Man." There were perhaps too many familiar tales of a small everyday world, a small town or a rural landscape, in which something terrible suddenly happens. Nursing homes recurred with faintly depressing frequency. Most surprisingly of all, there were several stories either wholly about, or else prominently featuring, the game of golf. A visitor from a galaxy far, far away, reading these stories to learn about America, might have concluded that golf was the country's national sport. I read no stories about baseball, football, basketball, or hockey, but there were maybe five or six in which golf played some part. What does this puzzling phenomenon reveal? I have no idea, really. I leave the question open.

Any anthology will be, to some extent, the product of its editor's predilections. None of us is wholly immune to his own taste. When we began our discussions, Heidi asked me if there were any authors I particularly liked or disliked, and any literary tics that grated on me. I replied, "I'm pretty broad church, really. Good is good and bad is bad. I do dislike the creative writingese that infects many short stories nowadays, that flat, polished sameness of tone that so many stories now have. Otherwise, I'm up for anybody, even **** ******, I suppose." (In the end, Mr. ****** didn't make the final cut.)

Old-fashioned naturalism was the dominant manner this year, and creative writingese, I have to say, was often in evidence. There were so many stories that were well observed, well crafted, full of well-honed phrases; so many rhythmic, allusive, technically sophisticated stories that knew when to leave matters unresolved and when it was right to bring events to a dramatic climax; so many stories that had everything one could wish for in a story . . . except for the sense that it had to be written, that is was necessary. This was what I had expected and perhaps feared: a widespread, humorless, bloodless competence.

But there were many compensating treasures, and, in the end, riches to choose from . . . forty-odd first-rate stories when we had room for only twenty. Some of the contenders were confidently topical: Jim Shepard memorably evoked Chernobyl; Ann Beattie, with equal skill, told of the hurricane in Key West. Others were more fanciful. Jonathan Lethem's "The King of Sentences," a story reminiscent of the antic genius of Donald Barthelme, which includes a comically unsatisfying encounter with a Barthelme-like writer, reminded me of my own disappointing meeting with a somewhat-too-well-oiled Barthelme at the PEN Congress in New York in 1986. Karen Russell's story "St. Lucy's Home for Girls Raised by Wolves" was included by Stephen King in *The Best American Short Stories 2007,* and I'm happy to see her continuing development, evidenced by the vampire story I've chosen here, into the true heir of the ferocious British fabulist Angela Carter.

The pure, muscular storytelling of Mark Wisniewski's "Straightaway" was irresistible. George Saunders's "Puppy" and Nicole Krauss's "From the Desk of Daniel Varsky" were among the first stories I read, and I couldn't get either of them out of my head, which made it impossible to leave either out of this book. When I first read Tobias Wolff's story "Bible," I wanted to get up and applaud. (Religion was another of the year's major themes — reflected here in "Missionaries" by Bradford Tice, a story that reminded me, in some moments, of Flannery O'Connor, and "Man and Wife," Katie Chase's story of an imaginary cult, which is, astonishingly, her first published fiction.)

There were some painful decisions, of course. One golf story, Brendan Mathews's "Dunn & Sons," hung in there until the very end, and I'm kind of sad to have left it out. André Aciman, David Foster Wallace, Rick DeMarinis, Beverly Jensen, Erin Soros, and Shena McAuliffe all have good reason to feel aggrieved. Andrew Sean Greer's story "Darkness" and Kevin Brockmeier's "The Year of Silence," very different in the telling, were built upon coincidentally similar metaphorical conceits. Rightly or wrongly, I decided I had to choose between the rival metaphors of darkness and silence, and silence won, but it was a hair's-breadth decision. (Brockmeier's story may require some readers to refer to the Morse code alphabet, which we have included on page 328. I should mention that when I tried to decode the message in the story, I got it wrong. As ever, Heidi Pitlor came gently but firmly to my rescue.)

The convention that each writer should be represented by only one story gave me some trouble, too, because there were two writers, the immensely fecund and original T. C. Boyle and the extraordinary Steven Millhauser, each of whom had two contenders so strong that it was, essentially, impossible to choose between them. Had I included Boyle's "Sin Dolor" instead of his "Admiral," and Millhauser's "A Report on Our Recent Troubles" instead of "The Wizard of West Orange," this collection would have lost nothing in quality.

The human being is a storytelling animal, or, actually, *the* storytelling animal, the only creature on Earth that tells itself stories in order to understand what sort of creature it is. Some of these stories are immense, the so-called "grand narratives" of nation, race, and faith, and others are small: family stories, and stories of elective affinities, of the friends we choose, the places we know, and the people we love; but we all live in and with and by stories, every day, whoever and wherever we are. The freedom to tell each other the stories of ourselves, to retell the stories of our culture and beliefs, is profoundly connected to the larger subject of freedom itself. The Nobel laureate Elias Canetti titled one volume of his autobiography *The Tongue Set Free,* and here, in these pages, you will find, I hope, twenty exhilarating proofs of the value of the lingually liberated imagination.

SALMAN RUSHDIE

The Best AMERICAN SHORT STORIES 2008

T. C. BOYLE

Admiral

FROM *Harper's Magazine*

SHE KNEW IN HER HEART it was a mistake, but she'd been laid off and needed the cash, and her memories of the Strikers were mostly on the favorable side, so when Mrs. Striker called — *Gretchen, this is Gretchen? Mrs. Striker?* — she'd said yes, she'd love to come over and hear what they had to say. First, though, she had to listen to her car cough as she drove across town (fuel pump, that was her father's opinion, offered in a flat voice that said it wasn't his problem, not anymore, not now that she was grown and living back at home after a failed attempt at life), and she nearly stalled the thing turning into the Strikers' block. And then did stall it as she tried, against any reasonable expectation of success, to parallel park in front of their great rearing fortress of a house. It felt strange punching in the code at the gate and seeing how things were different and the same, how the trees had grown while the flowerbeds remained in a state of suspended animation, everything in perpetual bloom and clipped to within a millimeter of perfection. The gardeners saw to that. A whole battalion of them that swarmed over the place twice a week with their blowers and edgers and trimmers, at war with the weeds, the insects, the gophers and ground squirrels, and the very tendency of the display plants to want to grow outside the box. At least that was how she remembered it. The gardeners. And how Admiral would rage at the windows, showing his teeth and scrabbling with his claws — and if he could have chewed through glass, he would have done it. "That's right, boy," she'd say, "that's right — don't let those bad men steal all your dead leaves and dirt. You go, boy. You go. That's right."

She rang the bell at the front door and it wasn't Mrs. Striker who answered it but another version of herself in a white maid's apron and a little white maid's cap perched atop her head, and she was so surprised she had to double-clutch to keep from dropping her purse. *A woman of color does not clean house,* that was what her mother always told her, and it had become a kind of mantra when she was growing up, a way of reinforcing core values, of promoting education and the life of the mind, but she couldn't help wondering how much higher a dog-sitter was on the socioeconomic scale than a maid. Or a sous-chef, waitress, aerobics instructor, ticket puncher, and tortilla maker, all of which she'd been at one time or another. About the only thing she hadn't tried was leech-gathering. There was a poem on the subject in her college text by William Wordsworth, the poet of daffodils and leeches, and she could summon it up whenever she needed a good laugh. She developed a quick picture of an old long-nosed white man rolling up his pant legs and wading into the murk, then squeezed out a miniature smile and said, "Hi, I'm Nisha? I came to see Mrs. Striker? And Mr. Striker?"

The maid — she wasn't much older than Nisha herself, with a placid expression that might have been described as self-satisfied or just plain vacant — held open the door. "I'll tell them you're here," she said.

Nisha murmured a thank-you and stepped into the tiled foyer, thinking of the snake brain and the olfactory memories that lay coiled there. She smelled dog — smelled Admiral — with an overlay of old sock and furniture polish. The great room rose up before her like something transposed from a cathedral. It was a cold room, echoing and hollow, and she'd never liked it. "You mind if I wait in the family room?" she asked.

The maid — or rather the girl, the young woman, the young woman in the demeaning and stereotypical maid's costume — had already started off in the direction of the kitchen, but she swung round now to give Nisha a look of surprise and irritation. For a moment it seemed as if she might snap at her, but then, finally, she just shrugged and said, "Whatever."

Nothing had changed in the paneled room that gave onto the garden, not as far as Nisha could see. There were the immense old high-backed leather armchairs and the antique Stickley sofa rescued from the law offices of Striker and Striker, the mahogany bar with the wine rack and the backlit shrine Mr. Striker had created in homage to the spirits of single-malt Scotch whisky, and overseeing it all, the oil portrait of Admiral with its dark heroic hues and golden patina of varnish. She remembered the day the painter had come to the house and posed the dog for the preliminary snapshots. Admiral uncooperative, Mrs. Striker strung tight as a wire, and the inevitable squirrel bounding across the lawn at the crucial moment. The painter had labored mightily in his studio to make his subject look noble, snout elevated, eyes fixed on some distant, presumably worthy object, but to Nisha's mind an Afghan — any Afghan — looked inherently ridiculous, like some escapee from *Sesame Street,* and Admiral seemed a kind of concentrate of the absurd. He looked goofy, just that.

When she turned round, both the Strikers were there, as if they'd floated in out of the ether. As far as she could see, they hadn't aged at all. Their skin was flawless, they held themselves as stiff and erect as the Ituri carvings they'd picked up on their trip to Africa, and they tried hard to make small talk and avoid any appearance of briskness. In Mrs. Striker's arms — *Call me Gretchen, please* — was an Afghan pup, and after the initial exchange of pleasantries, Nisha, her hand extended to rub the silk of the ears and feel the wet probe of the tiny snout on her wrist, began to get the idea. She restrained herself from asking after Admiral. "Is this his pup?" she asked instead. "Is this little Admiral?" The Strikers exchanged a glance. The husband hadn't said, *Call me Cliff,* hadn't said much of anything, but now his lips compressed. "Didn't you read about it in the papers?"

There was an awkward pause. The pup began to squirm. "Admiral passed," Gretchen breathed. "It was an accident. We had him — well, we were in the park, the dog park . . . you know, the one where the dogs run free? You used to take him there, you remember, up off Sycamore? Well, you know how exuberant he was . . ."

"You really didn't read about it?" There was incredulity in the husband's voice.

"Well, I — I was away at college, and then I took the first job I could find. Back here, I mean. Because of my mother. She's been sick."

Neither of them commented on this, not even to be polite.

"It was all over the press," the husband said, and he sounded offended now. He adjusted his oversized glasses and cocked his head to look down at her in a way that brought the past rushing back. "*Newsweek* did a story, *USA Today* — we were on *Good Morning America,* both of us."

She was at a loss, the three of them standing there, the dog taking its spiked dentition to the underside of her wrist now, just the way Admiral used to when he was a pup. "For what?" she was about to say, when Gretchen came to the rescue.

"This is little Admiral. Admiral II, actually," she said, ruffling the blond shag over the pup's eyes.

The husband looked past her, out the window and into the yard, an ironic grin pressed to his lips. "Two hundred and fifty thousand dollars," he said, "and it's too bad he wasn't a cat."

Gretchen gave him a sharp look. "You make a joke of it," she said, her eyes suddenly filling, "but it was worth every penny and you know it." She mustered a long-suffering smile for Nisha. "Cats are simpler — their eggs are more mature at ovulation than dogs' are."

"I can get you a cat for thirty-two thou."

"Oh, Cliff, stop. Stop it."

He moved to his wife and put an arm round her shoulders. "But we didn't want to clone a cat, did we, honey?" He bent his face to the dog's, touched noses with him, and let his voice rise to a falsetto: "Did we now, Admiral. Did we?"

At seven-thirty the next morning, Nisha pulled up in front of the Strikers' house and let her car wheeze and shudder a moment before killing the engine. She flicked the radio back on to catch the last fading chorus of a tune she liked, singing along with the sexy low rasp of the lead vocalist, feeling good about things — or better, anyway. The Strikers were giving her twenty-five dollars an hour, plus the same dental and health-care package they offered the staff at their law firm, which was a whole solid towering brick wall of improvement over what she'd been making as a waitress at Johnny's Rib Shack, sans health care, sans dental, and sans any tip she could remember above 10 percent of the pretax total because the people who came out to gnaw ribs were just plain cheap and no two ways about it. When she stepped out of the car, there was Gretchen coming down the front steps of the house with the pup in her arms, just as she had nine years ago when Nisha was a high school freshman taking on what she assumed was going to be a breeze of a summer job.

Nisha took the initiative of punching in the code herself and slipping through the gate to hustle up the walk and save Gretchen the trouble, because Gretchen was in a hurry, always in a hurry. She was dressed in a navy blue suit with a double string of pearls and an antique silver pin in the shape of a bounding borzoi that seemed eerily familiar — it might have been the exact ensemble she'd been wearing when Nisha had told her she'd be quitting to go off to college. *I'm sorry, Mrs. Striker, and I've really enjoyed the opportunity to work for you and Mr. Striker,* she'd said, hardly able to contain the swell of her heart, *but I'm going to college. On a scholarship.* She'd had the acceptance letter in her hand to show her, thinking how proud of her Mrs. Striker would be, how she'd take her in her arms for a hug and congratulate her, but the first thing she'd said was, *What about Admiral?*

As Gretchen closed on her now, the pup wriggling in her arms, Nisha could see her smile flutter and die. No doubt she was already envisioning the cream-leather interior of her BMW (a 750i in Don't-Even-Think-About-It Black) and the commute to the office and whatever was going down there, court sessions, the piles of documents, contention at every turn. Mr. Striker — Nisha would never be able to call him Cliff, even if she lived to be eighty, but then he'd have to be a hundred and ten and probably wouldn't hear her anyway — was already gone, in his matching Beemer, his and hers. Gretchen didn't say *Good morning* or *Hi* or *How are you?* or *Thanks for coming,* but just enfolded her in the umbrella of her perfume and handed her the dog. Which went immediately heavy in Nisha's arms, fighting for the ground with four flailing paws and the little white ghoul's teeth that fastened on the top button of her jacket. Nisha held on. Gave Gretchen a big grateful-for-the-job-and-the-health-care smile, no worries, no worries at all.

"Those jeans," Gretchen said, narrowing her eyes. "Are they new?"

The dog squirming, squirming. "I, well — I'm going to set him down a minute, okay?"

"Of course, of course. Do what you do, what you normally do." An impatient wave. "Or what you used to do, I mean."

They both watched as the pup fell back on its haunches, rolled briefly in the grass, and sprang up to clutch Nisha's right leg in a clumsy embrace. "I just couldn't find any of my old jeans — my mother probably threw them all out long ago. Plus" — a laugh — "I don't think I could fit into them anymore." She gave Gretchen a moment to ruminate on the deeper implications here — time passing, adolescents grown into womanhood, flesh expanding, that sort of thing — then gently pushed the dog down and murmured, "But I *am* wearing — right here, under the jacket? — this T-shirt I know I used to wear back then."

Nothing. Gretchen just stood there, looking distracted.

"It's been washed, of course, and sitting in the back of the top drawer of my dresser where my mother left it, so I don't know if there'll be any scent or anything, but I'm sure I used to wear it because Tupac really used to drive my engine back then, if you know what I mean." She gave it a beat. "But hey, we were all fourteen once, huh?" Gretchen made no sign that she'd heard her — either that or she denied the proposition outright. "You're going to be all right with this, aren't you?" she said, looking her in the eye. "Is there anything we didn't cover?"

The afternoon before, during her interview — but it wasn't really an interview because the Strikers had already made up their minds, and if she'd refused them they would have kept raising the hourly till she capitulated — the two of them, Gretchen and Cliff, had positioned themselves on either side of her and leaned into the bar over caramel-colored Scotches and a platter of ebi and maguro sushi to explain the situation.

Just so that she was clear on it. "You know what cloning is, right?" Gretchen said. "Or what it involves? You remember Dolly?"

Nisha was holding fast to her drink, her left elbow pressed to the brass rail of the bar in the family room. She'd just reached out her twinned chopsticks for a second piece of the shrimp but withdrew her hand. "You mean the country singer?"

"The sheep," the husband said.

"The first cloned mammal," Gretchen put in. "Or larger mammal."

"Yeah," she said, nodding. "Sure. I guess."

What followed was a short course in genetics and the method of somatic-cell nuclear transplant that had given the world Dolly, various replicated cattle, pigs, and hamsters, and now Admiral II, the first cloned dog made available commercially through SalvaPet, Inc., the genetic-engineering firm with offices in Seoul, San Juan, and Cleveland. Gretchen's voice constricted as she described how they'd taken a cell from the lining of Admiral's ear just after the accident and inserted it into a donor egg that had had its nucleus removed, stimulated the cell to divide through the application of an electric current, and then inserted the developing embryo into the uterus of a host mother — "The sweetest golden retriever you ever saw. What was her name, Cliff? Some flower, wasn't it?"

"Peony."

"Peony? Are you sure?"

"Of course I'm sure."

"I thought it was — oh, I don't know. You sure it wasn't Iris?"

"The point is," he said, setting his glass down and leveling his gaze at Nisha, "you can get a genetic copy of the animal, a kind of three-dimensional Xerox, but that doesn't guarantee it'll be like the one you, well, the one you lost."

"It was so sad," Gretchen said.

"It's nurture that counts. You've got to reproduce the animal's experiences, as nearly as possible." He gave a shrug, reached for the bottle. "You want another?" he asked, and she held out her glass. "Of course we're both older now — and so are you, we realize that — but we want to come as close as possible to replicating the exact conditions that made Admiral what he was, right down to the toys we gave him, the food, the schedule of walks and play, and all the rest. Which is where you come in —"

"We need a commitment here, Nisha," Gretchen breathed, leaning in so close Nisha could smell the Scotch coming back at her. "Four years. That's how long you were with him last time. Or with Admiral, I mean. The original Admiral."

The focus of all this deliberation had fallen asleep in Gretchen's lap. A single probing finger of sunlight stabbed through the window to illuminate the pale fluff over the dog's eyes. At that moment, in that light, little Admiral looked like some strange conjunction of ostrich and ape. Nisha couldn't help thinking of *The Island of Dr. Moreau,* the cheesy version with Marlon Brando looking as if he'd been genetically manipulated himself, and she would have grinned a private grin, fueled by the Scotch and the thundering absurdity of the moment, but she had to hide everything she thought or felt behind a mask of impassivity. She wasn't committing to anything for four years — four years? If she was still living here in this crap-hole of a town four years from now, she promised herself she'd go out and buy a gun and eliminate all her problems with a single, very personal squeeze of the trigger.

That was what she was thinking when Gretchen said, "We'll pay you twenty dollars an hour," and the husband said, "With health care — and dental," and they both stared at her so fiercely she had to look down into her glass before she found her voice.

"Twenty-five," she said.

And oh, how they loved that dog, because they never hesitated. "Twenty-five it is," the husband said, and Gretchen, a closer's smile blooming on her face, produced a contract from the folder at her elbow. "Just sign here," she said.

After Gretchen had climbed into her car and the car had slid through the gate and vanished down the street, Nisha sprawled out on the grass and lifted her face to the sun. She was feeling the bliss of déjà vu — or no, not déjà vu, but a virtual return to the past, when life was just a construct and there was nothing she couldn't have done or been and nothing beyond the thought of clothes and boys and the occasional term paper to hamper her. Here she was, gone back in time, lying on the grass at quarter of eight in the morning on a sunstruck June day, playing with a puppy while everybody else was going to work — it was hilarious, that's what it was. Like something you'd read about in the paper — a behest from some crazed millionaire. Or in this case, two crazed millionaires. She felt so good she let out a laugh, even as the pup came charging across the lawn to slam headfirst into her, all feet and pink panting tongue, and he was Admiral all right.

Admiral in the flesh, born and made and resurrected for the mere little pittance of a quarter-million dollars. For a long while she wrestled with him, flipping him over on his back each time he charged, scratching his belly and baby-talking him, enjoying the novelty of it, but by quarter past eight she was bored and she pushed herself up to go on into the house and find something to eat. *Do what you used to do,* Gretchen had told her, but what she used to do, summers especially, was nap and read and watch TV and sneak her friends in to tip a bottle of the husband's forty-year-old Scotch to their adolescent lips and make faces at one another before descending into giggles. Twice a day she'd take the dog to the doggy park and watch him squat and crap and run wild with the other mutts till his muzzle was streaked with drool and he dodged at her feet to snatch up mouthfuls of the Evian the Strikers insisted he drink. Now, though, she just wanted to feel the weight of the past a bit, and she went in the back door, the dog at her heels, thinking to make herself a sandwich — the Strikers always had cold cuts in the fridge, mounds of pastrami, capicolla, smoked turkey, and Swiss, individual slices of which went to Admiral each time he did his business outside where he was supposed to or barked in the right cadence or just stuck his goofy head in the door. She could already see the sandwich she was going to make — a whole deli's worth of meat and cheese piled up on Jewish rye; they always had Jewish rye — and she was halfway to the refrigerator before she remembered the maid.

There she was, in her maid's outfit, sitting at the kitchen table with her feet up and the newspaper spread out before her, spooning something out of a cup. "Don't you bring that filthy animal in here," she said, glancing up sharply.

Nisha was startled. There didn't used to be a maid. There was no one in the house, in fact, till Mrs. Yamashita, the cook, came in around four, and that was part of the beauty of it. "Oh, hi," she said, "hi, I didn't know you were going to be — I just . . . I was going to make a sandwich, I guess." There was a silence. The dog slunk around the kitchen, looking wary. "What was your name again?"

"Frankie," the maid said, swallowing the syllables as if she weren't ready to give them up, "and I'm the one has to clean up all these paw marks off the floor — and did you see what he did to that throw pillow in the guest room?"

"No," Nisha said, "I didn't," and she was at the refrigerator now, sliding back the tray of the meat compartment. This would go easier if they were friends, no doubt about it, and she was willing, more than willing. "You want anything?" she said. "A sandwich — or, or something?"

Frankie just stared at her. "I don't know what they're paying you," she said, "but to me? This is the craziest shit I ever heard of in my life. You think I couldn't let the dog out the door a couple times a day? Or what, take him to the park — that's what you do, right, take him to the doggy park over on Sycamore?"

The refrigerator door swung shut, the little light blinking out, the heft of the meat satisfying in her hand. "It's insane, I admit it — hey, I'm with you. You think I wanted to grow up to be a dog-sitter?"

"I don't know. I don't know anything about you. Except you got your degree — you need a degree for that, dog-sitting, I mean?" She hadn't moved, not a muscle, her feet propped up, the cup in one hand, spoon in the other.

"No," Nisha said, feeling the blood rise to her face, "no, you don't. But what about you — you need a degree to be a maid?"

That hit home. For a moment, Frankie said nothing, just looked from her to the dog — which was begging now, clawing at Nisha's leg with his forepaws — and back again. "This is just temporary," she said finally.

"Yeah, me too." Nisha gave her a smile, no harm done, just establishing a little turf, that was all. "Totally."

For the first time, Frankie's expression changed: she almost looked as if she were going to laugh. "Yeah, that's right," she said, "temporary help, that's all we are. We're the temps. And Mr. and Mrs. Striker — dog-crazy, plain crazy, two-hundred-and-fifty-thousand-dollar-crazy — they're permanent."

And now Nisha laughed, and so did Frankie — a low rumble of amusement that made the dog turn its head. The meat was on the counter now, the cellophane wrapper pulled back. Nisha selected a slice of Black Forest ham and held it out to him. "Sit!" she said. "Go ahead, sit!" And the dog, just like his father or progenitor or donor or whatever he was, looked at her stupidly till she dropped the meat on the tile and the wet plop of its arrival made him understand that here was something to eat.

"You're going to spoil that dog," Frankie said.

Nisha went unerringly to the cabinet where the bread was kept, and there it was, Jewish rye, a fresh loaf, springy to the touch. She gave Frankie a glance over her shoulder. "Yeah," she said. "I think that's the idea."

A month drifted by, as serene a month as Nisha could remember. She was making good money, putting in ten-hour days during the week and half days on the weekends, reading through all the books she hadn't had time for in college, exhausting the Strikers' DVD collection and opening her own account at the local video store, walking, lazing, napping the time away. She gained five pounds and vowed to start swimming regularly in the Strikers' pool but hadn't got round to it yet. Some days she'd help Frankie with the cleaning and the laundry so the two of them could sit out on the back deck with their feet up, sharing a bottle of sweet wine or a joint. As for the dog, she tried to be conscientious about the whole business of imprinting it with the past — or *a* past — though she felt ridiculous. Four years of college for this? Wars were being fought, people were starving, there were diseases to conquer, children to educate, good to do in the world, and here she was reliving her adolescence in the company of an inbred semi-retarded clown of a cloned Afghan hound because two childless rich people decreed it should be so. All right. She knew she'd have to move on. Knew it was temporary. Swore that she'd work up a new résumé and start sending it out — but then the face of her mother, sick from vomiting and with her scalp as smooth and slick as an eggplant, would rise up to shame her. She threw the ball to the dog. Took him to the park. Let the days fall round her like leaves from a dying tree.

And then one afternoon, on the way back from the dog park, Admiral jerking at the leash beside her and the sky opening up to a dazzle of sun and pure white tufts of cloud that made her feel as if she were floating untethered through the universe along with them, she noticed a figure stationed outside the gate of the Strikers' house. As she got closer, she saw that it was a young man dressed in baggy jeans and a T-shirt, his hair fanning out in rusty blond dreads and a goatee of the same color clinging to his chin. He was peering over the fence. Her first thought was that he'd come to rob the place, but she dismissed it — he was harmless; you could see that a hundred yards off. Then she saw the paint smears on his jeans and wondered if he was a painting contractor come to put in a bid on the house, but that wasn't it either. He looked more like an amateur artist — and here she had to laugh to herself — the kind who specializes in dog portraits. But she was nearly on him now, thinking to brush by him and slip through the gate before he could accost her, whatever he wanted, when he turned suddenly and his face caught fire. "Wow!" he said. "Wow, I can't believe it! You're her, aren't you, the famous dog-sitter? And this" — he went down on one knee and made a chirping sound deep in his throat — "this is Admiral. Right? Am I right?"

Admiral went straight to him, lurching against the leash, and in the next instant was flopping himself down on the hot pavement, submitting to the man's caresses. The rope of a tail whapped and thrashed, the paws gyrated, the puppy teeth came into play. "Good boy," the man crooned, his dreads riding a wave across his brow. "He likes that, doesn't he? Doesn't he, boy?"

Nisha didn't say anything. She just watched, the smallest hole dug out of the canyon of her boredom, till the man rose to his feet and held out his hand even as Admiral sprang up to hump his leg with fresh enthusiasm. "I'm Erhard," he said, grinning wide. "And you're Nisha, right?"

"Yes," she said, taking his hand despite herself. She was on the verge of asking how he knew her name, but there was no point: she already understood. He was from the press. In the past month there must have been a dozen reporters on the property, the Strikers stroking their vanity and posing for pictures and answering the same idiotic questions over and over — *A quarter-million dollars: that's a lot for a dog, isn't it?* — and she herself had been interviewed twice already. Her mother had even found a fuzzy color photo of her and Admiral (couchant, lap) on the Web under the semi-hilarious rubric CLONE SITTER. So this guy was a reporter — a foreign reporter, judging from the faint trace of an accent and the blue-eyed rearing height of him, German, she supposed. Or Austrian. And he wanted some of her time.

"Yes," he said, as if reading her thoughts. "I am from *Die Weltwoche,* and I wanted to ask of you — prevail upon you, beg you — for a few moments? Is that possible? For me? Just now?"

She gave him a long slow appraisal, flirting with him, yes, defi nitely flirting.

"I've got nothing but time," she said. And then, watching his grin widen: "You want a sandwich?"

They ate on the patio overlooking the pool. She was dressed casually in shorts and flip-flops and her old Tupac tee, and that wasn't necessarily a bad thing because the shirt — too small by half — lifted away from her hips when she leaned back in the chair, showing off her navel and the onyx ring she wore there. He was watching her, chattering on about the dog, lifting the sandwich to his lips and putting it down again, fooling with the lens on the battered old Hasselblad he extracted from the backpack at his feet. The sun made sequins on the surface of the pool. Admiral lounged beneath the table, worrying a rawhide bone. She was feeling good, better than good, sipping a beer and watching him back.

They had a little conversation about the beer. "Sorry to offer you Miller, but that's all we have — or the Strikers have, I mean."

"Miller High Life," he said, lifting the bottle to his mouth. "Great name. What person would not want to live the high life? Even a dog. Even Admiral. He lives the high life, no?"

"I thought you'd want a German beer, something like Beck's or something."

He set down the bottle, picked up the camera, and let the lens wander down the length of her legs. "I'm Swiss, actually," he said. "But I live here now. And I like American beer. I like everything American."

There was no mistaking the implication, and she wanted to return the sentiment, but she didn't know the first thing about Switzerland, so she just smiled and tipped her beer to him.

"So," he said, cradling the camera in his lap and referring to the notepad he'd laid on the table when she'd served him the sandwich, "this is the most interesting for me, this idea that Mr. and Mrs. Striker would hire you for the dog? This is very strange, no?"

She agreed that it was.

He gave her a smile she could have fallen into. "Do you mind if I should ask what are they paying you?"

"Yes," she said. "I do."

Another smile. "But it is good — worth your while, as they say?"

"I thought this was about Admiral," she said, and then, because she wanted to try it out on her tongue, she added, "Erhard."

"Oh, it is, it is — but I find you interesting too. More interesting, really, than the dog." As if on cue, Admiral backed out from under the table and squatted on the concrete to deposit a glistening yellow turd, which he examined briefly and then promptly ate.

"Bad dog," she said reflexively.

Erhard studied the dog a moment, then shifted his eyes back to her. "But how do you feel about the situation, this concept of cloning a pet? Do you know anything about this process, the cruelty involved?"

"You know, frankly, Erhard, I haven't thought much about it. I don't know really what it involves. I don't really care. The Strikers love their dog, that's all, and if they want to, I don't know, bring him back —"

"Cheat death, you mean."

She shrugged. "It's their money."

He leaned across the table now, his eyes locked on hers. "Yes, but they must artificially stimulate so many bitches to come into heat, and then they must take the eggs from the tubes of these bitches, what they call 'surgically harvesting,' if you can make a guess as to what that implies for the poor animals" — she began to object, but he held up a peremptory finger — "and that is nothing when you think of the numbers involved. Do you know about Snuppy?"

She thought she hadn't heard him right. "Snuppy? What's that?"

"The dog, the first one ever cloned — it was two years ago, in Korea? Well, this dog, this one dog — an Afghan, like your dog here — was the result of over a thousand embryos created in the laboratory from donor skin cells. And they put these embryos into one hundred and twenty-three bitches and only three clones resulted — and two died. So: all that torture of the animals, all that money — and for what?" He glanced down at Admiral, the flowing fur, the blunted eyes. "For this?"

A sudden thought came to her: "You're not really a journalist, are you?"

He slowly shook his head, as if he couldn't bear the weight of it.

"You're what — one of these animal people, these animal liberators or whatever they are. Isn't that right? Isn't that what you are?" She felt frightened suddenly, for herself, for Admiral, for the Strikers and Frankie and the whole carefully constructed edifice of getting and wanting, of supply and demand and all that it implied.

"And do you know why they clone the Afghan hound," he went on, ignoring her, "the very stupidest of all the dogs on this earth? You don't? Breeding, that is why. This is what they call an uncomplicated genetic line, a pure line all the way back to the wolf ancestor. Breeding," he said, and he'd raised his voice so that Admiral looked up at the vehemence of it, "so that we can have this purity, this stupid hound, this *replica* of nature."

Nisha tugged down her T-shirt, drew up her legs. The sun glared up off the water so that she had to squint to see him. "You haven't answered my question," she said. "Erhard. If that's even your name."

Again, the slow rolling of the head on his shoulders, back and forth in rhythmic contrition. "Yes," he said finally, drawing in a breath, "I am one of 'these animal people.'" His eyes went distant a moment and then came back to her. "But I am also a journalist, a journalist first. And I want you to help me."

That night, when the Strikers came home — in convoy, her car following his through the gate, Admiral lurching across the lawn to bark furiously at the shimmering irresistible discs of the wheels of first one car, then the other — Nisha was feeling conflicted. Her loyalties were with the Strikers, of course. And with Admiral too, because no matter how brainless and ungainly the dog was, no matter how many times he wet the rug or ravaged the flowerbed or scrambled up onto the kitchen table to choke down anything anyone had been foolish enough to leave untended even for thirty seconds, she'd bonded with him — she would have been pretty cold if she hadn't. And she wasn't cold. She was as susceptible as anyone else. She loved animals, loved dogs, loved the way Admiral sprang to life when he saw her walk through the door, loved the dance of his fur, his joyous full-throated bark, the feel of his wet whiskered snout in the cupped palm of her hand. But Erhard had made her feel something else altogether. What was it? A sexual stirring, yes, absolutely — after the third beer, she'd found herself leaning into him for the first of a series of deep, languid, adhesive kisses — but it was more than that. There was something transgressive in what he wanted her to do, something that appealed to her sense of rebellion, of anarchy, of applying the pin to the swollen balloon . . . but here were the Strikers, emerging separately from their cars as Admiral bounced between them, yapping out his ecstasy. And now Gretchen was addressing her, trying to shout over the dog's sharp vocalizations, but without success. In the next moment, she was coming across the lawn, her face set.

"Don't let him chase the car like that," she called, even as Admiral tore round her like a dust devil, nipping at her ankles and dodging away again. "It's a bad habit."

"But Admiral — I mean, the first Admiral — used to chase cars all the time, remember?"

Gretchen had pinned her hair up so that all the contours of her face stood out in sharp relief. There were lines everywhere suddenly, creases and gouges, frown marks, little embellishments round her eyes, and how could Nisha have missed them? Gretchen was old — fifty, at least — and the realization came home to Nisha now, under the harsh sun, with the taste of the beer and of Erhard still tingling on her lips. "I don't care," Gretchen was saying, and she was standing beside Nisha now, like a figurine the gardeners had set down amid that perfect landscape.

"But I thought we were going to go for everything, the complete behavior, good or bad, right? Because otherwise —"

"That was how the accident happened. At the dog park. He got through the gate before Cliff or I could stop him and just ran out into the street after some idiot on a motorcycle . . ." She looked past Nisha a moment, to where Admiral was bent over the pool, slurping up water as if his pinched triangular head worked on a piston. "So no," she said, "no, we're going to have to modify some behavior. I don't want him drinking that pool water, for one thing. Too many chemicals."

"Okay, sure," Nisha said, shrugging. "I'll try." She raised her voice and sang out, "Bad dog, bad dog," but it was halfhearted and Admiral ignored her.

The cool green eyes shifted to meet hers again. "And I don't want him eating his own" — she paused to search for the proper word for the context, running through various euphemisms before giving it up — "shit."

Another shrug.

"I'm serious on this. Are you with me?"

Nisha couldn't help herself, and so what if she was pushing it? So what?

"Admiral did," she said. "Maybe you didn't know that."

Gretchen just waved her hand in dismissal. "But this Admiral," she said. "He's not going to do it. Is he?"

Over the course of the next two weeks, as summer settled in with a succession of cloudless, high-arching days and Admiral steadily grew into the promise of his limbs, Erhard became a fixture at the house. Every morning, when Nisha came through the gate with the dog on his leash, he was there waiting for her, shining and tall and beautiful, with a joke on his lips and always some little treat for Admiral secreted in one pocket or another. The dog worshipped him. Went crazy for him. Pranced on the leash, spun in circles, nosed at his sleeves and pockets till he got his treat, then rolled over on his back in blissful submission. And then it was the dog park, and instead of sitting there wrapped up in the cocoon of herself, she had Erhard to sustain her, to lean into her so that she could feel the heat of him through the thin cotton of his shirt, to kiss her, and later, after lunch and the rising tide of the beer, to make love to her on the divan in the cool shadows of the pool house. They swam in the afternoons — he didn't mind the five pounds she'd put on; he praised her for them — and sometimes Frankie would join them, shedding the maid's habit for a white two-piece and careering through a slashing backstroke with a bottle of beer her reward, because she was part of the family too. Mama and Papa and Aunt Frankie, all there to nurture little Admiral under the beneficent gaze of the sun. Of course, Nisha was no fool. She knew there was a quid pro quo involved here, knew that Erhard had his agenda, but she was in no hurry, she'd committed to nothing, and as she lay there on the divan smoothing her hands over his back, tasting him, enjoying him, taking him inside her, she felt hope, real hope, for the first time since she'd come back home. It got so that she looked forward to each day, even the mornings that had been so hard on her, having to take a tray up to the ghost of her mother while her father trudged off to work, the whole house like a turned grave, because now she had Admiral, now she had Erhard, and she could shrug off anything. Yes. Sure. That was the way it was. Until the day he called her on it.

Cloudless sky, steady sun, every flower at its peak. She came down the walk with Admiral on his leash at the appointed hour, pulled back the gate, and there he was — but this time he wasn't alone. Beside him, already straining at the leash, was a gangling overgrown Afghan pup that could have been the twin of Admiral, and though she'd known it was coming, known the plan since the very first day, she was awestruck.

"Jesus," she said, even as Admiral jerked her forward and the two dogs began to romp round her legs in a tangle of limbs and leashes, "how did you — ? I mean, he's the exact, he's totally —"

"That's the idea, isn't it?"

"But where did you find him?"

Erhard gave her a look of appraisal, then his eyes jumped past her to sweep the street. "Let's go inside, no? I don't want that they should see us here, anyone — not right in the front of the house."

He hadn't talked her into it, not yet, not exactly, but now that the moment had come she numbly punched in the code and held the gate open for him. What he wanted to do, what he was in the process of doing with her unspoken complicity, was to switch the dogs — just for a day, two at the most — by way of experiment. His contention was that the Strikers would never know the difference, that they were arrogant exemplars of bourgeois excess, even to the point of violating the laws of nature — and God, God too — simply to satisfy their own solipsistic desires. Admiral wouldn't be harmed — he'd enjoy himself, the change of scenery, all that. And certainly she knew how much the dog had come to mean to him. "But these people will not recognize their own animal," he'd insisted, his voice gone hard with conviction, "and so I will have my story and the world will know it." Once inside the gate, they let the dogs off their leashes and went round back of the house where they'd be out of sight. They walked hand in hand, his fingers entwined with hers, and for a long while, as the sun rode high overhead and a breeze slipped in off the ocean to stir the trees, they watched as the two dogs streaked back and forth, leaping and nipping and tumbling in doggy rhapsody. Admiral's great combed-out spill of fur whipped round him in a frenzy of motion, and the new dog, Erhard's dog — the impostor — matched him step for step, hair for glorious hair. "You took him to the groomer, didn't you?" she said.

Erhard gave a stiff nod. "Yes, sure. What do you think? He must be exact."

She watched, bemused, for another minute, her misgivings buried deep under the pressure of his fingers, bone, sinew, the wedded flesh, and why shouldn't she go along with him? What was the harm? His article, or exposé, or whatever it was, would appear in Switzerland, in German, and the Strikers would never know the difference. Or even if they did, even if it was translated into English and grabbed headlines all over the country, they had it coming to them. Erhard was right. She knew it. She'd known it all along. "So what's his name?" she asked, the dogs shooting past her in a moil of fur and flashing feet. "Does he have a name?"

"Fred."

"Fred? What kind of name is that for a pedigree dog?"

"What kind of name is Admiral?"

She was about to tell him the story of the original Admiral, how he'd earned his sobriquet because of his enthusiasm for the

Strikers' yacht and how they were planning on taking Admiral II out on the water as soon as they could, when the familiar rumble of the driveway gate drawing back on its runners startled her. In the next moment, she was in motion, making for the near corner of the house where she could see down the long macadam strip of the drive. Her heart skipped a beat: it was Gretchen. Gretchen home early, some crisis compelling her, mislaid papers, her blouse stained, the flu, Gretchen in her black Beemer, waiting for the gate to slide back so she could roll up the drive and exert dominion over her house and property, her piss-stained carpets, and her insuperable dog. "Quick!" Nisha shouted, whirling round. "Grab them. Grab the dogs!"

She saw Erhard plunge forward and snatch at them, the grass rising up to meet him and both dogs tearing free. "Admiral!" he called, scrambling to his knees. "Here, boy. Come!" The moment thundered in her ears. The dogs hesitated, the ridiculous sea of fur smoothing and settling momentarily, and then one of them — it was Admiral, it had to be — came to him, and he got hold of it even as the other pricked up its ears at the sound of the car and bolted round the corner of the house.

"I'll stall her," she called.

Erhard, all six feet five inches of him, was already humping across the grass in the direction of the pool house, the dog writhing in his arms.

But the other dog — it was Fred, it had to be — was chasing the car up the drive now, nipping at the wheels, and as Nisha came round the corner, she could read the look on her employer's face. A moment and she was there, grabbing for the dog as the car rolled to a stop and the engine died. Gretchen stepped put of the car, heels coming down squarely on the pavement, her shoulders thrust back tightly against the grip of her jacket. "I thought I told you . . ." she began, her voice high and querulous, but then she faltered and her expression changed. "But where's Admiral?" she said. "And whose dog is *that?*"

In the course of her life, short though it had been, she'd known her share of embittered people — her father, for one; her mother, for another — and she'd promised herself she'd never go there, never descend to that hopeless state of despair and regret that ground you down till you were nothing but raw animus, but increasingly now everything she thought or felt or tasted was bitter to the root. Erhard was gone. The Strikers were inflexible. Her mother lingered. Admiral reigned supreme. When the car had come up the drive and Gretchen had stood there confronting her, she'd never felt lower in her life. Until Admiral began howling in the distance and then broke free of Erhard to come careening round the corner of the house and launch himself in one wholly coordinated and mighty leap right into the arms of his protector. And then Erhard appeared, head bowed and shoulders slumped, looking abashed.

"I don't think I've had the pleasure," Gretchen said, setting down the dog (which sprang right up again, this time at Erhard) and at the same time shooting Nisha a look before stepping forward and extending her hand.

"Oh, this is, uh, Erhard," she heard herself say. "He's from Switzerland, and I, well, I just met him in the dog park, and since he had an Afghan too —"

Erhard was miserable, as miserable as she'd ever seen him, but he mustered a counterfeit of his smile and said, "Nice to meet you," even as Gretchen dropped his hand and turned to Nisha.

"Well, it's a nice idea," she said, looking down at the dogs, comparing them. "Good for you for taking the initiative, Nisha . . . but really, you have to know that Admiral didn't have any — *playmates* — here on the property, Afghans or no, and I'm sure he wasn't exposed to anybody from *Switzerland,* if you catch my drift?"

There was nothing Nisha could do but nod her acquiescence.

"So," Gretchen said, squaring her shoulders and turning back to Erhard. "Nice to meet you," she said, "but I'm going to have to ask that you take your dog — what's his name?"

Erhard ducked his head. "Fred."

"Fred? What an odd name. For a dog, I mean. He does have papers, doesn't he?"

"Oh, yes, he's of the highest order, very well bred."

Gretchen glanced dubiously down at the dog, then back at Erhard. "Yes, well, he looks it," she said, "and they do make great dogs, Afghans — we ought to know. I don't know if Nisha told you, but Admiral is very special, very, very special, and we can't have any other dogs on the property. And I don't mean to be abrupt" — a sharp look for Nisha — "but strangers of any sort, or species, just cannot be part of this, this . . ." She trailed off, fighting, at the end, to recover the cold impress of her smile. "Nice meeting you," she repeated, and there was nowhere to go from there.

It had taken Nisha a while to put it all behind her. She kept thinking Erhard was lying low, that he'd be back, that there had been something between them after all, but by the end of the second week she no longer looked for him at the gate or at the dog park or anywhere else. And very slowly, as the days beat on, she began to understand what her role was, her true role. Admiral chased his tail and she encouraged him. When he did his business along the street, she nudged the hard little bolus with the tip of her shoe till he stooped to take it up in his mouth. Yes, she was living in the past and her mother was dying and she'd gone to college for nothing, but she was determined to create a new future — for herself and Admiral — and when she took him to the dog park she lingered outside the gate, to let him run free where he really wanted to be, out there on the street where the cars shunted by and the wheels spun and stalled and caught the light till there was nothing else in the world. "Good boy," she'd say. "Good boy."

KEVIN BROCKMEIER

The Year of Silence

FROM *Ecotone*

1.

SHORTLY AFTER TWO in the afternoon, on Monday, the sixth of April, a few seconds of silence overtook the city. The rattle of the jackhammers, the boom of the transformers, and the whir of the ventilation fans all came to a halt. Suddenly there were no car alarms cutting through the air, no trains scraping over their rails, no steam pipes exhaling their fumes, no peddlers shouting into the streets. Even the wind seemed to hesitate.

We waited for the incident to pass, and when it did, we went about our business. None of us foresaw the repercussions.

2.

That the city's whole immense carousel of sound should stop at one and the same moment was unusual, of course, but not exactly inexplicable. We had witnessed the same phenomenon on a lesser scale at various cocktail parties and interoffice minglers over the years, when the pauses in the conversations overlapped to produce an air pocket of total silence, making us all feel as if we'd been caught eavesdropping on one another. True, no one could remember such a thing happening to the entire city before, but it was not so hard to believe that it would.

3.

A handful of people were changed by the episode, their lives redirected in large ways or small ones. The editor of a gossip magazine, for instance, came out of the silence determined to substitute the next issue's lead article about a movie star for one about a fashion model, while her assistant realized that the time had come for her to resign her job and apply for her teaching license. A lifelong vegetarian who was dining in the restaurant outside the art museum decided to order a porterhouse steak, cooked medium rare. A would-be suicide had just finished filling his water glass from the faucet in his bathroom when everything around him seemed to stop moving and the silence passed through him like a wave, bringing with it a sense of peace and clarity he had forgotten he was capable of feeling. He put the pill bottle back in his medicine cabinet.

Such people were the exceptions, though. Most of us went on with our lives as though nothing of any importance had happened until the next incident occurred, some four days later.

4.

This time the silence lasted nearly six seconds. Ten million sounds broke off and recommenced like an old engine marking out a pause and catching spark again. Those of us who had forgotten the first episode now remembered it. Were the two occasions connected, we wondered, and if so, how? What was it, this force that could quell all the tumult and noise of the city — and not just the clicking of the subway turnstiles and the snap of the grocery-store awnings, but even the sound of the street traffic, that oceanic rumble that for more than a century had seemed as interminable to us as the motion of the sun across the sky? Where had it come from? And why didn't it feel more unnatural?

These questions nettled us. We could see them shining out of one another's eyes. But a few days passed before we began to give voice to them. The silence was unusual, and we were not entirely sure how to talk about it — not because it was too grave and not because it was too trivial, but because it seemed grave one moment and trivial the next, and so no one was quite able to decide whether it mattered enormously or not at all.

5.

A stand-up comedian performing on one of the late-night talk shows was the first of us to broach the subject, albeit indirectly. He waited for a moment in his act when the audience had fallen completely still and then halted in midsentence, raising one of his index fingers in a listening gesture. A smile edged its way onto his lips. He gave the pause perhaps one second too long, just enough time for a trace of self-amusement to show on his face, then continued with the joke he had been telling. He could not have anticipated the size of the laugh he would receive.

6.

The next morning's newspapers had already been put to bed by the time the comedian's routine was broadcast. The morning after that, though, the first few editorials about the silence appeared. Then the radio hosts and TV commentators began to talk about it, and soon enough it was the city's chief topic of conversation. Every family dinner bent around to it sooner or later, every business lunch, every pillow talk. The bars and health clubs all circulated with bets about the phenomenon: *Ten dollars says the government had something to do with it, twenty says it will never happen again.*

When two full weeks went by without another incident, our interest in the matter threatened to shrivel away. It might actually have done so had the next episode not occurred the following Sunday, surprising us all in the middle of our church services. There was another silence, more than ten seconds long, just a couple of days later, and a much shorter silence, like a hiccup, the day after that.

Every time one of the silences came to an end, we felt as though we had passed through a long transparent passageway, a tunnel of sorts, one that made the world into which we emerged appear brighter and cleaner than it had before, less troubled, more humane. The silence siphoned out of the city and into our ears, spilling from there into our dreams and beliefs, our memories and expectations. In the wake of each fresh episode a new feeling flowed through us, full of warmth and a lazy equanimity. It took us a while to recognize the feeling for what it was: contentment.

7.

The truth was that we enjoyed the silence, and more than that, we hungered for it. Sometimes we found ourselves poised in the doorways of our homes in the morning, or on the edges of our car seats as we drove to work, trying to hear something very faint beneath the clatter of sirens and engines. Slowly we realized that what we were waiting for was another incident to take place.

There were weeks when we experienced an episode of silence almost every day. One particular Wednesday saw three of them in the span of a single hour. But there were other weeks when what the papers took to calling a "silence drought" descended upon the city, and all our hopes for a cessation went in vain. If more than a few days passed without some minor lull to interrupt the cacophony, we would become irritable and overtender, quick to gnash at one another and then to rebuke ourselves for our failures of sympathy. On the other hand, a single interlude of silence might generate an aura of fellow feeling that could last for the better part of a day.

The police blotters were nearly empty in the hours following a silence. The drunks in the bars turned amiable and mild. The jails were unusually tranquil. The men who ran the cockfights in the warehouses down by the docks said that their birds lost much of their viciousness after the great roar of the city had stopped, becoming as useless as pigeons, virtually impossible to provoke to violence.

And there was another effect that was just as impressive: the doctors at several hospitals reported that their mortality rates showed a pronounced decline after each incident, and their recovery rates a marked increase. No, the lame did not walk, and the blind did not see, but patients who were on the verge of recuperating from an injury often seemed to turn the corner during an episode, as if the soundlessness had triggered a decision somewhere deep in the cells of their bodies.

Surely the most dramatic example was the woman at Mercy General who came out of a prolonged coma in the space of a five-second silence. First her hand moved, then her face opened up behind her eyes, and soon after the noise of the hospital reemerged, she moistened her lips and said, "Everything sounded exactly the same to me."

The doctors had a hard time convincing her that she was in fact awake.

8.

The silence proved so beneficial to us that we began to wish it would last forever. We envisioned a city where everyone was healthy and thoughtful, radiant with satisfaction, and the sound of so much as a leaf lighting down on the sidewalk was as rare and as startling as a gunshot.

9.

Who was the first person to suggest that we try generating such a silence ourselves, one that would endure until we chose to end it? No one could remember. But the idea took hold with an astonishing tenacity. Local magazines published laudatory cover stories on the Silence Movement. Leaflets with headings like PROMOTE SILENCE and SILENCE = LIFE appeared in our mailboxes. The politicians of both major parties began to champion the cause, and it wasn't long before a measure was passed decreeing that the city would make every possible effort "to muffle all sources of noise within its borders, so as to ensure a continuing silence for its citizens and their families."

The first step, and the most difficult, was the dampening of the street traffic. We were encouraged first of all to ride the subway trains, which were appointed with all the latest noise-alleviation devices, including soft-fiber pressure pads and magnetic levitation rails. Most of the cars that were left on the road were equipped with silently running electric engines, while the others had their motors fitted with mineral wool shells that allowed them to operate below the threshold of hearing. The roads themselves were surfaced with a reinforced open-cell foam that absorbed all but the lowest frequency sounds, a material that we also adapted for use on our sidewalks and in our parking garages.

Once the street traffic was taken care of, we turned our attention to the city's other sources of noise. We sealed the electrical generators behind thick layers of concrete. We placed the air-conditioning equipment in nonresonant chambers. We redesigned the elevators and cargo lifts, replacing their metal components with a clear durable plastic originally developed by zoos as a display barrier to prevent the roars of the lions from reaching the exhibits of the prey animals. Certain noises that weren't essential to either the basic operations or the general aesthetic texture of the city were simply banned outright: canned music, church bells, fireworks, ringtones.

10.

We were exultant when the roads fell silent and pleased when the elevators stopped crying out on their cables, but by the time the cell phones and the pagers ceased to chirp, we were faced with a problem of diminishing returns. The greater the number of sounds we extinguished, the more we noticed the ones that remained, until even the slightest tap or ripple began to seem like an assault against the silence.

A clock ticking inside a plastic casing.
Water replenishing itself in a toilet tank.
A rope slapping languidly against a flagpole.
A garbage disposal chopping at a stream of running water.
The flat buzzing of a fluorescent light.
A modem squealing its broken tune.
A deodorizer releasing its vapor into the air.
An ice maker's slow cascade of thumps.

One by one, perhaps, these sounds were of little account, but added together they grew into a single vast sonority, and no matter how many of them we were able to root out, we kept discovering others. Now and then, while we were working to eliminate the noise of a match taking light or a soda can popping open, another episode of true silence would occur, a bubble of total peace and calm enwrapping the city in its invisible walls, and we would be reminded of the magnitude of what we were striving for.

How inexcusably flimsy, we realized, was the quiet we had managed to create. We redoubled our efforts.

11.

We were more resourceful than we had imagined. It seemed that for every noise that cropped up, there was at least one person in the city who was prepared to counteract it. An engineer bothered by the medical helicopter that beat by his office a dozen times a day drew up plans for a special kind of rotor blade, one that would slice through the air as smoothly as a pin sliding into a pincushion. He handed the plans over to the hospital. Within a few weeks the helicopter drifted so quietly past his window that he was surprised each time he saw it there. A single mother raising an autistic son who was provoked to fits of punching by the tone of her doorbell devised an instrument that replaced the sound with a pulsing light. She said that her son liked to sit on the floor watching now as she pressed the button again and again, a wobbly grin spreading over his face like a pool of molasses. A carpenter designed a nail gun that would soak up the noise of its own thud. A schoolteacher created a frictionless pencil sharpener. An antiques dealer who liked to dabble in acoustic engineering invented a sonic filter that could comb the air of all its sounds before releasing it into a room.

Eventually every noise but the muffled sigh of our breathing and the ticking of our teeth in our mouths had been removed from the inside of our buildings. The wind continued to blow, and the rain continued to fall, and no one had yet proposed a method to keep the birds from singing, but as long as we did not venture outside, we remained sealed in a cocoon of silence.

12.

There were times when the silence was close to perfect. Whole minutes went by after the early morning light breached the sky when the surging, twisting world of sound left us completely alone, and we could lie there in our beds, simply following our ruminations. We came to know ourselves better than we had before — or if not better, then at least in greater stillness. It was easier for us to see the shapes we wished our lives to take. People changed their jobs, took up chess or poker, began new courses of exercise. A great many couples made their marriage vows, and not a few others filed for divorce. One boy, an eight-year-old who attended the Holy Souls Parochial Academy, left school as the rest of his class was walking to the lunchroom, rode the subway to the natural history museum, and found his way to the dinosaur exhibit. He waited until the room had emptied and then stole beneath the tyrannosaurus, using the giant ribs of the skeleton to climb up to the skull. He was found there late that evening by a security guard, sitting hungry but uninjured on the smoothly curving floor of the jaw. The boy had left a note in his teacher's paper tray explaining himself. He had dreamed that the dinosaur was still roaring, the note said, but so weakly that the sound could only be heard from directly inside its head. He wanted to find out if it was true.

13.

The boy who climbed the tyrannosaurus was not the first of us to feel that his dreams were blending together with his reality. There was something about the luxuriousness of our situation that made it tempting to imagine that the space outside our heads was conforming to the space inside. Yet we did not really believe that this was so. It was just that we were seeing everything with a greater clarity now, both our minds and our surroundings, and the clarity had become more important to us than the division.

14.

The silence was plain and rich and deep. It seemed infinitely delicate, yet strangely irresistible, as though any one of us could have broken it with a single word if we had not been so enraptured. Every so often another natural episode would take place, and for a few seconds the character of the silence would change slightly, the way the brightness of a room might alter as some distant roller in the current surged through a lightbulb, but the quiet we had generated was so encompassing by now that only the most sensitive among us could be sure that something had truly happened.

15.

In the abundant silence we proceeded into ourselves. We fell asleep each night, woke each morning, and went about our routines each day, doing the shopping and preparing our tax returns, making love and cooking dinner, filing papers and cupping our palms to our mouths to check the smell of our breath, all in the beautiful hush of the city. Everywhere we could see the signs of lives in fluctuation.

A librarian who had worked in the periodicals room for almost three decades began displaying her oil paintings at an art gallery — hundreds of them, all on lending slips she had scavenged from the library's in/out tray, each tiny piece of paper flexed with the weight of the paint that had hardened onto it. The fliers at the gallery door proclaimed that the woman had never had the nerve to show her work before the silence was established.

The bursar at the university was caught skimming money from the school's pension fund. In her letter of resignation, she said she was ashamed only that she had been found out. If there was one thing the silence had taught her, she wrote, it was that any grief which befell a professor emeritus could never be more than a fraction of what he deserved.

A visiting gymnast giving an exhibition on the pommel horse at the midtown sports club fractured his wrist while doing a routine scissor movement. But up until the moment of the accident, he reported, the audience in the city was the most respectful he had ever seen, barely a cough or a rustle among them.

16.

Gradually, as we grew used to the stillness, the episodes of spontaneous and absolute silence came less frequently. There might be a three-second burst one week, followed by a one-second flicker a few weeks later, and then, if the episodes were running exceptionally heavy, another one-second echo a week or two after that.

One of the physicists at the city's Lakes and Streams Commission came up with what he called a "skipping-rock model" to describe the pattern. The distribution of the silences, he suggested, was like that of a rock skipping over the water and then, if one could imagine such a thing, doubling back and returning to shore. At first such a rock would land only rarely, but as it continued along its path, it would strike down more and more rapidly, until eventually the water would seize it and it would sink. But then, according to the paradigm, the rock would be ejected spontaneously through the surface to repeat its journey in reverse, hitting the water with increasing rarity until it landed back in the hand of the man who had thrown it.

The physicist could not explain why the silence had adopted this behavior — or who, if anyone, had thrown it — he could only observe that it had.

17.

Some eight months after the first incident took place, it had been so long since anyone had noticed one of the episodes that it seemed safe to presume they were finished.

The city was facing an early winter. Every afternoon a snow of soft, fat flakes would drift gently down from the sky, covering the trees and the pavilions, the mailboxes and the parking meters, the streets and the sidewalks. Recalling the way the snow used to soften the noise of the traffic made us experience a flutter of helpless nostalgia. Everything was different now. The sound of our footsteps creaking over the fresh accumulation was like a horde of crickets scraping their wings together in an empty room.

Not until we walked through the snow did we really discover how accustomed we had grown to the silence.

18.

We might have been content to go on as we were forever, whole generations of us being born into the noiseless world, learning to crawl and stand and tie our shoes, growing up and then apart, setting our pasts aside, and then our futures, and finally dying and becoming as quiet in our minds as we had been in our bodies, had it not been for another event that came to pass.

It was shortly after nine A.M., on Tuesday, January the twenty-sixth, when a few seconds of sound overtook the city. There was a short circuit in the system of sonic filters we had installed in our buildings, and for a moment the walls were transparent to every noise. The engine of a garbage truck backfired. A cat began to yowl. A rotten limb dropped from a tree and shattered the veneer of ice over a pond. Ten thousand people suddenly struck their knees on the corner of a desk or remembered a loss they had forgotten or slid into an orgasm beneath the bodies of their lovers and cried out in pain or grief or sexual ecstasy.

The period of noise was abrupt and explosive, cleanly defined at both its borders. Instinctively we found ourselves twisting around to look for its source. Then the situation corrected itself, and just like that we were reabsorbed in the silence.

It seemed that the city had been opened like a tin can. So much time had gone by since we had heard our lives in their full commotion that we barely recognized the sound for what it was. The ground might have fallen in. The world might have ended.

19.

Four days later another such incident occurred, this one almost eight seconds long. It was followed the next week by a considerably shorter episode, as brief as a coal popping in a fire, which was itself followed a few days later by a fourth episode, and immediately after by a fifth and a sixth, and early the next afternoon by a seventh.

We were at a loss to account for the phenomenon.

A cryptographer employed by the police force announced his belief that both the episodes of silence and the episodes of clamor resembled communications taking the form of Morse code, though from whom or what he could not say. A higher intelligence? The city itself? Any answer he might give would be no more than speculation. His hunch was that the sender, whoever it was, had resorted to using noise because we had ceased to take note of the silence. He said that he was keeping a record of the dots and dashes and hoped to be able to decipher the message very soon.

20.

The cryptographer's theory bore all the earmarks of lunacy, and few of us pretended to accept it, but it was, at least, a theory. Every so often another event would transpire, interrupting the stillness with a burst of shouts and rumbles, and we would stop whatever we were doing, our arms and shoulders braced as if against some invisible blow, and wonder what was going on. Many of us began to look forward to these eruptions of sound. We dreamed about them at night. We awaited them with a feeling of great thirst. The head of the city's notary public department, for instance, missed the noise of the Newton's cradle he kept in his office, the hanging metal balls clicking *tac-tac-tac* against each other as they swayed back and forth. The cabdriver who began his circuit outside the central subway terminal every morning wished that he was still able to punch his horn at the couriers whose bicycles skimmed so close to his bumper. The woman who ran the Christian gift store in the shopping mall designed a greeting card with an illustration of a trio of kittens playing cymbals, bagpipes, and a tuba on the front. The interior caption read MAKE A JOYFUL NOISE UNTO THE LORD. She printed a hundred copies to stock by the cash register, along with twenty-three more to mail to the members of her Sunday school class.

21.

It turned out that in spite of everything the silence had brought us, there was a hidden longing for sound in the city. So many of us shared in this desire that a noise club began operating, tucked away in the depths of an abandoned recording studio. The people who went to the club did so for the pure excitement of it, for the way the din set their hearts to beating. Who needed serenity, they wanted to know? Who had ever asked for it? They stood in groups, listening to the club's switchboard operator laying sound upon sound in the small enclosed space of the room. The slanting note of a violin. The pulse of an ambulance siren. Gallons of water geysering from an open hydrant. A few thousand football fans cheering at a stadium.

Afterward, when the club's patrons arrived home, they lay on their pillows unable to fall asleep, their minds spinning with joy and exhilaration.

22.

The episodes continued into the spring, falling over the city at intervals none of us could predict. Whenever we became most used to the silence, it seemed, the fundamental turmoil of the world would break through the tranquility and present itself to us again. More and more people began to prefer these times of disruption. They made us feel like athletes facing a game, like soldiers who had finished their training, capable of accomplishing great things in battle. A consensus slowly gathered among us. We had given up something important, we believed: the fire, the vigor that came with a lack of ease. We had lost some of the difficulty of our lives, and we wanted it back.

23.

The city council drafted a measure to abolish the silence initiative. After a preliminary period of debate and consideration, it was adopted by common consent. The work of breaking the city's silence was not nearly as painstaking as the work of establishing it had been. With the flip of a few switches and the snip of a few wires, the sonic filters that had sheltered our buildings were disabled, opening our walls to every birdcall and thunderclap. Scrapers and bulldozers tore up the roads, and spreading machines laid down fresh black asphalt. The cloth was unwound from the clappers of the church bells. The old city buses were rolled out of the warehouses. A fireworks stand was erected by the docks, and a gun club opened behind the outlet mall. A man in a black suit carried an orange crate into the park one evening to preach about the dangers of premarital sex. A man with a tattoo of a teardrop on his cheek set three crisply folded playing cards on a table and began shuffling them in intersecting circles, calling out to the people who walked by that he would offer two dollars, two clean new, green new George Washington dollar bills, to anyone who could find that lovely lady, that lady in red, the beautiful queen of hearts.

24.

In a matter of weeks, we could hear cell phones ringing in restaurants again, basketballs slapping the pavement, car stereos pouring their music into the air. Everywhere we went we felt a pleasurable sense of agitation. And if our interactions with each other no longer seemed like the still depths of secluded pools, where enormous fish stared up at the light sifting down through the water — well, the noise offered other compensations.

We became more headstrong, more passionate. Our sentiments were closer to the surface. Our lives seemed no less purposeful than they had during the silence, but it was as if that purpose were waiting several corners away from us now, rather than hovering in front of our eyes.

For a while the outbreaks of sound continued to make themselves heard over the noise of the city, just as the outbreaks of silence had, but soon it became hard to distinguish them from the ongoing rumble of the traffic. There were a few quick flashes of noise during the last week of May, but if they carried on into the summer, we failed to notice them. In their place were dogs tipping over garbage cans, flatbed trucks beeping as they backed out of alleys, and fountains spilling into themselves again and again.

The quiet that sometimes fell over us in movie theaters began to seem as deep as any we had ever known. We had a vague inkling that we had once experienced our minds with a greater intimacy, but we could not quite recover the way it had felt.

25.

Every day the silence that had engulfed the city receded further into the past. It was plain that in time we would forget it had ever happened. The year that had gone by would leave only a few scattered signs behind, like the imprints of vanished shells in the crust of a dried lake bed: the exemplary hush of our elevators, the tangles of useless wire in our walls, and the advanced design of our subway lines, fading slowly into antiquation. That and a short item published in the Thursday, July the eighth, edition of the morning newspaper, a letter detailing the results of the log the police department's cryptographer had been keeping, a repeating series of dots and dashes whose meaning was explicit, he said, but whose import he could not fathom. Dot, dash, dot, dot. Dot, dot. Dot, dot, dot. Dash. Dot. Dash, dot. Dot, dash, dash. Dot. Dot, dash, dot, dot. Dot, dash, dot, dot.

KAREN BROWN

Galatea

FROM *Crazyhorse*

I MARRIED WILLIAM in upstate before he turned out to be the Collegetown Creeper. I took his last name and became Margaret Mary Bell. I was named after my father's aunt, who was a novice with the Benedictine sisters of Regina Laudis, in Bethlehem, Connecticut, when she died on the turnpike with three other sisters, all on their way back to the convent after a retreat. I often imagined them driving in a sky-blue sedan with the windows down and the bright sun on the hood. The air on their faces is cool and smells of cut grass. It catches in their wimples, invades the seams, and soothes their scalps. Their habits flap. They have the radio on, and the Searchers sing "Love Potion Number Nine," and they laugh. They are young women, wedded to God. Their mouths open and drink in the sun and the wind. Under the black fabric their bodies surge in secret, betraying their vows. Sometimes I wanted to be pinioned in that faith, in the rules of their love. I felt my heart drawn out in wild longing with the words: *devotion, ecstasy, rapture,* and *betrothal.*

I was going to graduate school then, and writing, and I met William Bell one day while my sister was visiting, and we went to a park playground by Cayuga Lake. The lake was dark and cold, and the wind gusted off of it in an unfriendly way, rattling the bare maple branches, clanking the chains of the mostly empty swings. The playground was the old-fashioned kind, with wooden seesaws and one of those spinning platforms with metal handles, and the few kids there were playing on that, all of them running in the worn circle of dirt, making it spin, feebly, and then jumping on. My sister and I didn't have children ourselves, but we remembered how fun it was when we were small, and so we told them to climb on, and we both grabbed one of the metal bars, and the kids held on with their mittens, and we ran and pushed with all our force. Some of the kids were too small, and the spinning made them afraid, and one even flew off. It was a sickening sight, the way he was flung into the dirt. My sister and I looked at each other in horror, and a few of the other mothers knelt down by the boy, who turned out to be William Bell's nephew, and I almost cried, I was so embarrassed. Then William came over and grabbed the boy by the arm and righted him, quickly, as if nothing was wrong.

"God, don't hate me," I said.

William had one of those smooth-cheeked faces that flush in cold weather. He brushed the dirt from the boy's pants knees and wiped his tear-stained face with his bare hand, and the whole time he kept glancing up at me, reassuring me no, really, not a big deal. Meanwhile the little boy whimpered, and I wondered if he'd bumped his head or sustained some injury of which William remained oblivious.

"Is he okay?" I asked. And sure enough his pants had torn, and his little knee was skinned and raw and bloody.

"Oh, shit," William said. "My sister will kill me."

The other mothers had silently reclaimed their children, and none of us really knew how to tend to the boy, so William was resigned to taking him home that way and suffering his sister's anger. He told me about it that night when he called me, how his sister's eyes panicked, and she grabbed the boy away from him so quickly, he felt like a criminal.

"You should have told her it was my fault," I said. I sat on my bed, pulled out from the couch. It had begun to snow. In the streetlight, I could see the snow whitening the branches of the big elm outside my window. I had written my phone number on a ski tag I tore from my sister's parka that afternoon. I was so happy he had called. I kept remembering his eyes looking at me in the park, and the way his cheeks reddened from the cold. My sister sat watching TV a few feet away from me, shushing me every so often so she could hear. We drank hot chocolate spiked with Kahlua and ate candy corn I bought in a moment of nostalgia on Halloween. I told William about my Women and Grief course, how we listened to tapes of keening women from Ireland and Greece.

"I can barely stand it," I said.

"Is it sad?" he asked me. "Is it awful?"

I tried to explain how it was so awful, I wanted to laugh, and how hard it was not to, did he think I was crazy? He told me no, of course not. You're interesting, he said. He lived with his sister and his nephew and was in between jobs because he'd been kicked out of the university's College of Engineering. He was an inventor, he said, who could not abide by someone else's schedule. He called every day that week, and our talking became whispered intimations, everything taking on some imagined double meaning. He said the moss on the rocks at the bottom of a shallow stream was the same color as my eyes, and asked if he could come over to my apartment, and I remembered he had called me *interesting,* so I said yes.

He came on a Friday night. I watched for him out of my window, through the branches of the elm. My apartment was only one large room upstairs in a house on Seneca Street. Downstairs lived a poet named Angela who was a student too. She was very tall and soft-spoken, one of those people you sit with late at night and tell everything to. I could see the light from her window, the way it shone out onto the snow. I often imagined what it would have been like to live in the entire house alone, to move freely through all the rooms, to traverse the stairs and wander into a dining room and a kitchen at the back of the house. Now someone living a separate life occupied these spaces — Angela, and Geoff and his dog Suzie downstairs, and Professor Harrow upstairs with me. Our lives invaded one another's in unwanted, unacknowledged ways. The floors were oak and they creaked, and I listened to Professor Harrow's insomniac footsteps back and forth when I couldn't sleep. I had a fireplace in my apartment. Angela had one downstairs in hers. We were not allowed to use them, but we put large lighted pillar candles in them, and it gave the illusion of the warmth that we desired.

The cold here was bitter, different than New England. Outside the city, the wind spilled across sweeping, open spaces dotted with abandoned farm machinery and old houses buckling in on themselves. You wouldn't think they were habitable, but once in a while there would be a tacked-up sheet in the doorway, or plastic nailed over the windows, and the narrow ribbon of smoke from a chimney. William Bell was not from anywhere else. He was born here, in Tompkins County, and lived here all his life. At one time his father sold and repaired lawnmowers in a shop behind their house, and before that he was an attorney. They had an enclosed front porch with an air hockey game, and gnome statuary on the front lawn that William, as a child, believed came alive at night. Before she died, his mother grew apples and sold them from a small roadside stand, Macoun and Winesap and Cortland. I imagined, from these aspects of his life, that I knew everything about him. When he pulled up to the curb, I found myself rushing down the stairwell to meet him at the door, tugging him by the arm in from the cold. It was still snowing, the light, fluttery, lake effect snow that went on for days. "Come here, you," I said. He smiled, slowly, unsure what to make of me. His cheeks held their usual flush. He wore a wide-brimmed beaver-skin hat. We stood on the old worn Persian rug in what once was the vestibule. The walls were papered in brown, with tiny pink roses. The woodwork was brown too, mahogany shining in the weak yellow overhead light. There was a coat rack and an umbrella stand and a small, rickety antique table. The whole downstairs smelled of Angela's incense.

He looked around, somewhat sheepish, and removed his hat with one hand, grabbing it at the crown. "I like this place," he said, nodding.

"Your hat is different," I told him.

He looked at it in his hand. "Well," he said. "It was my father's hat."

When he glanced up at me, his face was sad. I thought that, once, women met their lovers here and, pressed by decorum, demurely took their hats and coats. I wondered if the thought I had ever occurred to them — that if William Bell and I had sex, there might be some sweet added dimension of loss and sorrow conquered, for a moment, in my arms. I didn't know this person I had become. I had always assumed I would demand things of boys and men, dicker with my body, holding out interminably until they proved themselves in some way. But that night, I didn't wait to kiss him. I wanted to ease that sadness about his mouth with mine. His lips clung and trembled, kissing me back. Upstairs in my apartment, by the wavering fireplace candlelight, I undressed for him. All year, except the months of July and August when the summer heat rose to make a sweltering pocket, my apartment was cold. William slid his hands up and down my body and felt the raised bumps on my skin.

"I can't warm you up," he said. So we climbed into my bed, under the quilt and the blanket. That night the palms of his hands skimmed the surface of me, and he talked, his voice a soft hum that I had grown used to on the phone. I didn't know what he wanted with me. When I touched him, he took my hands away, sweetly, like a correcting parent. Then he fell asleep.

My bed was lumpy with springs, and I had a certain angle in which I slept. But with William taking up the space, and my body burning and bright from his fingertips, I could not. I imagined I was Auntie Sister, who at my age entered the abbey. I'd always pictured her alone in her chaste bed, consumed with desire for something ineffable and bodiless, but lying there I knew you could not separate the two — body and desire. I watched the shadows of the elm on my white plaster wall. I listened to the silence of the snow. The branches, sheathed in ice, clicked together like delicate bones. On my wall above my desk I have pasted a poem Angela gave to me, one of Sylvia Plath's, with its elm voice: *Clouds pass and disperse. Are those the faces of love, those pale irretrievables? Is it for such I agitate my heart?* I listened for Professor Harrow's slippered footfalls, their shushing across his oak flooring, back and forth. Sometimes a deliberate, thoughtful pacing. At others, a slow, anguished dragging. I rarely saw him in our upstairs hall. When I did, I must have worn an expression of sympathy, because he avoided me, and hurried down the stairs, as if he knew I knew, and he was ashamed of his wakefulness. The times we met, his face was white and startled. His hair was dark, combed back damply. He wore a camel overcoat with soiled elbows and smelled of the cigarettes I'd seen him smoke furtively, like a teenager, at his cracked window.

On the first night William slept with me, Professor Harrow was quiet. I envied him. I tried to breathe in and out, regularly, to feign sleep. I propped my head in my hands and looked at William Bell's face. Were we still strangers? I wondered. Or had something been forged about which we would never speak? I wouldn't know just then how he felt. His sleeping, slack expression revealed nothing, and I felt a small, pitiable stone of fear. How easily I could be abandoned. At least, in sleep, I would not have to wonder what I wanted. When I did sleep, it was near morning. I awoke to find William Bell watching me in the gray light. We were like sentries who had traded places.

I looked at him, looking at me. He seemed sad again, defeated.

"You could never love me," he said, somberly.

His cheeks were flushed again. His breath came out in a white cloud, and the candles in the fireplace had burned down to flat saucers of wax. He sat upright, with his bare chest exposed, and my grandmother's crocheted afghan swaddling his waist, multicolored and garish.

"Well," I said. I didn't know how to finish. I could not admit that I was thinking about his body below the covers. "You look cold."

He stared at me, his chest pale against the afghan. "I don't care," he said. "I don't care about anything right now."

He looked away. I heard him breathe, deeply. But he didn't make a move to get up and leave.

"You don't have to stay," I said. I rolled away from him, to the metal edge of the bed. I thought of Professor Harrow, waking, what his routine might be on a Saturday morning — toast, coffee in a china cup. I imagined him with buttery crumbs on his fingers, listening through the walls. William Bell sighed again and heaved himself out of bed. He was tall, and I heard his body unfold. I listened to him find his clothes, to his soft sighs retrieving them, and the sound of the fabric slipping over his arms and legs. Finally, he put on his shoes, big boots that clomped appallingly. I turned around, and he was standing over the bed.

"Tell me not to go," he said.

"Tell me you want to stay," I told him.

"Ask me to kiss you," he said.

"Do you want to kiss me?" I was confused. I saw it was useless to talk.

"I want to kiss you more than anyone I have ever met," he said, but he made no move toward the bed. His eyes were troubled and dark. He turned then and went out the door. I heard him thump down the stairs. I didn't get up and lock the door behind him. I lay there for a long time, wondering whether or not to believe him. Finally, I slept again. When I awoke, it must have been early afternoon. Weak sunlight shone across the end of the bed. And William Bell was there, sitting in the armchair I found in an antique store, its worn upholstered arms curving over wood inlaid with the carved heads of ducks. He was watching television without the sound. He ate from a carton I recognized from the Korean place in Collegetown. I thought I should be a little afraid of him, coming into my apartment without asking, but I was not.

I moved on the bed, and he glanced back at me. He smiled, wide and happy. I hadn't seen him smile like that before. There were many things I hadn't seen about him, things I couldn't know. None of that mattered then. My body was warm, my limbs slid across the soft sheets. He brought the food over to the bed and sat on the end. "Are you hungry?" he asked. I rose up onto my knees and put my arms around his shoulders. His face changed, quickly, like clouds moving over the sun and the shadows lengthening on a lawn. He set the food down on the floor. I smelled its spices on his mouth. I heard his breathing catch, felt his body's sudden shift, its tension, like something coiled and tight. His hands were cold. It felt wonderful, his hands on me, his mouth moving, his groans. I thought: he came into my room while I slept, and I grew breathless and greedy for him.

We stayed in bed all that day. I heard Professor Harrow come up the stairs and slip his key into his lock. William Bell held me in his hands. I felt my body transform, heighten and strain and sigh. What else would make me happier? Just then, I believed in anything — love, *irretrievables.* The light moved in its pale way across the foot of my bed, across the worn oak floor. It settled in the lap of the antique chair. We let the room grow dim and darken and match the outside. When the streetlight came on, we watched the snow falling in it.

"Does it ever stop snowing here?" I asked him. His hand was heavy, pressed to my bare stomach.

"It's winter," he said, as if this was an answer.

My stomach rumbled, and he said we needed to feed me, and so he pulled me up and my nakedness was light and airy in the dark. I stood on the foldout bed. He slid off the end and stood in front of me.

"Look at you," he said. "Galatea."

I posed, rigid, like marble.

William Bell reached up and put his hands on my hips. I remembered this moment for a long time after — the press of his thumbs, his cradling of me. He leaned in and kissed my hipbones, my thighs. I didn't need food. I wanted to be ravished. This was, for the most part, what became of us. His devotion, my submission. That night we dressed and went out into the snowy street. The houses lined up in their rows, their roofs thick and white, the lampposts and power lines and tree limbs all leaden with snow. The snow falling was eerie and oddly warm. He held my hand, and I let him. Every so often he stopped and pulled me in to kiss. A passing car's headlights would light us up.

"Isn't this being in love?" he said.

I told him I didn't know.

We stood on the sidewalk, under someone's porch light. Inside the house we saw people watching television, just their feet in socks propped up on a coffee table. They still had their jack-o'-lanterns on the porch. Though they were nearly buried, you could just make out the carved grimaces. I noticed, all around, things caught unprepared by snow — a rake propped against a fence, a child's bicycle tossed down on the grass. On the porch a pair of socks, pulled off and abandoned, frozen stiff in their contortions.

"You don't trust anything," he said, despondent. He let my hand drop. I had to retrieve his hand and tell him to stop it. I wondered if this was love, this constant reclamation, this rush to reassure. We kept walking and he steered me past the railroad tracks into an end of town I had never been to, not even with Angela in her Volvo. We stopped at the head of a path. Below us a creek, not yet frozen, rushed in the dark. To the right were scattered twinkling lights and a soft din of conversation. I sensed low-built dwellings coated with snow and imagined people in them. There were several fires burning. The place smelled of wood smoke and the dank creek mud.

William Bell took my hand. "Let's go," he said.

Of course, I would not. He looked back at me, calmly chastising. "These people know me," he said.

My feet had grown cold in my boots. I didn't know what he would need to say to make me walk down the path with him. He stepped toward me and slid his two hands up under my coat, under my sweater and T-shirt. His hands on my skin, the press of his fingertips, were somehow consoling, familiar.

"You must trust me," he said, softly, into my hair.

And I was not sure whether it was that I trusted him or that I worried if I didn't, he would take his hands away forever. He held my hand again and we went down the path worn muddy by others' footsteps. The enclave consisted of tents and tarps strung on two-by-fours. Strung bulbs, or Christmas lights, powered by a small generator, lit some of the dwellings. There were end tables with small, shaded lamps and tinny radios. Under the tarps, or around the fires, the people sat on aluminum chairs, the kind with plastic slats, low-slung canvas chairs, camp chairs, the type you took to an outdoor concert or a kid's sports game, or the beach. The people eyed us, warily. They were dressed for the weather, in layers of clothes that made them look lumpy, and all of the same size and sex. We kept walking down the narrow paths. The snow fell, landing in their fires and hissing. The mud sucked at my boots. From the tents came the smells of humans — stale breath, refuse, the odor of a dirty clothes hamper. We arrived at a fire removed from the others. Around it, the people laughed and passed a bottle around. They smoked, and their exhaling formed large clouds about their heads. When they saw William, they greeted him, all at once.

"Well, if it isn't Mr. Bell Junior," one said.

There were no chairs for us. We stood beside their group, feeling the warmth of their fire on our faces.

"What do you have for us?" someone else asked. I wondered if this was a kind of password or mode of entry, the bringing of something, like a gift. I still could not distinguish between the men and the women. Their voices were the same — deep and gravelly. They wore knitted caps, some with pompoms, some striped and bright. They seemed like children sitting by the fire.

"I've brought the woman I'm going to marry," William said.

I looked at him, quickly, and stepped away. "What?" I said.

There was a sudden quiet. A throat was cleared, raspy, horrible. Either William's announcement, or my objection, was out of place in their circle. I thought I saw one person roll his eyes.

"Oh Lord, get Billy Bell out here," another said.

Around us the snow blew softly. The sky was a black bowl, starless. I could see the shapes of trees, their remaining leaves withered and clinging, lonely shapes on slender twigs. A man emerged from one of the nearby tents. He was tall and well built. He wore a heavy tweed overcoat and lumbered up to us. In the firelight, I saw his eyes in his roughened face, exactly like William Bell's.

"What now?" he said, gruff, unforgiving.

He pulled a cigarette from his pocket and then looked to the group for a light. William took a silver Zippo from his own pocket and lit the man's cigarette. Both of their hands went up to cup the flame from the wind. Here was the man who lined up mowers on his front lawn with prices handwritten on cardboard placards, who with youthful earnestness argued cases in a courtroom in downtown Ithaca. I noticed he was unsteady, swaying in his long coat.

"Did you hear?" someone around the fire said. "He's brought the woman he is going to marry."

"Or not," snickered someone else. The group laughed, tentatively, not sure of what to make of this situation.

The tall man sighed. He wore a wool Burberry's scarf tucked into his collar. He would not look at either of us.

"Get out of here," he said, quietly. His voice was ominous, threatening.

William Bell stayed. They were nearly the same height.

"I thought you should meet," he said. I sensed the sarcasm in his voice, a kind of tremor. I saw that once, the older man would have put his hand on William's shoulder or taken him in his arms. I knew that William was waiting for all of these things.

Someone in the circle started singing a low, bawdy song. Something about *wedded* and *bedded, O.* Others joined in, creating a distraction, an odd background accompaniment. The older man turned and stumbled back into his tent. I figured he would have his place to sit there, his bottle. He could listen to our retreating footsteps in the mud and feel whatever it was he felt — compunction, sorrow. As we left, the other groups around their fires joined in the song. There was cackling laughter, not derisive, but a waylaid sadness. I imagined all of them having slipped down their own lives to this place, forsaken, or perhaps unwilling to let anyone lay claim to them. We made our way up the embankment, listening to the creek slough its banks. Soon the temperature would dip, and its surface would still and thicken. Underneath the rainbow trout would sit, dumb and cowed, waiting for spring.

I did not talk about the incident of that evening to William Bell. We returned to my apartment and it was dawn. We had walked home in silence. I had held his hand. Upstairs we met Professor Harrow in his plaid robe and slippers. His ankles were bare and white. He seemed dazed, standing on the landing. It was cold, and our breath came out around our heads.

"Good morning," he mumbled, standing there as if he'd been chased from his room by something to which he did not wish to return. I put my key in the lock and regretted seeing him like that. Inside the apartment it was still cold, still gray and dark. William Bell sat heavily on the end of the bed and put his face in his hands. The elm scraped my window. The snow fell, invisibly, blending into the whitish morning. I sat down beside William and felt I might save him with a profession of love. I pushed him down on the bed and looked into his face. He shook his head and tried to turn away.

"Look at me," I said, and he did.

We looked at each other for a long time, believing we knew what the other thought. I saw I could imagine anything about him, even a past he might never confess. I saw this was what love was.

"Will you?" he asked.

I kissed him. His hands fell back into place on my body. We both got what we wanted, I think. A notary in an old house on Tioga married us in a civil ceremony. Outside, the snow was like powdered sugar falling through a sieve. It didn't seem real. It was like stage snow, pretty and harmless. As we spoke our vows, though, it turned to ice, and slanted against the window, a vindictive tapping.

We had very little money. He worked for a few weeks at Agway, selling snow shovels and bags of salt and light bulbs, and I was proud of him, getting up at a normal hour, showering and putting on clean clothes. He came home sedate and smelling of loam, and I was happy. Then he quit. He acquired and left a succession of jobs, and I discovered that this was his pattern, and he saw nothing wrong with it. I stayed with him in Ithaca for the Christmas holiday. His sister had been furious when she'd found out we'd married, and she refused to have anything to do with us, so I hadn't yet told my own family. It seemed then the most foolish of things to do with my life.

We fell into a kind of decline. The apartment was cluttered and unclean. I had a small stove and a few pots that we washed out when we needed them. They sat on the burners with their previous contents congealing. William's bits of magnetized wire, bulbs and circuits and metal shavings littered the window ledges. The little Christmas tree still sat in its pot on the table by the window, its branches absent of any green life. The glass ornaments slipped off, one at a time, at night. In the darkness, they made small splashing sounds when they shattered, like spilling water.

Winter in upstate is interminable. Here the snow was a burden in piled banks, an endless tumbling of flakes. Icicles hung from the house's eaves, deadly threats you ducked under or knocked off with a shovel. The reaches of snow were vast, wide, white fields rolling on and on. There was a bitter wind that rattled the windows in their frames. I didn't think I could stand it, and I told William Bell, and he gave me his look of reproof. Consider the people in the encampment, his look said. We had not gone back there again, though I suspected that William did. When we shopped at Goodwill, looking for a writing table, he purchased clothing, and shoes that I never saw him wear. Often, Angela offered us food, extra loaves of bread, casseroles in disposable tins, and it disappeared. I didn't question him about anything. I let the undiscussed spaces in our life together flourish. I didn't care where he went or what he did, as long as he returned to me.

And then one afternoon I came home and the chairs that went around my small table were missing. Another day the lamp was gone, and then the table itself. These things were not acceptable, I told him. He stared at me, blankly, with his beautiful flushed cheeks. He did not return that night, or the next, or the next, when the snow stopped and things began to melt and drip. I called his sister but hung up on the answering machine. For two weeks I went to my classes and came home, and he was still gone. I began to imagine Sister Margaret Mary, her unrequited body prone on her narrow bed in her sparsely furnished room. There was her dark clothing in the closet and above the small chest of drawers the brassy body of Christ on the cross, the object onto which she safely fastened her own longing. And then I came back from class one evening and the hangers that once held his clothes were bare wires, and the bureau drawer where he kept his sweaters and balls of socks was empty.

I distracted myself with cleaning, left the windows open, and let the cold air blow through the place. I brushed William's magnetized pieces of wire and metal out the window into the snow below. I used bleach and scrubbed, borrowed Angela's mop. I loaded the blankets and sheets in her car and drove them to the Laundromat, maneuvering around the potholes in the streets, the slush spraying up onto the windshield. Outside, without William Bell, the world was changing.

At the Laundromat, I saw a boy I'd met when I first came to school. I could not remember his name, but he remembered mine, and he asked me what I was reading and what courses I was taking this semester, and then asked me more things, and I realized I wasn't answering him the way I normally might because I was married now, and I felt the boundaries of this, without really wanting to. The big hot dryers rolled and tumbled. Pieces of lint floated past. And I looked at his earnest expression, his eyes lit with genuine interest, and I looked at myself as he saw me: my hair too long, uncombed, my sweater with its unraveling wool hem, the smell of bleach on my hands. And I wondered, crazily, if he could love me. "Help me take my stuff to my car," I said.

He grabbed armfuls. I opened the Volvo's trunk and we put the sheets and blankets inside. And then we stood in the slush in the cold, filling the space between us with our fogging breath. "Come home with me and help me make the bed," I said.

He glanced around, as if someone might witness all of this occurring, as if he'd stepped into a story and been asked to play a role. He didn't smile and answer right away. Then I saw him bite the inside of his cheek.

"Are you serious?" he said, quietly, covertly.

I shrugged. "Of course," I told him.

Climbing into his car, he was eager and quick. He drove that way too, following too close behind, almost hitting me once at a stop sign. At my house I parked at the curb and he carried everything in his arms up the stairs. His footsteps were light, glancing off each step, careening up to the landing where he had to wait for me to unlock the door. I heard him breathing behind the pile of laundry.

Inside, the breeze had whipped things into a frenzy. Magazines and manuscript pages had blown onto the floor. The curtains were caught up in their rods. All of the old smells seemed resurrected — fireplace ashes, oak polish, the walls' dampened plaster. It wasn't unpleasant. It felt cold and fiercely alive.

"It is freezing in here," the boy said.

I imagined he dreaded removing his clothes.

I shut the windows and the room stilled. I turned to him and tried to remember his name. We were in the Native American class on the third floor of the Andrew White house. We read the story of the Lakota. He grinned at me from across the room. I saw he had no idea what to do, and without any complicity, neither did I.

"This is the bed," I said. The mattress was thin in the pitiless March light. He grabbed an end of a sheet, and we stretched it out from either side. From the pile of bed sheets we found the one to go on top, our heads bumping, sorting through everything. His hair smelled of shampoo. The room filled with the smell of clean laundry. We made the bed. He was very competent and serious, as if this was really what he had expected. When we were done he sat down on the edge.

"I want a cigarette," he said. He looked up at me, apologetically.

"I don't smoke," I told him. I sat down on the bed next to him.

"Maybe we should go out and have a few pitchers of beer," he said.

I took his hand and placed it on my leg. We both looked at it, a fine hand with long fingers and bulky knuckles. "There isn't a set way to go about this," I told him. "Either you want me more than a cigarette, or you don't."

He chuckled and ran his free hand through his hair. He would not look at me at all. "Do you do this a lot?" he asked. "I mean, you're a pretty girl. I could be the Creeper."

I asked him what he meant, and he told me the story of the Collegetown Creeper, how he showed up in women's unlocked apartments while they slept. They awoke to him standing over their beds or sitting idly in a chair, wearing a wide-brimmed hat. I imagined they did not look favorably on his presence or invite him to bed. They screamed, and swore at him, and called the authorities. I looked at the boy's fine-boned face, his eyebrows drawn together, telling his story.

"You aren't him," I said.

"Didn't you go to Wellesley?" he asked.

I told him he must have me confused with someone else.

"Didn't you go to Yale?" I asked him.

He laughed then. "No, I didn't," he said.

"Well then," I said. "We aren't who we thought we were."

The sheets smelled like laundry soap. The spot of sun on the bed was almost warm. "We are just imitations of what we thought," he said.

His hand on my leg heated it up. Our bodies touched at the shoulder and hip. They sank at varying depths into the too-thin mattress. "What if we kiss?" I suggested. Anything to stop his musing.

He put both of his hands on my face then and held it like a bowl you might tip and drink from. I felt my heart shift and give, dislodged from its winter hibernation. Most men exhibit at least one endearing gesture, and this was his. His mouth was soft and he closed his eyes. We kissed for a long time on the clean-smelling bed. He whispered my name like a summoning spell. I didn't even know his. I wouldn't have said it, anyway. I knew he wouldn't stay, that once he was through and his clothing back on, he would saunter out into the hallway, relieved to be done with me, grateful and changed, but still relieved. It was this way with all of them afterward. When they left, they always gave me something. "You're sweet," they'd say. I'd have put on his undershirt, and when I began to remove it, he'd tell me, "No, keep it." One gave me his St. Christopher's medal on a tarnished chain, another his L.L. Bean windbreaker. Often, when they spent the night, I dreamed I heard William's boots clomping up the stairs, scraping mud outside the door. He would come in and stand by the bed in the gray light. I'd search his face for some evidence of my betrayal, and find none. His eyes did their usual sad dance over the body he no longer held, and then he turned and left the room. Sometimes, in the dream, I chased after him. And sometimes, awake, I did the same, slipping out of bed and down the stairs, out the front door onto the porch. I'd stand there, shivering, half dressed, fooled by what was dream and what was real, no longer able to tell the difference.

At Easter I finally went home to visit, and when I returned to my apartment it had been emptied of its furnishings. Angela was out of town. When I knocked on Professor Harrow's door, he answered and placed a hand on my arm. His eyes held a blinking lasciviousness I had never noticed before. "Well, well," he said, and I pulled my arm away. "I assumed you'd moved out." There had been banging on the stairs, he told me, and a pickup truck at the curb. I knew William Bell had been there and taken everything. I would not go looking. I did not trust what I wanted to find — my duck-carved chair inside the flap of a tent, its legs sunk in muddied earth, the bed unfolded from the couch in the broad spring sunlight. I might have begged to stay, to lie down on the worn sheets that smelled of melting snow. At night the little strung lights must leave spangles on the canvas like stars. The bonfire smoke invades clothing and pores. The creek rushes its banks again with fervor. I no longer remembered the day we married. Only the day I knew we would, those moments with my heart warm and rapt, the silent promise of the frozen world, the elm chafing in its coat of ice.

KATIE CHASE

Man and Wife

FROM *The Missouri Review*

THEY SAY EVERY GIRL REMEMBERS that special day when everything starts to change.

I was lying under the tree in my parents' backyard, an oak old enough to give shade but too young to be climbed, when Dad's car pulled into the garage. All afternoon I'd been riding bikes with Stacie, but we had a fight when she proposed we play in my basement — it *was* getting too hot out, but I was convinced she was only using me for my Barbies. This was eight years ago. I was nine and a half years old.

Dad came out and stood in the driveway, briefcase in hand, watching me pull up grass. "Mary Ellen!"

I yanked one final clump, root and dirt dangling from my hands, and sat up.

"Come inside. I have wonderful news."

In the kitchen Dad was embracing my mother, his arms around her small, apron-knotted waist. "I can't believe it went through," she was saying. She turned to me with shiny eyes, cleared her throat, and said in her sharp voice, "Mary, go get down the good glasses."

I pushed a chair to the cupboards and climbed onto the countertop. Two glass flutes for my parents, and for myself a plastic version I'd salvaged from last New Year's, the first time I'd been allowed, and encouraged, to stay up past midnight and seen how close the early hours of the next day were to night.

Dad took down the last leftover bottle of champagne and popped it open, showering the kitchen floor. My mother laughed and wiped her hands on her polka-dotted apron, as if she'd gotten wet.

"Hold up your glass, Mary Ell," said Dad. He filled it halfway, and theirs to the rim. When in the past I'd been curious about alcohol, my parents had frowned, taken a drink, and feigned expressions of disgust. On New Year's, for instance, my cup had held plain orange juice, and the next morning, while my parents still slept, I'd had orange juice in it again.

"A toast." My mother held up her glass and waited.

I waited too. The champagne fizzed, bubbles rising.

"To Mary," said Dad, and then he stopped, choked up.

"Our own little girl, to be a woman," my mother said. "Bottoms up."

They clinked their glasses together, and mine met theirs dully, with a tap that brought an end to the pleasant ringing they'd created. I brought the champagne to my lips. I found that if ingested in small sips, it was quite drinkable, no worse than my mother's Diet Coke, and it had the welcome effect of making me feel I was floating away.

"Don't you want to hear what the big news is?" said Dad. My mother turned her back on us to the cutting board, where she was chopping a fresh salad.

In a small voice I said, "Yes." I tried to smile, but that feeling was in my stomach, made more fluttery by drink. I recognize the feeling now as a kind of knowledge.

"Well, do you remember Mr. Middleton? From Mommy and Daddy's New Year's party?"

At the party I'd been positioned, in scratchy lace tights and a crinoline-skirted dress, at the punch bowl to ladle mimosas for their guests. Many of their friends introduced themselves to me that night: Mr. Baker, Mr. Silverstein, Mr. Weir. Some bent to my height and shook my hand. Mr. Woodward scolded me for insufficiently filling his cup, and his young wife, Esmerelda, my former babysitter, led him away.

"Mr. Middleton — that nice man with the mustache? You talked together for quite some time."

Then I remembered. As I served other guests, he'd lingered with a glass of sweating ice water, talking about his business. He directed his words to the entire room, looking out over it rather than at me, but he spoke quietly, so only I could hear. He offered figures: annual revenue, percentages, the number of loyal clients. And then:

"My business is everything. It is my whole life." I looked up at him curiously, and his face reddened; his mustache twitched. When he finally left, patting my shoulder and thanking me for indulging him, I was relieved. I'd had little to say in return — no adult had ever spoken to me that way — and I'd felt the whole time, on the tip of my tongue, the remark that might have satisfied and gotten rid of him sooner.

"That's the good news," Dad said. "He's gone ahead and asked for your hand. And we've agreed to it."

My mother put down the knife and finished off her champagne. I wanted no more of mine.

"Well, don't be so excited," said Dad. "Do you understand what I'm saying? You're going to be a wife. You're going to live with Mr. Middleton, and he's going to take care of you, for the rest of your life. And, one day, when we're very old, he'll help out your mother and me too.

"Yep." He smiled. "It's all settled. Just signed the contract this afternoon. You'll really like him, I think. Nice man. You seemed to like him at the party, anyhow."

"He was okay," I managed to say. It was as I'd feared, somewhere, all along: the toast, the party, everything. But now he had a face, and a name. Now it was real: my future was just the same as any other girl's. Yet none of my friends had become wives yet, and it didn't seem fair that I should be the first taken. For one thing, I was too skinny. They say men first look for strength in a wife. Next they look for beauty, and even with braces and glasses yet to come, I was a homely little girl. It's last that men look for brains. You may notice that I skipped over wealth. While rumors of sex spread freely at school, it wasn't clear to me then just how money fit in. It was discussed only in negotiations, when lawyers were present and we were not. It was best that way for our parents, who tried to keep such things separate.

At dinner I pushed the food around on my plate, clearing a forkwide path and uncovering the blue-and-white pattern of little people kneeling in rice fields and pushing carts. My mother was on her third glass of champagne — she wouldn't last through *Jeopardy!* — and she was laughing at everything Dad said about his anxious day at the office.

A timer buzzed, and my mother rose from the table to pull out her raspberry pie. She approached me with the dish clasped in her oven mitts.

"Take a good look at that pie, Mary."

The crust was golden brown, its edges pressed with the evenly spaced marks of a fork prong. Sweet red berries seeped through the three slits of a knife.

"It's perfect," she said, with her usual ferocity.

The next morning Stacie acted like our fight hadn't happened, and I wanted to play along. We went to ride bikes while my mother showered. Dad's car had left already for work, and he'd dragged the garbage out to the curb. The champagne bottle poked from the recycling bin, ready to be taken away. It was another summer day.

"We had a celebration last night," I told Stacie. "Dad let me have booze."

"Oh, yeah? What for?" She pedaled ahead and moved onto the street, which her parents, and mine, forbade.

I had to shout, she was so far ahead. "Someone named Mr. Middleton wants to take me."

Stacie slammed on her brakes and turned her bike to face me. Once caught up, I kept going.

"When?" she demanded, appearing alongside. "You know he can't take you yet."

"Why not?" I said, but I assumed, as did Stacie, that there'd be a long period of engagement. In the fall we were to start the fifth grade, and it was rare for a girl still in elementary to be taken.

"He must really like you," Stacie said, in awe. We pedaled slowly, pensively. "But you're so skinny."

Mrs. Calderón, in her silken robe, was out watering her rose bushes. She waved.

"We'd better get on the sidewalk," I said.

When we reached Maple Court, we laid our bikes on the island and sprawled in the warm grass, making daisy chains from the flowering weeds. Stacie put her hand on my arm. It was rare for us to touch.

"Whatever happens," she said, "don't dump me."

"What do you mean?"

"I mean, ever since my sister went to live with Mr. Gordon, she never plays with me anymore. When she comes over, she just sits in the kitchen with my mom, drinking tea." She rolled her eyes. "They talk about recipes, and my mom gives her a frozen casserole that she pretends to Mr. Gordon she made by herself."

"Okay," I said. "I promise."

She held up her pinky, and I joined it with mine.

"I promise, when I live with Mr. Middleton, you can still come over and play Barbies."

"Not just Barbies," she said. "We'll still play everything. We'll still be best friends."

I hadn't even been sure we were best friends, since during school she spent her time with ratty-haired Cassandra, and I, in protest, with the studious Chan twins. But I remained solemn. Maybe she wasn't using me. Besides, although I couldn't really imagine what it would be like to be a wife, I knew I wouldn't want to be stuck with Mr. Middleton all the time. I began to laugh.

"What?"

"He has the stupidest mustache!" I drew a thin line above my mouth with my finger, sweeping up at the edges, to indicate the way it curled.

"Probably you can make him shave it off. My sister makes Mr. Gordon wear socks all the time, so she doesn't have to see his feet."

Stacie picked apart her chain and let the flowered weeds fall — she had a theory they could again take root. I wore mine around my wrist but lost it during the ride back. My mother was still in the bathroom, the mingled scent of her products floating out beneath the door.

After serving us tuna-and-pickle sandwiches, my mother sent Stacie home.

"But why?"

"Shhh," she said. "I need to talk to you."

I folded my arms across my chest and glared at her.

"Don't," she said. "Just don't. Come here with me."

In the living room, she sat and patted the couch beside her. The television wasn't on, which made the room feel too still and too quiet, like nothing happened in it when we weren't around.

"Now, I know Daddy explained that you're going to be a wife. But do you know what that means?"

I refused to look at her, though I could feel her eyes on my face. "Yeah. I'll go live with Mr. Middleton. I'll have to make him dinner."

"Yes," she said. "But you'll have to do more than that."

"Can I still play Barbies with Stacie? I promised her."

"You did, did you."

I nodded. I told my mother everything that Stacie had said. It made me proud that Stacie was jealous, and I thought it would make my mother proud too.

"I'm sorry to say, it's really up to Mr. Middleton when, and if, you can play with your friends. And he may not appreciate you, still just a little girl, telling him to shave off his mustache. He's had that thing for years." She halted a creeping smile. "What I'm trying to say is, you'll belong to him. You'll have to be very obedient — not that you haven't always been a good girl. Your father and I are very proud of you. You get such good grades and stay out of trouble."

She paused, frowning. "I don't think you realize just how lucky you are that Mr. Middleton has offered to take you. He's a very successful man, and he's made quite a generous offer, for little in return." She patted my leg. "I don't mean you, of course. Any man would be lucky to have you. But to be honest, I'm not sure why he's so eager to settle it."

I stared at the black television screen. "Can I go to Stacie's now?"

"Wait. We're not through." She stood and approached the bookshelf. On days when I stayed home sick, I'd lie on the couch and stare at that bookshelf. Each book's spine, its title and design, suggested something of its story, and their order and arrangement seemed fixed, like the sequencing of photographs along the hallway wall: from my parents' wedding — my mother thirteen and Dad twenty-seven — to the day of my birth to my fourth-grade class picture. But as my mother took out the Bible and a few romance paperbacks, I saw that behind them were more books, a whole hidden row; the shelf was deeper than I'd realized. She removed from hiding a slim volume called *Your Womanly Body,* its cover decorated in butterflies and soft-colored cut flowers blooming in vases.

"This will tell you *some* of what you need to know about being a wife. I imagine Mr. Middleton won't expect much from you at first. After all, you're still very young."

I began to turn the pages: there were cartoons of short and tall and skinny and fat women, their breasts different sizes and weights, with varying colors and masses of hair between their legs. The pictures weren't a shock to me. I'd seen my mother naked before, and Stacie had confirmed that her own looked much the same. Once I'd even seen Dad, when I surprised him by waiting outside the bathroom door for a Dixie cup of water late one night.

"You'll have a child someday, of course. But most people like to wait until they're older and know each other better. I, for instance, had you when I was eighteen. By today's standards, that's still a little young.

"It can be scary, at first." My mother's voice had turned soft, and she was staring out the window at the tree. "The important thing to remember is, even though he's in charge, you can have some control. Pay close attention: what he wants the most may be very small, and you can wait out the rest."

I already knew there were ways to put off sex: some girls "sucked" their husbands "off," others cried until left alone. And if a girl did become pregnant too soon, if it would be unseemly for her to keep the baby, I knew there were ways to get rid of it. But still, I'd rather not think about all that before I had to face it.

My mother was saying, "A man's life is spent waiting and preparing for the right girl. It can be very lonely. In a way, girls have it easy —"

"Mommy, when will I go live with Mr. Middleton?"

"I was getting to that, Mary. You can be so impatient." She lifted the book from my hands and turned to put it away. "You'll be going to him in the fall."

"Oh." I stared down at my bare summer feet, callused, tan, and dirty. "After school starts?"

"Mary. There'll be no school for you this fall. You'll have a house to take over."

The feeling was back in my stomach, more of an ache now, and all I wanted was to curl up on the couch while my mother brought Jell-O and chicken noodle soup. On sick days you could escape the movement of the world. It was always difficult to get back into it, to catch up on schoolwork and eat real food again, but this time I wasn't sure I ever wanted to rejoin the world.

Yet the books were different now. I wouldn't be able to not think about that.

"Of course, he'll probably let you go back soon. He'll want you to. That's what Mr. Middleton told us — that he admired your mind. He said he could tell you're a very bright girl.

"I should be so lucky," she added darkly. "Your father only saw my strength."

It became routine for Mr. Middleton to spend Sunday afternoons with us. At dawn my mother yanked open all the blinds, and the acrid smells of housecleaning began to fill the rooms. Even Dad was kept from sleeping in and given chores to do. I was ushered straight into the kitchen: "Do me one little favor," she said.

"Knead this dough. No, like this. Punch it, like you're pissed off."

"Check the stove. Has it reached the preheated temperature? Well, is it hot?"

"Okay, now we'll let that marinate. You know what's in this marinade? Just smell it — what does it smell like?"

Once I had completed my mother's "favor" ("Umm, it smells sweet." "Good! That's the honey"), I sneaked out while her back was turned.

I was to be scrubbed "my pinkest" in the shower. She showed me how to use Q-tips to clean out my ears, to rub lotion over my skin, and to pluck the little hairs I hadn't noticed before from between my eyebrows. She swore under her breath when she nicked me with the pink disposable razor — my legs slathered in a thick gel that smelled like baby powder. "Here," she said. "You finish."

I slid the blade along my leg, pressing as lightly as possible.

I was to wear "one of my prettiest dresses," which meant that I rotated among the three in my closet. Their straps dug into my shoulders, their crinoline scratched my bare legs. The first Sunday my mother threw onto my bed a package from Sears. Inside were three training bras. I didn't have anything resembling breasts, and when I finally did, years into my marriage, they were so small that I continued to wear the trainers for some time. My husband didn't seem to care or know the difference.

Every Sunday had the feel of a holiday — the boredom of waiting for the guest to arrive and the impatience of waiting for him to leave. Mr. Middleton always brought a bouquet of flowers, at the sight of which I was to feign surprise and gratitude. Every week, the same grocery-store assortment of wildflowers that smelled rank and bitter, like weeds. Mr. Middleton sat with my father in the living room while I trimmed and arranged the flowers in my mother's crystal vase. She had me stir something or taste it for salt before nudging me back out to join them.

Mr. Middleton would wear a full suit and tie, despite the fact that our house had no air conditioning. As the afternoon wore on, he would take off the suit jacket, loosen and remove the tie, roll up the sleeves of the dress shirt, and, lastly, undo the shirt's top button, revealing a tuft of dark, curly hair. The hair on his head was straight, and he'd run a hand through it, slicking it back with his sweat. Dad, in a short-sleeved polo shirt and khaki shorts, would watch, smiling to himself. My shaven skin felt cool and smooth. I had to stop myself from running my hands along my legs as I sat listening to them talk "business." Their tone was cordial, but they seemed to eye each other warily. I didn't consider it then, but Dad was likely sensitive to the fact that while he had to report to a boss, Mr. Middleton was his own.

"How's business?"

"Business is good. You?"

"Business is good. Clients?"

"Clients are good. Got to treat them right, keep them happy," Dad said.

"Of course."

In and out of the room bustled my mother. She refilled the pitcher of lemonade, replenished the dish of melting ice cubes, brought out bowls of mixed nuts and pretzels and onion dip. Before long, this became my job. I'd stand before Mr. Middleton with a tray of pickles and olives.

"Hmm, let's see." He'd mull over the choices, select a pimento-stuffed green olive. I'd turn to offer the tray to Dad, who had a penchant for sweet pickles, but then: "Please, wait just a moment — perhaps another. Hmm, let's see." And he'd choose a kalamata. The metal tray was heavy, but my arms grew stronger, and I learned to balance it on my shoulder.

Mr. Middleton rarely addressed me directly. Which is not to say he wasn't speaking to me. "Profit margins" and "quarterly analyses" were discussed with glances and smiles in my direction. But he never asked what I thought, how I was doing, how I had spent my week. Adults, I knew, just liked to humor children, and ordinarily those questions tired me, causing me to clam up on the pretense of feeling shy. But in this situation it was disconcerting. After all, wasn't Mr. Middleton supposed to like me? What were we going to say to each other when we were, one day, inevitably, alone? I knew I would be expected to say something; wives, especially as they grew up, didn't have to be invited to speak. They scolded their husbands for things they were doing wrong, or weren't doing at all. They had stories to tell, of what had happened that day at the market, of the rude cashier and the unmarked price of the fresh loaf of bread.

For then, I followed my mother's advice the best I could. I wouldn't speak unless spoken to. I sat up straight in the chair, didn't complain if the food at dinner was strange, didn't ask to turn on the television. I paid close attention to Mr. Middleton; I focused on his mustache, the way it moved with his mouth, studied the shine of his gold watch, viewed the gradual stripping of clothing, the sweat gathering on his forehead and alongside his nose, where his glasses slid. I suppose I may have already been following my mother's advice, but I don't remember thinking so. I never liked to admit I was doing as she suggested. I preferred to credit my own volition.

Mr. Middleton seemed to me older than my father, though he was almost a decade younger. Dad was strict, but he could be silly, wasn't afraid to be lazy, and had been known to watch cartoons that even I found stupid. Mr. Middleton was too polite and too proper. He was boring in the way a robot would be: never leaving to go to the bathroom, never saying anything Dad disagreed with or found ridiculous. They would have had much to argue about — they do now — their strategies in business so different: Dad doting on his clients, trying to keep them pleased each step of the way, Mr. Middleton acting with cool aggression against their wishes, with the long run in mind, the biggest possible profit. I suppose we were all on our best behavior.

By dinnertime the business talk had faltered, and the men punctuated their silence with compliments for the meal — something Dad never did when it was just the three of us. This was when my mother took over. "Thank you," she might say. "Mary Ellen helped prepare that."

"Did she? It's quite good," said Mr. Middleton.

"Oh, she's learning. Believe it or not, just a month ago even something this simple would have been beyond her."

Mr. Middleton smiled politely and chewed, his mustache moving up and down, a piece of couscous caught in the right-side curl.

"There is still so much for her to learn, I'm afraid. You mustn't — you mustn't expect too much, from the start."

"But of course Donna will get her up to speed," said Dad. "Won't you, honey?"

"Of course," my mother said. "All I meant was, Mary is such a fast learner. Why, just the other day the sauce was starting to stick, and instead of letting it burn or calling me, she just turned down the burner and gave it a stir. How about that?"

The heat from the kitchen was creeping into the dining room, and a bead of sweat slipped down Mr. Middleton's forehead. His top button, at that point, remained done. He offered nothing but another polite smile. Maliciously I wanted, in front of everyone, to call attention to the couscous still in his mustache. "Right there," I'd interrupt, pointing to a spot above my own lip. This was something a wife could do, scold or embarrass her husband for his own good. But I knew I hadn't earned it yet, and it would take years of waiting, quietly noting.

Mr. Middleton seemed oblivious to my parents' fears and cover-ups, but I've come to see that he was not, nor was he too polite to lead the conversation elsewhere. I can look back now with some sympathy. I can see myself in him: he was determined to behave in the way that was expected, in the belief, often false but sometimes accurate, that this gave him some autonomy. And after all, he was getting what he wanted.

One Saturday afternoon Mr. Middleton showed up while my parents were out. They were leaving me home alone more often in preparation for the days when I'd be keeping house, with Mr. Middleton off at work. Usually I found myself frozen, unable to act as I would if my parents were around. I had a great fear of doing something wrong, either accidentally (opening the door to a dangerous stranger or coming upon some matches, which would inadvertently scratch against something and become lit, igniting a raging fire) or purposely, overcome by the thrill of risk. The only way to ensure this wouldn't happen was to remain on the couch until they came back.

At the sound of a knock at the door, I lifted a slat of the blind and peered out at Mr. Middleton: no flowers in hand, no suit and tie. He wore blue jeans and sports sandals, a polo shirt like those Dad owned. His arms were covered in those dark, curly hairs. Through the peephole his nose was made long by the curved glass, and his mustache twitched nervously. It gave me a small thrill, making him wait. Just as he began to back away, I did as I should and opened the door.

"Mary Ellen. What a pleasant surprise."

"Hello," I said politely. "Would you like to come in?"

He looked down the block, both ways. It was quiet for a Saturday. Only Mrs. Calderón was out, pruning her blooming roses. She'd recently explained to me that she had to cut them back so they could grow. Mr. Middleton smiled in her direction and entered the house.

"I'm home alone," I said. It seemed best if I made that clear right away.

"I won't stay long. You see, I was just in the neighborhood and thought I'd drop by."

That was reasonable to me, but it seemed out of character for Mr. Middleton, who operated purely, I thought, on formality and routine. "Would you like a glass of iced tea with lemon?" I asked.

"No, thank you."

He wasn't sitting, so I didn't sit, unaware that I might have offered him a seat. The expression on his face was, as always, neutral, and he didn't return my stare. I felt I was doing something grossly wrong — I was still unfit to be a wife, unable to handle company on my own. My mother would scold me if she knew I'd received him in a T-shirt from last year's spelling bee and purple shorts stained with Kool-Aid.

I tried again. "How's business?"

He smiled and lowered himself to my height, his hands coming to rest on his knees. "Very well, thank you," he said. "But today, you see, I was thinking of you. I thought you might like to show me your Barbies."

No adult had ever asked to see them, and, to my knowledge, they'd never been mentioned in his presence. My mother allowed no visitors, other than my friends, into the basement. She had warned me that the Barbies would have to go when I went to Mr. Middleton. To head off my tears, Dad had added quietly that perhaps, for a while, they could leave them set up in the basement for when I came to visit.

I watched for some sign in Mr. Middleton that he was joking or only humoring me, but he reached out a hairy arm and took my hand. His wasn't sweaty, though the day was muggy and humid, and his skin was surprisingly soft. On the narrow stairway he didn't let go; my arm strained and pulled behind me as I led him into the basement. His knees cracked as he took the stairs.

The basement was unfinished, just hard tiles, exposed beams, and many-legged insects. Stacie complained about the centipedes, but they appeared less often than the spiders. Strips of sunlight came in through the windows along the driveway, where you could see feet pass on their way to the side door.

Mr. Middleton dropped my hand and approached the Barbies' houses slowly, as if in awe. The toys sprawled from one corner of the room to the other, threatening to take over even the laundry area; the foldout couch, which I maintained took up valuable space, sometimes served as a mountain to which the Barbies took the camper. There was one real Barbie house, pink and plastic; it had come with an elevator that would stick in the shaft, so I had converted the elevator to a bed. The other Barbie home was made of boxes and old bathroom rugs meant to designate rooms and divisions; this was the one Stacie used for her family. The objects in the houses were a mixture of real Barbie toys and other adapted items: small beads served as food, my mother's discarded tampon applicators were the legs of a cardboard table. On a Kleenex box my Barbie slept sideways, facing Ken's back; both were shirtless, her plastic breasts against him.

Mr. Middleton asked about the construction and decoration of the rooms. He said he admired my reuse of materials. "A creative way to cut costs," he noted.

I shrugged. "Mom and Dad won't buy me anything else."

He nodded thoughtfully. "You work well within limits."

"I guess," I said, but I was pleased. He was admiring my mind.

"Well, you have quite a talent for design — I've seen professional blueprints more flawed." He suggested that in the future we might have a home built, one I could help plan.

Then he leaned down and stroked Barbie's back with his index finger. "Do they always sleep this way?" he asked.

I blushed and only shook my head. Sometimes they lay entirely naked, as my parents slept. Sometimes Barbie slept on top of Ken, or vice versa.

"Can you show me another way they might sleep?" he asked.

I hesitated, then picked up the dolls and put their arms around each other's bodies in a rigid hug. I tilted Barbie's head and pressed her face against Ken's, as if they were kissing, and laid them back atop the Kleenex box. Mr. Middleton watched with his detached interest.

"Your Barbies must love each other very much," he observed.

I'd never really thought about it that way. They were just doing what my parents and people on television did because they were married. But sometimes, when I was alone, it gave me that fluttery, almost sick feeling deep in my stomach, and I took the dolls apart.

Mr. Middleton stood and turned away. He held up his wrist to the sun strip, examining his watch, for what seemed a long time. "Well, thank you for sharing them with me. But I should be on my way."

I nodded, then recovered my manners. "Can I walk you to the door?"

"No, thank you, Mary Ellen. I'll show myself out."

On Sundays he'd shake my parents' hands before he left, and now I wondered if I should offer mine. But instead he reached out and patted me on the head, once, twice, then the last time just smoothing my hair, as my mother would to fix a stray strand, but much gentler.

When I heard the front door close, I knelt in front of the Barbie house. It was difficult, as my Ken's arms were straight, not bent like some, but I moved his arm so that it stroked Barbie's back. I startled when my mother called from the top of the stairs. I hadn't seen feet in the windows or heard a key in the door.

I didn't tell them that Mr. Middleton had been over, and the next day when he came for Sunday dinner, he didn't mention it either. It didn't occur to me until years later that the whole thing might have been prearranged. I could find out now; Mr. Middleton tells me anything I ask. He may tease, but he knows when to stop. It's quite possible he's even learned to fear me. For all his skill in the world of business, I think he understands less about the world without than I do.

That September, with Stacie back at school, my days were spent alone with my mother. She was nervous about the upcoming ceremony and would sit with me at the kitchen table for hours with catalogs of flowers and dresses.

"Do you like these roses? Or something more unique — orchids? But so expensive."

I would shrug. "It doesn't matter."

Depending on her mood, she would either become angry ("If it doesn't matter to you, who does it matter to? Pick out some flowers!") or take my reticence as deference to what she thought was best ("The orchids are lovely, but we'd best be practical, hmm?").

Once, paging together through pictures of dresses, she became so frustrated with me that she disappeared into the bathroom for almost an hour. Finally I knocked on the door. "Mommy? I left it open to the one I like." I heard water running, and when she came out she caught me around the shoulders and held me against her, my face nuzzling her stomach. "That's my good girl," she whispered above my head.

One afternoon was spent sewing, another polishing silver. The cooking lessons took on new vigor, and she had me reducing wine-based sauces, braising meats, and chopping fresh herbs for most of the day.. Dad would come home, see everything that had been set out on the table and everything that still simmered on the stove and roasted in the oven, throw his hands up in the air and say, "I don't know how you expect us to consume all this, Donna. Maybe you could lay off her a bit." But then he'd sit down and attack the food with an appetite that had the air of duty, sighing and unbuttoning his pants for dessert.

Stacie came over after school a couple of times a week, but she brought Cassandra; the Chan twins had forsaken me, believing my imminent wifehood to have changed me already. With only two Barbie houses, Stacie, Cassandra, and I couldn't play together fairly. Besides, I didn't want Cassandra and her ratty hair anywhere near them. Instead we sat on the porch eating gingersnaps — just talking and not playing anything. Other girls who'd been promised spent their time in this way.

Cassandra wanted to hear about Mr. Middleton. She believed her parents to be sealing up a deal with a Mr. Crowley from the neighboring town. I recounted Mr. Middleton's afternoon visit to sate her interest and swore them to secrecy. They didn't seem particularly impressed or unnerved. I yearned for either response, to anchor my own.

"Well, is he cute?" Cassandra asked, twirling a dishwater-blond lock.

I didn't know how to answer her. Unlike Stacie and me, Cassandra had always liked boys — but husbands were not like boys. I didn't know how to make her understand what it was really like, but I also had the feeling that Cassandra would handle things much differently when it was her turn. I was thankful when Stacie changed the subject to school, with stories of pencils stolen from the teacher's desk and guest story-readers, even though they made me both wistful and angry, and Stacie knew it.

The night before the ceremony, my parents entertained their friends with chilled rosé wine and a CD of lulling, smooth jazz on repeat. My mother dusted my cheekbones with her dark blush and checked my back to make sure I wore a trainer. I was to greet guests at the door until everyone had arrived, and then Stacie and I could retreat to the basement to play Barbies together one last time. According to tradition, Mr. Middleton was not invited; it was to be his last bachelor night alone. But Mr. Woodward and Esmerelda came, and Mr. Silverstein, and Stacie's and Cassandra's parents, eager to know how it had all been pulled off. Mr. Baker said, as if surprised, "You look very pretty tonight, Mary Ellen," and then he and Mr. Weir stood together in the corner, shaking their heads. The Calderóns arrived last. Mr. Calderón was so old, his eyes constantly watered, and he could barely speak or hear anything. Mrs. Calderón was a young grandmother, her braided hair still long and black. She bent to me and whispered, "You're not getting cold feet now, are you, dear?"

"Cold feet?" I asked. I peered down at my slipper socks, embarrassed I'd removed the Mary Janes.

"I tried to run away from this one." She winked at her husband, but his expression didn't change. "But then, I always misbehaved."

Mr. Calderón held tight to her arm, and she guided him patiently toward the drinks. She kissed his shaking hand, then placed a glass of water in it.

In the basement, adult feet shifting above us, I understood that Mrs. Calderón had been saying that she knew me and that she understood. From tomorrow on, that would be me upstairs, like Esmerelda and even my mother, laughing a stupid laugh and making frequent trips to the bathroom, with an eye on my husband and his eye on me. Mrs. Calderón had issued me a playful dare and made no promises; but if it was the last childlike thing I did, I would take her up on it.

"Stacie, I need your help."

She stopped pushing her Barbie car, a convertible she'd acquired from me in a trade, and said with suspicion, "You do?"

As I explained what I wanted to do, Stacie's eyes began to gleam. At one point she took my hand. I felt close to her, until she said, "You won't be married first after all!" But still she was my confidante, my partner with her own stake.

What we came up with wasn't much of a plan, but we did identify the basic elements required in running away: a note, a lightly packed suitcase, and utter secrecy. My mother had already packed most of my clothes into a luggage set embroidered with my new initials, M.M. I removed the lightest bag from the pile by the side door and had Stacie sneak it back home with her. After slipping away, having deposited the note in a spot both clandestine and sure to be eventually discovered, I would call Stacie from a pay phone and have her meet me with the suitcase. For this purpose, I used my new skills to sew a quarter into the hem of my dress, which hung, long and white, like a ghost, outside my closet door.

Beneath the covers with a flashlight that night, I composed the note to Mr. Middleton. I could not tell him, as they did in fantasy romance movies, that I had met someone else. What I wrote was this:

Dear Mr. Middleton,

I am sorry to leave you at the alter. You seem very nice but I cannot be a wife. Please do not try to find me and please try to go on with your life.

Mary Ellen

I thought it sounded quite grown up and made running away on cold feet seem a serious and viable act. I wasn't worried that we hadn't decided where I would go. I didn't consider then that I knew of no woman who was not a wife, that anyone I might turn to would turn me in, that breach of contract was serious business and punishable by law. I believed two things: that getting away would be the hardest part of the game and that you could plan only as far as you could see. I don't know if I believed that I would make it, but I believed that I would try.

I might have left that very night, cutting Stacie's ties to my venture, but I had a romantic notion of wearing that dress. I pictured kicking off the white patent-leather shoes to run faster, and the small train flailing behind me. I pictured that the dress would get dirty as I ran; it would rip and tear, and then I would know I was free.

When we arrived at the chapel, I spied Mr. Middleton's car in the parking lot. During a covert trip to the "potty," I slipped the note beneath its windshield wipers. It had always made me laugh that my parents never noticed an advertisement attached in this way until they were driving.

In the bride's room, Dad, his eyes shiny and red-rimmed, was smoothing out the fold from the contract, to which my signature was to be added. "Why don't you go sit down, Frank?" my mother suggested, but she stayed with me, adjusting my dress and hair-spraying my hot-roller curls, until the final moments. She hovered in the doorway. "You are wearing, aren't you, all the things we talked about? You remember how it goes? Something old, something new, something borrowed, something blue, and a silver sixpence for your shoe?"

"I remembered," I said, thinking of the sewn quarter. If I wasn't careful to keep my skirt held as I walked, the coin hit the floor with the barest knock. "Mommy, can I have a few minutes alone? This is a very big day for me."

She looked surprised, but her face softened. "Boy, kid, you really have grown up." She kissed my cheek, then rubbed it furiously to remove any trace of lipstick. I felt sad, at that moment, to think that I would never see her again, and wondered if she would privately count me lucky or only be disappointed.

The air outside smelled like a fall barbecue, charring corn and sausages. In the bright blue sky flew a V of birds. Just as I took a breath to run, I spotted Mr. Middleton across the lot next to his car. The collar of his tuxedo was misaligned; he had skipped a buttonhole and set the whole thing off. Facing the sun, he held one hand to his face — to shield his eyes? — and in the other was my note. His shoulders seemed to be shaking with laughter. Had he been about to run away himself when he came upon my note? This possibility, however remote, might have been what led me to walk straight toward him, slowly, steadily, wholly of my own volition. I hate to believe, especially now, that it was as simple as holding to my nature; that I was just a good girl who did always as she was told, without hope and without design.

"Mary Ellen?" he said. "You're still here." I saw as I came closer that he'd actually been crying, not laughing; a tear dropped from the left-side curl of his mustache. I thought of something Dad often said, when, much younger, I'd get caught up in venturesome play with inevitable consequence: "It's all fun and games, isn't it, until someone gets hurt."

"I'm still here," I said. I raised my arms to indicate I should be lifted and let Mr. Middleton cradle me against his chest. I felt his wildly beating heart, and he began to stroke my hair as if I needed calming down. But my stomach felt only the faintest rumble of hunger, an emptiness. I knew that I had done the right thing, the only thing I could, but still, I felt foolish. If I was really as smart as everyone believed, I would never have found myself in this situation, with a ridiculous man I was obligated to care for. My escape would have been better planned and better executed. He would never have taken an interest in the first place.

"Mary," he said, "you do know that I —"

"What?" I struggled to sit up in his arms, impatient suddenly, and restless. I wanted to go inside, where everyone was waiting, and get it over with.

He set me down on the hood of his car and began again. "I think you'll be very pleased with the life I want to give you."

I stared through his windshield at the tan leather seats, sculpted to hug a body as the vehicle took the curves. I saw where the top would fold down. This car would take me to my new home.

"You do understand, don't you, that the deal is irrevocable? If you were to run off, your parents would owe me a great deal of money. They could never hope to come out of debt."

I knew that was a threat and thought lowly of him for it. But then he said something I look back on now as the beginning of my new understanding of my life. "I'm yours, Mary Ellen, and if you stay, all that is mine will be yours too."

In answer, I rebuttoned his shirt.

As I signed the contract, my eyes slid down the page, its tiny print in a formal, inscrutable language. The sum my parents had provided to Mr. Middleton seemed enormous, though I know it now to be less than the cost of my childhood home and much less than the worth of Mr. Middleton's company. Men who'd planned poorly would seek a much larger dowry and might suffer for it in their choice of wives. But it was our parents, always looking toward the future, who put money first. The dowry, like a child that would grow, was ultimately an investment.

I handed over the paper for the minister to stamp, and he pronounced us man and wife.

Mr. Middleton has kept my note folded in his sock drawer, and for years he has teased me for having misspelled *altar.* Putting away his clean laundry, I look at it sometimes, not with wistfulness or shame, but because I want to remember. The contract itself is in a safety deposit box; I'll receive a key for my eighteenth birthday, a day now close in sight. The Barbies, of course, are long gone. Dad succeeded in overriding my mother, and the toys stayed in the basement a year into my marriage. But I rarely played with them — they seemed to have lost their allure, and I never knew what they wanted to do or say or wear. Stacie still hadn't been promised, and I offered them to her, but she pretended not to be interested. She and Cassandra were thick as thieves then. "Save them for your kids," she said, and we couldn't help but dissolve into panicked laughter. By the time she was taken, at age fourteen, she was serious about having children. It is her husband who insists they wait. If we see each other now at the market, grocery baskets in hand, we merely nod in greeting. We have so little in common.

Mr. Middleton has made me apprentice to his business, which he says one day when he is dead, I will take over. Even if — and the decision to have children is entirely up to me, he says — one day we have a son. This is highly unusual and very progressive, Dad has told me. He patted my head and told me he was proud. I looked for something like greed or jealousy in his eyes, but found only love. My mother admitted, over afternoon tea, that she wishes Dad had done something similar for her. As far as I can see, he long ago reached his height on the ladder. What could he have done for her?

"I have good business sense, a ruthless mind," she insisted, and gestured to the piles of butterscotch-chip scones she'd baked for a block sale. "But I suppose I'm lucky, in that we fell in love."

I nodded in agreement, though I knew what would provoke her: *But isn't it easier if we don't think of love?*

Visiting is difficult because, although they think they act differently, my parents still treat me like a child, a newlywed bride. They don't recognize what I've become, but they won't argue when the time comes to face it, when Dad retires and I, with Mr. Middleton's money, am in charge of them. Their investment in me will have its rewards. I want the best for them, as they've managed for me.

After a morning spent at home with my private tutor, Ms. Dundee — whose husband succumbed when she was much younger and much prettier (she says) to a condition she won't speak of — I change into a navy skirt and Peter-Pan-collar blouse, hop on my bike, and head to the office. Mr. Middleton has given me a fine car, of course, but I normally prefer the exercise. So far I just prepare after-lunch coffee and bring it in on a tray, each cup made to the preference of each board member. Mr. Middleton sits at the head of the table. His mustache, after all these years, remains; he would shave it if I asked, but I suspect that issuing that demand would expose me somehow. Once situated beside him, I'm encouraged to listen in and, if so inclined, take notes. But it's the quiet power struggle that interests me, the way his inferiors look at him and how they cover their desires with neutral jargon, loyal reports. He takes for granted, I think, the way things are now.

"You've learned a lot so far from just watching and listening," he says to me, winking, as I take out my pad of paper. I turn away and roll my eyes: he believes we're always in on some joke. This one is meant to be in reference to the nights I join him in his bedroom, on the floor above mine. Mostly I just lie there while he touches my hair or my back, as he once demonstrated with the doll. He has mentioned in those moments love, and a feeling of fulfillment. For him they may be the same thing. Yet even with me around, taking care of things, I sense he's still a lonely man. I feel guilty sometimes, offering so little reimbursement for his attentions, though he receives more pleasure from them than I do, and I've made attempts to do for him what other girls and young wives have described. Now I believe that the hardest part of the game is staying in it, holding on to your stake. And that you can't plan too far into the future. I've taken this down in my notes: *The benefits mature with time.* I've begun to appreciate just how much work parents invest in their children, and wives in their husbands; it's only fair for the investor to become a beneficiary.

DANIELLE EVANS

Virgins

FROM *The Paris Review*

ME AND JASMINE AND MICHAEL were hanging out at Mr. Thompson's pool. We were fifteen and it was the first weekend after school started, and me and Jasmine were sitting side by side on one of Mr. Thompson's ripped-up green-and-white lawn chairs, doing each other's nails while the radio played "Me Against the World." It was the day after Tupac got shot, and even Hot 97, which hadn't played any West Coast for months, wasn't playing anything else. Jasmine kept complaining that Michael smelled like bananas.

"Sunscreen," Jasmine said, "is for white people. That's them white girls you've been hanging out with, got you wearing sunscreen. Black people don't burn."

Never mind that Michael was lighter than Jasmine and I was lighter than Michael, and really all three of us burned. Earlier, when Jasmine had gone to the bathroom, I'd let Michael rub sunscreen gently into my back. I guess I smelled like bananas too, but I couldn't smell anything but the polish, and I didn't think she could either. She went on about it anyway, though.

"You smell like food," she said. "I don't know why you wanna smell like food. Maybe that works in Bronxville, but ain't nobody here gonna lick you cause you smell like bananas."

"I don't want you to lick me," Michael said. "I don't know where your mouth has been. I know you don't never shut it."

Jasmine and Michael were my only real friends, and if they fought I'd have to fix it. I turned up the dial on Mr. Thompson's radio, which was big and old. The metal had deep scratches on it, and rust spots left by people like us who didn't watch to see whether or not we flicked drops of water on it. It had a good sound though, and the music was loud and heavy with bass. When the song was over they cut to some politician saying that it was a shame talented young black people kept dying, and it was time to do something about it. They'd been saying that all day. Mr. Thompson got up and cut off the radio.

"You live like a thug, you die like a thug," he said, looking at us. "It's nothing to cry over when people wake up in the beds they made." He walked back to the lawn chair where he'd been reading the paper. He let it crinkle loudly when he opened it again, like the sound of someone else reading would make us less ignorant.

Jasmine snorted. She lifted Michael's sweatshirt with the tips of her thumb and index finger so she didn't scratch her still-drying polish and pulled out the pictures he had been showing us before Mr. Thompson came over — photos of his latest girlfriend, a brunette with big eyes and enormous breasts, lying on a bed with a lot of ruffles on it.

"You live like a white girl, you act like a white girl," said Jasmine, frowning at the picture and making her voice deep like she was Mr. Thompson.

"She's not white," said Michael. "She's Italian."

"Italian people ain't white?"

"No."

"What the fuck are they then?"

"Italian."

"Mr. Thompson," Jasmine called across the yard. "Are Italian people white?"

"Ask the Ethiopians," said Mr. Thompson. None of us knew what he was talking about, so we all shut up.

The air started to feel cooler through our swimsuits, and Michael got up, putting his jeans on over his wet swim trunks and pulling his sweatshirt over his head. I followed Jasmine into the house, where we took turns changing in the downstairs bathroom. We said goodbye to Mr. Thompson, who grunted. "Girls," he nodded at us, and then, harsher, at Michael, "Boy."

Michael rolled his eyes. Michael wasn't bad. Mostly I thought he hung out with us because he was bored. He needed somebody when his white girls' parents were home, and we didn't get him in trouble as much as his boys did. We hung out with him because it was easier to have a boy around than not to. When you were alone, men were always wanting something from you. We even wondered about Mr. Thompson sometimes, or at least we never used his pool without Michael there. Mr. Thompson was retired, but he'd been our elementary school principal, which is how he was the only person we knew in Mount Vernon with a swimming pool in his backyard. It was small, and twenty minutes from our houses even if we walked fast, but he kept it clean, much nicer than the city pool, and we were the only ones he'd told could use it anytime. I thought it was because I'd been good in school, but Jasmine thought it was because her mom had worked there. She'd been one of the lunch ladies, with a hairnet cutting a line into her broad forehead and her face all covered in sweat. Even when she got home she'd smelled like grease. Mr. Thompson had always been nice to her, even when we'd gone out of our way to pretend not to know her.

We felt bad for letting him make us nervous. He was the smartest man we knew, and probably he was just being nice. But we'd had enough nice guys suddenly look at us the wrong way. My first kiss was with a boy who'd said he'd walk me home and a block later was licking my mouth. The first time a guy ever touched me, I was eleven and he was sixteen and a lifeguard at the city pool. We'd been chicken-fighting and when he put me down, he held me against the cement and put his fingers in me, and I wasn't scared or anything, just cold and surprised. When I told Jasmine later she said he did that to everyone, her too. Michael kept people like that out of our way. It was like he didn't even see us as girls, and that felt good sometimes.

Michael's brother Ron was leaned up against his car, waiting for him at the bottom of Mr. Thompson's hill. The car was a brown Cadillac that was older than Ron, who graduated from our high school last spring and worked at RadioShack. Ron was golden colored with curly hair and baby-doll eyelashes and the kind of smile where you could count all of his teeth. Jasmine always said how fine he was, but to me he looked like the kind of person who should be on television, not someone you'd actually want to talk to. Michael hopped in the front seat and waved bye to us.

"Man," Ron said, cuffing him on the back of his head. "You got two cute girls here, and you ain't even gonna try to take 'em with you? I thought I raised you better than that."

"I'm meeting people at the Galleria. You coming?" Michael called.

"Who's gonna be there?" Jasmine asked.

"Me, Darius, Eddie . . . probably some other people."

"Nuh uh," Jasmine said. "You're cool, but your boy Eddie ain't."

"What's wrong with my boy?" Michael asked, grinning.

Jasmine made a *tsk* sound. "He ignorant, that's what."

"Damn, son," said Ron as he walked back to the driver's side. "Your whole crew can't get no play." He got in, slammed the car door, and made a U-turn.

On his way past us he leaned out the window and called, "You get tired of messing with these fools, you come down to the mall and see *me*," then rolled up the amber window and drove off.

Jasmine's problem was that she had lost her virginity to Eddie four months before. He told her he would go with her afterward, but instead he went with Cindy Jackson. We saw them all over the city all summer, holding hands. It drove Jasmine crazy. She liked to pretend no one knew any of this, even though it had been written in both the boys' and girls' bathrooms at school: JASMINE FUCKED EDDIE AND NOW SHE'S PRESSED!! Cindy had written it in both places. I'd told Jasmine that Cindy was probably real familiar with the boys' bathroom, but all it did was make her madder.

When we got to Jasmine's apartment, we went straight to her room, which felt like it was my room too. We lived two blocks from each other and slept at each other's houses as much as we slept at our own. My schoolbooks were still piled on the corner of her floor, and my second bathing suit was hanging over her desk chair where I'd left it to dry the weekend before. We'd always shared everything, but this year it was getting to be a problem. When I put on a pair of her jeans, she said, "Look at you, stretching out my jeans wit your big old ass."

"You wish you had my ass," I said, which was true, because hers was flat like a board and people teased her about it. Jasmine had beautiful dark eyes and the most perfect nose I ever saw on anybody, and I had nice lips and a good shape, but that was it. We were the kind of girls who would always be beautiful *if*. We got dressed to go to the movies because there was nothing else to do, and even though Jasmine's pants were a little tight on me and the shirt I'd borrowed was pushing my chest up in my face, I looked all right, just maybe like I was trying too hard.

When we got to the movie theater, Jasmine said the new red carpet in the lobby looked cheap and tacky, and speaking of cheap and tacky, look who was here. Cindy was wearing tight jeans and a shirt that said BABY GIRL and showed off the rhinestone she had stuck to her bellybutton. She was with Eddie, and Michael was there too, and a bunch of their friends, and they waved us over.

"Look what Eddie gave me," said Cindy, all friendly. She pulled a pink teddy bear out of her purse and squeezed its belly. It sang "You Are My Sunshine" in a vibrating robot voice.

"That's nice," said Jasmine, her voice so high that she sounded almost like the teddy bear. Cindy smiled and walked off with Eddie, swinging her hips back and forth.

"I don't have a teddy bear neither," said Eddie's friend Tre, putting an arm around Jasmine. She pushed him off. Tre was the kind of boy my mother would have said to stay away from, but she said to stay away from all men.

"C'mon, Jasmine," Tre said. "I lost my teddy bear, can I sleep with you tonight?"

Jasmine looked at Tre like he was stupid. Michael put an arm around each of our shoulders and kissed us both on the cheek, me first, then Jasmine.

"You know these are my girls," he said to Tre. "Leave 'em alone."

His friends mostly left me alone anyway, because they knew I wasn't good for anything but a little kissing. But I was glad he'd included me. Michael nodded goodbye as he and his friends walked toward their movie. Eddie and Cindy stayed there, kissing, like that's what they had paid admission for. I grabbed Jasmine's hand and pulled her toward the ticket counter.

"That's nasty," I said. "She looks nasty all up on him in public like that."

"No one ever bought me a singing teddy bear," said Jasmine. "Probably no one ever will buy me a singing teddy bear."

"I'll buy you a singing teddy bear, you silly bitch," I said.

"Shut up," she said. She'd been sucking on her bottom lip so hard, she'd sucked the lipstick off it, and her lips were two different colors. "Don't you ever want to matter to somebody?"

"I matter to you. And Michael."

Jasmine clicked her tongue. "Say Michael had to shoot either you or that Italian chick who's letting him hit it right now. Who do you think he would save?"

"Why does he have to shoot somebody?" I said.

"He just does."

"Well, he'd save me then. She's just a girl who's fucking him."

"And you're just a girl who isn't," Jasmine said. "That's your problem, Erica. You don't understand adult relationships."

"Where are there adults?" I asked, turning in circles with my hand to my forehead like a sea captain looking for land.

"You're right," she said. "I'm tired of these little boys. Next weekend we're going to the city. We're gonna find some real niggas who know how to treat us."

That was not the idea I meant for Jasmine to have.

We had our cousins' IDs, and we'd gone clubbing a few times nearby, but it was usually just a bar with a DJ, and we never stayed that long or got into any trouble. People would appear out of nowhere, all *Ain't you Miss Trellis's daughter?* or *Didn't you used to be friends with my little sister?* If we flirted even a little bit, someone would say *Yo, those are some baby girls right there,* and our guy would vanish, and the bouncer would tell us it was time to go home. *You had your fun, girls,* he'd say, and the thing was, usually we had.

Clubbing in the city was something else. It hadn't finished turning into night yet when we got on the train, but Jasmine had made me take my glasses off and I couldn't see straight. She wouldn't let me wear pantyhose either, because I'd borrowed her shoes that opened at the toe and laced up my leg from my ankles to just below my knee, and I felt naked — her skirt was too short on me. The only thing Jasmine let me do right was bring Michael with us, and he was standing there in his brother's shoes, since he only owned Tims and sneakers. He also had his brother's ID, even though he and his brother didn't look at all alike. Michael was smaller and copper colored and looked like he should have been wearing glasses, even though he didn't.

"Money-earnin' Mount Vernon's not good enough for you two anymore?" he asked, his hands stuffed in the pockets of his jeans.

"Mount Vernon's not good enough for anybody," said Jasmine. "And do you know anybody here who earns any real money?"

When we got off in the city, it was starting to get chilly, and I got little bumps on my legs from the cold. We ordered slices of pizza from Famous Ray's and sat in the window. Our reflections in the glass looked watery, like we were melting at the edges.

"All right," said Jasmine. "Who are we tonight?"

"Serene and Alexis, same as always," I said. I was thinking of the names on our IDs. "And Michael, you're Ron I guess."

"No, stupid. I mean who are we when guys ask questions."

"Seniors?"

"Nah, we're in college."

"What college?"

"You two? Clown college," said Michael. Jasmine threw a dirty napkin at him.

"That's you, Michael," she said. "We're in City College. I'm a fashion major, and I'm gonna get rich selling people nice clothes so girls don't go around lookin' like Cindy Jackson, lookin' trifling all the time, and so you, Erica, can find some pants that actually fit your ass in them. I got a man, and he's fine, and he plays ball, but I may have to kick him to the curb because lately he's jealous of me, so I'm at the club looking for someone who can handle me."

"What's he jealous for?" I asked.

"He's jealous of my success, dummy. Who are you?"

I thought about what I would be if I could be anything.

"I'm at City College too, I guess. What do you major in to be a teacher?"

"Teaching," said Jasmine.

"Ain't no major in teaching," said Michael.

"You ever been to college?" said Jasmine. "Your brother ain't even been to college."

"I'm not stupid," said Michael. "I'm gonna have a degree. I was over at Mr. Thompson's today talking about books and stuff while you two were putting a bunch of makeup on your faces."

"Whatever," I said. "Teaching. I'm majoring in teaching then."

"What about your man?" Jasmine said.

"He's great," I said. "He's in college too, and he's gonna be a doctor, but he also writes me love poems. And paints pictures of me. He's a painter too."

"He so great, why you at the club?" said Michael.

"Umm — he's dead?" I said.

"Dead?" said Jasmine.

"Dead." I nodded. "I just finished grieving. I burned all his poems and now I wish I still had them."

"Check this chick," said Jasmine. "Even when she imagines shit, her life is all fucked up."

*

Michael gave me his jacket on the way from Ray's to the club, and I wrapped it around me and felt warmer. He was talking about earlier, when he was over at Mr. Thompson's.

"Did you know?" said Michael. "That the Ethiopians beat the Italian army?"

"Do I care?" Jasmine asked. "No wonder I never meet nobody, hanging out with you."

Michael made a face at Jasmine behind her back, but we were quiet for the rest of the walk.

I didn't know why Jasmine needed to meet people besides us anyway. Jasmine thought just because people were older, they were going to be more interesting. They didn't look any more interesting, all lined up outside the club like we did on school picture day. At the door one of the bouncers checked Jasmine's ID, then looked her up and down and waved her in. He barely looked at mine, just glanced at my chest and stamped my hand. But he didn't even take Michael's, just shook his head at him and laughed.

"Not tonight," he said.

Michael didn't look too surprised, but he reached for my wrist when he saw I was waiting there, like I would have left with him if he asked me.

"You be careful with yourself, all right?"

I nodded. The bouncer turned around like he might change his mind about letting me in. "Bye, Ron," said Jasmine, and she took off.

I ran in after her. "You didn't have to just leave him like that."

She rolled her eyes. "Whole room full of people and you're worried about Michael. He can take care of himself."

I knew Michael would be all right. It was me I was worried about. The dance floor was full, and the strobe light brought people in and out of focus like holograms. Up on the metal platforms girls were dancing in shorts and bikini tops. The one closest to me had her body bent in half, her hands on her ankles and her shiny-gold-short-covered butt in the air. I wondered how you got to be a girl like that. Did you care too much what other people thought, or did you stop caring?

Me and Jasmine did what we always did at a club, moved to the center of the dance floor and moved our hips to the music. At school they got mad about dancing like that, but we never learned any other kind of dancing except the steps from music videos, and good luck finding a boy who could keep up with that. By the end of the first song two men had come up behind us and started grinding. I looked up at Jasmine to make sure it wasn't Godzilla behind me, and when she nodded and gave me a thumbs-up, I pressed into the guy harder, winding forward and backward.

After we'd been dancing for an hour and I was sweaty and my thighs were tired, I signaled to Jasmine and we went to the bathroom to clean ourselves up. I let Jasmine fix my makeup. I could feel her fingers on my face, touching up my eye shadow, smoothing on lip gloss. I remembered a book we'd read in middle school and said, "It's like I'm Helen Keller, and you're Teacher."

"You're the teacher," Jasmine said. "I'm Alexis, the fashion designer."

"We're not," I said, because it seemed important all of a sudden, but Jasmine was already on her way out the door.

When we left the bathroom, we stood by the bar awhile and waited for people to buy us drinks. A lawyer from Brooklyn brought me something too strong when I told him to surprise me, and he kept talking about the river view from his apartment while I tried to drink it in little tiny sips. A construction worker from Queens told me he'd been waiting all his life for me, which must've been a pretty long time because he was old. A real college student, from Harlem, walked away from me when I couldn't answer his questions about City College. *Go home sweetie,* he said, and I realized that I wanted to. But I didn't see Jasmine. I listened for her, but all I could hear was other people talking, and the boom of music from the speakers above me. Then I heard Jasmine laugh on the other side of the bar and start to sing along with Foxy Brown, *Ain't no nigga like the one I got . . .* She was sitting on a silver bar chair, and there were guys all around her. One of them was telling her how pretty she sang, which was a lie — she had no voice to begin with, plus she was making it sound all stupid and breathy on purpose. When she saw me, she waved.

"Yo," she said, smiling big like she had the only other time I'd seen her drunk. "Serene."

I'd forgotten the name I was answering to and looked at her funny for a minute. I walked closer and one of the men put his arm around me.

"She can come too," he said, and Jasmine smiled.

"Where?" I said.

"After party," she giggled. "In the Bronx. The valet is getting their car. I was just about to look for you."

I shook my head.

"Yes," she said, putting her arms around me and kissing me on the forehead. One of the guys whistled.

I followed her outside. The valet pulled the car up, and I counted the men as they got in. There were four of them.

"There's no room," I said. "Let's go." I pulled Jasmine's hand, but the man by the far window patted his lap, and Jasmine crawled into the car and sat there and put her arms around him.

"Room now," Jasmine said, and because I was out of excuses I got in the car, and five minutes later we were speeding up the West Side Highway. For a minute I thought about what my mother would say, but Jasmine's new friends didn't look dangerous. They looked like they'd spent more time getting dressed than me and Jasmine had. The one Jasmine was sitting on had a sparkly diamond earring. The one next to me had on a beige linen shirt. They all smelled like cologne beneath sweat. My sheets had smelled like that once after Michael took a nap in my bed, and I didn't want to wash them until it had faded. Jasmine was kissing the man with the earring. She was kissing him deep, and his hands were tracing the top of her shirt. He fingered the chain she always wore around her neck, and stopped kissing her to look at it.

"Princess," he mumbled. "Are you a princess?"

Jasmine giggled. Her chain glittered like a dime at the bottom of a swimming pool.

"Are you a princess too?" the man next to me asked. He looked down at me, and I could see that his eyes were a pretty green, but bloodshot.

"No," I said. I folded my arms across my chest.

"Man, look who we got here," said the one in the passenger seat, turning around. "College girl with a attitude problem. How'd we end up with these girls again? Y'all are probably virgins, aren't you?"

"No," Jasmine said. "Like hell we are. We look like virgins to you?"

"Nah," he said, and I didn't know whether to feel pissed off or pretty.

The car stopped in front of an apartment building, and I followed them into the lobby, and into the elevator, and earring guy still had his arms around Jasmine and pretty-eyes guy was still looking at me. If I'd wanted to lose my virginity to a random guy in the Bronx, I would've done it already, not just let Jasmine give it away. I knew if she saw my face, she would know how mad I was, but she had her head in earring guy's neck. The clicks and dings in the elevator seemed like they were saying something in a language I didn't speak. I thought about pulling her off of him. I thought about hitting her. They'd pushed the button for the eighth floor, but the doors opened on five. There was nobody standing there and I kept waiting for the thing that would stop us, and then I thought, nothing will stop this but me. So I ran, out of the elevator and down the stairs and out the front door and down to the bodega on the corner.

There was a whole pile of fruit lit up outside, like what anybody really needed in the middle of the night was a mango. Inside, it was comforting just looking at the rows and rows of bread and cereal and soup all crammed together, and I stared at them for a while. The man behind the counter was old. He looked like how I would have imagined my grandfather looking if I'd known him.

"You all right?" he said. "You need some aspirin? Some ginger ale?"

I shook my head.

"You need to call somebody?"

I pointed at the pay phone outside on the corner, and the man shrugged. When I realized Jasmine wasn't coming after me, I walked back outside. The door jingled when I opened it, and I was mad at it for sounding so happy. I didn't know who else to call at two-thirty in the morning, so I beeped Michael and pushed in the pay phone number. I was afraid he wouldn't call back, but he did, ten minutes later.

"Just come get me," I said, and all he asked for was the street name.

When Ron's car pulled up, Michael got out and gave me a hug.

"You all right?" he asked. "Did something happen?"

I nodded, then shook my head. I was starting to feel stupid, because I knew I looked a mess, and nothing bad had really happened to me.

"Where's your girl?"

"Up in one of those buildings, with some guys she met at the club."

"Do we need to go get her?"

I thought of Jasmine in that man's lap, Jasmine laughing and saying *Like hell we are,* Jasmine letting me run out of the elevator by myself. "No. Leave that trick where she is." Once I said the words, I was sorry. They seemed like the kind of thing you couldn't take back. I wanted Michael to be mad at me, to say he was Jasmine's friend too and he wouldn't leave her like that, but he just shrugged at his brother and opened the car door.

"Uh uh," said Ron, when Michael started to get in. "Let the lady up front."

I sat beside him while Michael scowled and got in the back.

"I guess we can't take you to your mom's or you'll be in trouble, huh?" Ron asked.

"No," I said. "I'm supposed to be at Jasmine's."

"No doubt," he said, and he squeezed my knee, looking at me so hard that I thought of my mother saying no one does you a favor who doesn't want something back.

At Michael and Ron's house, they put me on the downstairs couch and gave me a blanket. When Ron said good night and went into his bedroom in the basement, I thought maybe I'd only imagined the look he gave me earlier. I unlaced my shoes and took down my hair and curled up in the blanket, trying not to think about Jasmine and what kind of a mess I'd left her in. I thought of her laughing, thought of the look on her face when she had closed her eyes and let that man kiss her, and for a second I hated her and then a second later I couldn't remember anything I'd ever hated more than leaving her. I was sitting there in the dark when Ron came back and put an arm around me.

"You know you're too pretty for me to leave you on the couch like that," he said, pulling me toward him. I didn't know that, but I did understand then that there was no such thing as safe, only safer, that this, if it didn't happen now, would happen later but not better. I was safer than Jasmine right now, safer than I might have been. He kissed me, hard, like he was trying to get to the last drop of something, and I kissed him back, harder, like I wanted to get it all back. The noise in my head stopped and I didn't have to think about anything but where to put all the pieces of my body next.

He grabbed my hand and led me to the bedroom, and he kissed me again and pushed my skirt up around my hips. "You're beautiful," he said, which must've been a lie by this time of night. I sat on the bed and pulled my underwear off and realized they were Jasmine's. I thought how mad she'd be that it was me and not her doing this. I kissed him and he kept going and I didn't stop him.

Afterward I was embarrassed because he was embarrassed, and I knew I couldn't stay there, but instead of going back to the couch I walked upstairs to Michael's room and climbed into his bed. He smelled the way I remembered him. I just wanted to touch him really, and not to wake up alone. But he thought I meant something by it, and I let him. I let him kiss me until he felt under my shirt and his fingers found my bra hook, which was still undone because I hadn't bothered to fasten it.

"What happened?" he asked.

"Nothing," I said.

"Right," he said. He turned away from me and faced the wall. I looked at the back of his ears and reached for his shoulders to pull myself toward him.

ALLEGRA GOODMAN

Closely Held

FROM *Ploughshares*

MOLLY'S FATHER WAS A PHYSICIST, and not the garden-variety kind. He had been in one of Orion's college textbooks as the Eisenstat Principle of something or other. Matter? Motion? Orion didn't remember, although it was assumed he knew which. The Eisenstats assumed many things. "I take it the two of you are planning to get married," Carl Eisenstat told Orion once, with scientific bluntness. Orion had started back, offended that Carl would touch on a matter so private and confusing, but Molly's father pressed on, implacably, "and I make that assumption because you've been seeing each other for so long."

Not counting their time at Harvard, Orion and Molly had been together for almost five years. After graduation in 1995, the college sweethearts had never left Cambridge, and whenever they saw their classmates and heard about their friends' adventures in South Africa and Russia and Wall Street, Orion and Molly felt both old and childish. They lived off Putnam Avenue in a third-floor warren with a ramshackle but surprisingly large roof deck. They kept a hibachi there, aluminum lawn chairs, and a camping table they'd found on the street. On summer nights, when people came up for drinks, they passed around a pair of tweezers for the splinters that split off the sun-warped railings.

They had talked about getting engaged, of course. Molly's plan was to get married when Orion finished grad school, and he had always liked this idea — keeping marriage at an indeterminate distance along with his dissertation. Then Orion took a leave from school to help start a little Internet security company called ISIS.

VC money came flooding in, businesses stampeded to sign on for ISIS's cryptographic service, LockBox, and the premium data protection package, ChainLinx. Future earnings were shooting through the roof, and Orion's professional and financial prospects, once pleasantly vague, were now unavoidably bright. This was not lost on Molly's father. Nothing was. Carl and Deborah drove up from Princeton often and made Orion squirm with their approval.

One chilly April afternoon, the Eisenstats took Orion and Molly to Sunday brunch at Henrietta's Table. Lanky, white-haired Carl forged the way at the buffet, loading his plate with lox and whitefish, eggs and sausages. Orion and Molly hurried to the carving board where a chef stood slicing slabs of meat, and Molly's mother, Deborah, brought up the rear, pausing wistfully at the waffle station, but settling on yogurt, fruit salad, and a tiny dish of steel-cut Irish oatmeal. The resemblance between Deborah and Molly was striking: dark eyes, a heart-shaped face, lovely from the front, less so in profile. Molly had her mother's slight bump in the nose and tiny chin. They were both petite, but Deborah was also zaftig, a short, wide gerontologist who wore tunic-length sweaters and long necklaces, silk cords hung with unusual pendants: a woven bag or many-hinged locket, a miniature kaleidoscope bouncing like a buoy on her vast bosom.

"Well, this is nice," said Deborah, when they reconvened at the table.

Molly and Orion, who had already started eating, nodded and kept at it.

"How's ISIS?" Deborah inquired warmly, as if Orion's company was a person.

"Fine," Orion said.

"More than fine," corrected Carl Eisenstat. "You've been getting a lot of press," he informed Orion, who ducked his head, something between a nod and a shrug. The four ISIS founders had just appeared in the March 2000 issue of *Fortune* magazine under the heading "Tycoons in Training."

"I hear you're talking about going public," said Carl.

"No, no, not yet," Orion demurred, although that was all anyone at ISIS did talk about. At the computers, at the vending machines, in the elevators, Orion heard the programmers discussing what they'd do after the company's IPO.

"I'd get a boat."

"Motorboat!"

"Speedboat!"

"Nah, boats suck! Get a Harley."

"Yeah!"

"A Ferrari!"

"Sweet!"

Some of the guys — they were almost all young men — were still undergraduates, working at ISIS in between classes. When they talked money, they sounded like teenagers boasting what they'd do to girls.

Now, at brunch, even Carl Eisenstat had a gleam in his eye. He actually whipped out that morning's *Boston Globe* and began to read: "*The closely held company does not* . . . wait . . . it's down here: *Asked about his heroes, company cofounder Orion Klingenstein cites computer pioneer Donald Knuth, and maverick Free Software activist Richard Stallman* . . . Did you see this?" Carl asked.

How different Molly's father seemed from the man Orion had first met, almost eight years before. The Eisenstats had driven up to see their daughter, and she'd brought her new boyfriend to breakfast. On that occasion, he and Molly had shared one side of a booth, like brother and sister facing their parents. Orion wore jeans and a T-shirt, and his wet blond hair fell in his eyes. Molly was dressed more formally in jeans and a button-down plaid shirt; her short curls were damp, her eyes magnified by round wire-rimmed glasses. He and Molly looked a little too clean to be entirely innocent, having just come from Mather House, where they'd shared a shower, but they sat straight with the seam of the upholstered booth running up between them. Molly's mother had tried to make conversation, but Professor Eisenstat kept his eyes on Orion at all times. Under Carl's gaze, Orion had tried not to eat so fast or gulp his juice, although he was famished and thirsty. He had tried not to think of the night before, lest some memory of warmth and dark nakedness flash across his face. Concentrating on his omelet, he'd attempted to seem thoughtful and interesting and utterly unlustful. Still, Carl gazed at him with a grim, penetrating look, as Deborah chatted about where Orion was from: Middlebury. Where he'd gone to high school: Putney.

"Are there astronomers in your family?" Deborah had asked.

"Nope," said Orion. "My mom just liked the name."

"Do you have siblings?"

"No." Orion tried a little humor. "Were you thinking they'd be called Sagittarius?"

"I have a question for you," Carl broke in. His voice was taut and slightly amused, as though he were sharpening cruel ironic skewers and looking forward to running Orion through. "How is it, majoring in an auxiliary field?"

Orion looked up in surprise. "Auxiliary? You mean computer science?" He had been so busy guarding against attacks on his character, that at first he didn't recognize Carl's scientific gambit as such.

"Right. Auxiliary in that computer science is not a true science in itself, but a handmaid to physics, math, biology . . ."

"Oh, don't be such a snob," Molly the premed scolded her father. "Just because we aren't all unlocking secrets of the universe . . ."

"I like CS," Orion said stoutly.

"But that's my question," Carl pressed. "What exactly do you like about it?"

Orion paused. "Programming," he said.

"Hmm." Carl sipped his coffee.

"I don't mind being a handmaid. I think I'd like to . . ." Orion's voice trailed off.

There he'd been, squirming, twenty years old and utterly ridiculous. He'd gazed across the table at Molly's father with a mixture of resentment and misery. How had Carl known that Orion had come to Harvard intending to study astronomy? Did it show that as a child Orion stayed out late stargazing with his birthday telescope?

Orion had once dreamed of peering into space to glimpse the oldest stars. He had imagined studying the origins of the universe, but he wasn't good enough at physics to pursue the idea properly. Where he excelled was in building little computer systems piece by piece. Orion loved to tinker. He was a puzzle solver, no deep-thinking puzzle maker. He did well in his CS courses: programming, distributed systems, hardware, algorithms, graphics, where he rendered a faceted crystal vase filled with water and a single red rose, which cast an accurate shadow on a wood-grain tabletop. Were these exercises at all important? In Carl's presence he'd felt acutely that computer science lacked a certain — he would never say the word aloud — but yes, the field lacked a certain majesty.

These days, Molly's famous father seemed thrilled with Orion's programming habit. When he spoke of ISIS, Carl sounded eager, almost boyish. He found the whole business absolutely delightful and looked upon his daughter's future fiancé with such benevolent pride that Orion almost missed the Carl of old, the fire-breathing academician. What a strange effect money, or even the idea of money, had on people.

Orion hadn't set out to be wealthy; he hadn't begun his research project on Internet security to make serious money, although he had ended it that way — incorporating with Jonathan, Aldwin, and Jake. Truly, his goal a year ago was to put together some code for fun and make a pile of money along the way — but only money in the lighthearted sense, not funds involving lawyers and trusts and lockups and talk of writing wills. There was a big difference between money and being rich. Money meant freedom — endless quarters for the laundromat and no worries about rent or going out to dinner or the movies. Money was spontaneous: flying last minute to Paris, buying all the comic books and games you wanted, laying down cash at Pandemonium for the latest Neal Stephenson in hardback. Being rich, however, was all about paperwork and contingencies. Money was pleasure. Richness was just sick. He hadn't realized before ISIS that the two went together; sometimes he forgot. At other times — at the table now — he quailed at the way one followed the other. Money was a joy ride, and afterward you got rich all over.

He was going to be wealthy. He couldn't avoid it. No more long vague years of graduate school. No obstacles to marrying. How could he put off shopping for a ring? In a year, he could afford any ring or bracelet or necklace; he could afford anything. Orion looked at Carl's smooth close-shaven cheeks and his hawkish gray eyes, and he saw what wealth would mean: not just traveling the world and buying toys, but paying huge complicated taxes and living in a house with Molly forever — not forever in the romantic sense — forever like her parents, with a loud dog and yellowing houseplants. Molly would gain a hundred pounds, and Orion would have to start collecting humongous ugly paintings. They'd have a three-car garage and seven bathrooms, and they would sit around at night and debate whether it was better to time-share or buy planes.

"How many employees are you up to now?" Carl asked.

"I think we're at . . ." Orion hesitated, distracted by the cell phone in his pocket, buzzing against his leg. "Eighty-three?" he ventured, checking the caller ID. "Ninety-three?" It was Jonathan, but Orion ignored the call. He and Jonathan were close friends, and ISIS cofounders and all that, but lately they hadn't been getting along. "Maybe a hundred in Cambridge," said Orion.

Deborah focused on Orion with a look of quiet pride. Carl leaned forward, keen and curious. Only their daughter paid no attention. Orion realized with annoyance that Molly, who was now an intern and post-call, had closed her eyes and left him to entertain her parents' expectations on his own. She was still sitting upright in her chair, but she had fallen fast asleep.

All the way home in the back of the Eisenstats' car, Orion had to talk to Carl and Deborah. Their daughter's eyes fluttered, but Orion had to answer. Molly had been working at the hospital, saving lives for so long, that she just could not stay awake. He tried to remember their last real conversation. He thought it was about getting a cat. Or maybe not. Maybe it was last summer before her internship began. The power was out on their street, and they'd walked to Toscanini's for ice cream and air conditioning. They'd been discussing the khulfee flavor — a mixture of pistachio and cardamom. "No, I'm not getting that," Orion told Molly as they stood in line.

"Oh, come on. Just a taste! You never try anything new," she'd accused him. "You hate new things."

"Not true," he protested.

"You won't move," she pointed out. "You won't take Dad's Volvo. You don't want to —"

"We don't need to move," he reasoned. "We don't need a car."

"Try it. You'll like it," she teased him, whispering in his ear.

He looked at Molly now, slumped over in the car, and he hated her for being away all the time. She was always gone — even now, when she sat at his side.

"So you'll be coming down for Memorial Day weekend?" Deborah asked from the front seat.

"I don't know," Orion muttered.

"You don't have plans already!" Deborah exclaimed.

"Molly's brother will be home," Carl said in a voice that decided the matter.

"We can't make plans till we know Molly's call schedule," Orion countered, undeciding the matter as best he could.

"Molly — what's your schedule in May?" Deborah asked, looking searchingly at her daughter slumped in the back seat.

"I'm sure she could get someone to cover for her," Carl said.

Orion stared out the window at the budding trees and Victorian houses of Cambridgeport. He gazed at his neighbors' cars rusting quietly in their driveways, and the flaming tulips opening in side gardens.

"Well, she could get someone if she arranged it early," Deborah speculated.

"What?" Molly roused herself.

"I said if you arranged it with someone early, you could get a friend to cover you for . . ."

"Your brother will be home," Carl reiterated.

Orion wished briefly for the rented car to hit a pothole and flip over. He wished for an accident. Nothing serious — just enough to shake everybody upside-down.

Orion helped Molly up the stairs and unlocked the door of their apartment. She dropped her bag just inside the door and bolted for the bedroom. "Wait," he said. "Molly?"

Gone again. Fully clothed, she lunged for the bed, seized her pillow, and smiling blissfully she closed her eyes.

"Aren't you going to take off your shoes?" Orion tugged at one shoe and then the other. Her legs were dead weights in his hands. He reached around her waist, unbuckled her belt, and unzipped her pants. "Ouch," he murmured. Her belt had cut into her soft stomach and left red marks. He tried to turn her over all the way to unbutton her blouse, but she clung to her pillow, and he couldn't get it off. "I give up," he said. He waited a moment to see if she would answer.

There was a reason he and Molly avoided inviting her parents up to the apartment. The floor was covered with dirty clothes, the table strewn with bills and mail, bank statements from Fleet. Orion didn't bother looking at them. Despite his huge equity in ISIS, he had, of course, no money to speak of in his account. The kitchen counters were stacked with dishes, the television coated with dust. The answering machine was blinking, as usual. He opened his notebook computer, scanned his seven hundred new e-mails — two from Jonathan, subject: URGENT, message: "get your butt over here NOW." He snapped the computer shut again. He thought briefly about taking some laundry downstairs. Then he stuffed his computer into his backpack and put on his fisherman sweater, stretched out and worn to threads at the elbows. He strode into the bedroom. "Okay, Molly, I'm going," he said. He bent down over her curly head. "Bye."

She stirred and turned. Her face was tender with sleep. She reached out and wrapped her arms around him. She drew him close, and she was warm, her skin smoother than the silky blouse she was wrinkling. Her eyes opened. Her lips parted, and he was about to kiss her, when suddenly she spoke. "Get milk," she said.

At the bottom of the stairwell, he couldn't find the bicycle pump. He'd had a slow leak for a while, and now his front tire was too mushy to get far. He thought about walking his bike to Broadway Bicycle School. Then, remembering that they were closed on Sunday, he shouldered his backpack and set out on foot for ISIS. It was almost four in the afternoon by the time he made it to the offices in Kendall Square.

"Where the hell have you been?" demanded Jonathan as soon as he got off the elevator. It was uncanny, as if Jonathan had been there standing all the time, waiting for the elevator doors to open.

"Having brunch," Orion said.

"Brunch?" Jonathan echoed in disbelief, as if he'd never heard the word before.

They were walking through what had recently been a great open space, the top-floor wilderness of the company. At one time Jonathan and Orion had played a form of indoor badminton here, but new cubicles were now installed, and programmers packed in together. There were private offices as well for Dave, the company CEO, Aldwin, the CFO, and Jonathan, the CTO. Jake was the chief programmer, or something like that. CPO? No, that wasn't right. Only Orion wasn't chief of anything. That had been his choice. They'd offered him some sort of vice presidency, but at the time, the whole thing had sounded too ridiculous, like one of those old movies about tiny pretend countries, as if ISIS were Ruritania or he was going to be communications minister of the Duchy of Grand Fenwick. Of course, Orion had been wrong about this. The titles meant membership on the executive board. The CFO and CTO were, in fact, piloting the company, and ISIS was a cash-rich powerhouse, no fictional grand duchy. But Orion told himself he'd stick to writing code. He knew far more about the inner workings of the ISIS system than Dave ever would, with all his business experience and his "Statement of Values" — his credos posted everywhere like something out of Orwell's Ministry of Love: "We are a community. We value excellence. We honor truthfulness. We believe in the capacity of each individual to make a difference."

"We need to talk to you. Now," said Jonathan.

"Why?" asked Orion, as he picked his way through the maze of cubicles.

"Get in the conference room." Jonathan had the broad shoulders, thick neck, and small blue eyes of a former wrestler. He came from Nebraska, and he and his sisters had gone to a one-room school where they were half the students. As a teenager he'd spent summers working on ranches and reading Ayn Rand. His ambitions had been to become president, go to Harvard, play professional football, and make a gazillion dollars — not necessarily in that order. While he hadn't gotten into Harvard, and had stopped playing football after high school, he hadn't yet ruled out the presidency. The gazillion dollars went without saying.

Jonathan had been a lot of fun in grad school. His first days in Cambridge he ran around with a camera, photographing everything in sight. "What are you doing?" Orion had asked him.

"Taking pictures of the ivy," Jonathan explained. When they'd entered the university's business competition with their plan for ISIS, Jonathan and Orion had taken the T downtown and bought suits for their presentation. Horrible navy suits from Filene's Basement — too short in the arms for Orion, too narrow in the chest for Jonathan. They chose ties as well, the loudest ones they could find. Orion picked swirly purple, and Jonathan bought a nasty green one with a scaly design like iguana skin. Now that he was CTO, however, and working around the clock at ISIS, Jonathan's sense of humor was sadly diminished. He reminded Orion of Molly when she came home post-call with a headache and looked at the apartment and screamed that Orion never took care of the simplest things.

Jonathan marched into the conference room, and Orion took his time following. He glanced at the programmers, leaned in, and scanned their screens. He saw Clarence typing away, and Umesh, and Nadav, but the one he looked for was the new girl who'd just started on the LockBox team. He was always conscious of her, working among the guys. Her name was Sorel, like the plant. She was waiflike and English, a master's student of some kind. Her skin was fair, her blond hair straight and fine. She wore odd black clothes and had the palest eyes he'd ever seen; he wasn't sure of the color — they were like water. She had a wonderful accent. Sometimes he talked to her, just to get her to say things like "corollary," which she pronounced with the stress in the middle, a little bump and then a rush of speed at the end, "cor*oll*ery," like a model train chugging up and then shooting around a tiny mountain. She glanced at him quizzically as he passed by.

"I'm going to the principal's office," he told her.

"Oh," Sorel said, suppressing laughter as she turned back to her computer. "I won't be seen talking to you, then."

He knew everyone would see him and Jonathan, however. The conference room cut right into the open-plan programmers' space, and the walls were glass, another of Dave's brilliant ideas.

Jonathan and Aldwin perched atop the oval table with the *Globe* strewn before them.

"I've been getting e-mails all morning from investors," Jonathan accused him.

"About what?" asked Orion.

"About what? About this!" Jonathan shook the newspaper at Orion.

"You cite Richard Stallman as your hero," Aldwin said.

"Well, what's wrong with that? I happen to admire Stallman's ideas about information sharing."

Aldwin folded his hands paternally on his knee. With his baby face and mild manners, his well-groomed curly hair, clean clothes, and matching socks, he seemed, literally, best suited of the founding four for corporate life. He was Dave's favorite. Everyone knew that. Of course the very idea of Dave picking one of the founders as his favorite was strange, to say the least. After all, the four of them had hired Dave. At the time, Jonathan had privately conceded Orion's contention that Dave wasn't particularly bright. They'd picked their CEO from the lineup for looks and experience, since he was old, and the established companies had heard of him. "You do see that we are in business?" Aldwin asked Orion now.

"ISIS is not the local branch of the Free Software Foundation," Jonathan snapped.

"You do see that our investors are hoping to make money here?" Aldwin continued.

"Free Software is free as in freedom," Orion insisted. "Not free as in free lunches. I never said I didn't want to make money."

"What the hell is wrong with you?" Jonathan exploded. "We are selling a proprietary security system. You are going to reporters, scaring our investors, talking about giving stuff away."

"I never said anything about giving stuff away. I mentioned Richard Stallman's *name.*"

"He's a crazy anarchist."

"Not true," said Orion. "He happens to be a visionary — and I personally find his questions very interesting. Like, when you think about it, the whole notion of intellectual property is an oxymoron. How can you own something intangible? It's like, you can't own souls, can you?"

"Are you trying to make me angry?" Jonathan asked.

"Maybe you should take your name off our patents," Aldwin suggested.

"I said I admired him. I never said I wanted to be him. Jesus."

"We are in the process of filing for our IPO," Aldwin said. "This is a particularly sensitive time."

"We have one shot," said Jonathan.

"Why?" asked Orion. "Why do we have one shot? LockBox has issues. ChainLinx is still buggy — you're selling this stuff before its time."

"No, you don't understand," Aldwin said. "This is the time. This is our window of opportunity."

"Have you studied the marketplace?" Jonathan demanded.

"I've studied our code. I don't give a shit about the marketplace."

"And this is exactly the kind of statement I'm talking about," Jonathan broke in. "Do not talk to reporters again." Jonathan pointed his index finger directly at Orion's chest, but Orion didn't flinch.

He had been an athlete too, although his sport was skiing and involved no contact — only swift descents. "Do not talk to anyone," Jonathan said. "When you get phone calls, refer them to Amanda. That's her job."

"I think you're overreacting," Orion said.

Jonathan glared at him. "We're trying to build something here. We have created an entity here from nothing. You, on the other hand, spend your time whining, or shooting off your mouth, or breaking stuff —"

"Exposing problems," Orion countered.

"Aldwin and I have been in Mountain View all week," Jonathan said. "Jake is still in Singapore. We are taking care of customers and signing partners. The three of us have not been home. We have not had brunch. And we do not want to come in here and find that you — with your five million shares — have been bullshitting reporters again about free software."

Orion turned away slightly from the CTO and CFO, once his buddies, his closest friends. He gazed through the glass wall at the programmers in their cubicles. Several guys were crowded around Sorel's desk. Had she got the new high score in Quake III? She was keeping her head down, her thin shoulders hunched. "I happen to have ideas," Orion murmured. "I have my own opinions."

"Your ideas are — occasionally — great," Jonathan told him. "Your opinions suck."

"So let's review," said Aldwin. "I'm a reporter. Hello. Orion Klingenstein? I'd like to speak to you about the Free Software Movement."

They were turning on Sorel. Orion could see the guys spinning her swivel chair around, forcing her to look at them.

"Now," said Aldwin. "You say . . ."

"Go to hell," Orion snapped, and left the conference room.

Aldwin's voice floated after him. "And actually, that answer would be preferable to . . ."

"What's going on?" Orion asked Clarence. There were three of them standing over Sorel.

"She crashed the system," Clarence said.

"Really?" Orion asked Sorel.

"I did not," she countered reflexively.

"You're lying," Clarence told her.

"She checked in code that crashed the system," Umesh said.

"And so," said Nadav, "she gets the rubber chicken." Menacingly, he swung the rubber chicken in Sorel's face. It was the sort of plucked rubber chicken you got in joke shops. Its limp body was yellow and gelatinous, its neck long and scrawny.

"No," Sorel said, attempting irony and sounding pathetic, "anything but that."

But the programmers had their rituals. "You crash the system," said Clarence, "you get the chicken."

Nadav pitched the rubber bird directly into Sorel's lap.

"Give it back to him," Orion told Sorel.

She picked up the bird and held it out to Clarence.

"She crashed the system," Clarence insisted.

"You said that already," said Orion. "Now put the chicken nicely on her desk."

Clarence glared at Orion. Orion acted like one of the guys, and now, suddenly, he pulled rank on them. Sullenly, Clarence threw the chicken down on Sorel's desk.

"Get back to work," Orion said.

"System's down," Clarence reminded him.

"We are a community," said Orion, quoting Dave's "Statement of Values."

"She's got to get the bug out," Umesh said.

And Nadav quoted Dave snarkily, "We value the contribution of each individual."

The little crowd dispersed, and Orion pulled up a chair next to Sorel. Her face was white, her hands tiny on the keyboard as she scrolled through code on the screen. She wouldn't look at him. She just stared straight in front of her.

"It's okay," he whispered.

"Go away, please," she said.

"I break stuff all the time," he told her.

"Yeah, I'm sure you . . . don't," she retorted.

"In college — in the summers — when I was at Microsoft," he said, "you got Tootsie Pops when you screwed up."

She kept her eyes on the screen. Then, after a moment, she asked, "Why?"

"Because you were a sucker."

"At least you could eat them," she said.

"Let's fix your code."

"I thought you only did new projects, and, sort of, meta-programming. Aren't you terribly busy?"

He thought of Jonathan and Aldwin and Jake flying around; he thought of Molly working her thirty-hour shifts. "Yeah, I guess I'm supposed to be busy," he said, "but I'm really not. Move over." She edged her swivel chair to one side so he could squeeze his in.

Slowly, they checked the LockBox system. They combed the program line by line. First they used her machine, and then he took the workstation next to hers, and they worked in parallel on separate computers. As they searched, they turned up little items and oddities they hadn't expected, missing comments, obscure bugs, strange bits of circuitous reasoning, the dust bunnies in the code. Hours passed. They didn't speak, but mumbled to themselves. "What happens when this line executes?"

"And what happens here?"

"What's the value of the variable now?"

"Now stop and try to run . . ."

They kept working until numbers seemed to imprint themselves on Orion's eyes, so that whenever he turned from the computer screen he saw those digits everywhere. The chambers of the program drew Orion and Sorel deeper and deeper into the software's formal logic. They counted their steps as they descended into dark passageways. The voices all around them grew muffled, the ambient light on the floor began to dim. Orion's phone rang, but he didn't even glance at it.

Night came. Programmers went home, and others took their place. Jonathan and Aldwin were long gone. Still, Orion and Sorel kept hunting underground, watching for errors, listening for rushing water, tapping walls.

"Why are you smiling?" Sorel asked at one point.

"I'm just concentrating," he murmured, half to himself. Then he confessed, "Actually I love doing small repetitive things."

"I don't," she admitted.

"You can go," he said. "I'll finish."

"I don't want to go," she said. "I just need a bit of fresh air."

"Okay," he told her, and kept on working. She pulled on a black coat much too big for her. She was heading for the elevators when he realized she would be going down alone into the dark.

"Wait," he called, and she held open the door. "I'll come down with you."

"No, don't come."

He slipped inside, anyway. The doors closed, and the elevator carried them down to the lobby of the building.

"I just wanted to smoke," she confessed, as she pushed the glass doors of the lobby open and stepped outside. She took a pack of cigarettes from her pocket. "You don't mind, do you?"

"No," he said, even though he hated smokers.

"Sorry." She fussed with her lighter. "It's a habit from when I was younger. I grew up sort of running away from a very — religious family."

"In England?"

"In Golder's Green. Why are you laughing?"

He stopped and then confessed, "It's just the name Golder's Green together with your name, Sorel, like the plant."

She shot him a look, earnest and slightly disgruntled. "It's not Sorel like the plant, it's Sorel like the Yiddish version of Sarah. My father is a rabbi, and he's terribly religious. Both my parents are. I went to a girls' yeshiva where we didn't learn anything. I wasn't supposed to go to college."

"What were you supposed to do?" He stepped back as she exhaled. It was all he could do not to fan the smoke away with his hand.

"What kind of question is that? I was supposed to get married. I'm already twenty-four, and I'm an old maid! I'm not supposed to be in America or working, or anything like that. I was a bad girl when I was younger. I sneaked out after school and got a job at a pharmacy. I was earning extra money my parents didn't know about. I had a secret life, and I didn't even believe in God, but I won all the prizes for praying at school."

"How could they have prizes for praying?" Orion asked.

"You had to pray with the most spirit, and they gave you a prize. Whenever we had silent prayers, I mumbled each word under my breath so it looked like I was praying extra hard, and then I got awards. I lied a lot," she added matter-of-factly.

"You're very strange," Orion said.

"I'm very hungry," she countered. "I think we've missed dinner."

They took the elevator back up and raided the company kitchen.

"What do we have here? Chips. Salt and vinegar. Barbecue." He tossed her two bags. "Granola bars. Jelly Bellies. These are good."

"I wish there were more black ones," she said, picking through her bag of jellybeans.

"Oh, black cherry soda," he told her, taking four cans from the fridge. "This is good stuff. Let's go."

"You actually like working all night," she said, as they settled back in front of her workstation.

"I'm good at it," Orion told her. He was showing off a little, but he was also telling the truth. He was good at staying up until a job was done. He was no scientist or businessman, but he had an eye for detail, an understanding of the small picture, the obsessive game-playing mind of a superb hacker. "I can finish," he said. "You don't need to stay."

"Yes, I do," she said. "I got the chicken."

"Doesn't matter."

"No, I'm not going. It wouldn't be right."

They shared her computer now, and the monitor glowed before them. They sipped their drinks and traded jellybeans, and slowly found their way back inside the code. They read the lines aloud, mumbling statements to themselves. They made their way without a map; the program was their map, spreading in rivulets before them, diagramming underground rivers and branching tributaries. Their hands hovered over the keyboard and overlapped; his hand covered hers as they divined for the source of her mistake. And then she found it. Sorel found the bug. "Stupid, stupid," she groaned. "Over there. I forgot the array bounds check."

"Aha!" cried Orion. She'd neglected to specify enough computer memory for the number of items in her piece of the LockBox system.

"It's not even an interesting mistake," she griped, as she typed in proper array bounds. "Wait. Why isn't it working now?"

"Be patient," he said. "Let me."

By the time he had the system up and running again, Sorel was resting her head on the laminate desktop.

"Got it," Orion said, basking for a moment in accomplishment. "We got it back up," he announced to the nearly empty room.

"Cool," somebody said politely from across the way.

"Look," Orion called to Sorel as he danced toward the windows. "Sunrise."

"Lovely," she said, without moving.

"Come on." He dragged her over to the windows and made her look at the rosy rooftops of East Cambridge. "I love a sunrise," he said, "as long as I don't have to wake up for it." He felt joyous, masterful after the all-nighter. "I knew I'd get to the bottom of this."

"I was the one who found the bug," she reminded him.

They drifted back to her desk. He took the rubber chicken off and held it for a moment. Then he said, "Let's go up to the roof and throw this."

"You can't go up there," she said. "It's locked."

Still, he ran upstairs, and gamely she followed him. Orion pushed hard, and the door should have opened. That would have been dramatic, poetic justice to take the rubber chicken and throw it off, but as Sorel predicted, the door was locked, and so they trudged back down again to her cubicle.

He contemplated the chicken as he swung and spun it from its rubber neck. Then he knew what to do. "Let's go down to the river and drown it."

She laughed at that and hunted under her desk and pulled out the black heap that was her coat. Sleepily, she turned the coat here and there, trying to figure out which end was up. A couple of quarters and her pack of cigarettes fell out of the pockets.

"Here," he said, and held the coat for her the right way. He stuck the cigarettes far back on her desk behind the computer monitor. She didn't notice.

"Don't you have a jacket?" she asked.

"It's not bad out," he insisted. He felt warm and talkative as they took the elevator down and began walking between the half-built laboratories and biotech offices of Kendall Square. "Did you see all that ugly code?" he asked her. "Disgusting, wasn't it? Sloppy. We need standards. Somebody should be doing what we did every night. I'm going to —"

"Are you always quite so cheerful?" Squinting into the sun, Sorel shaded her eyes as she looked up at him.

"I like working," he said.

"I suppose soon you won't have to," she said.

He frowned. "We'll see."

"Don't you want to be rich?" she asked. "I would."

"I think I'd like to buy my dad a house," he told her. "He probably wouldn't stay in it, but I'd buy him one just to have."

"Why wouldn't he stay in it?"

"He's a little bit . . . He's an emeritus professor," he said. "He's old, and he sort of sleeps in his office a lot of the time."

"What did he teach?" Sorel asked.

"Poetry," he said. "He's a pretty well known poet among some people. My mother was his student. He wrote a whole book of poems about her."

"How lovely."

"And about their divorce."

"Hmm. Did he write any for you?"

"I guess so. Yeah."

"Do you know any?" she asked in a very proper voice.

"No, of course not." He was embarrassed by the question, although he couldn't have explained why. "Sometimes he falls asleep on park benches on campus," Orion confided. "It's no big deal. The guards all know him. The only thing is, since he doesn't dress that well, sometimes he looks kind of — homeless. Once he fell asleep on a bench, and when he woke up, he found two dollars in his hat."

"Oh no!" She laughed, and as she looked at him, sidelong, the light caught in her eyes.

"Wait, stop a minute," Orion said. They stopped walking, and right there on the sidewalk, he looked into her eyes. "Green."

"Yes, thanks, I knew that." She shook her head a little and hurried on. Her pale skin was pink in the fresh air, her hair spilled over the top of her coat. Her hand was so small, he scarcely noticed taking it in his.

The river was still and misty. Park benches were spaced evenly on the muddy bank, facing the water. Sorel took the rubber chicken from her coat pocket and then fumbled some more. Orion sat on a bench and watched her search for her cigarettes.

"Don't you want to throw it?" he asked her.

"I suppose." She was a little distracted, irritated she hadn't found what she was looking for. They walked right up to the edge of the riverbank, and she balanced on a wobbly rock. "You throw it," she said.

"No, you can do the honors," he told her.

She lifted the rubber chicken like a football and then stopped. "It's not littering, is it?"

"Oh, it probably is, but so what?" Orion asked.

"I just don't want to get arrested," she explained, "because I'm on a student visa."

"Throw the damn chicken!" he burst out. "I'll search." He looked up and down. "Okay, I see geese. I see a guy in a sleeping bag. I see the bridge. No cops. Now throw."

She hurled the rubber chicken into the air with all her strength. It sailed briefly above the water and then splashed down and floated sickly yellow on the surface.

"It looks terrible," she said. "It's not biodegradable. That was a dreadful idea."

"You worry too much," he said. They were standing a little closer than absolutely necessary, but it was cold.

"Don't you worry?" she asked him.

"No," he said. "Not now," he added, more truthfully. The water glowed, and the night chill was burning off; the whole riverbank was damp and greening.

"Why not now?" she pressed. She was wondering about him, waiting for him to explain exactly what he meant, standing there with her.

He looked into her questioning eyes. For a moment he saw the possibilities in front of him, each spreading outward, the branches of a decision tree. He could keep quiet. Or he could turn the question back on her. "What do you mean?" He could lie to her. He could say something, anything. He could make some excuse to leave. He could kiss her. He imagined kissing her, breaking the stillness, flustering her like that.

He pushed the hair off her face, bent down, and told her his secret instead. "I don't want to grow up," he whispered in her ear.

She laughed. "Are you already having your midlife crisis?" she asked. "Since you're about to be so rich? It's not very original."

"I don't want to be rich," he retorted.

"Poor you!" she said. "When the time comes, you'll just have to find the strength."

"You think it's funny?" he demanded.

"Yes, of course."

He pulled her toward him so she almost lost her balance there at the water's edge.

"Stop!" she cried out. "I won't tease you anymore, promise. Even if you do deserve it."

Laughing, he wrapped his arm around her shoulders, and she

leaned against him. Her cheek brushed his sweater. He'd helped her fix her code; together they'd vanquished all the other programmers, and she was grateful. He felt a wave of sleepiness, or possibly just contentment, holding her. She was so small, and he felt chivalrous. He knew she'd found the bug herself. Still, he loved the idea of protecting someone. Maybe there was a hacker's form of chivalry, no order of temperance or holiness — just good solid code.

"Do you like geese?" he asked her, as they watched the black geese waddle down the riverbank.

"No," she said. "They're nasty. They're like big pigeons."

"Do you like ISIS?" He spoke quietly, almost dreamily, thinking aloud.

"I can't tell you that," she said. "You'd have to fire me."

"Nah, I don't fire anybody," he said. "There's a whole department for that."

"Do you like ISIS?" she asked him.

"Not as much as I . . ."

"Just because you were fighting with Jonathan?"

He didn't answer.

"I saw you through the window," she said.

"I liked the company in theory," he confessed, "but not in practice."

"You can afford not to," she pointed out. "I have to worry about funding."

"Are you trying to get a research fellowship?"

"I'm applying to Ph.D. programs in physics," she said.

"Oh, physics. Molly's father would like you, then," he mused.

"Who's Molly's father?"

"Carl Eisenstat," he said.

She gasped and stepped back, breaking his embrace. "You know Carl Eisenstat?" she asked reverentially.

And there was Molly's father again, with Orion in his clutches. There was Carl, back on the scene, sometimes disdainful, sometimes delighted, always examining Orion with his quick hawk's eye.

"The Eisenstat Principle of Viscosity," said Sorel.

"Oh, that's what it's a principle of," Orion said.

"You didn't know that?" she asked him. And then, "Who's Molly?"

"My girlfriend," he said, darting a look at her. He hesitated. Subtly, almost imperceptibly, the space between them had grown. "I probably should have mentioned her earlier."

"But she didn't come up," Sorel said.

"No."

She smiled and thrust her hands into her pockets. "Right. I should get breakfast."

"I'll come with you," he told her.

"No, don't come," she said. "I'm in a rush. I have to be somewhere this morning. I have an appointment at the dentist's at nine o'clock."

"That's in three hours," he pointed out.

"But I should get home first," she said, and added formally, "Thanks for all your help. Goodbye, good morning, and all that."

"Don't smoke," he told her.

"Why are you telling me not to smoke?" she asked. Her voice was more puzzled than angry. "You hardly know me."

"It's not good for you," he said idiotically.

"You'll have to explain about the rubber chicken," she said, as she climbed up the riverbank.

"Just say it came to a bad end," Orion told her.

"It was your idea to drown it." She turned back toward him with her funny reproachful look. "Really, you should be the one to tell them."

"Okay," he called after her as she hurried away, "I'll send mail I donated the LockBox chicken to the Free Software Foundation. Everyone will understand."

When she was gone, Orion stood at the water's edge and gazed out to where Sorel had thrown the rubber chicken. He imagined the bird falling through the water, drifting until it lodged in slimy plants where fish nosed its orange feet. He wished he could swim underwater with Sorel; he wished he could disappear with her again, if only to learn the bird's fate.

On the surface, a lone rower dimpled the river with his oars. "Motorboat! Speedboat! Sweet!" the programmers chorused in his mind.

The full sun warmed his shoulders as he trudged up to the street. His stomach rumbled, and cars zipped by as he waited to cross Memorial Drive. He walked to Central Square and ducked into the Store 24 near the bus stop. He bought coffee there and two doughnuts, and a huge tuna sub in plastic wrap. The only other person in the store was the cashier, a young Muslim woman who wore a headscarf. The scarf was pinned to her hair with bobby pins decorated with tiny rhinestone diamonds, and she was talking on the phone. She paused for a moment and turned to Orion. "Anything else?"

"No, thanks," Orion said. Even as he spoke, Orion glanced around the store at the bags of chips and pretzels, the candy bars. He saw the dairy section behind glass, the shelves of butter and yogurt and American cheese, but he forgot the one thing Molly wanted.

A. M. HOMES

May We Be Forgiven

FROM *Granta*

WAS THERE EVER a time you thought — I am doing this on purpose, I am fucking up and I don't know why?

The warning sign. Two years ago, Thanksgiving at their house. Twenty or thirty people at tables spreading from the dining room into the living room and stopping abruptly at the piano bench. He was at the head, picking turkey out of his teeth. I kept watching him as I went back and forth carrying plates into the kitchen — the edges of my fingers dipping into repulsive goo — cranberry sauce, sweet potatoes, a cold pearl onion, gristle. With every trip back and forth from the dining room to the kitchen, I hated him more. Every sin of our childhood came back. He was born eleven months after me, he was at first sickly, not enough oxygen along the way, and got too much attention and then, despite what I tried to tell him about how horrible he was, always acted as though he believed he was a gift of the gods. They named him George. Geo he liked to be called, like that was something cool, something scientific, mathematical, analytical. Geode I called him — like a sedimentary rock. Despite the fact that he was perpetually oblivious to everyone but himself, his preternatural confidence, his divinely arrogant head dappled with blond threads of hair lifted high, drew the attention of others, gave the impression that he knew something. People solicited his opinions, his participation, while I never saw the charm. As much as he and I plotted against each other and blamed the other for our misdeeds, we were surprisingly similar under the surface, which was all the more annoying. By the time we were ten and eleven, he was taller than me, broader, stronger. "You sure he's not the butcher's boy?" my father would ask jokingly. No one laughed.

I was bringing in plates and platters, casseroles caked with the debris of dinner, and no one, not George, not my wife, Claire, and all the kids, not his awful friends, seemed to notice that help was needed. His wife, Jane, had been at it all day: cooking, cleaning, and serving, and now scraping bones and slop into a giant trash bin.

Jane scraped the plates, piling dirty dishes one atop the other and dropping the slimy silver into a sink of steamy soapy water. Glancing at me, she brushed her hair away with the back of her hand and smiled. I went back for more.

The turkey platter was in the center of the table. I reached over my wife's shoulder and lifted; despite the meat being down to the bone, the tray was heavy and wobbled. I willed myself to stay strong and was able to carry out the mission while balancing a casserole of Brussels sprouts and bacon in the crook of my other arm.

I stood in their kitchen, picking at the carcass while Jane did the dishes, bright blue gloves on, up to her elbows in suds. My fingers were deep in the bird, the hollow body still warm, the best bits of stuffing packed in. I dug with my fingers and brought stuffing to my lips. She looked at me — my mouth moist, greasy, my fingers curled into what would have been the turkey's g-spot if they had such things — lifted her hands out of the water and came toward me, planting one on me. Not friendly. The kiss was serious, wet, full of desire. It was terrifying and unexpected. She did it, then snapped off her gloves and walked out of the room. I was holding the counter, gripping it with greasy fingers. Hard.

From Thanksgiving through Christmas and on into the New Year, I thought of George fucking Jane. George on top of her, or, for a special occasion, George on the bottom, and once, fantastically, George having her from the back. I couldn't stop thinking about it. I was convinced that despite his charms, George wasn't very good and that all he knew about sex he learned from the pages of a magazine read furtively while shitting. I thought of my brother fucking his wife — constantly. And whenever I saw her — the nephew's birthday, Christmas Eve, New Year's — I was hard. I wore baggy, pleated pants and double pairs of jockey shorts to contain my treasonous enthusiasm. The effort created bulk, and I worried that it gave me the appearance of having gained weight.

It is almost nine when Jane calls. Claire is still at her office — one or two nights a week she works late, "preparing, rehearsing, reviewing, strategizing." Another man would think his wife was having an affair — I think Claire is just smart. "I need your help," Jane says.

"Don't worry," I say, before I even know what the worry is. I imagine her calling me from the kitchen phone. The long curly cord wrapping around her body.

"He's at the police station."

"Did he do something wrong?" I ask.

"Apparently. And now I'm supposed to go and get him."

I glance at the New York skyline. From the outside our building is ugly, postwar white brick, dull. But we're up high, the windows are broad, and there's a small terrace where we used to sit and have our morning toast. Now the table is rusting and we've got the cat's litter box under it and a bin where we keep recyclables.

"Can you pick him up?" she asks.

Within minutes I'm on the street. When we bought the apartment, the idea of an extra $20,000 for a parking spot seemed outrageous, but over time it's felt like the deal of the century. I call Claire from the car. "I'm in the car," I say, "on my way to George's. There's some kind of problem and I've got to pick him up. I had my dinner — there's some for you in the fridge. Call later."

A fight. On the way to the police station that's what I'm thinking. George has it in him: a kind of atomic reactivity that stays under the surface until some small something triggers him and he erupts, throwing over a table, smashing his fist through a wall or into something. More than once I've been the recipient of his frustrations: a baseball hurled at my back, striking me at kidney level and dropping me to my knees; in my grandmother's kitchen, a shove hurling me backward, through a full-length pane of glass, as George blocks me from getting the last of the brownies. I imagined that he'd gone out or had a drink after work and gotten on the wrong side of something.

Thirty-three minutes later, inside the suburban police station, I announce myself to the two cops. "I'm the brother of the man you called his wife about," which gets me nowhere. "I'm here on behalf of Geo Stone. Has a crime been committed?"

"We wanted to take him to the hospital, but he wouldn't go; just kept repeating that he was a dangerous man and we should take him downtown, lock him up, and be done with it. He's in the back, sitting in the cell. Personally, I think the man needs a doctor — you don't walk away from something like that unscathed."

"So he got into a fight?"

"Car accident, bad one. Doesn't appear he was under the influence, passed a breath test, and consented the blood and urine, but really he should see a doctor."

"Was it his fault?"

"He ran a red light, ploughed into a minivan, husband and daughter were killed on impact, the wife was alive at the scene in the back seat next to the surviving boy. Rescue crew used the Jaws of Life to free the wife, upon release she lost consciousness and expired at the scene."

"Her legs fell out of the car," someone adds in the background.

"The boy is in a fair condition. He'll survive," the younger cop says, going into the back to get George.

"Is my brother being charged with a crime?"

"Not at the moment. He was going pretty fast, just plowed right into them. Officers noted that he appeared disoriented at the scene. Take him home, get him a doctor and a lawyer — these things can get ugly."

"He won't come out," the younger cop says.

"Tell him we don't have room for him," the older one says. "Tell him that the real criminals are coming soon, and if he doesn't come out now he's staying in and they'll butt-fuck him in the middle of the night."

George comes out. "How come you're here?" he asks me.

"Jane called, and besides you only had the one car."

"She could have taken a taxi."

"It's late."

I lead George through the small parking lot and into the night, feeling compelled to take his arm, to guide him by his elbow — not sure if I'm preventing him from escaping or just steadying him. George doesn't pull away — he lets himself be led.

"Where's Jane?"

"At the house."

"Does she know?"

I shake my head — no.

"It was awful. There was a light."

"Did you see the light?"

"I think I may have seen it, but it was like it didn't make sense."

"Like it didn't apply to you?"

"Like I just didn't know." He gets into the car. "Where's Jane?" he asks again.

"At the house," I repeat.

In the driveway, the headlights cut through the house and catch Jane in the kitchen, holding a pot of coffee.

"Are you all right?" she asks when we are inside.

"How could I be?" he says. George empties his pockets onto the kitchen counter. He takes off his shoes, socks, pants, boxers, jacket, shirt, undershirt, and stuffs all of it into the kitchen trash can.

"Would you like some coffee?" Jane asks.

Naked, George stands with his head tilted as if he's hearing something.

"Coffee?" she asks again, gesturing with the pot.

He doesn't answer. He walks from the kitchen through the dining room and into the living room, and sits in the dark — naked in a chair.

"Did he get into a fight?" Jane asks.

"Car accident. You'd better call your insurance company and your lawyer. Do you have a lawyer?"

"George, do we have a lawyer?"

"Do I need one?" he asks.

"Something is wrong with him," Jane says.

"He killed people."

There is a pause.

She pours George a cup of coffee and brings it into the living room along with a dishtowel that she drapes over his genitals like putting a napkin in his lap.

The phone rings.

"Don't answer it," George says.

"Hello," she says. "I'm sorry. He's not home right now. May I take a message?" Jane listens. "Yes, I hear you, perfectly clear," she says and then hangs up. "Do you want a drink?" she asks no one in particular and then pours one for herself.

"Who was it?" I ask.

"Friend of the family," she says, and in a moment I realize that she means a friend of the family that was killed.

For a long time he sits in the chair, the dishtowel shielding his privates, the cup of coffee daintily on his lap. Beneath him a puddle forms.

"George," Jane implores, when she hears what sounds like water running, "you're having an accident."

Tessie, the old dog, gets up from her bed, comes over, and sniffs it. Jane hurries into the kitchen and comes back with a wad of paper towels. "It will eat the finish right off the floor," she says.

Through it all George looks blank, empty, like a husk left by a reptile who has shed his skin.

Jane takes the coffee cup from George and hands it to me. She takes the wet dishtowel from his lap, helps him to stand, and then wipes the back of his legs and his ass with paper towels. "Let me help you upstairs."

I watch as they climb the steps. I see my brother's body, slack, his stomach sagging slightly, the bones of his hips, his pelvis, his flat ass, all so white they appear to glow in the dark. As they climb, I see below his ass and tucked between his legs, his low, pinkish purple nut sac swaying like an old lion.

I sit on their couch. Where is my wife? Isn't she curious to know what happened? Why hasn't she called?

The room smells of urine. The wet paper towels are on the floor. Jane doesn't come back to clean up the pee. I do it and then sit back down on the sofa.

I want to go home. I hate this living room. I hate this house. I remember helping them find the house. I remember when they bought it. I remember helping them do things to fix it up. Why do they still live here? Their children are grown, the place is empty, the dog is old.

In the morning there are hurried phone calls and hushed conversations. We will take him to the hospital and they will look for something, some invisible explanation that will relieve him of responsibility.

"Am I going deaf, or what the fuck is going on around here?" George wants to know.

"George," she says clearly, "we have to go to the hospital. Pack your bag."

And he does.

I drive them. He sits next to me wearing clothes from the wrong season, well-worn corduroy pants, a flannel shirt he's had for fifteen years. He's unevenly shaven.

I drive self-consciously, worried that his complacent mood might shift, that he might flash back, erupt, and try to grab the wheel. The seat belts are good; they discourage sudden movements.

"Simple Simon met a pieman going to the fair; Said Simple Simon to the pieman, 'Let me taste your ware,'" George intones. "Simple Simon went a-fishing for to catch a whale; All the water he had got was in his mother's pail. Watch out," he says to me, "or you'll get what you asked for."

In the emergency room Jane goes to the counter with their insurance information, with the description from the police that her husband was involved in a fatal car accident the afternoon before and appeared disoriented at the scene.

"That's not what happened," George bellows. "The fucking SUV was like a big white cloud in front of me, I couldn't see over it, couldn't see around it, I couldn't help but punch through it like a cheap piece of aluminum, like a fat fucking pillow. The airbag punched me back, slammed me, knocked the wind right outta me, and when I finally got out, there were people pushed together like lasagne. The boy in the back doesn't stop crying. I wanted to just punch him, but his mother was looking at me, her eyes popping out of her head."

As George is talking, two large men make their way toward him from the rear. He doesn't see it coming. They grab him. He fights back. He's strong. They're strong. In the end they win. And I wonder, was it necessary?

The next time we see George, he's in a cubicle in the back of the emergency room, arms and legs tied to a gurney.

"Do you know why you're here?" a doctor asks him.

"I've got bad aim," George says.

"Can you remember what happened?"

"It's more like I'll never forget. I left work at about eight, drove toward home, decided to stop for a bite, which is not something I normally do, but I was tired, I can admit that. I didn't see her. As soon as I realized I'd hit something, I stopped. I stayed with her. I held on to her. She was slipping out from under herself, fluid was leaking out, like a broken engine. I felt sick. And I hated her. I hated her for how stunned she looked, how gray, the pool forming beneath her — I didn't even know where exactly it was coming from. It started to rain. There were people with blankets — where did the blankets come from? I heard sirens. People in cars drove around us. I saw them staring."

"What is he talking about?" I insist. "That's not what happened. That's not this accident. Perhaps it's another one, but it's not his."

"George," Jane says. "I read the police report, that's not the right story. Are you thinking of something else? Something you dreamed or something you saw on television?"

"Any history of mental or neurological symptoms?" the doctor asks. We all shake our heads. "What line of work are you in?"

"Law," George says. "I studied law."

"Why don't you leave him with us for now? We'll order some tests," the doctor says, "and then we'll talk further."

The next morning we go to see him. "Is this the right place for him, a psych ward?" I ask.

"It's the suburbs," she says. "How dangerous could a suburban psych ward be?"

He is alone in his room.

"Good morning," Jane says.

"Is it — I wouldn't know."

"Did you have your breakfast?" she asks, seeing the tray in front of him.

"It's dog food," he says. "Take it home to Tessie."

"Your breath stinks — did you brush your teeth?" I ask.

"Don't they do it for you?" George asks. "I've never been in a mental hospital before."

"It's not a mental hospital," Jane says. "You just happen to be in the mental unit."

"I can't go into the bathroom," he says. "I can't look at myself in the mirror — I can't." He begins to sound hysterical.

"Do you need me to help you? I can help you clean up." Jane opens the toilet kit they have left for him.

"Don't make her do this," I say. "You're not an infant. Snap out of it — stop acting like a zombie."

He begins to cry. I walk out of the room. As I leave, Jane is running water on a washcloth.

In the evening after work, Claire comes to the hospital bringing Chinese food from the city for the four of us. We reheat it in the microwave marked FOR PATIENT USE — NO MEDICAL PRODUCTS. We clean our hands with the bottles of foaming cleanser that are on every wall of every room. I worry about putting anything down, touching any surfaces — suddenly I fear I could be eating deadly germs.

"You have a big trip coming up," Jane says, making conversation with Claire.

"I'm going to China for a few days," Claire says.

"No one goes to China for a couple of days," George growls.

Refusing to eat, he will only allow himself to suck the hot mustard directly from the plastic packets — self-punishment. No one stops him.

"When are you leaving?" Jane asks.

"Friday."

I pass another packet of mustard to George.

Later, in private, Claire tells me not to leave Jane alone — it's all too strange. "I wouldn't be surprised if she comes home one night and the family of the family is camped out on her lawn, or worse, inside her house. George destroyed them — he took their lives and they're going to want something back. Do Jane and George have a gun? If not, they should get one."

"What are you saying? You sound so paranoid. And even if it were true, you'd want me to be there to do what — scare them away or shoot them?"

"She's very vulnerable. Imagine if it were you: if you went nuts, wouldn't you want someone to stay home with me and keep an eye on the house?"

"We live in an apartment with a doorman. If I went crazy, you'd be fine."

"That's true, but Jane is not me. She needs someone. Also you should visit the surviving boy. The lawyer is going to tell you not to, but just do it. There is a reason I'm a lawyer," Claire says. "I'm always thinking."

And so without telling anyone, I do it. I go and visit the boy.

"Are you from the insurance company?" someone asks.

I nod — is a nod the same as a lie?

"Do you have everything you need?" I ask, and I'm not sure why.

They don't answer.

*

It's funny how quickly something becomes a routine, a way of doing business. I stay with Jane, and it is as though we are playing house. At night I take out the trash, lock the door, she makes a snack, we watch a little television and read. I read whatever it was that George had been reading; his newspapers and magazines and a big history of Thomas Jefferson that sits beside the bed.

The accident happened and then it happened. It didn't happen the night of the accident or the night we all visited. It happened the night after that, the night after Claire told me not to leave Jane alone, the night after Claire left for China. Claire went on her trip, George went downhill, and then it happened. It was the thing that was never meant to happen.

The evening visit to the hospital went badly. For reasons that were not clear, George was locked in a padded room, his arms bound to his body. We took turns peering through the small window. He looked horrible. Jane asked to go in and see him. The nurse cautioned her against it, but she insisted. Jane went to him, called his name. He looked at her; she swept his hair out of his face, wiped his furrowed brow, and he turned on her, he pinned her with his body and bit her again and again, breaking the skin in several places. The aides rushed in and pulled him off her. She was taken downstairs and treated in the emergency room, the wounds cleaned and dressed. She was given some kind of a shot, like a rabies vaccination.

We came back to the house, had our tea, and went about our business. I changed out of my clothes, the same clothes I'd been wearing for days and washing every night. I put on a pair of his pyjamas and went upstairs.

I hugged her. I wanted to be comforting. I was in his pyjamas, she was still dressed, and I didn't think anything would happen. "I apologize," I said, without knowing what I was saying. And she was against me; she put her hands on the sides of her skirt and slid it down. Jane pulled me toward her.

There was one time that I almost told Claire about Thanksgiving — in fact I tried to tell her. It was one night just after sex when I was feeling particularly close to her. As I started to tell the story, Claire sat up straight; she pulled the sheet tight against her body, and I backed away from what I was about to say. I changed it. I left out the kiss. And I just mentioned something about Jane brushing against me.

"You were in her way, and she was trying to get past you and not get to you," Claire said.

I didn't mention that I felt the head of my cock pressing against my sister-in-law's tight skirt, her hips, her thighs pressed together.

"Only you would think she was making a pass," Claire said, disgusted.

"Only me," I repeated.

She pulled me to her; her hips were narrow. My hand slid down into her panties. It was a new jungle, new wildlife. She sighed. The feel of her, this private softness, was incredible. I remember thinking, This is not really going to happen — is it?

Her mouth was on me. She reached for something, some kind of cream; it started cold and then went warm. She stroked me, looking me straight in the eye. And then again her mouth was on me and there was no way of saying no. She pulled my trousers out from under, quickly had me down, and was upon me, riding me. It was like nervous heaven. I exploded.

Drenched in her scent but too shaken to shower or to fall asleep in their bed, I waited until she was asleep and then went downstairs into the kitchen and washed myself with dish soap. I was in my brother's kitchen at three in the morning, soaping my cock at his sink, drying myself with a dishtowel that said HOME SWEET HOME.

It happened again in the morning when she found me on the sofa, and then again in the afternoon after we visited him.

"What happened to your hand?" George asked her. He was back in his room, with no memory of the night before.

Jane began to cry.

"You look like hell," he said. "Get some rest."

"It's been a difficult time," I said. That evening we opened a bottle of wine and did it again, more slowly, deliberately, intentionally.

Somehow the hospital let him out, or perhaps he just decided to leave. Inexplicably, he was able to walk out unnoticed in the middle of the night. He comes home in a taxi, using money that he's found wrinkled at the bottom of his pocket. He can't find his keys, so he rings the bell and the dog barks.

I think I remember that part — the dog barking.

Or maybe he didn't ring the bell and the dog didn't bark. Maybe he took the spare key from under the mat, or from inside the fake rock in the garden by the door, and like an intruder he came silently into his own house.

He comes upstairs thinking he'll crawl into his bed, but his spot is taken. I don't know how long he stood there. I don't know how long he waited before he lifted the lamp from her side of the bed and smashed it onto her head.

That's when I woke up.

She was screaming. The one blow wasn't enough. She tried to get up; the lamp wasn't even broken. George looked at me and then picked the lamp up again and swung it at her, a big blow like a baseball bat. The porcelain vase that was the base exploded against her head. By then I was out of bed. He dropped what remained of the lamp — blood streaming down his fingers — picked up the telephone, and tossed it to me.

"Call it in," he said.

I stood facing him. We were the same. We have the same gestures, the same faces, the family chin, my father's brow, the same mismatched selves. I was staring at him, not knowing how this was going to work out. An awful gurgling sound prompted me to dial the phone.

Accidentally, I drop the phone. I bend to pick it up, and my brother's foot catches me under the chin, kicking me hard. My head snaps back. I am down as he leaves the room. I see his hospital gown under his clothes, hanging out like some kind of tail. She is making a horrible noise. I can't get up. I dial 0. I dial 0 like it is a hotel, like I expect someone to answer. There is a long recording, a kind of spoken-word essay about what the 0 button can do for you, and I realize it will be forever before a real person comes on. I hang up and after several shaky starts am able to call the police.

"A woman has been beaten. Hurry," I say, and give them the address.

I go into the bathroom and get a washcloth as though that will help, as though I can just wipe the blood away. I couldn't even find the spot, her head was a mash, blood and hair and bone and lamp, and I just held the washcloth there and waited.

And it took forever.

*

Later when I went downstairs, George was in the kitchen, drinking a cup of coffee. There was blood on his hands and flecks of something on his face — pieces of the lamp, I realized later, shards.

"May I have some clothing?" George asked.

"Escort him," one of the cops said. "Take the clothes he's wearing as evidence and search what he wants to put on."

When George comes back, he's wearing my clothes, the ones I've been wearing for days. The ones I washed and had folded and draped over a chair.

"Those are my clothes," I say.

"And those are my pyjamas," he says, looking at me. "Now you've gone and done it."

"I'm not going to be able to help you this time," I tell him.

"Have I committed a crime?"

"It's hard to know, isn't it?" one of the cops says.

I dress. The cops take George, the ambulance takes Jane, and an extra cop waits for me. I take the house key and her purse; it has her cell phone, it has whatever information will be needed.

"Are we going to the hospital or the police station?"

"Station," he says.

Before we go, I call Claire in China. "There's been an accident. Jane has been injured."

"Should I come there?" Claire asks.

"No," I say. I am hating her for how willing she was to let me go. Why did she send me into Jane's arms: was she testing me? Did she really trust me that much?

At the police station, I am told that I am not a suspect, that they just need to ask a couple of questions to fill in the story.

"Did you have sex with her?"

"I'm going to decline to answer that."

"Were you having sex with her when your brother came home?"

"No."

"Had you been having a relationship with your brother's wife?"

"No. I was there because my brother has been in the hospital."

"And your wife?"

"She's in China. It was her suggestion that I stay with my brother's wife."

"How would you describe your relationship with your brother?"

"Close but competitive. I remember when they bought the house. I remember helping them to pick things out — the kitchen tiles. After the accident I comforted her."

The cop drives me to the hospital. The doctors tell me that if Jane survives she will never be the same. "Even in the short time she's been with us, there has been a decline. She is retreating as if folding into herself. We have taken her into the operating room to clean the wound; we'll drill holes to accommodate the swelling. The prognosis is poor."

I have to call the children and say, "Your mother is in a coma and your father is in jail."

I dial the oldest one first. "I comforted her — after the accident. I was asleep in your parents' bed when he came home."

"Did he walk in on you?" the boy asks.

"He came home unexpectedly. He saw us sleeping. Your father has gone insane — they're not even going to be able to hold him responsible. Maybe you should come home or maybe you don't want to come home. Maybe you never want to come home again. Whatever it is, we all understand. I remember when your parents bought the house, I remember picking out things."

The boy tells me that he will call his sister — I am grateful for that, for not having to go through this again.

When Jane comes out of surgery I see her. They bring her down the hall attached to a huge mechanical ventilator — her head wrapped like a mummy, her eyes black and blue, broken nose. Her face looks like a meatball. There is a hose coming out from under the blanket, urine back at the end of the bed.

I kissed her there last night — she said no one had ever done that before — and then I kissed her again, deeply. I made out with her down there. I used my tongue — no one will ever know that.

I am telling myself that I did what I was told. Claire told me to stay. Jane wanted me — she pulled me toward her. Why am I being so weak? Why am I blaming the victim? I ask myself, Did you ever think you should stop yourself or someone else but in the moment you couldn't or didn't? Now I understand the meaning of — it just happened. Or — it was an accident.

A police officer comes to find me in the waiting room. "Does your brother have a history of violence?"

"Not really," I say. "Why?"

"We found these in his pocket." He hands me a wad of newspaper clippings: LOVE TRIANGLE GONE WRONG. TRYST AWRY. CUCKOLDED HUSBAND PLUNGES 20 FLOORS. THE BEST DUMPLINGS IN HONG KONG. WESTCHESTER LOVE NEST RANSACKED. Scribbled on the clips are little notations: "I would have done it differently," "Good job," "Next time don't forget Grandma." The handwriting looks familiar.

"Someone has been in a library looking things up. Someone has been doing a lot of thinking."

"Where did you find these?" I ask.

"In the pocket of the pants he wore to the station. What were you thinking?"

I shrug. "I suppose we all try to make sense of things."

I visit George on Tuesdays. They bring him to the visiting area in shackles; we speak through holes drilled in thick Plexiglas, holes filled with the spittle of every criminal's family that has come before us.

"How are you?" I ask.

"How could I be?"

"It was an accident," I say.

"I am not asking for your opinion," George says.

"How are my roses?" he asks.

"They have black spot. I'll spray again tonight if it doesn't rain."

NICOLE KRAUSS

From the Desk of Daniel Varsky

FROM *Harper's Magazine*

IN THE WINTER of 1972 R and I broke up, or I should say he broke up with me. His reasons were vague, but the gist, as I remember it now, was that he had a secret self, a cowardly self he found despicable that he could never show me, and that he needed to be alone like a sick animal until he could improve this self and bring it up to a standard he judged deserving of my or anyone else's company. Obviously I argued with him — we had been together almost two years, his secrets were my secrets, if there was a little animal in him, a cruel or cowardly ferret, I of all people would know — but it was useless. About three weeks after he'd moved out, I got a postcard from him without a return address saying (needlessly, I thought) that he felt our decision, as he called it, hard as it was, had been the right one, and I had to admit to myself that our relationship was over for good.

Things got worse then for a while, as they say, before they got better. I won't go into it except to say that I didn't go out, not even to see my grandmother, and I didn't let anyone come to see me either. The only thing that helped, oddly, was the fact that the weather was stormy, and so I had to keep running around the apartment with a strange little brass wrench made especially for tightening the bolts on either side of the antique window frames, because they always got loose in windy weather and then the windows would shriek. There were six windows altogether, and just as I finished tightening the bolts on one, another would start to howl, so I would run with the wrench to that one, and then maybe I would have a half-hour of silence, silence but for the rain hitting the glass, during which I would sit on the only chair left in the apartment, clutching the little special wrench, waiting to spring into action. For a while, at least, it seemed that all there was of the world was that long rain and the need to keep the bolts fastened. When the weather finally cleared (it had been the end of a hurricane up from the south), I went out for a walk. Everything was flooded, and there was a feeling of calm from all that still, reflecting water. I walked for a long time, six or seven hours at least, through neighborhoods that I had never been to before and have never been back to since. By the time I got home I was exhausted, but I felt that I had purged myself of something, and though I was still sad I was also, in a way, sick of R.

Not long after that his grand piano was lowered through the window, the same way it had come in. It was the last of his possessions to go, and as long as the piano had been there, it was as if R hadn't really left. Both shared the qualities of being at once silent and imposing. In the weeks that I lived alone with the piano, before they came to take it away, I would sometimes pat it as I passed, in just the same way that I had patted R. The only difference is that R always did, eventually, speak. Softly, it's true, in contradiction with the words themselves, which often contained a trapdoor through which you might fall, if you weren't careful, and break a leg.

A few days later an old friend of mine named Paul Alpers called to tell me about a dream he'd had. In it he and the great poet César Vallejo were at a house in the country that had belonged to Vallejo's family since he was a child. It was empty, and all the walls were painted a bluish white. The whole effect was very peaceful, Paul said, and in the dream he thought Vallejo lucky to be able to go to such a place to work. This looks like the holding place before the afterlife, Paul told him. Vallejo didn't hear him, and he had to repeat himself twice. Finally the poet (who in real life died at forty-six, penniless, in a rainstorm, just as he had predicted, in Paris) understood and nodded. Before they entered the house he'd told Paul a story about his uncle and how the uncle used to dip his fingers in the mud to make a mark on Vallejo's forehead — something to do with Ash Wednesday. And then, Vallejo said (said Paul), he would do something I never understood. To illustrate, Vallejo dipped his two fingers in the mud and drew a mustache across

Paul's upper lip. They both laughed. Throughout the dream, Paul said, most striking was the complicity between them, as if they had known each other for many years.

Naturally Paul had thought of me when he'd woken up, because when we were sophomores in college, or I was a sophomore and Paul was a junior, we'd met in a seminar on avant-garde poets taught by the son of a tobacco farmer who had grown up, unpredictably, to be a brilliant, if somewhat elusive, professor of Spanish and Italian literature. We'd become friends because we always agreed with each other in class, while everyone else disagreed with us, more and more vehemently as the semester progressed, and with time a bunkered alliance had formed between Paul and me that after all these years (seven) could still be unfolded and inflated instantly. He asked how I was, alluding to the breakup, which someone must have told him about. I said I was okay except that I thought maybe my hair was falling out. I also told him that along with the piano, the sofa, chairs, bed, and even the silverware had gone with R, since when I met him I'd been living more or less out of a suitcase, whereas he had been like a sitting Buddha surrounded by all of the furniture he'd inherited from his mother. Paul said he thought he might know someone, a poet who was a friend of a friend's, who was going back to Chile and might be getting rid of his furniture. A phone call was made, and it was confirmed that the poet, Daniel Varsky, did indeed have some items he didn't know what to do with, not wanting to sell them in case he changed his mind and decided to return to New York. Paul gave me his number and said Daniel Varsky was expecting me to get in touch. I put off making the call for a few days, mostly because there was something awkward about asking a stranger for his furniture, even if the way had already been paved, and also because in the month since R and all of his many belongings had gone, I'd become accustomed to a spare existence. Problems arose only when someone else came over and I would see, reflected in the look on my guest's face, that from the outside the conditions, my conditions, appeared sad and pathetic.

When I finally called Daniel Varsky, he picked up after one ring. There was a cautiousness in that initial greeting, before he knew who it was on the other end, that I later came to associate with Daniel Varsky, and with Chileans, few as I've met, in general. It took a minute for him to sort out who I was, a minute for the light to go on, revealing me as a friend of a friend's and not some loopy woman calling — about his furniture? she'd heard he wanted to get rid of it? or just give it out on loan? — a minute in which I considered apologizing, hanging up, and carrying on as I had been, with just a mattress, plastic utensils, and the one chair. But once the light had gone on (Ah-hah! Of course! Sorry! It's all waiting right here for you) his voice softened and became louder at the same time, giving way to an expansiveness that I also came to associate with Daniel Varsky and, by extension, everyone who hails from that dagger pointing at Antarctica, as Henry Kissinger once called it.

He lived all the way uptown, on the corner of 101st Street and Central Park West. On the way, I stopped to visit my grandmother, who lived in a nursing home on West End Avenue. She no longer recognized me, but once I'd gotten over the sadness of this I found myself able to enjoy being with her. We normally sat and discussed the weather from eight or nine different angles, before moving on to my grandfather, who a decade after his death continued to be a subject of fascination to her, as if with each year of his absence his life, or their life together, became more of an enigma to her. She liked to sit on the sofa, marveling at the lobby (All of this belongs to me? she'd periodically ask, waving in a gesture that took in the whole place) and wearing all of her jewelry at once. Whenever I came, I brought her a chocolate babka from Zabar's. She always ate a little out of politeness, and the cake would flake onto her lap and stick to her lips, and after I left I think she gave the rest away to the nurses.

When I got to 101st Street, Daniel Varsky buzzed me in. As I waited for the elevator in the dingy lobby, it occurred to me that I might not like his furniture, that it might be dark or otherwise oppressive, and that it would be too late to back out gracefully. But on the contrary, when he opened the door my first impression was of light, so much so that I had to squint, and for a moment I couldn't see his face because it was in silhouette. There was also the smell of something cooking, which later turned out to be an eggplant dish he'd learned to make in Israel. Once my eyes adjusted I was surprised to find that Daniel Varsky was young. I'd expected someone older, since Paul had said his friend was a poet, and though we both wrote poetry, or tried to write it, we made a point of never referring to ourselves as poets, whom we considered only those whose work had been judged by those in a position of authority to be worthy of publication, not just in an obscure journal or two, but in an actual book that could be purchased in a bookstore. In retrospect this turns out to have been a very narrow, not to mention conventional, definition of a poet, and though Paul and I and others we knew prided ourselves on our literary sophistication, in those days we were still walking around with our ambition intact, and in certain ways it blinded us.

Daniel was twenty-four, a year younger than I, and though he hadn't yet published a book of poems, he seemed to have spent his time better, or more imaginatively, or maybe what could be said is that he felt a pressure to go places, meet people, and experience things that whenever I have encountered it in someone has always made me envious. He had traveled for the past four years, living in different cities, on the floors of people he met along the way, and sometimes apartments of his own when he could convince his mother or maybe it was his grandmother to wire him money, but now at last he was going home to take his place alongside the friends he had grown up with who were fighting to build a beautiful world, or at least socialism, in Chile.

The eggplant was ready, and while Daniel set the table he told me to look around at the furniture. The apartment was small, but there was a large south-facing window through which all the light came. The most striking thing about the place was the mess — papers all over the floor, some of them torn, coffee-stained Styrofoam cups, notebooks, plastic bags, cheap rubber shoes, dirty socks, records missing their sleeves. Anyone else would have felt compelled to say, Excuse the mess, or joked about a herd of wild pigs passing through, but Daniel didn't mention the state of the apartment at all. The only more or less empty surface was the walls, bare aside from a few maps he'd tacked up of the cities he had lived in — Jerusalem, Berlin, Mexico City, Barcelona — and on certain avenues, corners, and squares he had scribbled notes that I didn't immediately understand because they were in Spanish, and it would have seemed rude to have gone up and tried, while my host and benefactor set down the silverware, to decipher them. So I turned my attention to the furniture, or what I could see of it under the mess — a sofa, a wooden desk with lots of drawers, some big and some small, so small you would have to be ingenious to think of what to put in them, a pair of bookshelves crammed with volumes in Spanish, French, and English, and, possibly the nicest piece, a kind of chest or trunk with iron braces that looked like it had been rescued from a sunken ship, which had been put to use as a coffee table. He must have acquired everything secondhand, none of it looked new, but all the pieces shared a kind of sympathy, and the fact that they were suffocating under papers and books made them more attractive rather than less. Suddenly I felt awash in gratitude to their owner, as if he were handing down to me not just some wood and upholstery but the chance at a new life, leaving it up to me to rise to the occasion. I'm embarrassed to say that my eyes actually filled with tears, though as is so often the case the tears sprang from older, more obscure regrets I had delayed thinking about, which the gift, or loan, of a stranger's furniture had somehow unsettled.

We must have talked for seven or eight hours at least. Maybe more. It turned out that we both loved Rilke, even if there was evidence that as a person he was selfish, hysterical, and even a jerk, because (we agreed) the personality and life of the poet shouldn't be considered when judging his or her work. We also liked Auden, though I liked him more — both more than Daniel and more than I do now that I'm older, or one might even say old — and neither of us cared much for Yeats, but both felt secretly guilty about this, in case it suggested some sort of personal failure at the level where poetry lives and matters. The only moment of disharmony came when I raised the subject of Neruda, the one Chilean poet I knew, to which Daniel responded with a flash of anger. Why is it, he asked, that wherever a Chilean goes in the world, Neruda and his fucking seashells have already been there and set up a monopoly? He held my gaze, waiting for me to counter him, and as he did I got the feeling that where he came from, it was commonplace to talk as we were talking, and even to argue about poetry to the point of inevitable violence, and for a moment I felt brushed by loneliness. Just a moment, though, and then I jumped to apologize, and swore up and down to read the abbreviated list of great Chilean poets he scribbled on the back of a paper bag (at the top of which, in capital letters overshadowing the rest, was Nicanor Parra), and also to never again raise the ugly head of Neruda, either in his presence or anyone else's.

We talked then of Polish poetry, of Russian poetry, of Turkish and Greek and Argentine poetry, of Sappho and the lost notebooks of Pasternak, of the death of Ungaretti, the suicide of Weldon Kees, and the disappearance of Arthur Cravan, who Daniel Varsky claimed was still alive, cared for by the whores of Mexico City. Sometimes, in the dip or hollow between one rambling sentence and the next, a dark cloud would cross his face, hesitate for a moment as if it might stay, and then slide past, dissolving toward the edges of the room, and at those moments I almost felt I should turn away, since though we talked a lot about poetry, we had not yet talked much about ourselves.

At a certain point Daniel jumped up and went rifling through the desk with all the drawers, opening some and closing others, in search of a cycle of poems he'd written. It was called *Forget Everything I Ever Said,* or something like that, and he had translated it himself. He cleared his voice and began to read aloud in a voice that coming from anyone else might have seemed affected or over-the-top, touched as it was with a faint tremolo, but in Daniel seemed completely natural. He didn't apologize or hide behind the pages. Just the opposite. He straightened up like a pole, as if he were borrowing energy from the poem, and looked up frequently, so frequently that I began to suspect that he had memorized what he'd written. It was at one of these moments, as we met eye-to-eye across a word, that I realized he was actually quite good-looking. He had a big nose, a big Chilean-Jewish nose, and big hands with skinny fingers, and big feet (I don't know about the toes), but there was also something delicate about him, something to do with his long eyelashes or his bones. The poem was good, not great but good, or maybe it was even great, it was hard to tell without being able to read it myself. It seemed to be about a girl who had broken his heart, though it could just as easily have been about a dog or even a weasel; halfway through I got lost and started to think first about Athens, where I had once been, and then about how R always used to wash his narrow feet before he got into bed because the floor of our apartment was dirty, and though he never told me to wash mine it was implicit, since if I hadn't the sheets would have gotten dirty, making his own washing pointless. I didn't like sitting on the edge of the tub or standing at the sink with one knee to my ear, watching the black dirt swirl in the white porcelain, but it was one of those countless things one does in life to avoid an argument, and now the thought of it made me want to laugh or cry or possibly choke, one of the three, as did the entire subject of R.

By then Daniel Varsky's apartment had gotten dim and aquatic, the sun having gone down behind a building, and the shadows that had been hiding behind everything began to creep out. I remember there were some very large books on his shelf, fine books with tall cloth spines. I don't remember any of their titles, perhaps they were a set, but they seemed somehow to be in collusion with the darkening hour. It was as if the walls of his apartment were suddenly carpeted like the walls of a movie theater to keep the sound from getting out, or other sounds from getting in, and inside that tank, in what light there was, we were both the audience and the picture. Or it was like we alone had been cut loose from the island and were now drifting in uncharted waters, black waters of unknowable depth. I was considered attractive in those days, some people even called me beautiful, though my skin was never good, and it was this that I noticed when I looked in the mirror, this and a faintly perturbed look, a slight wrinkling of the forehead that I hadn't known I was doing. But before I was with R, and while I was with him too, there were plenty of men who made it clear they would've liked to go home with me, either for a night or longer, and as Daniel and I got up and moved, swam would be a better word, to the living room, I wondered whether he was one of them.

I think it was then that he told me the desk had been used, briefly, by Lorca. I didn't know if he was joking or not, as it seemed highly improbable that this young traveler from Chile could have gotten hold of such a valuable item, but I decided to assume that he was serious so as not to risk offending someone who had shown me only kindness. When I asked how he had gotten it, he shrugged and said he had bought it, but he did not elaborate. I thought he was going to say, And now I am giving it to you, but he didn't, he just gave one of the legs a little kick, not a violent one but a gentle one, full of respect, and kept walking.

Either then or later we kissed, but when it happened it was anticlimactic. It wasn't that the kiss was bad. In many ways it was a good kiss, even a passionate one. But if we were kissing then we couldn't talk, and the more we talked, the more there was to say. The kiss was just a note of punctuation in our long conversation, a parenthetical remark made in order to assure each other of a deeply felt agreement, a mutual offer of companionship, which is so much more rare than sexual passion or even love. His lips were bigger than I expected, not big on his face but big when I closed my eyes and they touched mine, and for a split second I felt as if they were smothering me. More than likely it was just that I was so used to R's lips, thin non-Semitic lips that often turned blue in the cold. With one hand Daniel Varsky squeezed my thigh, and I touched his hair, which smelled like a dirty river. I think by then we'd arrived, or were about to arrive, at the cesspool of politics, and at first angrily, then almost on the edge of tears, Daniel Varsky railed against Nixon and Kissinger and their sanctions and ruthless machinations that were, he said, trying to strangle all that was new and young and beautiful in Chile, all the hope that had swept the doctor Allende into Moneda Palace. Workers' wages up by 50 percent, he said, and all these pigs care about is their copper and their multinationals! Just the thought of a democratically elected Marxist president makes them shit in their pants! Why don't they just leave us alone and let us get on with our lives, he said, and for a minute his look was almost pleading or imploring, as if I somehow held sway with the shady characters at the helm of that dark ship, the dark ship of my country. I didn't know much about what was happening in Chile, at least not then, not yet. Much later, years later, after I got a phone call from Paul Alpers saying that Daniel Varsky had been taken in the middle of the night by Manuel Contreras's secret police, I knew. But in the spring of 1972, sitting in his apartment on 101st Street in the last of the evening light, while General Augusto Pinochet Ugarte was still the demure, groveling army chief of staff who tried to get his friends' children to call him Tata, I didn't know much.

What's strange is that I don't remember how the night (by then it was already night, an enormous New York City night) ended. Obviously we must have said goodbye, after which I left his apartment, or maybe we left together and he walked me to the subway or hailed me a cab, since in those days the neighborhood, or the city in general, wasn't exactly safe. I just don't have any recollection of it. A few weeks later a moving truck arrived at my apartment and unloaded the furniture, though someone else must have arranged it, because by that time Daniel Varsky had already gone home to Chile.

Three or maybe even four years passed. In the beginning I used to get postcards — first from Santiago, then Concepción, and then more obscure places, towns on the edge of the Atacama, though in the end the postmarks all said Iquique. At first they were warm and even jovial: Everything is fine. I'm thinking of joining the Chilean Speleological Society, but don't worry, it won't interfere with my poetry, if anything the two pursuits are complementary. I may have a chance to attend a mathematics lecture by Parra. The political situation is going to hell, if I don't join the Speleological Society I'm going to join the MIR. Take good care of Lorca's desk, one day I'll be back for it. Besos, D. V. After the coup they became somber, and then they became cryptic, and then, about six months before I heard he'd disappeared, the postcards stopped coming altogether. I kept them all in one of the drawers of his desk. I didn't write back, because there was no address to write back to. In those years I was still writing poetry, and I wrote a few poems addressed, or dedicated, to Daniel Varsky. My grandmother died and was buried too far out in the suburbs for anyone to visit. I went out with a number of men, moved apartments twice, and wrote my first novel at Daniel Varsky's desk. Sometimes I forgot about him for months at a time. I don't know if I knew about Villa Grimaldi yet, almost certainly I hadn't heard of 38 Calle Londres, or Cuatro Alamos, or the Discoteca also known as Venda Sexy because of the sexual atrocities performed there and the loud music the torturers favored, but whatever the case I knew enough that at other times, having fallen asleep on Daniel's sofa as I often did, I had nightmares about what they did to him. Sometimes I would look around at his furniture, the sofa, desk, coffee table, bookshelves, and chairs, and be filled with a crushing despair, and sometimes just an oblique sadness, and sometimes I would look at it all and become convinced that it amounted to a riddle, a riddle he had left me that I was supposed to crack.

Many years have passed since then. I was married for a while, but now I live alone again, though not unhappily. There are moments when a kind of clarity comes over you, and suddenly you can see through walls to another dimension that you'd forgotten or chosen to ignore in order to continue living with the various illusions that make life, particularly life with other people, possible. And that's where I am now, or where I have arrived. Generally I don't think about Daniel Varsky, or very rarely, though I am still in possession of his bookshelves, his desk, and the trunk of a Spanish galleon or the salvage of an accident on the high seas, now quaintly used as a coffee table. The sofa began to rot, I don't remember exactly when, but it began to rot, and I had to throw it away. In certain ways I would be glad to be rid of the rest too. It reminds me, when I am in a certain mood, of things I would rather forget. For example, sometimes I am asked by the occasional journalist who wishes to interview me why I stopped writing poetry. Either I say that the poetry I wrote wasn't any good, perhaps it was even terrible, or I say that a poem has the potential for perfection and this possibility finally silenced me, or sometimes I say that I felt trapped in the poems I tried to write, which is like saying one feels trapped in the universe, or trapped by the inevitability of death, but the truth of why I stopped writing poetry is not any of these, not nearly, not exactly. The truth is that if I could explain why I stopped writing poetry then I might write it again. What I am saying is that Daniel Varsky's desk, which became my desk, my desk of now more than thirty years, reminds me of these things. I've always considered myself only a temporary guardian and had assumed a day would come, after which, albeit with mixed feelings, I would be relieved of my responsibility, the responsibility of living with and watching over the furniture of my friend, the dead poet Daniel Varsky, and that from then on I would be free to move as I wished, possibly even to another country. It isn't exactly that the furniture has kept me in New York, but if pressed I have to admit that this is the excuse I've used to myself for not leaving all these years, long after it became clear that the city had nothing left for me.

From time to time, I have met people, mostly Chileans, who knew or had heard of Daniel Varsky. For a short time after his death his reputation grew, and he was counted among the martyred poets silenced by Pinochet — Pinochet who once said that not a leaf fell in Chile that he didn't know about. But of course the ones that tortured and killed Daniel Varsky had never read his poetry; it's possible they didn't even know that he wrote poetry at all. A few years after he disappeared, with the help of Paul Alpers, I wrote letters to a few of Daniel's friends, asking if they had any poems of his that they could send to me. I had the idea that I could get them published somewhere as a kind of memorial to him. But I received only one letter back, a short reply from an old school friend saying he didn't have anything. I put it in the drawer with Daniel's postcards; it must still be there, though I haven't looked. For a while I even thought of writing to his mother, but in the end I never did.

There's one thing I forgot to say about the desk. Among the many drawers, some being very small, as I said, and some of average size, there is also one with a small cylindrical lock. If you were sitting at the desk the lock would be located just above your right knee. The drawer has been locked for as long as I can remember, and though I've looked many times I've never found the key. Often I've wished it were a different drawer that was locked, since the one on the top right is the most practical, and whenever I go to look for something in one of the many drawers, I always instinctively reach for it first, awakening a fleeting unhappiness, a kind of orphaned feeling that I know has nothing to do with the drawer but that has somehow come to live there. For some reason I always assumed that the drawer contained letters from the girl in the poem Daniel Varsky once read to me, or if not her, then someone like her. But as I write this it occurs to me that I don't know where I ever got that idea. In fact, I have no memory of whether the desk arrived to me with the drawer locked. It's possible that I unknowingly pushed in the cylindrical lock years ago, and that whatever is in there belongs to me.

JONATHAN LETHEM

The King of Sentences

FROM *The New Yorker*

THIS WAS THE TIME when all we could talk about was sentences, sentences — nothing else stirred us. Whatever happened in those days, whatever befell our regard, Clea and I couldn't rest until it had been converted into what we told ourselves were astonishingly unprecedented and charming sentences: "Esther's cleavage is something to be noticed" or "You can't have a contemporary prison without contemporary furniture" or "I envision an art which will make criticism itself seem like a cognitive symptom, one which its sufferers define to themselves as taste but is in fact nothing of the sort" or "I said I want my eggs scrambled, not destroyed." At the explosion of such a sequence from our green young lips, we'd rashly scribble it on the wall of our apartment with a filthy wax pencil, or type it twenty-five times on the same sheet of paper and then photocopy the paper twenty-five times and then slice each page into twenty-five slices on the paper cutter in the photocopy shop and then scatter the resultant 625 slips of paper throughout the streets of our city, fortunes without cookies.

We worked in bookstores, the only thing to do. Nobody who didn't — and that included every one of our customers — knew what any of the volumes throbbing along those shelves was worth, not remotely. Nor did the bookstores' owners. Clea and I were custodians of a treasury of sentences much bigger on the inside than on the outside. Though we mostly handled the books only by their covers (or paged briefly through to ascertain that no dunce had striped the pages yellow or pink with a Hi-Liter), we communed deeply with them, felt certain that only we deserved to abide with them. Any minute we'd read them all cover to cover, it was surely about to happen. Meanwhile, every customer robbed us a little. At the cash registers we spoke sentences tailored to convey our disdain, in terms so subtle it was barely detectable. If our customers blinked a little at the insults we embedded in our thank-yous, we believed, they just might be worthy of the marvels their grubby dollars entitled them to bear away.

We disparaged modern and incomplete forms: gormless and garbled jargon, graffiti, advertising, text-messaging. No sentence conveyed by photons or bounced off satellites had ever come home intact. Punctuation! We knew it was holy. Every sentence we cherished was sturdy and biblical in its form, carved somehow by hand-dragged implement or slapped onto sheets by an inky key. For sentences were sculptural, were we the only ones who understood? Sentences were bodies too, as horny as the flesh-envelopes we wore around the house all day. Erotically enjambed in our loft bed, Clea patrolled my utterances for subject, verb, predicate, as a chef in a five-star kitchen would minister to a recipe, insuring that a soufflé or sourdough would rise. A good brave sentence ("I can hardly bear your heel at my nape without roaring") might jolly Clea to instant climax. We'd rise from the bed giggling, clutching for glasses of cold water that sat in pools of their own sweat on bedside tables. The sentences had liberated our higher orgasms, nothing to sneeze at. Similarly, we were also sure that sentences of the right quality could end this hideous endless war, if only certain standards were adopted at the higher levels. They never would be. All the media trumpeted the administration's lousy grammar.

But we were chumps and we knew it. As makers of sentences we were practically fetal, beneath notice, unlaunched, fooling around in our spare time or on somebody else's dime. Nobody loved our sentences as we loved them, and so they congealed or grew sour on our tongues. We barely glanced at our wall-scribblings for fear of what a few weeks or even hours might expose in our infatuations. Our photocopied fortune slips we'd find in muddy clogs in storm drains, tangled with advertising fliers, unheeded. Our manuscripts? Those were unspeakable secrets, kept not only from the world but from each other. My pages were shameful, occluded everywhere with xxxxxx's of regret. I scurried to read Clea's manuscript every time she left the apartment but never confessed that I even knew it existed. Her title was "Those Young Rangers Thought Love Was a Scandal Like a Bald White Head." Mine was "I Heard the Laughter of the Sidemen from Behind Their Instruments."

Others might hail kings of beer or burgers — we bowed to the King of Sentences. There was just one. We owned his titles in immaculate firsts and tattered reading copies and odd variant editions. It thrilled us to see the pedestrian jacket copy and salacious cover art on his early mass-market paperbacks: to think that he'd once been considered fodder for dime-store carousels! The newest editions of the titles he'd allowed to be reprinted (four early novels had been suppressed from republication) were splendidly austere, their jackets, from the small presses that published him now, bearing text only, no graven images. The progress of his editions on our shelf was like a cartoon of evolution, a slug crawling from the surf to become a mammal, a monkey, and then at last a hairless noble fellow gazing into the future.

The King of Sentences gave no interviews, taught nowhere, condescended to appear at no panels or symposia. His tastes, hobbies, and heartbreaks were unknown, and we extrapolated them from his books at our peril. His digital footprint was pale: people like that didn't care about people like him. Google, for what it was worth, favored a famous painter of wildlife scenes — beaver dams, heron hideaways — with the same name. The King of Sentences only wrote, beavering away himself on a dam of quintessence, while wholly oblivious of public indifference and of a sales record by now likely descending to rungs occupied by poets. His author photograph, identical on twenty years of jackets and press clippings until it stopped circulating at all, arrested him somewhere in the mid-1960s, turtlenecked, holding a cocktail glass forever. His last cocktail, maybe.

In the same loft where we entangled, Clea and I drove ourselves mad reading the King of Sentences' books aloud, by candlelight, when we ought to have been sleeping. We'd tear the book from each other's hands for the pleasure of running his words like gerbils in the Habitrails of our own mouths. We'd alternate chapters, pages, paragraphs, finally sentences, at last agree to read him in unison. He could practically hear us as we intoned his words, we'd swear they reached his ears. But not really. Really, we were vowing to ourselves and to each other that we'd make a day trip in search of the King of Sentences, that we'd flush him out, propel ourselves into his company and confidence, buoy him with our love and bind ourselves (and our secret manuscripts, oh yeah!) to his greatness. We each had what the other needed, of this we were positive. Maybe we'd watch him write. Maybe he'd watch us dance, or fuck, who knew? We'd buy him lunch. He was surely mortal enough for lunch. He'd want us at least for lunch.

He lived, we'd learned, north of the city, having drawn from his days as a Greenwich Village flâneur whatever inspiration he'd needed, and departed around the time of that last photograph and cocktail. (We figured that his departure from the narrow town house on Jane Street marked an expiration date on anything west of Second Avenue as an authentic locale.) Minimal detective work pinned him to a P.O. box in Hastings-on-Hudson — how clever and coy he had been to find a place name that was itself, with the mere insertion of an apostrophe, a sentence, and a faintly lascivious one too. So it was that we knew he'd summoned us to his hiding place: Clea could play Hudson, and I'd be Hasting.

We sent a postcard warning, addressed to his box. No return address, so he couldn't refuse. No fancy sentences, fearing his judgment of those. Just fragments: "coming in two weeks," "get ready," "can't wait to meet in person" (as if we'd already met on other planes, for we had). The appointed day came upon us like a sickness, and though each in our privacy might have preferred to stay in bed and sweat it out, we couldn't have looked each other in the eye if we hadn't staggered out of doors, to the subway, up to Grand Central Terminal. During the short ride we held hands, fever-sweaty at the palms. Exiting Metro-North's Hastings-on-Hudson station under a thundercloud-clotted sky, we found ourselves the sole travelers not claimed by family members waiting in Subarus or bleeping their driver-side doors unlocked as they crossed the parking lot with cell phones clammed to their ears. The train continued on behind us, and the station depopulated as if neutron-bombed.

"This is the town of the King of Sentences."

"This little town."

"He could be watching us now, don't act stupid. With a telescope."

We blundered along something called Main Street, seeking the post office, until a passerby directed us to Warburton Avenue. Inside the mediocre lobby we staked out a position near the numbered boxes, innocuously pretending to screw up our change-of-address forms so that we had to start over again a dozen times. His box, which we surveilled with peripheral vision only, pulsed with risk and possibility — our own postcard had been handled there, a precursor to this encounter.

Losing patience, we sidled to the main counter. "What time on the average day does the box holder typically, you know, pick up?"

"Box mail goes up at ten-thirty."

"Right, sure, but mostly when do citizens appear and begin to gather it up, take it to their private homes?"

"Whenever they care to."

"Sure, right, this is America, isn't it?"

"Sure is."

"Thank you."

We resumed charades with the chained pen. Two, three, five, eight, eighteen Hastings-on-Hudsonians lumbered in to check their boxes, sort circulars into recycling bins, greet the postmistress, and trade coins for stamps, each of comically tiny denominations. Everyone in this hamlet, it seemed, had just found a sixteen- or twenty-three-cent stamp in a dusty drawer, and had chosen today to supplement it up to viability using car-seat nickels and pennies.

Yet somehow between transactions the postmistress had sneaked away for a tattling phone call, or so we surmised from the blinking patrol car that now swept up in front of the P.O. Into the lobby strode a cowboyesque figure, a man, late-fiftyish, wearing a badge in the manner of a star, lean, and, when he spoke, laconic. Clea read my mind, saying, "You the sheriff in these parts?"

"Chief of police."

"Not the sheriff of Hastings-on-Hudson?"

"No, ma'am, there isn't one. Can I ask what you're doing here?"

"Waiting."

"Have you folks got postal business today?"

"No," I said. "But we've got business with someone who might have postal business, if that's okay."

"I suppose it might be, sir, but I'm forced to wonder who we're talking about."

"The King of Sentences."

"I see. You wouldn't happen to be the authors of a certain unsigned and borderline-ominous postcard?"

"Might happen to be, though there was hardly ominous intent."

"I see. And now you're waiting, I'm guessing, for the addressee."

"In the manner of free Americans in a federally controlled public space, yes. We checked with the postmistress."

"I see. You mind if I wait a bit myself?"

"By definition we can't."

Soon enough he appeared. The King of Sentences, unmistakably, though withered like a shrunken-apple fetish of the noble cipher in the photograph. He wore a gray sweatshirt and caramel corduroys with the knees and thighs bald, like a worn radial tire. Absurd black Nikes over gray dress socks. Hair white and scant. Eyes tiny and darting. They darted to the not-sheriff, who nodded minimally. The King nodded back with equal economy.

We collapsed, as planned, to our knees, conveying the beautiful anguish of our subjection to the sole King of Sentences — bowed heads, fingers wriggling as if combing the air for particles of his greatness. A chapter of "I Heard the Laughter of the Sidemen from Behind Their Instruments," secreted in the waistband of my underwear, buckled as I knelt there. The King stood inert, if anything sagged slightly. The chief turned and shook his head, a little appalled.

"You okay?" he asked the King.

"Sure. Let me talk to them a minute."

"Anything you say." The law went outside, to stand and take a cigarette beside his cruiser. He watched us through the window. We nodded and waved as we scrambled back to our feet.

"Who sent you?" the King said.

"You, you, you," Clea said. "It was you."

"We weren't so much sent as drawn," I said. "You gave us the gift of your work, and now we're here, a gift in return."

"Take us," Clea said.

"No, thank you," the King said. His eyes shifted nervously from Clea, settling on me.

"We anointed you the King of Sentences," I told him. "We're the ones who did that. Nobody else." I didn't want to bully him with news of how scarcely his name circulated, how stale and marked-down the assembly of his hardcovers on used-bookstore shelves.

"I didn't tell you to come."

"No, but you are responsible for our presence."

"Let me be clear. I have nothing for you."

"Take us home."

"Not on your life."

"We came all this way."

He shrugged. "When's the next train back?"

The sentences that emerged from his mouth were flayed, generic, like lines from black-and-white movies. I tried not to be disappointed in this stylistic turn. He had something to teach us, always.

"We don't care. We don't have tickets. We came for you."

"I don't fraternize. This kind of intrusion is the last thing I need."

"Lunch," I begged. "Just lunch."

"I eat only what my housekeeper prepares. A disproportion of sodium could murder me at this point."

Clea hugged herself with pleasure. I heard her murmur the line, cherishing it privately, ". . . disproportion . . . sodium . . . murder me." The King craned on his Nike toes, checking that the cop was still outside.

"Forget lunch. An hour of your time."

"We're to hover in the post-office lobby for an hour? Doing what, exactly?"

"No, let's go somewhere," Clea said. "A hotel room, if you won't have us in your house."

"Or the bar," I said, offering a check on Clea's presumption. "The bar in the lobby of a hotel, a public setting. For a cocktail."

The King laughed for the first time, a cackle edged, like a burnt cookie, with bitterness. "What largesse. You'd take me to one of our town's fine hotels. They're as superb as the restaurants. Motel 6 or Econo Lodge, I believe those are your options."

"Anywhere," Clea panted.

The King's weary gaze again shunted: Clea, myself, the disinterested postmistress, the chief outside, who now ground a butt into the curb with his heel and turned his head to follow the progress of some retreating buttocks. The King's voice edged down an octave. "Econo Lodge," he said. "On Lower Brunyon. I'll find you there in fifteen minutes."

"We don't have a vehicle."

"Too bad."

"Can we ride with you?"

"No way, José."

"How do we get there?"

"Figure it out." The King of Sentences departed the P.O. and skulked around the corner and out of view, presumably to his car. I couldn't have entirely imagined the extra little kick in his step as he went. The King had been energized, if only slightly, by meeting his subjects. It was a start, I thought.

On the sidewalk we teetered with excitement, blinking in the glare that now filtered through the gnarled clouds. The chief looked us up and down again. We offered charming smiles.

"Can I give you folks a lift back to the station?"

"No, thanks, we're looking for Lower Brunyon. Care to point us in the right direction?"

"Why Lower Brunyon?"

"The Econo Lodge, if you must know. Is it walking distance?"

"Longish, I'd say. Why not let me escort you?"

"Sure."

We sat behind a cage. The back seat smelled of smoke, perfume, and vomit, raising interesting questions about the definition of police work in Hastings-on-Hudson. The chief took corners smoothly, in the prowling, snaky manner of a driver unconcerned about regulating his speed.

"You two in the regular habit of doing junk like this?"

"What do you mean by 'junk'?"

"Putting yourselves in the hands of a customer like your friend in there?"

"I'd be junk in his hands any day," Clea said defiantly.

"Well, he's old and likely pretty harmless by now," the chief said. "I saw him the other day in the pharmacy, getting himself one of those inflatable doughnuts for sitting on when you've got anal discomfort. I'd say from what I've heard those sort of troubles are his just desserts. We're not dummies around here, you know. When he moved up here from the city a certain number of stories trailed after him. He's been a bad boy."

"He's the greatest maker of sentences in the United States of America," I said.

"I've had a look," the chief said. "He's not bad. I'm just wondering if you ever troubled with the content of his books, as opposed to just the sentences."

"Sentences *are* content," Clea said.

The chief lifted his hands in mock surrender. "Fair enough then, I've said my piece. Just understand this — whatever my personal views of either his character or his prose, he's under my protection surely as any other citizen in this town. *Comprende?*"

"Does everyone up here speak Spanish? Is this a bilingual metropolis?" Clea said.

"That's enough out of you, young lady. Here's the Econo Lodge, and a good day to you both."

"Thanks, chief."

We crept inside the Econo Lodge's slumbering atrium. A uniformed teenage clerk blinked hello, raised his hand. We ignored him. The King of Sentences hovered beside a counter bearing urns of complimentary coffee labeled "Premium," "Diesel," and "Jet Fuel." The King nodded mutely, beckoned to us with a tilt of his chin. We trailed him down a corridor with a tongue-hued carpet. I worked not to visualize an anal doughnut.

"Inside," he said.

The King lit only a lamp at the bedside in the windowless room. We crowded in, the room a mere margin to the queen-size bed. The air conditioner rumbled and hummed. The temperature was frigid. The King took the only chair, gestured us to the bed's edge. We sat.

Clea and I began simultaneously, tangling aloud. "We're —" I said.

Clea said, "You're the —"

"Let's not waste time," the King interrupted. He spoke in an exhausted snarl, all redemptive possibility purged from his voice and manner. Our rendezvous had taken on the starkness of an endgame. "Do you want money?"

"Money?" I said.

"That's right." He reached into his shirt pocket and revealed a packet of twenties, obviously prepared in advance. It occurred to me wildly that he'd taken us for blackmailers. Perhaps he was blackmailed routinely, had cash on hand for regular payouts. "How much will it take to make you go away?" He began counting out piles: "Twenty, forty, sixty, eighty, one hundred, twenty, forty, sixty, eighty, two hundred —"

"We don't want your money!" I nearly shouted. "You've given us enough, you've given us everything! We're here to give something back!"

"I suppose I'm meant to be glad to hear it." He repocketed his money carelessly.

"We'd like you to be glad, yes."

He only cocked an eyebrow. "What have you got for me?"

I untucked my polo shirt and withdrew my chapter, the pages a mass curled and baked in its secret compression against my belly.

"I knew you looked funny!" Clea cried. I ignored her, handed the pages across to the King. He accepted them, his expression sour.

"For a moment there I thought you were about to undress," he said.

"Would you like that?" Clea blurted. "Should we undress?"

The King examined us starkly. He placed my chapter ignominiously on the carpet beneath his chair. Perhaps now we were at the crossroads, perhaps we had his attention at last. "Yes," he said cautiously. "I think that could be . . . advantageous."

We stripped, racing to be the first bared to his view. I'd lose the race either way, for Clea had rigged the game: she had written a sentence on her stomach in blue marker. *The sorcerer lately couldn't recall whether he was a capable sleeper or an insomniac.* Brilliant, I thought bitterly. The King stared. I saw Clea's pubic hair through the eyes of the King. Clea's bush was full and crazy. I thought, I will never see it again without seeing the pubic hair at which the King of Sentences once glanced. The King said, "Insomniac, I believe."

Clea blushed around the sentence, her flesh blazing like neon.

"Hand me your clothes, please."

We handed the King our clothes. He began immediately rending them, in a weary frenzy of destruction, tearing both our shirts sleeve from sleeve, shredding Clea's bra and underwear, slicing at her skirt with his nicotine teeth. He struggled to do any damage to my jeans. I felt I wanted to help him somehow, but stood jellied in my nakedness, doing nothing, not wishing to insult him, to draw attention to his feebleness. It was a mighty enough display, given his age. The hands that had forged the supreme sentences in contemporary American writing were now dismembering the syntax of my underwear.

Soon enough our daily costumes lay in an unseemly ruined pile at our feet. My chapter scattered beneath the clothes and chair legs, forgotten. He hadn't looked at even one sentence, never would. I knew I would have to forgive him. So I did it right then and there: I forgave him.

The King moved to the door. We stood in our bare feet, wobbling slightly, goose-pimpled, still breathing out clouds of expectation like frost-breath.

"That's all?" Clea said.

"That's all, you ask? Yes, that's all. That's more than enough."

"You're leaving us here."

"I am."

He closed the door carefully, not slamming it. Clea and I waited an appropriate interval, then turned and clung to each other in a kind of rapture. Understanding, abruptly and at last, just what it takes to be King. How much, in the end, it actually costs.

REBECCA MAKKAI

The Worst You Ever Feel

FROM *Shenandoah*

WHEN THE NINE-FINGERED violinist finally began playing, Aaron hid high up on the wooden staircase, as far above the party as the ghosts. The exact, oak-floored center of the universe. He was a spider reigning high above the web of oriental rug, that bursting star of red and black and gold, and from his limbs stretched forty-three invisible fibers, winding light and sticky around the forty guests, around his parents, around Radelescu the violinist. There were thinner strands too, between people who had a history of love or hate, and all three ghosts were tied to Radelescu, to his arcing bow. But Aaron held the thickest strings, and when he thought, *Breathe,* all the people breathed.

After dinner, his mother had not nodded him up to his toothpaste and away from the increasingly drunken conversation as she had when he was eight, nine, ten, and Aaron wondered whether she'd forgotten, with the wine and noise, or whether this was something new, something he could expect from now on. To be safe he'd changed to pajama pants and a white T-shirt, so if caught he could claim he'd come down for water. He remembered to mess his hair, staticky enough on its own but now a halo of rough brown in the bedroom mirror. Through the balusters, he watched the man and his violin duck in and out of the yellow cone of light that fell from the lamp hanging over the piano. Yesterday morning Aaron's mother had brought Radelescu a plate of scrambled eggs and parsley as he sat at the bench, slowly picking out the chords of the accompaniment. Tonight, she played the accompaniment for him.

Aaron guessed that by moving in and out of the light, Radelescu was blinding himself to the room, to the eager faces and cradled wineglasses of forty-two greedy listeners. Now, as the old man began to play faster, Aaron felt very tired, and he needed to use the bathroom, but he also knew he wouldn't be able to move himself from the wooden step and away from the music. His throat had been sore all day, glue and needles, but now he was able to forget that. He squinted to see the stump of Radelescu's chopped-off finger, to see if he held the bow differently than other people, but the arm moved too fast.

Behind Radelescu, leaning against the fireplace, Aaron's father rolled the cup of his empty wineglass back and forth between his hands, eyes closed. Aaron's father was the luckiest man in the world. Exhibit A: He was rescued from drowning three different times. Exhibit B: The third time was by a beautiful American pianist much younger than he was, a woman so beautiful he married her and she became Aaron's mother. Exhibit C: He left the university, and Iaşi, and Moldavia, and all of Romania on June 20, 1941, exactly nine days before the Iaşi pogrom. Exhibit D: He left because he had won a scholarship to Juilliard, and it took a long time to cross the ocean in an ocean liner, especially in the uncertain time of war, and once you've gone to Juilliard you have connections, and connections are what matter in life — more than talent.

Aaron could not hear much difference between this music and that on Radelescu's last record, the one from 1966 with no cover. The man had aged twenty-four years since then, and this perhaps accounted for the small moments of shakiness, the vibratos that warbled on the far side of control. He was old; the hair stuck out from his head in white, wavy lines. The wrinkles on his face were deep, and the ones across his forehead were as wavy as his hair. Radelescu spoke only a little English, and Aaron spoke no Romanian at all, so at dinner the night before, Aaron and his mother had sat quietly while the two men spoke. Occasionally, Aaron's father would translate something for them, but it was only about the concert preparations or the delicious food. Later, when Radelescu overheard Aaron talking to his mother about the book report due on Monday, the old man began to laugh. Aaron's father translated that he was amused to hear a child speak English so quickly and so fluently. All day today, Aaron had tried to speak faster and louder and use long words. "Indubitably," he had said at lunch today; and "pathetic" and "electrocution" and "cylinder."

This afternoon, Aaron had gone with the two men to the grocery store. He had assumed they were there to pick up some last things for the party, but when they simply went and stood in the middle of the produce section, he realized the real purpose was to show Radelescu an American supermarket. They stood a long time beside the bins of different-colored apples, pointing at mushrooms and grapefruits and bananas and speaking Romanian. Radelescu was laughing, but there was something else on his face too, and Aaron tried to read it. Devastation, maybe. When a lady walked by with her plastic basket, Aaron pretended to look at the stand of tomatoes. Finally they got a cart and began to walk through the aisles, grabbing olive oil, seltzer, five kinds of cheese. When they returned to the produce section, Aaron's father put four bunches of green onions in the cart and then handed Radelescu a bright tangerine. Radelescu said something, laughed, and then, pressing his mouth to the orange skin, kissed the fruit.

Aaron could feel now that the people in the room below were breathing less, as if afraid to knock the old man back to Romania on the wind of their exhalations.

And no, he could not actually see the three ghosts with their violins — the three students who died in June 1941 — but he knew where they would go and he traced their flight with his eyes, over the crowd, around the light, against the ceiling. Until he was ten, whenever Aaron was sick or bleeding, his father would say the same thing: "May this be the worst pain you ever feel." By which he meant: "This is nothing. American boys will never receive thin-papered letters by airmail, telling them that their mother, father, two sisters, one brother, grandparents, uncles and aunts, thirteen cousins, have all been killed. You do not know pain." But then, two years ago, they all went to West Germany before his father's concert in Bonn. It was the closest Aaron had ever been to Romania, although now that things were different, his father promised a trip before the year was out. As they pulled their suitcases through the streets of Bonn, jetlagged, Aaron had felt a spook, a chill, something that made him want to run, and in his walking half-sleep he dropped his backpack to break off around the corner and down the alley until he came to a park. He did not picture dead bodies, he did not see ghosts or hear voices, but he felt something terrible and haunted, the feeling you have when you are alone in a house and you press your back to the wall so nothing can get behind you. When his father caught him hard by the arm and asked what he was doing, Aaron said, "This is where all the people died." He did not even really mean it, didn't believe it, but these words were the only way he could express his nausea, the feeling that he was surrounded by a graveyard. His eyes must have been scared and honest enough, because when they finally found the hotel, his mother asked the old, long-nosed concierge about the history of the square. "Yes, there was a synagogue," he said. "A terrible massacre." And his parents looked at each other, and his father said something in German to the concierge, and his mother's face was lighter than her hair. Aaron was as shocked as his parents, and he spent the rest of the trip wondering whether this was luck, maybe inherited from his father, or a real kind of vision he just hadn't known enough to trust fully. He always tried now to focus on the things he felt but couldn't see. It was people's sadness, mostly, that he tried to feel, the ghosts that surrounded them, the place where a finger used to be but no longer was. He imagined people's pain traveling through the air on radio waves. If he positioned himself in a room and concentrated and listened, he could catch it all.

Since their visit to Bonn, his father had not belittled his fevers and broken bones. Aaron knew his father suspected that he was haunted, that he saw ghosts and fires and the evils of the world, past, present, and future. He would sometimes ask Aaron what he was thinking, then wait for the answer with squeezed eyebrows. He would sit by his bed on nights when Aaron couldn't sleep.

But Aaron was half a liar. When he felt something — for instance, that a woman on the train was sick — he wouldn't say it out loud until later, when there was no way his parents could ask if she was all right, if she needed help. It was something his mother would do, going up to a stranger like that. Most times, he never found out himself whether he was right or wrong; and he didn't want to know, because if he were wrong once or twice, he'd stop trusting himself. For the same reason, when his father asked him for lottery numbers, he just shook his head. "But think!" his father would say. "With my luck and your psychic powers!" It was the only time he joked of this. When he told the story of Bonn at parties, as he had tonight, it was with reverence. He called Aaron "our little rabbi," but it was not a way of teasing.

The six best things about parties were: (1) Having so many people to watch. (2) The job of opening the door for guests, and waiting for the curbs to fill with parked cars so yours was the house everyone passed and said, "Oh, they must be having a party tonight!" (3) Pastries. (4) The people who brought chocolates. (5) Watching people get drunk. (6) The music.

Radelescu stopped, and people clapped. Aaron decided to pay more attention to the next piece, to follow the music itself rather than what it made him think of. This might be impossible, he knew, to hear only the notes and not daydream or feel thirsty. Perhaps this habit was the fault of Aaron's first violin teacher, Mrs. Takebe, who insisted that every piece tells a story. As he played, he would guess what they were: One was about a Chinese spy. Another told of a man who lost his wife in an art gallery and spent the rest of his life looking for her hidden in the paintings.

Aaron knew that no one in the room could listen without thinking of Radelescu's missing finger, of how he almost starved to death, of how he kept his arms strong in prison. A minute into the piece, Aaron knew he too could not focus on the music alone, and so he willed himself to feel — more than anyone else in the room — the old man's memory. *This piece tells the story of his life,* he decided, and he tried to feel each note as a separate moment, to hear what thoughts Radelescu himself pulled into them.

He knew what his father had told him about the university in Iași — the oldest in Romania — where the young Radelescu had taught only two semesters before quitting in a rage, setting up his own studio in an old two-story building behind campus. He brought many students with him, including Aaron's father, who secretly left the university grounds for lessons three times a week. Soon a piano teacher joined him, and the little house was full of music. Wherever in the thin-walled building you took your violin, you could still hear the piano; and so the two teachers began to specialize in the teaching of duets, because what else could you do? Aaron imagined that the building smelled old, that mildewed rugs covered the floors, but that the piano was impeccably tuned. Aaron's father had always spoken of the two teachers in one breath: Radelescu and Morgenstern and their Famous Music Factory.

Morgenstern, he said, had fingers like tree branches and legs like a stick insect's. When he reached for notes, the piano looked small as a child's tin keyboard. On the record shelves, next to Radelescu's old record, were several of Morgenstern's: 1965, 1972, 1980, 1986. Aaron enjoyed flipping through the jackets in chronological order to watch the man's hair go from black to gray to white and see his jowls slowly drop.

The music factory's star violin student was Aaron's father, and on the last day before he set off for America, they had a party with a small cake. They must have known there was danger around them. There had been pogroms in other towns in Romania. Aaron imagined a stack of newspapers sitting on the lid of the piano, largely ignored. They might have put the little cake right on top of the papers. They might have said, "Be careful on your journey." No one would need to say why.

The piece ended — very softly — before Aaron could continue the story. No one clapped this time; they sighed and nodded and closed their eyes and looked at each other, smiling. Aaron hoped the next piece would be full of noise and minor keys so he could feel how Iaşi turned on itself, how the followers of the Iron Guard rampaged for nine days through the town, finding every Jew. The Iron Guard were worse than Nazis, because they were men the Jews had trusted; some of Radelescu's old students and colleagues would have been among them. Aaron could not picture the Guard without imagining men in suits of armor. His father had corrected this notion long ago but still the picture remained.

But the next piece was quiet and tense, and so instead Aaron imagined the inside of the music school, where Radelescu, Morgenstern, and six students had barricaded themselves. Four of the students were Jewish; both teachers were. Around him in the room, Aaron felt the swaying of the forty-one people who were not Radelescu, and he felt them try to imagine his time locked in the little school. They would be wrong.

Radelescu's hair would have been wavy, still, but black and thick, catching the light of the building's scattered light bulbs, refracting it back into the darkest corners. Aaron imagined the musicians would have chosen one single room, the one with the piano, and although the entrances to the building were locked, they would have locked this other, smaller door too, in case the Iron Guard broke through the first barrier. They would have moved the piano against the door. In here, they were safe; since the building was brick, they might even survive a fire. And since the little school was new and almost entirely unknown, chances were the Guard would not even think to batter down the doors and shoot through the windows and douse the porch with gas. Aaron knew from what Radelescu told his father that the eight of them survived on only the small, sour candies Radelescu kept in a bowl on his desk. Aaron did not know whether there was running water. There must have been something, because humans do not survive for ten days with no water.

On the seventh day, the only female student, a young Jewish woman whom Aaron's father had once dated, collapsed from hunger and exhaustion. He used to take her for coffee across the street; he used to study his poetry and his math downstairs while he waited for her lesson to finish. She had strong little fingers, perfect for the violin. She would live to stagger out of the building at the end, but she would die the day after from having eaten too much too quickly. Aaron tried to feel her hunger in his stomach, but his bladder was full, and his stomach pressed out into the elastic of his pajamas. He imagined instead being bloated with starvation, but this didn't fit with his picture of the small, dark woman in a flowered spring dress, lying in the corner among fallen sheaves of music.

They were sick, all of them, and not able to stay awake much. If they had indeed moved the piano to block the door, they must have worried they wouldn't have strength to move it back when the fires and gunshots were over. At some point, they had to accept that they would likely die in the room. Those who were married, like Morgenstern the pianist, would have written farewell letters to spouses they feared were already dead. Aaron tried to feel despair in the music — in the scratches, audible below the note, of bow against string.

The first student to die was Zoltan, the Hungarian, who was not Jewish but who, like the other gentile in the room, had stayed — maybe out of loyalty and maybe out of a musician's fear of violence. Violinists need thin hands; they tend to be small people, Aaron knew. As he himself grew larger and broader this year, his fingers had started to overreach the strings and bump each other. Aaron's teacher talked of switching him to cello.

On the eighth day, when terrible smells rose from the streets, thicker and muskier than the burning before, Zoltan had vanished into the supply closet for several minutes. When they heard him coughing, they called his name. He came out with his lips and chin and hands covered in a light, yellow powder. He began to cry, and the tears made lines through the yellow. Radelescu was the first to realize he had been eating from the cake of cheap rosin. If they had water, they must have given him some, but during the night he died — whether from the rosin or starvation or fear, they didn't know. Aaron wondered what they did with the body. His picture of a room barricaded by a piano gave them no choice but to keep it there or throw it out the window. If he could find a way, he would ask his father if he knew what they did with the body. His father did not mind questions.

The next day, the streets had begun to quiet down. There were no more gunshots. In the afternoon they sent out one of the students, a Jewish boy Aaron's father hadn't known — the youngest student, sixteen and brave. To do this, they must have moved the piano and gone downstairs. Aaron imagined the boy would have forged some system of communication to tell them either to stay put or to run out the door and through the streets to the house of the second gentile student, the star pianist. Ilinca, his wife, would be waiting for him, hoping he was alive, and she would keep them all safe. They might have had a string, a long string like Theseus used in the labyrinth, which the student dragged out the door by one end. If he tugged once, it meant to stay put. Two tugs meant run. In any case, the boy was gone two minutes, and then they heard a gunshot.

It may have been the last gunshot of the pogrom, but they did not know this. They stayed an extra day, a day the collapsed girl could have used to find a doctor. They stayed, and then using the last of their strength they stumbled through the streets, and (Aaron's father's famous luck perhaps with them) found Ilinca at home.

As Aaron finished his story, the piece ended. He took this as a sign that he was right about the string, about the piano against the door; he *had* been tuned to the right frequency.

The five times Aaron knew for certain he had been right, in chronological order: (1) The synagogue in Bonn. (2) When his aunt was pregnant. (3) His teacher was getting a divorce. (4) The fish was going to get sick. (5) Right now.

A young couple he didn't know had sat down on the second stair from the bottom, and the woman was leaning against the man, her head on his shoulder. People whispered to each other while Radelescu and Aaron's mother shuffled through sheets of music, and Aaron heard the man say to the woman, "He'll never fully have it back."

"Astounding, though," the woman said.

Aaron hadn't thought there was anything missing at all, anything besides the finger. Concentrating on the room now, he felt that many people were saying, "No, he'll never have it back," and he imagined the three ghosts — the woman, the young boy, the yellow-faced Hungarian — crying silently for the way Radelescu's hands had changed. The Hungarian ghost shook his head, and invisible rosin snowed over the room.

The ghosts and Aaron's father alone would know the real difference, and so Aaron watched his father's face a long time. What he saw there, he was certain, wasn't disappointment but a host of other terrible things: guilt, sadness, anger, fear. Primarily guilt, which Aaron guessed was from his leaving, from his luck.

Aaron watched as his father and Radelescu whispered together. *Breathe,* Aaron commanded the people in the room, and he could feel them all exhale.

"Mr. Radelescu has invited our young rabbi to join him," Aaron's father announced to the room, and then looked right at him, on the stairs, and so did all the guests. He didn't know how his father had seen him sitting in the darkness, but now he felt all the threads of everyone's vision surround him, tie him in a knot. He was the fly now in the web, not the spider. He shouldn't have changed his clothes.

Aaron stayed still a moment, but he knew from his father's look that he could not remain on the stairs. In his pajamas and bare feet, he stood and walked down, between the parted couple, to join his father at the fireplace. He felt like the boy he'd been at five years old, when he routinely came down in his pajamas to kiss the guests and be admired. He wanted to glare at his father, to express his embarrassment in some public way, but he knew this was the worst night for that, and so he pulled himself up and held it in. Radelescu said something in Romanian, and ten or eleven people in the room understood and laughed.

"First violin of the 'Trout' Quintet," his father whispered. "Mr.

Radelescu and your mother will fill in the other parts." It was what he'd been practicing for two months now, sometimes with his mother taking the piano part, and so he was relieved. Aaron got his violin from inside the cabinet and quickly tuned. He guessed his father had planned this trio but kept from saying anything so Aaron would not get nervous; he knew how his son thought too much.

As he started to play, Aaron's throat was worse, a dryness now that made him want to swallow just as a test, but he knew he could ignore it. He angled himself so he could see Radelescu's right hand. He could see, as he'd seen last night at dinner, the stub that extended just beyond the first knuckle, hardly a bigger bump than if the finger had just been closed in a fist.

Once he relaxed into it, the music beside him made his own playing better, and he found himself taking rubatos where he never had before, the accompaniment holding his notes suspended in the air until he felt the moment to move on. He knew his tone was not perfect, his fingering not exact, but this was what people meant when they talked about playing with passion and feeling. He hoped his father could hear.

Really, most people in the room would not be thinking about those ten days in the music school, but about the twenty years Radelescu had spent in prison, unable to play the violin. Aaron knew they all felt privileged to be here, to witness the great man's exclusive, private return. He'd been out of prison only the four months since Ceausescu's fall, and here, in this suburban living room, he tried the steadiness of his hands.

When the Soviets came in 1944 they at least made things safe for the Jews, despite the bread lines and the men like Ceausescu and the posters telling you to work harder. "They rescued us from Hell to Hades," Aaron's father said. He always said "us," although he'd never been back. And by the end of the war Radelescu, recovered from malnutrition, returned to his old university post. The Communists favored him, sponsored his concerts, and then put him in prison. What he had done to fall out of their graces, Aaron did not quite understand, but then his father knew many people they put in jail; it was something the Communists tended to do.

Aaron suddenly stumbled back into the consciousness of his own playing, and wished he hadn't. Before, his instinct was carrying him along, but now he had to stop and think where he was, second-guess, catch up, count. He felt everyone's eyes on him except Radelescu's; the old man was lost in the music. Radelescu did not close his eyes when he played, but he squeezed his face tight and gazed into the middle distance.

Everyone knew the story of Radelescu's time in jail, and so there wasn't much for Aaron to figure out. When they first took him there, they wanted to ensure that he would never play violin again. The guards observed which hand he ate with, and when they were sure it was the right, they took him to a room and chopped off the smallest finger of that hand. They weren't, any of them, musicians, or they would have known that he used his right hand for bowing, his left for fingering. He had to make adjustments, of course, and he would never be the same. But after the bandage came off, Radelescu set about making a violin in his jail cell. From the cuffs of his prison uniform, he pulled out a great many threads and braided them together to make the strings. He knew the thickness of each by heart. Next, from the wooden base of his bed, he took a thin board. He rubbed down the sides until it was the width of a violin neck, then took a nail from the bed and carved notches for the strings. And then with more wood and more gray linen threads, he made a bow. Every few months, the guards would find the violin hidden in his bed and take it away, but he would make a new one. All the beds in the building were made of wood, so they could not stop his efforts to wrench instrument after instrument from the bones of the prison. Aaron wondered why they didn't take it all away and make him sleep on the floor, but perhaps even the Communists had rules of fair treatment. Perhaps they liked the game. With a nail, Radelescu carved onto the back of each model the name of his fellow teacher, the pianist, as if that man were the maker of the instrument: Morgenstern, it said, in place of Stradivari.

It hadn't occurred to Aaron before just now that of course the piano teacher had been Radelescu's lover. He didn't receive this as a vision so much as recognize the clues, now that he was old enough to know about these things. This was the reason his father had always spoken of the two men together, as one entity, but in a voice that held some unspeakable tragedy. And Radelescu was here alone. Either the pianist had died or had left Radelescu during the long prison sentence. But Morgenstern's last album, the one from 1986, showed a healthy older man, his eyes bright and his cheeks rosy in the cheaply colorized photo. So he had left him. While Radelescu had been carving the pianist's name, that man had forged out some other, different life that was not made only of prison and loss and memory.

Five times a day, immediately after the guards had passed, Radelescu would take his violin from its hiding place and play one of the pieces he remembered. His cell would be silent but for the scraping of string on string. What Aaron tried to feel, now, was what real music would sound like to the old man, what that first raw scratch of violin sounded like after twenty years of silence. As rough and raw as a dried-out throat.

Again, suddenly, he was back in the music, picturing the notes on the page, and he heard himself play a note that was wrong — not just wrong to him, but audibly wrong to everyone in the room. He waited a beat to rejoin the music on the right note, but found it was like a train he'd missed and couldn't jump onto. Radelescu glanced at him and then seamlessly picked up the melody. He turned so Aaron could see his fingers on the strings; Aaron copied him until he got back the stream of things, and Radelescu returned to floating between the structural notes and motifs of the other three string parts.

Looking out at the gathered faces, Aaron saw that they were all smiling indulgently, that it was of no consequence to them whether or not he flubbed his part. He realized they did not see him and Radelescu as two musicians, but saw Aaron as youth personified, a living example of what the old man had lost. They were thinking, He Has His Whole Life Ahead of Him. They were thinking, Oh, How He Must Be Inspired Now to Work for the Things Radelescu Lost. They were thinking, Lucky American Boy, He Does Not Know Pain.

Aaron kept playing, but not as well as before. He took no risks with the tempo now, but tried to keep steady and count.

His father had moved out to the front of the crowd, and it was easy for Aaron to read his mind: he was giving a gift. Maybe this was all a gift to Aaron, something he felt his son would understand more as he grew older and treasure as a memory, or maybe it was a gift for Radelescu, a younger version of himself returned to the master teacher. Aaron saw in his father's bright eyes and in the clench of his jaw how he was willing together the old and the new. The ghosts flew like kites above his head.

Aaron could not stand his father's face like that, and he looked away, but not in time. Nausea flooded over him, perhaps even more strongly than on that day in Bonn, and the flow of the music was lost to him. He was shaking, and the bow flailed loose in his hand.

In an instant he realized two things, and the first of them, most starkly, most obviously, was the core of the guilt in his father's face: His father was not simply lucky, but had *looked* to leave Romania, had left early for Juilliard on purpose, had left behind his family and girlfriend, his teacher — not in order to study, but in order to save himself. And what was wrong with that? What was wrong with getting out? It was the same thing Morgenstern the pianist must have done, moving his piano across town, never walking by the jail, and even Radelescu had saved himself in that little building from the gunshots that killed the women and rounded the men onto the Death Train. And so what was wrong with getting out? Except that escaping is its own special brand of pain, and tied to you always are the strings of the souls that didn't save themselves.

But the second and more devastating thing he saw was this: That these were not divine revelations available only to Aaron. They were common sense, floating for anyone to see, more tangible and opaque than any ghost. He'd missed them simply because he lived here in America and in the present, and the air was filled with things he would keep missing forever unless they happened to hit him, suddenly and accidentally, like an errant knife.

It was when Radelescu stopped playing and turned with concerned eyes that Aaron began to cry like a much younger child. He was tired like he'd never been, and the room was a storm-tossed boat, and when he sank to the ground he felt warm urine on his leg and ankle. He still gripped the violin in his left hand and the bow in his right, remembering somehow not to let them drop.

His father was above him, touching his hair and forehead, first saying "No matter, no matter," then whispering words like an incantation: "May this be the worst you ever feel."

Behind him, among the drunken guests, the ones who'd heard the story of Bonn at dinner, who'd seen the quiet, pale boy grow paler and fall, rose a murmur: He has seen a vision, they were saying. The young rabbi has seen a vision.

STEVEN MILLHAUSER

The Wizard of West Orange

FROM *Harper's Magazine*

OCTOBER 14, 1889. But the Wizard's on fire! The Wizard is wild! He sleeps for two hours and works for twelve, sleeps for three hours and works for nineteen. The cot in the library, the cot in Room 12. Hair falling on forehead, vest open, tie askew. He bounds up the stairs, strides from room to room, greeting the experimenters, asking questions, cracking a joke. His boyish smile, his sharp eye. Why that way? Why not this? Notebook open, a furious sketch. Another. On to the next room! Hurls himself into a score of projects, concentrating with fanatical attention on each one before dismissing it to fling himself into next. The automatic adjustment for the recording stylus of the perfected phonograph. The speaking doll. Instantly grasps the essential problem, makes a decisive suggestion. Improved machinery for drawing brass wire. The aurophone, for enhancement of hearing. His trip to Paris has charged him with energy. Out into the courtyard! — the electrical lab, the chemical lab. Dangers of high-voltage alternating current: tests for safety. Improved insulation for electrical conductors. On to the metallurgical lab, to examine the graders and crushers, the belt conveyors, the ore samples. His magnetic ore-separator. "Work like hell, boys!" In Photographic Building, an air of secrecy. Excitement over the new Eastman film, the long strip in which lies the secret of visual motion. The Wizard says kinetoscope will do for the eye what phonograph does for the ear. But not yet, not yet! The men talk. What else? What next? A method of producing electricity directly from coal? A machine for compacting snow to clear city streets? Artificial silk? He hasn't slept at home for a week. They say the Wizard goes down to the Box, the experimental room in basement. Always kept locked. Rumors swirl. Another big invention to rival the phonograph? Surpass the incandescent lamp? The Wizard reads in library in the early mornings. From my desk in alcove I see him turn pages impatiently. Sometimes he thrusts at me a list of books to order. Warburton's *Physiology of Animals.* Greene and Wilson, *Cutaneous Sensation.* Makes a note, slams book shut, strides out. Earnshaw says Wizard spent three hours shut up in the Box last night.

OCTOBER 16. Today a book arrived: Kerner, *Archaeology of the Skin.* Immediately left library and walked upstairs to experimental rooms. Room 12 open, cot empty, the Wizard gone. On table an open notebook, a glass battery, and parts of a dissected phonograph scattered around a boxed motor: three wax cylinders, a recording stylus attached to its diaphragm, a voice horn, a cutting blade for shaving used cylinders. Notebook showed a rough drawing. Identified it at once: design for an automatic adjustment in recording mechanism, whereby stylus would engage cylinder automatically at correct depth. Wizard absolutely determined to crush Bell's graphophone. From window, a view of courtyard and part of chemical lab.

Returned to corridor. Ran into Corbett, an experimental assistant. The Wizard had just left. Someone called out he thought Wizard heading to stockroom. I returned down the stairs. Passed through library, pushed open double door, and crossed corridor to stockroom.

Always exhilarating to enter Earnshaw's domain. Those high walls, lined from floor to ceiling with long drawers — hides, bones, roots, textiles, teeth. Pigeonholes, hundreds of them, crammed with resins, waxes, twines. Is it that, like library itself, stockroom is an orderly and teeming universe — a world of worlds — a finitude with aspirations to allness? Earnshaw hadn't seen him, thought he might be in basement. His hesitation when I held up Kerner and announced my mission. Told him the Wizard had insisted it be brought to him immediately. Earnshaw still hesitant as he took out ring of keys. Is loyal to Wizard, but more loyal to me. Opened door leading to basement storeroom and preceded me down into the maze.

Crates of feathers, sheet metal, pitch, plumbago, cork. Earnshaw hesitated again at locked door of Box. Do not disturb: Wizard's strict orders. But Wizard had left strict orders with me: deliver book immediately. Two unambiguous commands, each contradicting the other. Earnshaw torn. A good man, earnest, but not strong. Unable to resist a sense of moral obligation to me, owing to a number of trifling services rendered to him in the ordinary course of work. In addition, ten years younger. In my presence instinctively assumes an attitude of deference. Rapped lightly on door. No answer. "Open it," I said, not unkindly. He stood outside as I entered.

Analysis of motives. Desire to deliver book (good). Desire to see room (bad). Yielded to base desire. But ask yourself: was it only base? I revere the Wizard and desire his success. He is searching for something, for some piece of crucial knowledge. If I see experiment, may be able to find information he needs. Analyze later.

The small room well-lit by incandescent bulbs. Bare of furnishings except for central table, two armchairs against wall. On table a closed notebook, a copper-oxide battery, and two striking objects. One a long stiff blackish glove, about the length of a forearm, which rests horizontally on two Y-shaped supports about eight inches high. Glove made of some solid dark material, perhaps vulcanized rubber, and covered with a skein of wires emerging from small brass caps. The other: a wooden framework supporting a horizontal cylinder, whose upper surface is in contact with a row of short metal strips suspended from a crossbar. Next to cylinder a small electric motor. Two bundles of wire lead from glove to battery, which in turn is connected to cylinder mechanism by way of motor. On closer inspection I see that interior of glove is lined with black silky material, studded with tiny silver disks like heads of pins. "Sir!" whispers Earnshaw.

I switch off lights and step outside. Footsteps above our heads. I follow Earnshaw back upstairs into stockroom, where an experimental assistant awaits him with request for copper wire. Return to library. Am about to sit down at desk when Wizard enters from other door. Gray gabardine laboratory gown flowing around his legs, tie crooked, hair mussed. "Has that book — ?" he says loudly. Deaf in his left ear. "I was just bringing it to you," I shout. Holding out Kerner. Seizes it and throws himself down in an armchair, frowning as if angrily at the flung-open pages.

October 17. A quiet day in library. Rain, scudding clouds. Arranged books on third-floor gallery, dusted mineral specimens in their glass-doored cabinets. Restless.

October 18. That wired glove. Can it be a self-warming device, to replace a lady's muff? Have heard that in Paris, on cold winter nights, vendors stand before the Opera House, selling hot potatoes for ladies to place in their muffs. But the pinheads? The cylinder? And why then such secrecy? Wizard in locked room again, for two hours, with Kistenmacher.

October 20. This morning overheard a few words in courtyard. Immediately set off for stockroom in search of Earnshaw. E's passion — his weakness, one might say — is for idea of motion photography. Eager to get hold of any information about the closely guarded experiments in Photographic Building and Room 5. Words overheard were between two machinists, who'd heard an experimental assistant speaking to so-and-so from chemical lab about an experiment in Photographic Building conducted with the new Eastman film. Talk was of perforations along both edges of strip, as in the old telegraph tape. The film to be driven forward on sprockets that engage and release it. This of course the most roundabout hearsay. Nevertheless not first time there has been talk of modifying strip film by means of perforations, which some say the Wizard saw in Paris: studio of Monsieur Marey. Earnshaw thrives on such rumors.

Not in stockroom but down in storeroom, as I knew at once by partially open door. In basement reported my news. Excited him visibly. At that instant — suddenly — I became aware of darker motive underlying my impulse to inform Earnshaw of conversation in courtyard. Paused. Looked about. Asked him to admit me for a moment — only a moment — to the Box.

An expression of alarm invading his features. But Earnshaw particularly well qualified to understand a deep curiosity about experiments conducted in secret. Furthermore: could not refuse to satisfy an indebtedness he felt he'd incurred by listening eagerly to my report. Stationed himself outside door. Guardian of inner sanctum. I quickly entered.

The glove, the battery, the cylinder. I detected a single difference: notebook now open. Showed a hastily executed drawing of glove, surrounded by several smaller sketches of what appeared to be electromagnets, with coils of wire about a core. Under glove a single word: haptograph.

Did not hesitate to insert hand and arm in glove. Operation somewhat impeded by silken lining, evidently intended to prevent skin from directly touching any part of inner structure. When forearm was buried up to elbow, threw switch attached to wires at base of cylinder mechanism.

The excitement returns, even as I write these words. How to explain it? The activated current caused motor to turn cylinder on its shaft beneath the metal rods suspended from crossbar, which in turn caused silver points in lining of glove to move against my hand. Was aware at first of many small gentle pointed pressures. But — behold! — the merely mechanical sensation soon gave way to another, and I felt — distinctly — a sensation as of a hand grasping my own in a firm handshake. External glove had remained stiff and immobile. Switched off current, breathed deep. Repeated experiment. Again the motor turning the cylinder. Sensation unmistakable: I felt my hand gripped in a handshake, my fingers lightly squeezed. At that moment experienced a strange elation, as if standing on a dock listening to water lap against piles as I prepared to embark on a longed-for voyage. Switched off current, withdrew hand. Stood still for a moment before turning suddenly to leave room.

OCTOBER 21. Books borrowed by Kistenmacher, as recorded in library notebook, Oct. 7 – Oct. 14: *The Nervous System and the Mind, The Tactile Sphere, Leçons sur la physiologie du système nerveux, Lezioni di fisiologia sperimentale, Sensation and Pain.* The glove, the cylinder, the phantom handshake. Clear — is it clear? — that Wizard has turned his attention to sense of touch. To what end, exactly? Yet even as I ask, I seem to grasp principle of haptograph. "The kinetoscope will do for the eye what the phonograph does for the ear." Is he not isolating each of the five senses? Creating for each a machine that records and plays back one sense alone? Voices disembodied, moving images without physical substance, immaterial touches. The phonograph, the kinetoscope, the haptograph. Voices preserved in cylinders of wax, moving bodies in strips of nitrocellulose, touches in pinheads and wires. A gallery of ghosts.

Cylinder as it turns must transmit electrical impulses that activate the silver points. Ghosts? Consider: the skin is touched. A firm handshake. Hello, my name is. And yours? Strange thoughts on an October night.

OCTOBER 24. This morning, after Wizard was done looking through mail and had ascended stairs to experimental rooms, Kistenmacher entered library. Headed directly toward me. Have always harbored a certain dislike for Kistenmacher, though he treats me respectfully enough. Dislike the aggressive directness of his walk, arms swinging so far forward that he seems to be pulling himself along by gripping onto chunks of air. Dislike his big hands with neat black hairs growing sideways across fingers, intense stare of eyes that take you in without seeing you, his black stiff hair combed as if violently sideways across head, necktie straight as a plumbline. Kistenmacher one of the most respected of electrical experimenters. Came directly up to my rolltop desk, stopping too close to it, as if the wood were barring his way.

"I wish to report a missing book," he said.

Deeper meaning of Kistenmacher's remark. It happens — infrequently — that a library book is temporarily misplaced. The cause not difficult to wrest from the hidden springs of existence. Any experimenter — or assistant — or indeed any member of staff — is permitted to browse among all three tiers of books, or to remove a volume and read anywhere on premises. Instead of leaving book for me to replace, as everyone is instructed to do, occasionally someone takes it upon self to reshelve. An act well-meant but better left undone, since mistakes easy to make. Earnshaw, in particular, guilty of this sort of misplaced kindness. Nevertheless I patrol shelves carefully, several times a day, not only when I replace books returned by staff, or add new books and scientific journals ordered for library, but also on tours of inspection intended to ensure correct arrangement of books on shelves. As a result quite rare for a misplaced volume to escape detection. Kistenmacher's statement therefore not the simple statement of fact it appeared to be, but an implied reproach: You have been negligent in your duties.

"I'm quite certain we can find it without difficulty," I said. Rising immediately. "Sometimes the new assistants —"

"Giesinger," he said. "*Musculo-Cutaneous Feeling.*"

A slight heat in my neck. Wondered whether a flush was visible.

"You see," I said with a smile. "The mystery solved." Lifted from my desk *Musculo-Cutaneous Feeling* by Otto Giesinger and handed it to Kistenmacher. He glanced at spine, to make certain I hadn't made a mistake, then looked at me with interest.

"This is a highly specialized study," said he.

"Yes, a little too specialized for me," I replied.

"But the subject interests you?"

Hesitation. "I try to keep abreast of — developments."

"Excellent," he said, and suddenly smiled — a disconcerting smile, of startling charm. "I will be sure to consult with you." Held up book, tightly clasped in one big hand, gave a little wave with it, and took his leave.

The whole incident rich with possibility. My responsibility in library is to keep up with scientific and technical literature, so that I may order books I deem essential. Most of my professional reading confined to scientific journals, technical periodicals, and institutional proceedings, but peruse many books as well, in a broad range of subjects, from psychology of hysteria to structure of the constant-pressure dynamo; my interests are wide. Still, it cannot have failed to strike Kistenmacher that I had removed from shelves a study directly related to his investigations in Box. Kistenmacher perfectly well aware that everyone knows of his secretive experiments, about which many rumors. Is said to enjoy such rumors and even to contribute to them by enigmatic hints of his own. Once told Earnshaw, who reported it to me, that there would soon be no human sensation that could not be replicated mechanically. At time I imagined a machine for production of odors, a machine of tastes. Knows of course that I keep a record of books borrowed by staff, each with name of borrower. Now knows I have been reading Giesinger on musculo-cutaneous feeling.

What else does he know? Can Earnshaw have said something?

OCTOBER 26. A slow day. Reading. From my desk in alcove I can see Wizard's rolltop desk with its scattering of books and papers, the railed galleries of second and third levels, high up a flash of sun on a glass-fronted cabinet holding mineral specimens. The pine-paneled ceiling. Beyond Wizard's desk, the white marble statue brought back from Paris Exposition. Winged youth seated on ruins of a gas streetlamp, holding high in one hand an incandescent lamp. The Genius of Light. In my feet a rumble of dynamos from machine shop beyond stockroom.

OCTOBER 28. In courtyard, gossip about secret experiments in Photographic Building, Room 8, the Box. A machine for extracting nutrients from seaweed? A speaking photograph? Rumors of hidden workrooms, secret assistants. In courtyard one night, an experimental assistant seen with cylinders under each arm, heading in direction of basement.

OCTOBER 29. For the Wizard, there is always a practical consideration. The incandescent lamp, the electric pen, the magnetic ore-separator. The quadruplex telegraph. Origin of moving photographs in study of animal motion: Muybridge's horses, Marey's birds. Even the phonograph: concedes its secondary use as instrument of entertainment, but insists on primary value as business machine for use in dictation. And the haptograph? A possible use in hospitals? A young mother dies. Bereft child comforted by simulated caresses. Old people, lingering out their lives alone, untouched. Shake of a friendly hand. It might work.

NOVEMBER 3. A momentous day. Even now it seems unlikely. And yet, looked at calmly, a day like any other: experimenters in their rooms, visitors walking in courtyard, a group of schoolchildren with their teacher, assistants passing up and down corridors and stairways, men working on grounds. After a long morning decided to take walk in courtyard, as I sometimes do. Warmish day, touch of autumn chill in the shade. Walked length of courtyard, between electrical lab and chemical lab, nodding to several men who stood talking in groups. At end of yard, took a long look at buildings of Phonograph Works. Started back. Nearly halfway to main building when aware of sharp footsteps not far behind me. Drawing closer. Turned and saw Kistenmacher.

"A fine day for a walk," he said. Falling into step beside me.

Hidden significance of Kistenmacher's apparently guileless salutation. His voice addressed to the air — to the universe — but with a ripple of the confidential meant for me. Instantly alert. Common enough of course to meet an experimenter or machinist in courtyard. Courtyard after all serves as informal meeting place, where members of staff freely mingle. Have encountered Kistenmacher himself innumerable times, striding along with great arms swinging. No, what struck me, on this occasion, was one indisputable fact: instead of passing me with habitual brisk nod, Kistenmacher attached himself to me with tremendous decisiveness. So apparent he had something to say to me that I suspected he'd been watching for me from a window.

"My sentiment exactly," I replied.

"I wonder whether you might accompany me to Room 8," he then said.

An invitation meant to startle me. I confess it did. Kistenmacher knows I am curious about experimental rooms on second floor, just upstairs from library. These rooms always kept open — except Room 5, where photographic experiments continue to be conducted secretly, in addition to those in new Photographic Building — but there is general understanding that rooms are domain of experimenters and assistants, and of course of the Wizard himself, who visits each room daily in order to observe progress of every experiment. Kistenmacher's invitation therefore highly unusual. At same time, had about it a deliberate air of mystery, which Kistenmacher clearly enjoying as he took immense energetic strides and pulled himself forward with great swings of his absurd arms.

Room 8: Kistenmacher's room on second floor. On a table: parts of a storage battery and samples of what I supposed to be nickel hydrate. No sign of haptograph. This in itself not remarkable, for experimenters are engaged in many projects. Watched him close door and turn to me.

"Our interests coincide," he said, speaking in manner characteristic of him, at once direct and sly.

I said nothing.

"I invite you to take part in an experiment," he next remarked. An air of suppressed energy. Had sense that he was studying my face for signs of excitement.

His invitation, part entreaty and part command, shocked and thrilled me. Also exasperated me by terrible ease with which he was able to create inner turmoil.

"What kind of experiment?" I asked: sharply, almost rudely.

He laughed — I had not expected Kistenmacher to laugh. A boyish and disarming laugh. Surprised to see a dimple in his left cheek. Kistenmacher's teeth straight and white, though upper left incisor is missing.

"That," he said, "remains to be seen. Nine o'clock tomorrow night? I will come to the library."

Noticed that, while his body remained politely immobile, his muscles had grown tense in preparation for leaving. Already absolutely sure of my acceptance.

When I returned to library, found Wizard seated at his desk, in stained laboratory gown, gesturing vigorously with both hands as he spoke with a reporter from the *New York World.*

NOVEMBER 5. I will do my utmost to describe objectively the extraordinary event in which I participated on the evening of November 4.

Kistenmacher appeared in library with a punctuality that even in my state of excitement I found faintly ludicrous: over fireplace the big clock-hands showed nine o'clock so precisely that I had momentary grotesque sense they were the false hands of a painted clock. Led me into stockroom, where Earnshaw had been relieved for night shift by young Benson, who was up on a ladder examining contents of a drawer. Looked down at us intently over his shoulder, bending neck and gripping ladder rails, as if we were very small and very far away. Kistenmacher removed from pocket a circle of keys. Held them up to inform Benson of our purpose. Opened door that led down to basement. I followed him through dim-lit cellar rooms piled high with wooden crates until we reached door of Box. Kistenmacher inserted key, stepped inside to activate electrical switch. Then turned to usher me in with a sweep of his hand and a barely perceptible little bow, all the while watching me closely.

The room had changed. No glove: next to table an object that made me think of a dressmaker's dummy, or top half of a suit of armor, complete with helmet. Supported on stand clamped to table edge. The dark half-figure studded with small brass caps connected by a skein of wires that covered entire surface. Beside it the cylinder machine and the copper-oxide battery. Half a dozen additional cylinders standing upright on table, beside machine. In one corner, an object draped in a sheet.

"Welcome to the haptograph," Kistenmacher said. "Permit me to demonstrate."

He stepped over to figure, disconnected a cable, and unfastened clasps that held head to torso. Lifted off head with both hands. Placed head carefully on table. Next unhooked or unhinged torso so that back opened in two wings. Hollow center lined with the same dark silky material and glittery silver points I had seen in glove.

Thereupon asked me to remove jacket, vest, necktie, shirt. My hesitation. Looked at me harshly. "Modesty is for schoolgirls." Turning around. "I will turn my back. You may leave, if you prefer."

Removed my upper clothing piece by piece and placed each article on back of a chair. Kistenmacher turned to face me. "So! You are still here?" Immediately gestured toward interior of winged torso, into which I inserted my arms. Against my skin felt silken lining. He closed wings and hooked in place. Set helmet over my head, refastened clasps and cable. An opening at mouth enabled me to breathe. At level of my eyes a strip of wire mesh. The arms, though stiff, movable at wrists and shoulders. I stood beside table, awaiting instructions.

"Tell me what you feel," Kistenmacher said. "It helps in the beginning if you close your eyes."

He threw switch at base of machine. The cylinder began to turn.

At first felt a series of very faint pinpricks in region of scalp. Gradually impression of separate prickings faded away and I became aware of a more familiar sensation.

"It feels," I said, "exactly as if — yes — it's uncanny — but as though I were putting a hat on my head."

"Very good," Kistenmacher said. "And this?" Opened my eyes long enough to watch him slip cylinder from its shaft and replace with new one.

This time felt a series of pinpricks in region of right shoulder. Quickly resolved into a distinct sensation: a hand resting on shoulder, then giving a little squeeze.

"And this?" Removed cylinder and added another. "Hold out your left hand. Palm up."

Was able to turn my armored hand at wrist. In palm became aware of a sudden sensation: a roundish smooth object — ball? egg? — seemed to be resting there.

In this manner — cylinder by cylinder — Kistenmacher tested three additional sensations. A fly or other small insect walking on right forearm. A ring or rope tightening over left biceps. Sudden burst of uncontrollable laughter: the haptograph had re-created sensation of fingers tickling my ribs.

"And now one more. Please pay close attention. Report exactly what you feel." Slipped a new cylinder onto shaft and switched on current.

After initial pinpricks, felt a series of pressures that began at waist and rose along chest and face. A clear tactile sensation, rather pleasant, yet one I could not recall having experienced before. Kistenmacher listened intently as I attempted to describe. A kind of upward-flowing ripple, which moved rapidly from waist to top of scalp, encompassing entire portion of body enclosed in haptograph. Like being repeatedly stroked by a soft encircling feather. Or better: repeatedly submerged in some new and soothing substance, like un-wet water. As cylinder turned, same sensation — same series of pressures — recurred again and again. Kistenmacher's detailed questions before switching off current and announcing experiment had ended.

At once he removed headpiece and set it on table. Unfastened back of torso and turned away as I extracted myself and quickly began to put on shirt.

"We are still in the very early stages," he said, back still turned to me as I threw my necktie around collar. "We know far less about the tactile properties of the skin than we do about the visual properties of the eye. And yet it might be said that, of all the senses" — here a raised hand, an extended forefinger — "touch is the most important. The good Bishop Berkeley, in his *Theory of Vision,* maintains that the visual sense serves to anticipate the tangible. The same may be said of the other senses as well. Look here."

Turned around, ignoring me as I buttoned my vest. From his pocket removed an object and held it up for my inspection. Surprised to see a common fountain pen.

"If I touch this pen to your hand — hand, please! — what do you feel?"

Extended hand, palm up. He pressed end of pen lightly into skin of my palm.

"I feel a pressure — the pressure of the pen. The pressure of an object."

"Very good. And you would say, would you not, that the skin is adapted to feel things in that way — to identify objects by the sense of touch. But this pen of ours is a rather large, coarse object. Consider a finer object — this, for example."

From another pocket: a single dark bristle. Might have come from a paintbrush.

"Your hand, please. Concentrate your attention. I press here — yes? — and here — yes? — and here — no? No? Precisely. And this is a somewhat coarse bristle. If we took a very fine bristle, you would discover even more clearly that only certain spots on the skin give the sensation of touch. We have mapped out these centers of touch and are now able to replicate several combinations with some success."

He reached over to cylinders and picked one up, looking at it as he continued. "It is a long and difficult process. We are at the very beginning." Turning cylinder slowly in his hand. "The key lies here, in this hollow beechwood tube — the haptogram. You see? The surface is covered with hard wax. Look. You can see the ridges and grooves. They control the flow of current. As the haptogram rotates, the wax pushes against this row of nickel rods: up here. Yes? This is clear? Each rod in turn operates a small rheostat — here — which controls the current. You understand? The current drives the corresponding coil in the glove, thereby moving the pin against the skin. Come here."

He set down cylinder and stepped over to torso. Unfastened back. Carefully pulled away a strip of lining.

"These little devices beneath the brass caps — you see them? Each one is a miniature electromagnet. Look closely. You see the wire coil? There. Inside the coil is a tiny iron cylinder — the core — which is insulated with a sleeve of celluloid. The core moves as the current passes through the coil. To the end of each core is attached a thin rod, which in turn is attached to the lining by a fastener that you can see — here, and here, and all along the lining. Ah, those rods!"

He shook his head. "A headache. They have to be very light, but also stiff. We have tried boar's bristle — a mistake! — zinc, too soft, steel, too heavy. We have tried whalebone and ivory. These are bamboo."

Sighing. "It is all very ingenious — and very unsatisfactory. The haptograms can activate sequences of no more than six seconds. The pattern then repeats. And it is all so very — clumsy. What we need is a different approach to the wax cylinder, a more elegant solution to the problem of the overall design."

Pause — glance at sheet-draped object. Seemed to fall into thought. "There is much work to do." Slowly reached into pocket, removed ring of keys. Stared at keys thoughtfully. "We know nothing. Absolutely nothing." Slowly running his thumb along a key. Imagined he was going to press tip of key into my palm — my skin tingling with an expected touch — but as he stepped toward door I understood that our session was over.

NOVEMBER 7. Last night the Wizard shut himself up in Room 12: seven o'clock to three in the morning. Rumor has it he is still refining the automatic adjustment for phonograph cylinder. Hell-bent on defeating the graphophone. Rival machine produces a less clear sound but has great practical advantage of not requiring the wax cylinder to be shaved down and adjusted after each playing. The Wizard throws himself onto cot for two hours, no more. In the day, strides from room to room on second floor, quick, jovial, shrewd-eyed, a little snappish, a sudden edge of mockery. A university man and you don't know how to mix cement? What do they teach you? The quick sketch: fixed gaze, slight tilt of head. Try this. How about that? Acid stains on his fingers. The Phonograph Works, the electrical lab, the Photographic Building. Alone in a back room in chemical lab, quick visit to Box, up to Room 5, over to 12. The improved phonograph, moving photograph, haptograph. Miniature phonograph for speaking doll. Ink for the blind, artificial ivory. A machine for extracting butter directly from milk. In metallurgical lab, Building 5, examines the rock crushers, proposes refinements in electromagnetic separators. A joke in the courtyard: the Wizard is devising a machine to do his sleeping for him.

I think of nothing but the haptograph.

NOVEMBER 12. Not a word. Nothing.

NOVEMBER 14. Haptograph will do for skin what phonograph does for ear, kinetoscope for eye. Understood. But is comparison accurate? Like phonograph, haptograph can imitate sensations in real world: a machine of mimicry. Unlike phonograph, haptograph can create new sensations, never experienced before. The upward-flowing ripple. Any combinations of touch-spots possible. Why does this thought flood my mind with excitement?

NOVEMBER 17. Still nothing. Have they forgotten me?

NOVEMBER 20. Today at a little past two, Earnshaw entered library. Saw him hesitate for a moment and look about quickly — the Wizard long gone, only Grady from chemical lab in room, up on second gallery — before heading over to my desk. Handed me a book he had borrowed some weeks before: a study of the dry gelatin process in making photographic plates. Earnshaw's appetite for the technical minutiae of photography insatiable. And yet: has never owned a camera and unlike most of the men appears to have no desire to take photographs. Have often teased him about this passion of his, evidently entirely mental. He once said in reply that he carries two cameras with him at all times: his eyes.

Touché.

"A lot of excitement out there," I said. Sweeping my hand vaguely in direction of Photographic Building. "I hear they're getting smooth motions at sixteen frames a second."

He laughed — a little uncomfortably, I thought. "Sixteen? Impossible. They've never done it under forty. Besides, I heard just the opposite. Jerky motions. Same old trouble: sprocket a little off. This is for you."

He reached inside jacket and swept his arm toward me. Abrupt, a little awkward. In his hand: a sealed white envelope.

I took envelope, while studying his face. "From you?"

"From" — here he lowered his voice — "Kistenmacher." Shrugged. "He asked me to deliver it."

"Do you know what it is?"

"I don't read other people's mail!"

"Of course not. But you might know anyway."

"How should — I know you've been down there."

"You saw me?"

"He told me."

"Told you?"

"That you'd been there too."

"Too!"

Looked at me. "You think you're the only one?"

"I think our friend likes secrets." I reached for brass letter-opener. Slipped it under flap.

"I'll be going," Earnshaw said, nodding sharply and turning away. Halfway to door when I slit open envelope with a sound of tearing cloth.

"Oh there you are, Earnshaw." A voice at the door.

Message read: "Eight o'clock tomorrow night. Kmacher."

It was only young Peters, an experimental assistant, in need of some zinc.

NOVEMBER 20, LATER. Much to think about. Kistenmacher asks Earnshaw to deliver note. Why? Might easily have contrived to deliver it himself, or speak to me in person. By this action therefore wishes to let Earnshaw know that I am assisting in experiment. Very good. But: Kistenmacher has already told Earnshaw about my presence in room. Which means? His intention must be directed not at Earnshaw but at me: must wish me to know that he has spoken to Earnshaw about me. But why? To bind us together in a brotherhood of secrecy? Perhaps a deeper intention: wants me to know that Earnshaw has been in room, that he too assists in experiment.

NOVEMBER 21, 3:00. Waiting. A walk in the courtyard. Sunny but cold: breath-puffs. A figure approaches. Bareheaded, no coat, a pair of fur-lined gloves: one of the experimenters, protecting his fingers.

NOVEMBER 21, 5:00. It is possible that every touch remains present in skin. These buried hapto-memories capable of being reawakened through mechanical stimulation. Forgotten caresses: mother, lover. Feel of a shell on a beach, forty years ago. Memory-cylinders: a history of touches. Why not?

NOVEMBER 21, 10:06 P.M. At two minutes before eight, Earnshaw enters library. I rise without a word and follow him into stockroom. Down stairway, into basement. Unlocks door of experimental room and leaves without once looking at me. His dislike of Box is clear. But what is it exactly that he dislikes?

"Welcome!" Kistenmacher watchful, expectant.

Standing against table: the dark figure of a human being, covered with wires and small brass caps. On table: a wooden frame holding what appears to be a horizontal roll of perforated paper, perhaps a yard wide, partially unwound onto a second reel. Both geared to a chain-drive motor.

A folding screen near one wall.

"In ten years," Kistenmacher remarks, "in twenty years, it may be possible to create tactile sensations by stimulating the corresponding centers of the brain. Until then, we must conquer the skin directly."

A nod toward screen. "Your modesty will be respected. Please remove your clothes behind the screen and put on the cloth."

Behind screen: a high stool on which lies a folded piece of cloth. Quickly remove my clothes and unfold cloth, which proves to be a kind of loincloth with drawstring. Put it on without hesitation. As I emerge from behind screen, have distinct feeling that I am a patient in a hospital, in presence of a powerful physician.

Kistenmacher opens a series of hinged panels in back of figure: head, torso, legs. Hollow form with silken lining, dimpled by miniature electromagnets fastened to silver points. Notice figure is clamped to table. Can now admit a man.

Soon shut up in haptograph. Through wire mesh covering eye holes, watch Kistenmacher walk over to machine. Briskly turns to face me. With one hand resting on wooden frame, clears throat, stands very still, points suddenly to paper roll.

"You see? An improvement in design. The key lies in the series of perforations punched in the roll. As the motor drives the reel — here — it passes over a nickel-steel roller: here. The roller is set against a row of small metallic brushes, like our earlier rods. The brushes make contact with the nickel-steel roller only through the perforations. This is clear? The current is carried to the coils in the haptograph. Each pin corresponds to a single track — or circular section — of the perforated roll. Tell me exactly what you feel." Throws switch.

Unmistakable sensation of a sock being drawn on over my left foot and halfway up calf. As paper continues to unwind, experience a similar but less exact sensation, mixed with prickles, on right foot and calf. Kistenmacher switches off current and gives source reel a few turns by hand, rewinding perforated paper roll. Switches on current. Repeats sensation of drawn-on socks, making small adjustment that very slightly improves accuracy in right foot and calf.

Next proceeds to test three additional tactile sensations. A rope or belt fastened around my waist. A hand: pressing its spread fingers against my back. Some soft object, perhaps a brush or cloth, moving along upper arm.

Switches off current, seems to grow thoughtful. Asks me to close eyes and pay extremely close attention to next series of hapto-graphic tests, each of which will go beyond simple mimicry of a familiar sensation.

Close my eyes and feel an initial scattering of prickles on both el-bows. Then under arms — at hips — at chin. Transformed gradu-ally into multiple sensation of steady upward pushes, as if I've been gripped by a force trying to lift me from ground. Briefly feel that I am hovering in air, some three feet above floor. Open my eyes, see that I haven't moved. Upward-tugging sensation remains, but illu-sion of suspension has been so weakened that I cannot recapture it while eyes remain open.

Kistenmacher asks me to close eyes again, concentrate my atten-tion. At once the distinct sensation of something pressing down on shoulders and scalp, as well as sideways against ribcage. A feeling as if I were being shut up in a container. Gradually becomes uncom-fortable, oppressive. Am about to cry out when suddenly a sen-sation of release, accompanied by feeling of something pouring down along my body — as though pieces of crockery were break-ing up and falling upon me.

"Very good," says Kistenmacher. "And now one more?"

Again a series of prickles, this time applied simultaneously all over body. Prickles gradually resolve themselves into the sensation — pleasurable enough — of being lightly pressed by something large and soft. Like being squeezed by an enormous hand — as if a fraternal handshake were being applied to entire surface of my skin. Enveloped in that gentle pressure, that soft caress, I feel soothed, I feel more than soothed, I feel exhilarated, I feel an odd and unaccountable joy — a jolt of well-being — a stream of bliss — which fills me to such bursting that tears of pleasure burn in my eyes.

When sensation stops, ask for it to be repeated, but Kisten-macher has learned whatever it was he wanted to know.

Decisively moves toward me. Disappears behind machine. Un-latches panels and pulls them apart.

I emerge backward, in loincloth. Carefully withdraw arms from torso. Across room see Kistenmacher standing with back to me. Yel-lowish large hands clasped against black suit jacket.

Behind screen begin changing. Kistenmacher clears his throat.

"The sense of sight is concentrated in a single place — two places, if you like. We know a great deal about the structure of the eye. By contrast, the sense of touch is dispersed over the entire body. The skin is by far the largest organ of sense. And yet we know almost nothing about it."

I step out from behind screen. Surprised to see Kistenmacher still standing with back to me, large hands clasped behind.

"Good night," he says: motionless. Suddenly raises one hand to height of his shoulder. Moves it back and forth at wrist.

"Night," I reply. Walk to door: turn. And raising my own hand, give first to Kistenmacher, and then to haptograph, an absurd wave.

NOVEMBER 22. Mimicry and invention. Splendor of the haptograph. Not just the replication of familiar tactile sensations, but capacity to explore new combinations — pressures, touches, never experienced before. Adventures of feeling. Who can say what new sensations will be awakened, what unknown desires? Unexplored realms of the tangible. The frontiers of touch.

NOVEMBER 23. Conversation with Earnshaw, who fails to share my excitement. His unmistakable dislike of haptograph. Irritable shrug: "Leave well enough alone." A motto that negates with masterful exactitude everything the Wizard represents. And yet: his passion for the slightest advance in motion photography. Instinctive shrinking of an eye-man from the tangible? Safe distance of sight. Noli me tangere. The intimacy, the intrusiveness, of touch.

NOVEMBER 24. Another session in Box. Began with several familiar sensations, very accurate: ball in palm, sock, handshake, the belt. One new one, less satisfactory: sensation of being stroked by a feather on right forearm. Felt at first like bits of sand being sprinkled on my arm; then somewhat like a brush; finally like a piece of smooth wood. Evidently much easier for pins to evoke precise sensations by stimulating touch-spots in limited area than by stimulating them in sequence along a length. Kistenmacher took notes, fiddled with metallic brushes, adjusted a screw. Soon passed on to sensations of uncommon or unknown kind. A miscellaneous assortment of ripples, flutters, obscure thrusts and pushes. Kistenmacher questioned me closely. My struggle to describe. Bizarre sensation of a pressure that seemed to come from inside my skin and press outward, as if I were going to burst apart. At times a sense of disconnection from skin, which seemed to be slipping from my body like clothes removed at night. Once: a variation of constriction and release, accompanied by impression that I was leaving my old body, that I was being reborn. Immediately followed by sensation, lasting no more than a few seconds, that I was flying through the air.

NOVEMBER 26. Walking in courtyard. Clear and cold. Suddenly aware of my overcoat on my shoulders, the grip of shoe leather, clasp of hat about my head. Throughout day, increased awareness of tactile sensations: the edges of pages against my fingers, door handle in palm. Alone in library, a peculiar sharp impression of individual hairs in my scalp, of fingernails set in their places at ends of my fingers. These sensations vivid, though lasting but a short time.

NOVEMBER 27. The Wizard's attention increasingly consumed by his ore-separating machinery and miniature mechanisms of speaking doll. The toy phonograph — concealed within tin torso — repeatedly malfunctions: the little wax cylinders break, stylus becomes detached from diaphragm or slips from its groove. Meanwhile, flying visits to the Box, where he adjusts metallic brushes, studies take-up reel, unhinges back panels, sketches furiously. Leaves abruptly, with necktie bunched up over top of vest. Kistenmacher says Wizard is dissatisfied with design of haptograph and has proposed a different model: a pine cabinet in which subject is enclosed, except for head, which is provided with a separate covering. The Wizard predicts haptograph parlor: a room of cabinet haptographs, operated by nickel-in-slot mechanism. Cabinet haptograph to be controlled by subject himself, by means of a panel of buttons.

NOVEMBER 28. Another encounter with Earnshaw. Distant. Won't talk about machine. So: talked about weather. Cold today. Mm hmm. But not too cold. Uh huh. Can't tell what makes him more uncomfortable: that I know he takes part in experiment, or that he knows I do. Talked about frames per second. No heart in it. Relieved to see me go.

NOVEMBER 29. Fourth session in Box. Kistenmacher meticulous, intense. Ran through familiar simulations. Stopped machine, removed roll, inserted new one. Presented theory of oscillations: the new roll perforated in such a way as to cause rapid oscillation of pins. Oscillations should affect kinesthetic sense. At first an unpleasant feeling of many insects attacking skin. Then: sensation of left arm floating away from body. Head floating. Body falling. Once: sensation of flying through air, as in previous session, but much sharper and longer lasting. My whole body tingling. Returned to first roll. Skin as if rubbed new. Heightened receptivity. Seemed to be picking up minuscule touches hidden from old skin. Glorious.

NOVEMBER 29, LATER. Can't sleep for excitement. Confused thoughts, sudden lucidities. Can sense a new world just out of reach. Obscured by old body. What if a stone is not a stone, a tree not a tree? Fire not fire? Face not face? What then? New shapes, new touches: a world concealed. The haptograph pointing the way. Oh, what are you talking about? Shut up. Go to bed.

NOVEMBER 30. Kistenmacher says Earnshaw has asked to be released from experiment — the Wizard refuses. Always the demand for unconditional loyalty. In it together. The boys. "Every man jack of you!"

Saw Earnshaw in courtyard. Avoiding me.

DECEMBER 1. This morning the Wizard filed a caveat with Patents Office, setting forth design of haptograph and enumerating essential features. A familiar stratagem. The caveat protects his invention, while acknowledging its incompleteness. In the afternoon, interviews in library with the *Herald,* the *Sun,* and the *Newark News.* "The haptograph," the Wizard says, "is not yet ready to be placed before the public. I hope to have it in operation within six months." As always, prepares the ground, whets the public appetite. Speaks of future replications: riding a roller coaster, sledding down a hill. Sensations of warmth and cold. The "amusement haptograph": thrilling adventures in complete safety of the machine. The cabinet haptograph, the haptograph parlor. Shifts to speaking doll, the small wax cylinders with their nursery rhymes. In future, a doll that responds to a child's touch. The Wizard's hands cut through the air, his eyes are blue fire.

The reporters write furiously.

Kistenmacher says that if three more men are put on job, and ten times current funds diverted to research, haptograph might be ready for public in three years.

DECEMBER 2. Lively talk in courtyard about haptograph, the machine that records touch. Confusion about exactly what it is, what it does. One man under impression it operates like phonograph: you record a series of touches by pressing a recording mechanism and then play back touches by grasping machine. Someone makes a coarse joke: with a machine like that, who needs a woman? Laughter, some of it anxious. The Wizard can make anything. Why not a woman?

DECEMBER 3. Arrived early this morning. Heard voices coming from library. Entered to find Wizard standing at desk, facing Earnshaw. Wizard leaning forward, knuckles on desk. Nostrils flared. Cheek-ridges brick-red. Earnshaw pale, erect — turns at sound of door.

I, hat in hand: "Morning, gentlemen!"

DECEMBER 5. Fifth session in Box. Kistenmacher at work day and night to improve chain-drive mechanism and smooth turning of reels. New arrangement responsible for miracles of simulation: ball in palm, handshake, the sock, the hat. Haptograph can now mimic perfectly the complex sensation of having a heavy robe placed on shoulders, slipped over each arm in turn, tied at waist. Possible the Wizard's predictions may one day be fulfilled.

But Kistenmacher once again eager to investigate the unknown. Change of paper rolls: the new oscillations. "Please. Pay very close attention." Again I enter exotic realms of the tactile, where words become clumsy, obtuse. A feeling — wondrous — of stretching out to tremendous length. A sensation of passing through walls that crumble before me, of hurtling through space, of shouting with my skin. Once: the impression — how to say it? — of being stroked by the wing of an angel. Awkward approximations, dull stammerings which cannot convey my sense of exhilaration as I seemed to burst impediments, to exceed bounds of the possible, to experience, in the ruins of the human, the birth of something utterly new.

December 6. Is it an illusion, a trick played by haptograph? Or is it the revelation of a world that is actually there, a world from which we have been excluded because of the limitations of our bodies?

December 6, later. Unaccustomed thoughts. For example. Might we be surrounded by immaterial presences that move against us but do not impress themselves upon the touch-spots of our skin? Our vision sharpened by microscopes. Haptograph as the microscope of touch.

December 7. Ever since interview, the Wizard not once in Box. His attention taken up by other matters: plans for mining low-grade magnetite, manufacture of speaking dolls in Phonograph Works, testing of a safe alternating current. The rivalry with Westinghouse. Secret experiments in Photographic Building.

December 8. My life consumed by waiting. Strong need to talk about haptograph. In this mood, paid visit to stockroom. Earnshaw constrained, uneasy. Hasn't spoken to me in ten days. I pass on some photographic gossip. Won't look me in the eye. Decide to take bull by horns. So! How's the experiment going? Turns to me fiercely. "I hate it in there!" His eyes stern, unforgiving. In the center of each pupil: a bright point of fear.

December 9. There are documented cases in which a blind person experiences return of sight. Stunned with vision: sunlight on leaves, the blue air. Now imagine a man who has been wrapped in cotton for forty-five years. One day cotton is removed. Suddenly man feels sensations of which he can have had no inkling. The world pours into his skin. The fingers of objects seize him, shake him. Touch of a stone, push of a leaf. The knife-thrust of things. What is the world? Where is it? Where? We are covered in cotton, we walk through a world hidden away. Blind skin. Let me see!

December 10. This afternoon, in courtyard, looked up and saw a hawk in flight. High overhead: wings out, body slowly dipping. The power of its calm. A sign. But of what? Tried to imagine hawkness. Failed.

DECEMBER 11. Long morning, longer afternoon. Picked up six books, read two pages in each. Looked out window four hundred times. Earnshaw's face the other day. Imprint of his ancestors: pale clerics, clean-cheeked, sharp-chinned, a flush of fervor in the white skin. Condemning sinners to everlasting hellfire.

DECEMBER 12. A night of terrors and wonders. Where will it end?

Kistenmacher tense, abrupt, feverish-tired. Proceeded in his meticulous way through familiar mimicries. Repeated each one several times, entered results in notebook. Something perfunctory in his manner. Or was it only me? But no: his excitement evident as he changed rolls. "Please. Tell me exactly." How to describe it? My skin, delicately thrummed by haptograph, gave birth to buried powers. Felt again that blissful expansion of being — that sense of having thrown off old body and assumed a new. I was beyond myself, more than myself, un-me. In old body, could hold out my hand and grasp a pencil, a paperweight. In new body, could hold out my hand and grasp an entire room with all its furniture, an entire town with its chimneys and saltshakers and streets and oak trees. But more than that — more than that. In new skin I was able to touch directly — at every point on my body — any object that presented itself to my mind: a stuffed bear from childhood, wing of a hawk in flight, grass in a remembered field. As though my skin were chock-full of touches, like memories in the brain, waiting for a chance to leap forth.

Opened my eyes and saw Kistenmacher standing at the table. Staring ferociously at unwinding roll of paper. Hum and click of chain-drive motor, faint rustle of metallic brushes. Closed my eyes . . .

. . . and passed at once into wilder regions. Here, the skin becomes so thin and clean that you can feel the touch of air — of light — of dream. Here, the skin shrinks till it's no bigger than the head of a pin, expands till it stretches taut over the frame of the universe. All that is, flowing against you. Drumming against your skin. I shuddered, I rang out like a bell. I was all new, a new creature, glistening, emerging from scaly old. My dull, clumsy skin seemed to break apart into separate points of quivering aliveness, and in this sweet cracking open, this radiant dissolution, I felt my body melting, my nerves bursting, tears streamed along my cheeks, and I cried out in terror and ecstasy.

A knock at the door — two sharp raps. The machine stopped. Kistenmacher over to door.

"I heard a shout," Earnshaw said. "I thought —"

"Fine," Kistenmacher said. "Everything is fine."

DECEMBER 13. A quiet day, cold. Talk of snow. The sky pale, less a color than an absence of color: unblue, ungray: tap water. Through the high arched windows, light traffic on Main. Creak of wagons, knock of hooves. In library fireplace, hiss and crackle of hickory logs. Someone walking in an upper gallery, stopping, removing a book from a shelf. A dray horse snorts in the street.

DECEMBER 14. A sense within me of high anticipation, mixed with anxiousness. Understand the anticipation, but why the other? My skin alert, watchful, as before a storm.

DECEMBER 15. A new life beckons. A shadow-feeling, an on-the-vergeness. Our sensations fixed, rigid, predictable. Must smash through. Into what? The new place. The there. We live off to one side, like paupers beside a railroad track. The center cannot be here, among these constricting sensations. Haptograph as a way out. Over there. Where?

Paradise.

DECEMBER 17. Disaster.

On evening of 16th, Kistenmacher came to fetch me at eight o'clock. Said he hadn't been in Box for two days — a last-minute snag in automatic adjustment of phonograph required full attention — and was eager to resume our experiments. Followed him down steps to basement. At locked door of Box he removed his ring of keys. Inserted wrong one. Examined it with expression of irritable puzzlement. Inserted correct one. Opened door, fumbled about. Switched on lights. At this point Kistenmacher emitted an odd sound — a kind of terrible sigh.

Haptograph lay on floor. Wires ripped loose from fastenings. Stuck out like wild hair. Back panels torn off, pins scattered about. On the floor: smashed reels, a chain from the motor, a broken frame. Wires like entrails. Gashed paper, crumpled lumps. In one corner I saw the dark head.

Kistenmacher, who had not moved, strode suddenly forward. Stopped. Looked around fiercely. Lifted his right hand shoulder-high in a fist. Suddenly crouched down over haptograph body and began touching wires with great gentleness.

Awful night. Arrived at library early morning. Earnshaw already dismissed. Story: On night of December 16, about seven o'clock, a machinist from precision room, coming to stockroom to pick up some brass tubing, saw Earnshaw emerging from basement. Seemed distracted, fidgety, quite unlike himself. After discovery of break-in, machinist reports to Wizard. Wizard confronts Earnshaw. E. draws himself up, stiff, defiant, and in sudden passionate outburst resigns, saying he doesn't like goings-on "down there." Wizard shouts, "Get out of here!" Storms away. End of story.

Kistenmacher says it will take three to five weeks to repair haptograph, perforate a new roll. But the Wizard has ordered him to devote himself exclusively to speaking doll. The Wizard sharp-tempered, edgy, not to be questioned. Dolls sell well but are returned in droves. Always same complaint: the doll has stopped speaking, the toy phonograph concealed in its chest has ceased to operate.

DECEMBER 18. No word from Kistenmacher, who shuts himself up in Room 8 with speaking doll.

DECEMBER 19. The Wizard swirling from room to room, his boyish smile, a joke, laughter. Go at it, boys! Glimpse of Kistenmacher: drooping head, a big, punished schoolboy. Can Wizard banish disappointment so easily?

DECEMBER 20. Earnshaw's destructive rage. How to understand it? Haptograph as devil's work. The secret room, naked skin: sin of touch. Those upright ancestors. Burn, witch!

DECEMBER 20, LATER. Saw Kistenmacher walking in courtyard. Forlorn. Didn't see me.

DECEMBER 20, LATER. Or did he?

DECEMBER 20, STILL LATER. Worried about fate of haptograph. Felt we were on the verge. Of what? A tremendous change. A revolution in sensation, ushering in — what, exactly? What? Say it. All right. A new universe. Yes! The hidden world revealed. The haptograph as adventure, as voyage of discovery. In comparison, the phonograph nothing but a clever toy: tunes, voices.

Haptograph: instrument of revelation.

Still no word.

DECEMBER 21. The Wizard at his desk, humming. Sudden thought: is that a disappointed man? The haptograph destroyed, Kistenmacher brokenhearted, the Wizard humming. A happy man, humming a tune. How could I have thought? Of course only a physical and temporary destruction. The machine easily reconstructed. But no work ordered. Takes Kistenmacher off job. Reign of silence. Why this nothing? Why?

Perhaps this. Understands that haptograph is far from complete. Protected by caveat. Sees Kistenmacher's growing obsession. Needs to wrest his best electrical experimenter from a profitless task and redirect his energies more usefully. So: destruction of machine an excuse to put aside experiment. Good. Fine. But surely something more? Relief? Shedding of a tremendous burden? The machine eluding him, betraying him — its drift from the practical, its invitation to heretical pleasures. Haptograph as seductress. Luring him away. A secret desire to be rid of it. No more! Consider: his sudden cheerfulness, his hum. Ergo.

And Earnshaw? His hostility to experiment serves larger design. By striking in rage at Wizard's handiwork, unwittingly fulfills Wizard's secret will. Smash it up, bash it up. Earnshaw as eruption of master's darkness, emissary of his deepest desire. Burn! Die! The Wizard's longing to be rid of haptograph flowing into Earnshaw's hatred of haptograph as wicked machine. Two wills in apparent opposition, working as one. Die! Inescapable conclusion: arm raised in rage against Wizard's work is the Wizard's arm.

Could it be?

It could be.

Kistenmacher entombed with speaking doll. The Wizard flies from room to room, busies himself with a hundred projects, ignores haptograph.

No one enters the Box.

DECEMBER 30. Nothing.

FEBRUARY 16, 1890. Today in courtyard overheard one of the new men speak of haptograph. Seemed embarrassed when I questioned him. Had heard it was shaped like a life-sized woman. Was it true she could speak?

Already passing into legend. Must harden myself. The experiment has been abandoned.

Snow in the streets. Through the high windows, the clear sharp jingle of harness bells.

Perhaps I dreamed it all?

Have become friendly with Watkins, the new stockroom clerk. A vigorous, compact man, former telegraph operator, brisk, efficient, humorous; dark blond side-whiskers. His passion for things electrical. Proposes that, for a fee, the owner of a telephone be permitted to listen to live musical performances: a simple matter of wiring. The electric boot, the electric hat. Electric letter opener. A fortune to be made. One day accompanied him down to storeroom, where he searched for supply of cobalt and magnesium requested by an assistant in electrical lab who was experimenting on new storage battery. Saw with a kind of sad excitement that we were approaching a familiar door. "What's in there?" — couldn't stop myself. "Oh that," said Watkins. Takes out a ring of keys. Inside: piles of wooden crates, up to ceiling. "Horns and antlers," he said. "Look: antelope, roebuck, gazelle. Red deer. Walrus tusks, rhino horns." Laughter. "Not much call for these items. But heck, you never can tell."

A dream, a dream!

No: no dream. Or say, a dream, certainly a dream, nothing but a dream, but only as all inventions are dreams: vivid and impalpable presences that haunt the mind's chambers, escaping now and then into the place where they take on weight and cast shadows. The Wizard's laboratory a dream garden, presided over by a mage. Why did he abandon haptograph? Because he knew in his bones that it was commercially unfeasible? Because it fell too far short of the perfected phonograph, the elegant promise of kinetoscope? Was it because haptograph had become a terrible temptress, a forbidden delight, luring him away from more practical projects? Or was it — is it possible — did he sense that world was not yet ready for his haptograph, that dangerous machine which refused to limit itself to the familiar feel of things but promised an expansion of the human into new and terrifying realms of being?

Yesterday the Wizard spent ten hours in metallurgical lab. Adjustments in ore-separator. "It's a daisy!" Expects it to revolutionize the industry. Bring in a handsome profit.

The haptograph awaits its time. In a year — ten years — a century — it will return. Then everyone will know what I have come to know: that the world is hidden from us — that our bodies, which seem to bring us the riches of the earth, prevent the world from reaching us. For the eyes of our skin are closed. Brightness streams in on us, and we cannot see. Things flow against us, and we cannot feel. But the light will come. The haptograph will return. Perhaps it will appear as a harmless toy in an amusement parlor, a playful rival of the gustograph and the odoroscope. For a nickel you will be able to feel a ball in the palm of your hand, a hat sitting on your head. Gradually the sensations will grow more complex — more elusive — more daring. You will feel the old body slipping off, a new one emerging. Then your being will open wide and you will receive — like a blow — like a rush of wind — the in-streaming world. The hidden universe will reveal itself like fire. You will leave yourself behind forever. You will become as a god.

I will not return to these notes.

Snow on the streets. Bright blue sky, a cloud white as house paint. Rumble of dynamos from the machine shop. Crackle of hickory logs, a shout from the courtyard. An unremarkable day.

DANIYAL MUEENUDDIN

Nawabdin Electrician

FROM *The New Yorker*

HE FLOURISHED ON a signature ability: a technique for cheating the electric company by slowing down the revolutions of its meters, so cunningly performed that his customers could specify to the hundred-rupee note the desired monthly savings. In this Pakistani desert, behind Multan, where the tube wells pumped from the aquifer day and night, Nawab's discovery eclipsed the philosopher's stone. Some thought he used magnets, others said heavy oil or porcelain chips or a substance he found in beehives. Skeptics reported that he had a deal with the meter men. In any case, this trick guaranteed Nawab's employment, both off and on the farm of his patron, K. K. Harouni.

The farm lay strung along a narrow and pitted farm-to-market road, built in the 1970s, when Harouni still had influence in the Islamabad bureaucracy. Buff or saline-white desert dragged out between fields of sugar cane and cotton, mango orchards and clover and wheat, soaked daily by the tube wells that Nawabdin Electrician tended. Beginning the rounds of Nurpur Harouni on his itinerant mornings, summoned to a broken pump, Nawab and his bicycle bumped along, decorative plastic flowers swaying on wires sprouting from the frame. His tools, notably a three-pound ball-peen hammer, clanked in a greasy leather bag suspended from the handlebars. The farmhands and the manager waited in the cool of the banyans, planted years earlier to shade each of the tube wells. "No tea, no tea," Nawab insisted, waving away the steaming cup.

Hammer dangling from his hand like a savage's ax, Nawab entered the oily room housing the pump and its electric motor. Silence. The men crowded the doorway till he shouted that he must have light. He approached the offending object warily but with his temper rising, circled it, pushed it about a bit, began to take liberties with it, settled in with it, called for a cup of tea next to it, and finally began disassembling it. With his long, blunt screwdriver he cracked the shields hiding the machine's penetralia, a screw popping loose and flying into the shadows. He took the ball-peen and delivered a crafty blow. The intervention failed. Pondering the situation, he ordered one of the farmworkers to find a really thick piece of leather and to collect sticky mango sap from a nearby tree. So it went, all morning and into the afternoon, Nawab trying one thing and then another, heating the pipes, cooling them, joining wires together, circumventing switches and fuses. And yet somehow, in fulfillment of the local genius for crude improvisation, the pumps continued to run.

Unfortunately or fortunately, Nawab had married early in life a sweet woman of unsurpassed fertility, whom he adored, and she proceeded to bear him children spaced, if not less than nine months apart, then not that much more. And all daughters, one after another after another, until finally the looked-for son arrived, leaving Nawab with a complete set of twelve girls, ranging from toddler to age eleven, and one odd piece. If he had been governor of the Punjab, their dowries would have beggared him. For an electrician and mechanic, no matter how light-fingered, there seemed no question of marrying them all off. No moneylender in his right mind would, at any rate of interest, advance a sufficient sum to buy the necessary items for each daughter: beds, a dresser, trunks, electric fans, dishes, six suits of clothes for the groom, six for the bride, perhaps a television, and on and on and on.

Another man might have thrown up his hands — but not Nawabdin. The daughters acted as a spur to his genius, and he looked with satisfaction in the mirror each morning at the face of a warrior going out to do battle. Nawab, of course, knew that he must proliferate his sources of revenue — the salary he received from K. K. Harouni for tending the tube wells would not even begin to suffice. He set up a one-room flour mill, run off a condemned electric motor — condemned by him. He tried his hand at fish farming in a pond at the edge of one of his master's fields. He bought broken radios, fixed them, and resold them. He did not demur even when asked to fix watches, although that enterprise did spectacularly badly and earned him more kicks than kudos, for no watch he took apart ever kept time again.

K. K. Harouni lived mostly in Lahore and rarely visited his farms. Whenever the old man did visit, Nawab would place himself night and day at the door leading from the servants' sitting area into the walled grove of ancient banyan trees where the old farmhouse stood. Grizzled, his peculiar aviator glasses bent and smudged, Nawab tended the household machinery, the air conditioners, water heaters, refrigerators, and pumps, like an engineer tending the boilers on a foundering steamer in an Atlantic gale. By his superhuman efforts, he almost managed to maintain K. K. Harouni in the same mechanical cocoon, cooled and bathed and lighted and fed, that the landowner enjoyed in Lahore.

Harouni, of course, became familiar with this ubiquitous man, who not only accompanied him on his tours of inspection but could be found morning and night standing on the master bed rewiring the light fixture or poking at the water heater in the bathroom. Finally, one evening at teatime, gauging the psychological moment, Nawab asked if he might say a word. The landowner, who was cheerfully filing his nails in front of a crackling rosewood fire, told him to go ahead.

"Sir, as you know, your lands stretch from here to the Indus, and on these lands are fully seventeen tube wells, and to tend these seventeen tube wells there is but one man, me, your servant. In your service I have earned these gray hairs" — here he bowed his head to show the gray — "and now I cannot fulfill my duties as I should. Enough, sir, enough. I beg you, forgive me my weakness. Better a darkened house and proud hunger within than disgrace in the light of day. Release me, I ask you, I beg you."

The old man, well accustomed to these sorts of speeches, though not usually this florid, filed away at his nails and waited for the breeze to stop.

"What's the matter, Nawabdin?"

"Matter, sir? Oh, what could be the matter in your service? I've eaten your salt for all my years. But, sir, on the bicycle now, with my old legs, and with the many injuries I've received when heavy machinery fell on me — I cannot any longer bicycle about like a bridegroom from farm to farm, as I could when I first had the good fortune to enter your service. I beg you, sir, let me go."

"And what is the solution?" Harouni asked, seeing that they had come to the crux. He didn't particularly care one way or the other, except that it touched on his comfort — a matter of great interest to him.

"Well, sir, if I had a motorcycle, then I could somehow limp along, at least until I train up some younger man."

The crops that year had been good, Harouni felt expansive in front of the fire, and so, much to the disgust of the farm managers, Nawab received a brand-new motorcycle, a Honda 70. He even managed to extract an allowance for gasoline.

The motorcycle increased his status, gave him weight, so that people began calling him Uncle and asking his opinion on world affairs, about which he knew absolutely nothing. He could now range farther, doing much wider business. Best of all, now he could spend every night with his wife, who early in the marriage had begged to live not in Nawab's quarters in the village but with her family in Firoza, near the only girls' school in the area. A long straight road ran from the canal headworks near Firoza all the way to the Indus, through the heart of the K. K. Harouni lands. The road ran on the bed of an old highway built when these lands lay within a princely state. Some hundred and fifty years ago, one of the princes had ridden that way, going to a wedding or a funeral in this remote district, felt hot, and ordered that rosewood trees be planted to shade the passersby. Within a few hours, he forgot that he had given the order, and in a few dozen years he in turn was forgotten, but these trees still stood, enormous now, some of them dead and looming without bark, white and leafless. Nawab would fly down this road on his new machine, with bags and streamers hanging from every knob and brace, so that the bike, when he hit a bump, seemed to be flapping numerous small vestigial wings; and with his grinning face, as he rolled up to whichever tube well needed servicing, with his ears almost blown off, he shone with the speed of his arrival.

Nawab's day, viewed from the air, would have appeared as aimless as that of a butterfly: to the senior manager's house in the morning, where he diligently paid his respects, then to one or another of the tube wells, kicking up dust on the unpaved field roads, into the town of Firoza, zooming beneath the rosewoods, a bullet of sound, moseying around town, sneaking away to one of his private interests — to cement a deal to distribute ripening early-season honeydews from his cousin's vegetable plot, or to count before hatching his half share in a flock of chickens — then back to Nurpur Harouni, and out again. The maps of these days, superimposed, would have made a tangle, but every morning he emerged from the same place, just as the sun came up, and every evening he returned there, tired now, darkened, switching off the bike, rolling it over the wooden threshold of the door leading into the courtyard, the engine ticking as it cooled. Nawab leaned the bike on its kickstand each evening and waited for his girls to come, all of them, around him, jumping on him. His face at this moment often had the same expression — an expression of childish innocent joy, which contrasted strangely and even sadly with the heaviness of his face and its lines and stubble. He would raise his nose and sniff the air to see if he could guess what his wife had cooked for dinner, and then he went in to her, finding her always in the same posture, making him tea, fanning the fire in the hearth.

"Hello, my love, my chicken piece," he said tenderly one evening, walking into the dark hut that served as a kitchen, the mud walls black with soot. "What's in the pot for me?" He opened the cauldron, which had been displaced by the kettle onto the beaten-earth floor, and began to search around in it with a wooden spoon.

"Out! Out!" she said, taking the spoon and, dipping it into the curry, giving him a taste.

He opened his mouth obediently, like a boy receiving medicine. The wife, despite having borne thirteen children, had a lithe strong body, her vertebrae visible beneath her tight tunic. Her long mannish face still glowed from beneath the skin, giving her a ripe ochre coloring. Even now that her hair was thin and graying, she wore it in a single long braid down to her waist, like a young woman in the village. Although this style didn't suit her, Nawab saw in her still the girl he had married twenty years before. He stood in the door, watching his daughters playing hopscotch, and when his wife went past he stuck out his butt, so that she rubbed against it as she squeezed through.

Nawab ate first, then the girls, and finally his wife. He sat out in the courtyard, burping and smoking a cigarette, looking up at the crescent moon just visible on the horizon. I wonder what the moon is made of? he thought, without exerting himself. He remembered listening to the radio when the Americans said they had walked on it. His thoughts wandered off onto all sorts of tangents. The dwellers around him in the hamlet had also finished their dinners, and the smoke from cow-dung fires hung over the darkening roofs, a harsh spicy smell, like rough tobacco. Nawab's house had numerous ingenious contrivances — running water in all three rooms, a duct that brought cool air into the rooms at night, and even a black-and-white television, which his wife covered with a doily that she had embroidered with flowers. Nawab had constructed a gear mechanism so that the antenna on the roof could be turned from inside the house to improve reception. The children sat inside watching it, with the sound blaring. His wife came out and sat primly at his feet on the sagging ropes of the woven bed, swinging her legs.

"I've got something in my pocket — would you like to know what?" He looked at her with a pouting sort of smile.

"I know this game," she said, reaching up and straightening his glasses on his face. "Why are your glasses always crooked? I think one ear's higher than the other."

"If you find it, you can have it."

Looking to see that the children were still absorbed in the television, she kneeled next to him and began patting his pockets. "Lower . . . lower . . . ," he said. In the pocket of the greasy vest that he wore under his kurta, she found a wrapped-up newspaper holding chunks of raw brown sugar.

"I've got lots more," he said. "Look at that. None of this junk you buy in the bazaar. The Dashtis gave me five kilos for repairing their sugarcane press. I'll sell it tomorrow. Make us some parathas. For all of us? Pretty please?"

"I put out the fire."

"So light it. Or, rather, you just sit here — I'll light it."

"You can never light it. I'll end up doing it anyway," she said, getting up.

The smaller children, smelling the ghee cooking on the griddle, crowded around, watching the brown sugar melt, and finally even the older girls came in, though they stood haughtily to one side.

Nawab, squatting and huffing on the fire, gestured to them. "Come on, you princesses, none of your tricks. I know you want some."

They began eating, pouring the brown crystallized syrup onto pieces of fried bread, and after a while Nawab went to his motorcycle and pulled from the panniers another hunk of the sugar, challenging the girls to see who would eat most.

One evening a few weeks after his family's little festival of sugar, Nawab was sitting with the watchman who kept guard over the grain stores at Nurpur Harouni. A banyan planted alongside the threshing floor only thirty years ago had grown a canopy of forty or fifty feet, and all the men who worked in the stores tended it carefully, watering it with cans. The old watchman sat under this tree, and Nawab and the other younger men would sit with him at dusk, teasing him, trying to make his violent temper flare up, and joking around with one another. They would listen to the old man's stories, of the time when only dirt tracks led through these riverine tracts and the tribes stole cattle for sport, and often killed each other while doing it, to add piquancy.

Although spring weather had come, the watchman still kept a fire burning in a tin pan to warm his feet and to give a center to the group that gathered there. The electricity had failed, as it often did, and the full moon climbing the sky lit the scene indirectly, reflecting off the whitewashed walls, throwing dim shadows around the machinery strewn about, plows and planters, drags, harrows.

"Here it is, old man," Nawab said to the watchman. "I'll tie you up and lock you in the stores to make it look like a robbery, and then I'll top off my tank at the gas barrel."

"Nothing in it for me," the watchman said. "Go on, I think I hear your wife calling you."

"I understand, sire. You wish to be alone."

Nawab jumped up and shook the watchman's hand, making a bow, touching his hands deferentially to the old man's knee, as he would to the feudal K. K. Harouni — a running joke, lost on the watchman these past ten years.

"Be careful, boy," the watchman said, standing up and leaning on his bamboo staff, clad in steel at the tip.

Nawab leapt on the kick-starter of his motorcycle, and in one smooth motion flicked on the lights and shot out of the threshing-floor gates, onto the quarter-mile driveway leading from the heart of the farm to the road. He felt cold and liked it, knowing that at home the room would be baking, the two-bar heater running day and night on pilfered electricity, the family luxuriating in excess warmth, even though the spring weather had come. Turning onto the dark main road, he sped up, outrunning the weak headlight, obstacles appearing faster than he could react, feeling as if he were racing forward in the flame of a moving lantern. Nightjars perching on the road as they hunted moths ricocheted into the dark, almost under his wheel. Nawab locked his arms, fighting the bike as he flew over potholes, enjoying the pace, standing on the pegs. Among low-lying fields, where the sugarcane had been heavily watered, mist rose and cool air enveloped him. He slowed, turning onto the smaller road running beside the canal, hearing the water rushing over the locks of the headworks.

A man stepped from beside one of the locks, waving down at the ground, motioning Nawab to stop.

"Brother," the man said, over the puttering engine, "give me a ride into town. I've got business, and I'm late."

Strange business at this time of night, Nawab thought, the taillight of the motorcycle casting a reddish glow around them on the ground. They were far from any dwellings. A mile away, the village of Dashtian crouched beside the road — before that there was nothing. He looked into the man's face.

"Where are you from?" The man looked straight back at him, his face pinched and therefore overstated, but unflinching.

"From Kashmor. Please, you're the first person to come by for over an hour. I've walked all day."

Kashmor, Nawab thought. From the poor country across the river. Every year, those tribes came to pick the mangoes at Nurpur Harouni and other nearby farms, working for almost nothing, let go as soon as the harvest thinned. The men would give a feast, a thin feast, at the end of the season, a hundred or more going shares to buy a buffalo. Nawab had been several times and was treated as if he was honoring them, sitting with them and eating the salty rice flecked with bits of meat.

He grinned at the man, gesturing with his chin to the seat behind him. "All right, then, get on the back."

Balancing against the weight behind him, which made driving along the rutted canal road difficult, Nawab pushed on, under the rosewood trees.

Half a mile from the headworks, the man shouted into Nawab's ear, "Stop!"

"What's wrong?" Nawab couldn't hear over the rushing wind.

The man jabbed something hard into his ribs.

"I've got a gun. I'll shoot you."

Panicked, Nawab skidded to a stop and jumped to one side, pushing the motorcycle away from him, so that it tipped over, knocking the robber to the ground. The carburetor float hung open, and the engine raced for a minute, the wheel jerking, until the engine sputtered and died, extinguishing the headlight.

"What are you doing?" Nawab babbled.

"I'll shoot you if you don't stand back," the robber said, rising up on one knee, the gun pointed at Nawab.

They stood obscured in the sudden woolly dark, next to the fallen motorcycle, which leaked raw-smelling gasoline into the dust underfoot. Water running through the reeds in the canal beside them made soft gulping sounds as it swirled along. His eyes adjusting to the dark, Nawab saw the man sucking at a cut on his palm, the gun held in his other hand.

When the man went to pick up the bike, Nawab approached a step toward him.

"I told you, I'll shoot you."

Nawab put his hands together in supplication. "I beg you, I've got little girls, thirteen children. I promise, thirteen. I tried to help you. I'll drive you to Firoza, and I won't tell anyone. Don't take the bike — it's my daily bread. I'm a man like you, poor as you."

"Shut up."

Without thinking, a flash of cunning in his eyes, Nawab lunged for the gun, but missed. For a moment the two men grappled, until the robber broke free, stepped back, and fired. Nawab fell to the ground, holding his groin with both hands, entirely surprised, shocked, as if the man had slapped him for no reason.

The man dragged the bike away, straddled it, and tried to start it, bobbing up and down, pitching his weight onto the lever, the engine whirring but not catching. It had flooded, and he held the throttle wide open, which made it worse. At the sound of the shot, the dogs in Dashtian had begun to bark, the sound fitful in the breeze.

Lying on the ground, at first Nawab thought the man had killed him. The pale moonlit sky, seen through the branches of the rosewood tree, tilted back and forth like a bowl of swaying water. He had fallen with one leg bent under him, and now he straightened it. His hand came away sticky when he touched the wound. "O God, O Mother, O God," he moaned, not very loudly, in a singsong voice. He looked at the man, whose back was turned, vulnerable, kicking wildly at the starter, not six feet away. Nawab couldn't let him take it away — not the bike, his toy, his freedom.

He stood up again and stumbled forward, but his injured leg buckled and he fell, his forehead hitting the rear bumper of the motorcycle. Turning in the seat, holding the gun at arm's length, the robber fired five more times, one two three four five, with Nawab looking up into his face in disbelief, seeing the repeated flame in the revolver's mouth. The man had never used weapons, had fired this unlicensed revolver only one time, to try it out when he bought it from a bootlegger. He couldn't bear to point at the torso or the head, but shot at the groin and the legs. The last two bullets missed wildly, throwing up dirt in the road. The robber rolled the motorcycle forward twenty feet, grunting, and again tried to start it. From Dashtian a torch jogged quickly down the road. Throwing the bike to the ground, the man ran into a stand of reeds that bordered a field.

Nawab lay in the road, not wanting to move. When the bullets first hit him, they didn't so much hurt as sting, but now the pain grew worse. The blood felt warm in his pants.

It seemed very peaceful. In the distance, the dogs kept barking, and all around the cicadas called, so many of them that they blended into a single gentle sound. In a mango orchard across the canal, some crows began cawing, and he wondered why they were calling at night. Maybe a snake up in the tree, in the nest. Fresh fish from the spring floods of the Indus had just come onto the market, and he kept remembering that he had wanted to buy some for dinner, perhaps the next night. As the pain grew worse, he thought of that, the smell of frying fish.

Two men from the village came running up, one much younger

than the other, both of them bare-chested. The elder, potbellied, carried an ancient single-barreled shotgun, the butt mended crudely with wire.

"Oh God, they've killed him. Who is it?"

The younger man kneeled down next to the body. "It's Nawab, the electrician, from Nurpur Harouni."

"I'm not dead," Nawab said insistently, without raising his head. He knew these men, a father and son — he had arranged the lighting at the son's wedding. "The bastard's right there in those reeds."

Stepping forward, aiming into the center of the clump, the older man fired, reloaded, and fired again. Nothing moved among the green leafy stalks, which were head high and surmounted by feathers of seed.

"He's gone," the young man said, sitting next to Nawab, holding his arm.

The father walked carefully forward, holding the gun to his shoulder. Something moved, and he fired. The robber fell forward into the open ground. He called, "Mother, help me," and got up on his knees, holding his hands to his waist. Walking up to him, the father hit him once in the middle of the back with the butt of the gun, and then threw down the gun and dragged him roughly by his collar onto the road. Raising the bloody shirt, he saw that the robber had taken half a dozen buckshot pellets in the stomach — black angry holes seeping blood in the light of the torch. The robber kept spitting, without any force.

The son got up and started the motorcycle by pushing it down the road with the gears engaged, until the engine came to life. Shouting that he would get some transport, he raced off, and Nawab winced, hearing the man, in his hurry, shifting without using the clutch.

"Do you want a cigarette, Uncle?" the old villager said to Nawab, offering the pack.

Nawab rolled his head back and forth. "Fuck, look at me."

In the silence, a forgotten thought kept bothering Nawab, something important. Then he remembered.

"Find the guy's revolver, Bholay. You're going to need it for the cops."

"I can't leave you," he said. But after a minute he threw away his cigarette and got up.

The old man was still searching in the reeds when the lights of a pickup materialized at the canal headworks and bounced wildly down the road. The driver, doubtful of the whole affair, stood by while the father and son lifted Nawab and the motorcycle thief into the back. They drove to Firoza, to a private clinic there, run by a mere pharmacist, who nevertheless kept a huge clientele because of his abrupt and sure manner and his success at healing all the prevalent diseases with the same few medicines.

The clinic smelled of disinfectant and of bodily fluids, a heavy sweetish odor. Four beds stood in a room, dimly lit by a fluorescent tube. As the father and son carried him in, Nawab, alert to the point of strain, observed blood on some rumpled sheets, a rusty blot. The pharmacist, who lived above the clinic, had come down wearing a loincloth and undershirt. He seemed perfectly unflustered, if anything slightly cross at having been disturbed.

"Put them on those two beds."

"*As salaam aleikum,* Dr. Sahib," said Nawab, who felt as if he were speaking to someone very far away. The pharmacist seemed an immensely grave and important man, and Nawab spoke to him formally.

"What happened, Nawab?"

"He tried to snatch my motorbike, but I didn't let him."

The pharmacist pulled off Nawab's shalwar, got a rag, and washed away the blood, then poked around quite roughly, while Nawab held the sides of the bed and willed himself not to scream. "You'll live," he said. "You're a lucky man. The bullets all went low."

"Did it hit . . ."

The pharmacist dabbed with the rag. "Not even that, thank God."

The robber must have been hit in the lung, for he kept breathing up blood.

"You won't need to bother taking this one to the police," the pharmacist said. "He's a dead man."

"Please," the robber begged, trying to raise himself up. "Have mercy, save me. I'm a human being also."

The pharmacist went into the office next door and wrote the names of drugs on a pad, sending the villager's son to a dispenser in the next street.

"Wake him and tell him it's Nawabdin the electrician. Tell him I'll make sure he gets the money."

Nawab looked over at the robber for the first time. There was blood on his pillow, and he kept snuffling, as if he needed to blow his nose. His thin and very long neck hung crookedly on his shoulder, as if out of joint. He was older than Nawab had thought, not a boy, dark-skinned, with sunken eyes and protruding yellow smoker's teeth, which showed whenever he twitched for breath.

"I did you wrong," the robber said weakly. "I know that. You don't know my life, just as I don't know yours. Even I don't know what brought me here. Maybe you're a poor man, but I'm much poorer than you. My mother is old and blind, in the slums outside Multan. Make them fix me, ask them to and they'll do it." He began to cry, not wiping away the tears, which drew lines on his dark face.

"Go to hell," Nawab said, turning away. "Men like you are good at confessions. My children would have begged in the streets."

The robber lay heaving, moving his fingers by his sides. The pharmacist seemed to have gone away somewhere.

"They just said that I'm dying. Forgive me for what I did. I was brought up with kicks and slaps and never enough to eat. I've never had anything of my own, no land, no house, no wife, no money, never, nothing. I slept for years on the railway station platform in Multan. My mother's blessing on you. Give me your blessing, don't let me die unforgiven." He began snuffling and coughing even more, and then started hiccuping.

Now the disinfectant smelled strong and good to Nawab. The floor seemed to shine. The world around him expanded.

"Never. I won't forgive you. You had your life, I had mine. At every step of the road I went the right way and you the wrong. Look at you now, with bubbles of blood stuck in the corner of your lips. Do you think this isn't a judgment? My wife and children would have wept all their lives, and you would have sold my motorbike to pay for six unlucky hands of cards and a few bottles of poison home brew. If you weren't lying here now, you would already be in one of the gambling camps along the river."

The man said, "Please, please, please," more softly each time, and then he stared up at the ceiling. "It's not true," he whispered. After a few minutes, he convulsed and died. The pharmacist, who had come back in by then and was cleaning Nawab's wounds, did nothing to help him.

Yet Nawab's mind caught at this, at the man's words and his death, like a bird hopping around some bright object, meaning to peck at it. And then he didn't. He thought of the motorcycle, saved, and the glory of saving it. Six shots, six coins thrown down, six chances, and not one of them had killed him, not Nawabdin Electrician.

ALICE MUNRO

Child's Play

FROM *Harper's Magazine*

I SUPPOSE THERE was talk in our house, afterward.

How sad, how *awful.* (My mother.)

There should have been supervision. Where were the Counselors? (My father.)

Just think, it might have — it might have been — (My mother.)

It wasn't. Just put that idea out of your head. It wasn't. (My father.)

It is even possible that if we ever passed the yellow house, my mother said, "Remember? Remember you used to be so scared of her? The poor thing."

My mother had a habit of hanging on to — even treasuring — the foibles of my distant infantile state.

Every year, when you're a child, you become a different person. Generally it's in the fall, when you reenter school, take your place in a higher grade, leave behind the muddle and lethargy of the summer vacation. That's when you register the change most sharply. Afterward you are not sure of the month or year, but the changes go on, just the same. For a long while the past drops away from you easily and, it would seem, automatically, properly. Its scenes don't vanish so much as become irrelevant. And then there's a switchback, what's been all over and done with sprouting up fresh, wanting attention, even wanting you to do something about it, though it's plain there is not on this earth a thing to be done.

Marlene and Charlene. People thought we must be twins. There was a fashion in those days for naming twins in rhyme. Bonnie and

Connie. Ronald and Donald. And then of course we — Charlene and I — had matching hats. Coolie hats, they were called, wide shallow cones of woven straw with some sort of tie or elastic under the chin. They became familiar later on in the century, from television shots of the war in Vietnam. Men on bicycles riding along a street in Saigon would be wearing them, or women walking in the road against the background of a bombed village.

It was possible at that time — I mean the time when Charlene and I were at camp — to say *coolie* without a thought of offense. Or *darkie,* or to talk about *jewing* a price down. I was in my teens, I think, before I ever related that verb to the noun.

So we had those names and those hats, and at the first roll call the Counselor — the jolly one we liked, Mavis, though we didn't like her as well as the pretty one, Pauline — pointed at us and called out, "Hey, Twins," and went on calling out other names before we had time to deny it.

Even before that we must have noticed the hats and approved of each other. Otherwise one or both of us would have pulled off those brand-new articles and been ready to shove them under our cots, declaring that our mothers had made us wear them and we hated them, and so on.

I may have approved of Charlene, but I was not sure how to make friends with her. Girls nine or ten years old — that was the general range of this crop, though there were a few a bit older — do not pick friends or pair off as easily as girls do at six or seven. I simply followed some other girls from my town — none of them my particular friends — to one of the cabins where there were some unclaimed cots, and dumped my things on top of the brown blanket. Then I heard a voice behind me say, "Could I please be next to my twin sister?"

It was Charlene, speaking to somebody I didn't know. The dormitory cabin held perhaps two dozen girls. The girl she had spoken to said, "Sure," and moved along.

Charlene had used a special voice. Ingratiating, teasing, self-mocking, and with a seductive merriment in it, like a trill of bells. It was evident right away that she had more confidence than I did. And not simply confidence that the other girl would move and not say sturdily, "I got here first." Or — if she was a roughly brought up sort of girl (and some of them were that, having their way paid by the Lions Club or the church and not by their parents) she might have said, "Go poop your pants, I'm not moving." No. Charlene had confidence that anybody would *want* to do as she asked, not just agree to do it. With me too she had taken a chance, for could I not have said, "I don't want to be twins," and turned back to sort my things? But of course I didn't. I felt flattered, as she had expected, and I watched her dump out the contents of her suitcase with such an air of celebration that some things fell on the floor.

All I could think of to say was "You got a tan already."

"I always tan easy," she said.

The first of our differences. We applied ourselves to learning them. She tanned, I freckled. We both had brown hair but hers was darker. Hers was wavy, mine bushy. I was half an inch taller, she had thicker wrists and ankles. Her eyes had more green in them, mine more blue. We did not grow tired of inspecting and tabulating even the moles or notable freckles on our backs, length of our second toes (mine longer than the first toe, hers shorter). Or of recounting all the illnesses or accidents that had befallen us so far, as well as the repairs or removals performed on our bodies. Both of us had our tonsils out — a usual precaution in those days — and both of us had had measles and whooping cough but not mumps. I had had an eyetooth pulled because it was growing in over my other teeth, and she had a thumbnail with an imperfect half-moon because her thumb had been slammed under a window.

And once we had the peculiarities and history of our bodies in place we went on to the stories — the dramas or near-dramas or distinctions — of our families. She was the youngest and only girl in her family and I was an only child. I had an aunt who had died of polio in high school and she — Charlene — had an older brother who was in the navy. For it was wartime, and at the campfire sing-song we would choose "There'll Always Be an England" and "Hearts of Oak" and "Rule Britannia," and sometimes "The Maple Leaf Forever." Bombing raids and battles and sinking ships were the constant, though distant, backdrop of our lives.

And once in a while there was a near strike, frightening but solemn and exhilarating, as when a boy from our town or our street would be killed, and the house where he had lived without having any special wreath or black drapery on it seemed nevertheless to have a special weight inside it, a destiny fulfilled and dragging it down. Though there was nothing special inside it at all, maybe just a car that didn't belong there parked at the curb, showing that some relatives or a minister had come to sit with the bereaved family.

One of the camp Counselors had lost her fiancé in the war and wore his watch — we believed it was his watch — pinned to her blouse. We would like to have felt for her a mournful interest and concern, but she was sharp-voiced and bossy and she even had an unpleasant name. Arva.

The other backdrop of our lives, which was supposed to be emphasized at camp, was religion. But since the United Church of Canada was officially in charge there was not so much harping on that subject as there would have been with the Baptists or the Bible Christians, or so much formal acknowledgment as the Roman Catholics or even the Anglicans would have provided. Most of us had parents who belonged to the United Church (though some of the girls who were having their way paid for them might not have belonged to any church at all), and being used to its hearty secular style, we did not even realize that we were getting off easily with just evening prayers and grace sung at meals and the half-hour special talk — it was called a Chat — after breakfast. Even the Chat was relatively free of references to God or Jesus and was more about honesty and loving-kindness and clean thoughts in our daily lives, and promising never to drink or smoke when we grew up. Nobody had any objection to this sort of thing or tried to get out of attending, because it was what we were used to and because it was pleasant to sit on the beach in the warming sun and a little too cold yet for us to long to jump into the water.

Grown-up women do the same sort of thing that Charlene and I did. Not the counting the moles on each other's backs and comparing toe lengths, maybe. But when they meet and feel a particular sympathy with each other they also feel a need to set out the important information, the big events whether public or secret, and then go ahead to fill in all the blanks between. If they feel this warmth and eagerness it is quite impossible for them to bore each other. They will laugh at the very triviality and silliness of what they're telling, or at the revelation of some appalling selfishness, deception, meanness, sheer badness. There has to be great trust, of course, but that trust can be established at once, in an instant.

I've observed this. It's supposed to have begun in those long periods of sitting around the campfire, stirring the manioc porridge or whatever, while the men were out in the bush deprived of conversation because it would warn off the wild animals. (I am an anthropologist by training, though a rather slack one.) I've observed but never taken part in these female exchanges. Not truly. Sometimes I've pretended because it seemed to be required, but the woman I was supposed to be making friends with always got wind of my pretense and became confused and cautious.

As a rule, I've felt less wary with men. They don't expect such transactions and are seldom really interested.

This intimacy I'm talking about — with women — is not erotic, or pre-erotic. I've experienced that as well, before puberty. Then too there would be confidences, probably lies, maybe leading to games. A certain hot temporary excitement, with or without genital teasing. Followed by ill-feeling, denial, disgust.

Charlene did tell me about her brother, but with true repugnance. This was the brother now in the navy. She went into his room looking for her cat and there he was doing it to his girlfriend. They never knew she saw them.

She said they slapped, as he went up and down.

You mean they slapped on the bed, I said.

No, she said. His thing slapped when it was going in and out. It was sickening.

And his bare white bum had pimples on it. Sickening. I told her about Verna.

Up until the time I was seven years old my parents had lived in what was called a double house. The word *duplex* was perhaps not in use at that time, and anyway the house was not evenly divided. Verna's grandmother rented the rooms at the back and we rented the rooms at the front. The house was tall and bare and ugly, painted yellow. The town we lived in was too small to have residential divisions that amounted to anything, but I suppose that as far as there were divisions, that house was right on the boundary between decent and fairly dilapidated. I am speaking of the way things were just before the Second World War, at the end of the Depression. (That word, I believe, was unknown to us.)

My father, being a teacher, had a regular job but little money. The street petered out beyond us between the houses of those who had neither. Verna's grandmother must have had a little money because she spoke contemptuously of people who were On Relief. I believe my mother argued with her, unsuccessfully, that it was Not Their Fault. The two women were not particular friends, but they were cordial about clothesline arrangements.

The grandmother's name was Mrs. Home. A man came to see her occasionally. My mother spoke of him as Mrs. Home's friend.

You are not to speak to Mrs. Home's friend.

In fact I was not even allowed to play outside when he came, so there was not much chance of my speaking to him. I don't even remember what he looked like, though I remember his car, which was dark blue, a Ford V-8. I took a special interest in cars, probably because we didn't have one.

Then Verna came.

Mrs. Home spoke of her as her granddaughter and there is no reason to suppose that not to be true, but there was never any sign of a connecting generation. I don't know if Mrs. Home went away and came back with her, or if she was delivered by the friend with the V-8. She appeared in the summer before I was to start school. I can't remember her telling me her name — she was not communicative in the ordinary way and I don't believe I would have asked her. From the very beginning I had an aversion to her unlike anything I had felt up to that time for any other person. I said that I hated her, and my mother said, How can you, what has she ever done to you?

The poor thing.

Children use that word *hate* to mean various things. It may mean that they are frightened. Not that they feel in danger of being attacked — the way I did, for instance, of certain big boys on bicycles who liked to cut in front of you, yelling fearsomely, as you walked on the sidewalk. It is not physical harm that is feared — or that I feared in Verna's case — so much as some spell, or dark intention. It is a feeling you can have when you are very young even about certain house faces, or tree trunks, or very much about moldy cellars or deep closets.

She was a good deal taller than I was and I don't know how much older — two years, three years? She was skinny, indeed so narrowly built and with such a small head that she made me think of a snake. Fine black hair lay flat on this head, and fell over her forehead. The skin of her face seemed as dull to me as the flap of our old canvas tent, and her cheeks puffed out the way the flap of that tent puffed in a wind. Her eyes were always squinting.

But I believe there was nothing remarkably unpleasant about her looks, as other people saw her. Indeed my mother spoke of her as pretty, or almost pretty (as in, *isn't it too bad, she could be pretty*). Nothing to object to either, as far as my mother could see, in her behavior. *She is young for her age.* A roundabout and inadequate way of saying that Verna had not learned to read or write or skip or play ball, and that her voice was hoarse and unmodulated, her words oddly separated, as if they were chunks of language caught in her throat.

Her way of interfering with me, spoiling my solitary games, was that of an older not a younger girl. But of an older girl who had no skill or rights, nothing but a strenuous determination and an inability to understand that she wasn't wanted.

Children of course are monstrously conventional, repelled at once by whatever is off-center, out-of-whack, unmanageable. And being an only child I had been coddled a good deal (also scolded). I was awkward, precocious, timid, full of my private rituals and aversions. I hated even the celluloid barrette that kept slipping out of Verna's hair, and the peppermints with red or green stripes on them that she kept offering to me. In fact she did more than offer — she would try to catch me and push these candies into my mouth, chuckling all the time in her disconnected way. I dislike peppermint flavoring to this day. And the name Verna — I dislike that. It doesn't sound like spring to me, or like green grass or garlands of flowers or girls in flimsy dresses. It sounds more like a trail of obstinate peppermint, green slime.

I didn't believe my mother really liked Verna either. But because of some hypocrisy in her nature, as I saw it, because of a decision she had made, as it seemed, to spite me, she pretended to be sorry for her. She told me to be kind. At first she said that Verna would not be staying long and at the end of the summer holidays would go back to wherever she had been before. Then, when it became clear that there was nowhere for Verna to go back to, the placating message was that we ourselves would be moving soon. I had only to be kind for a little while longer. (As a matter of fact it was a whole year before we moved.) Finally, out of patience, she said that I was a disappointment to her and that she would never have thought I had so mean a nature.

"How can you blame a person for the way she was born? How is it her fault?"

That made no sense to me. If I had been more skilled at arguing, I might have said that I didn't blame Verna, I just did not want her to come near me. But I certainly did blame her. I did not question that it was somehow her fault. And in this, whatever my mother might say, I was in tune to some degree with an unspoken verdict of the time and place I lived in. Even grown-ups smiled in a certain way, there was some irrepressible gratification and taken-for-granted superiority that I could see, in the way they mentioned people who were *simple,* or *a few bricks short of a load.* And I believed my mother must be really like this, underneath.

I started school. Verna started school. She was put into a special class in a special building in a corner of the school grounds. This was actually the original school building in the town, but nobody had any time for local history then, and a few years later it was pulled down. There was a fenced-off corner in which pupils housed in that building spent recess. They went to school a half-hour later than we did in the morning and got out a half-hour earlier in the afternoon. Nobody was supposed to harass them at recess, but since they usually hung on the fence watching whatever went on in the regular school grounds there would be occasions when there was a rush, a whooping and brandishing of sticks, to scare them. I never went near that corner, hardly ever saw Verna. It was at home I still had to deal with her.

First she would stand at the corner of the yellow house, watching me, and I would pretend that I didn't know she was there. Then she would wander into the front yard, taking up a position on the front steps of the part of the house that was mine. If I wanted to go inside to the bathroom, or because I was cold, I would have to go so close as to touch her and to risk her touching me.

She could stay in one place longer than anybody I ever knew, staring at just one thing. Usually me.

I had a swing hung from a maple tree, so that I either faced the house or the street. That is, I either had to face her or to know that she was staring at my back, and might come up to give me a push.

After a while she would decide to do that. She always pushed me crooked, but that was not the worst thing. The worst was that her fingers had pressed my back. Through my coat, through my other clothing, her fingers like so many cold snouts.

Another activity of mine was to build a leaf house. That is, I raked up and carried armloads of leaves fallen from the maple tree that held the swing, and I dumped and arranged these leaves into a house plan. Here was the living room, here was the kitchen, here was a big soft pile for the bed in the bedroom, and so on. I had not invented this occupation — leaf houses of a more expansive sort were laid out, and even in a way furnished, every recess in the girls' playground at school, until the janitor finally raked up all the leaves and burned them.

At first Verna just watched what I was doing, with her squinty-eyed expression of what seemed to me superior (how could she think herself superior?) puzzlement. Then the time came when she moved closer, lifted an armful of leaves that dripped all over because of her uncertainty or clumsiness. And these came not from the pile of spare leaves but from the very wall of my house. She picked them up and carried them a short distance and let them fall — dumped them, in the middle of one of my tidy rooms.

I yelled at her to stop, but she bent to pick up her scattered load again, and was unable to hang on to them, so she just flung them about and when they were all on the ground began to kick them foolishly here and there. I was still yelling at her to stop, but this had no effect, or else she took it for encouragement. So I lowered my head and ran at her and bunted her in the stomach. I was not wearing a cap, so the hairs of my head came in contact with the woolly coat or jacket she had on, and it seemed to me that I had actually touched bristling hairs on the skin of a gross hard belly. I ran hollering with complaint up the steps of the house, and when my mother heard the story she further maddened me by saying, "She only wants to play. She doesn't know how to *play.*"

By the next fall we were in the bungalow and I never had to go past the yellow house that reminded me so much of Verna, as if it had positively taken on her narrow slyness, her threatening squint. The yellow paint seemed to be the very color of insult, and the front door, being off-center, added a touch of deformity. The bungalow was only three blocks away from that house, close to the school. But my idea of the town's size and complexity was still such that it seemed I was escaping Verna altogether. I realized that this was not true, not altogether true, when a schoolmate and I came face to face with her one day on the main street. We must have been sent on some errand by one of our mothers. I did not look up, but I believed I heard a chuckle of greeting or recognition as we passed.

The other girl said a horrifying thing to me.

She said, "I used to think that was your sister."

"What?"

"Well, I knew you lived in the same house, so I thought you must be related. Like cousins, anyway.

"Aren't you? Cousins?"

"No."

The old building where the Special Classes had been held was condemned, and its pupils were transferred to the Bible Chapel, now rented on weekdays by the town. The Bible Chapel happened to be across the street and around a corner from the bungalow where my mother and father and I now lived. There were a couple of ways that Verna could have walked to school, but the way she chose was past our house. And our house was only a few feet from the sidewalk, so this meant that her shadow could practically fall across our steps. If she wished, she could kick pebbles onto our grass, and unless we kept the blinds down she could peer into our hall and front room.

The hours of the Special Classes had been changed to coincide with ordinary school hours, at least in the morning — they still went home earlier in the afternoon. Once they were in the Bible Chapel, it must have been felt that there was no need to keep them free of the rest of us on the way to school. This meant, now, that I had a chance of running into Verna on the sidewalk. I would always look in the direction from which she might be coming, and if I saw her, I would duck back into the house with the excuse that I had forgotten something, or that one of my shoes was rubbing my heel and needed a plaster, or a ribbon was coming loose on my hair. I would never have been so foolish now as to mention Verna and hear my mother say, "What's the problem, what are you afraid of, do you think she's going to eat you?"

What was the problem? Contamination, infection? Verna was decently clean and healthy. And it was hardly likely that she was going to attack and pummel me or pull out my hair. But only adults would be so stupid as to believe she had no power. A power, moreover, that was specifically directed at me. I was the one she had her eye on. Or so I believed. As if we had an understanding between us that could not be described and was not to be disposed of. Something that clings, in the way of love, though on my side it felt like hate.

When I told Charlene about her, we had got into the deeper reaches of our conversation — that conversation that seems to have been broken only when we swam or slept. Verna was not so solid an offering, not so vividly repulsive as Charlene's brother's pimpled bum, and I remember saying that she was awful in a way that I could not describe. But then I did describe her, and my feelings about her, and I must have done not too bad a job, because one day toward the end of our two-week stay at camp Charlene came rushing into the dining hall at midday, her face lit up with horror and strange delight.

"She's here. She's here. That girl. That awful girl. Verna. She's *here.*"

Lunch was over. We were in the process of tidying up, putting our plates and mugs on the kitchen shelf to be grabbed away and washed by the girls on kitchen duty that day. Then we would line up to go to the Tuck Shop, which opened every day at one o'clock. Charlene had just run back to the dormitory to get some money. Being rich, with a father who was an undertaker, she was rather careless, keeping money in her pillowcase. Except when swimming I always had mine on my person. All of us who could in any way afford to went to the Tuck Shop after lunch, to get something to take away the taste of the desserts we hated but always tried, just to see if they were as disgusting as we expected. Tapioca pudding, mushy baked apples, slimy custard.

Verna? How could Verna be here?

This must have been a Friday. Two more days at camp, two more days to go. And it turned out that a contingent of Specials — here too they were called Specials — had been brought in to enjoy with us the final weekend. Not many of them — maybe twenty altogether — and not all from my town but from other towns nearby. In fact as Charlene was trying to get the news through to me, a whistle was being blown, and Counselor Arva had jumped up on a bench to address us.

She said that she knew we would all do our best to make these visitors — these new campers — welcome, and that they had brought their own tents and their own Counselor with them. But they would eat and swim and play games and attend the Morning Chat with the rest of us. She was sure, she said, with that familiar warning or upbraiding note in her voice, that we would all treat this as an opportunity to make new friends.

It took some time to get the tents up and these newcomers and their possessions settled. Some apparently took no interest and wandered off and had to be yelled at and fetched back. Since it was our free time, or Rest Time, we got our chocolate bars or licorice whips or sponge toffee from the Tuck Shop and went to lie on our bunks and enjoy them.

Charlene kept saying, "Imagine. Imagine. She's here. I can't believe it. Do you think she followed you?"

"Probably," I said.

"Do you think I can always hide you like that?"

When we were in the Tuck Shop line I had ducked my head and made Charlene get between me and the Specials as they were being herded by. I had taken one peek and recognized Verna from behind. Her drooping snaky head.

"We should think of some way to disguise you."

From what I had said, Charlene seemed to have got the idea that Verna had actively harassed me. And I believed that was true, except that the harassment had been more subtle, more secret, than I had been able to describe. Now I let Charlene think as she liked because it was more exciting that way.

Verna did not spot me immediately, because of the elaborate dodges Charlene and I kept making, and perhaps because she was rather dazed, as most of the Specials appeared to be, trying to figure out what they were doing here. They were soon taken off to their own swimming class, at the far end of the beach.

At the supper table they were marched in while we sang.

> The more we get together, together, together,
> The more we get together,
> The happier we'll be.

They were then deliberately separated, and distributed among the rest of us. They all wore nametags. Across from me there was one named Mary Ellen something, not from my town. But I had hardly time to be glad of that when I saw Verna at the next table, taller than those around her but, thank God, facing the same way I was, so she could not see me during the meal.

She was the tallest of them, and yet not so tall, not so notable a presence, as I remembered her. The reason was probably that I had had a growing spurt during the past year, while she had perhaps stopped her growing altogether.

After the meal, when we stood up and collected our dishes, I kept my head bowed, I never looked in her direction, and yet I knew when her eyes rested on me, when she recognized me, when she smiled her sagging little smile or made that odd chuckle in her throat.

"She's seen you," said Charlene. "Don't look. Don't look. I'll get between you and her. Move. Keep moving."

"Is she coming this way?"

"No. She's just standing there. She's just looking at you."

"Smiling?"

"Sort of."

"I can't look at her. I'd be sick."

How much did she persecute me in the remaining day and a half? Charlene and I used that word constantly, though in fact Verna never got near us. *Persecute.* It had an adult, legal sound. We were always on the lookout, as if we were being stalked, or I was. We tried to keep track of Verna's whereabouts, and Charlene reported on her attitude or expression. I did risk looking at her a couple of times, when Charlene had said, "Okay. She won't notice now."

At those times Verna appeared slightly cast down, or sullen, or bewildered, as if, like most of the Specials, she had been set adrift and did not completely understand where she was or what she was doing there. Some of them had caused a commotion by wandering away into the pine and cedar and poplar woods on the bluff behind the beach, or along the sandy road that led to the highway. After that a meeting was called, and we were all asked to watch out for our new friends, who were not so familiar with the place as we were. Charlene poked me in the ribs at that. She of course was not aware of any change, any falling away of confidence or even a diminishing of physical size in this Verna, and she continually reported on her sly and evil expression, her look of menace. And maybe she was right — maybe Verna saw in Charlene, this new friend or bodyguard of mine, this stranger, some sign of how everything was changed and uncertain here, and that made her scowl, though I didn't see it.

"You never told me about her hands," said Charlene.

"What about them?"

"She's got the longest fingers I have ever seen. She could just twist them round your neck and strangle you. She could. Wouldn't it be awful to be in a tent with her at night?"

I said that it would be. Awful.

There was a change, that last weekend, a whole different feeling in the camp. Nothing drastic. The meals were announced by the dining-room gong at the regular times, and the food served did not improve or deteriorate. Rest time arrived, game time and swimming time. The Tuck Shop operated as usual and we were drawn together as always for the Chat. But there was an air of growing restlessness and inattention. You could detect it even in the Counselors, who might not have the same reprimands or words of encouragement on the tip of their tongues and would look at you for a second as if recalling what it was they usually said. And all this seemed to have begun with the arrival of the Specials. Their presence had changed the camp. There had been a real camp before, with all its rules and deprivations and enjoyments set up, as inevitable as school or any part of a child's life, and then it had begun to crumple at the edges, to reveal itself as something provisional. Play-acting.

Was it because we could look at the Specials and think that if they could be campers, then there was no such thing as real campers? Partly it was that. But it was partly that the time was coming very soon when all this would be over, the routines would be broken up and we would be fetched by our parents to resume our old lives, and the Counselors would go back to being ordinary people, not even teachers. We were living in a stage set about to be dismantled, and with it all the friendships, enmities, rivalries that had flourished in the past two weeks. Who could believe it had been only two weeks?

Nobody knew how to speak of this, but a lassitude spread among us, a bored ill-temper, and even the weather reflected this feeling. It was probably not true that every day during the past two weeks had been hot and sunny, but most of us would certainly go away with that impression. And now, on Sunday morning, there was a change. While we were having the Outdoor Devotions (that was what we had on Sundays instead of the Chat) the clouds darkened. There was no change in temperature — if anything, the heat of the day increased, but there was in the air what some people called the smell of a storm. And yet such stillness. The Counselors, and even the Minister who drove out on Sundays from the nearest town, looked up occasionally and warily at the sky.

A few drops did fall, but no more. The service came to its end and no storm had broken. The clouds grew somewhat lighter, not so much as to promise sunshine but enough so that our last swim would not have to be canceled. After that there would be no lunch — the kitchen had been closed down after breakfast. The shutters on the Tuck Shop would not be opened. Our parents would begin arriving shortly after noon to take us home, and the bus would come for the Specials. Most of our things were already packed, the sheets were stripped and the rough brown blankets, which always felt clammy, were folded across the foot of each cot. Even when it was full of us, chattering and changing into our bathing suits, the inside of the dormitory cabin revealed itself as makeshift and gloomy.

It was the same with the beach. There appeared to be less sand than usual, more stones. And what sand there was seemed gray. The water looked as if it might be cold though in fact it was quite warm. Nevertheless our enthusiasm for swimming had waned and most of us were wading about aimlessly. The Swimming Counselors — Pauline and the middle-aged woman in charge of the Specials — had to clap their hands at us.

"Hurry up, what are you waiting for? Last chance this summer."

There were good swimmers among us who usually struck out at once for the raft. And all who were even passable swimmers — that included Charlene and me — were supposed to swim out to the raft at least once and turn around and swim back, in order to prove that we could swim at least a couple of yards in water over our heads. Pauline would usually swim out there right away, and stay in the deeper water, to watch out for anybody who got into trouble and also to make sure that everybody who was supposed to do the swim had done it. On this day, however, fewer swimmers than usual seemed to be doing as they were supposed to, and Pauline herself, after her first cries of encouragement or exasperation, was just bobbing around the raft, laughing with and teasing the faithful ones who had made their way out there. Most of us were still paddling around in the shallows, swimming a few feet or yards, then standing on the bottom and splashing each other or turning over and doing the dead man's float, as if swimming was something hardly anybody could be bothered with anymore. The woman in charge of the Specials was standing where the water came barely up to her knees — most of the Specials themselves went no farther than where the water came up to *their* knees — and the top part of her flowered skirted bathing suit had not even got wet. She was bending over and making little hand-splashes at her charges, laughing and telling them *isn't this fun.*

The water Charlene and I were in was probably up to our chests and no more. We were in the ranks of the silly swimmers, doing the dead man's float, and flopping about backstroking or breaststroking, with nobody telling us to stop fooling around. We were trying to see how long we could keep our eyes open under water, we were sneaking up and jumping on each other's back. All around us were plenty of others yelling and screeching with laughter as they did the same things.

During this swim some parents or collectors of campers had arrived early, and let it be known they had no time to waste, so the campers who belonged to them were being summoned from the water. This made for some extra calling and confusion.

"Look. Look," said Charlene. Or sputtered, in fact, because I had pushed her underwater and she had just come up soaked and spitting. I looked, and there was Verna making her way toward us, wearing a pale-blue rubber bathing cap, slapping at the water with her long hands and smiling, as if her rights over me had suddenly been restored.

I have not kept up with Charlene. I don't even remember how we said goodbye. If we said goodbye. I have a notion that both sets of parents arrived at around the same time and that we scrambled into separate cars and gave ourselves over — what else could we do? — to our old lives. Charlene's parents would certainly have had a car not so shabby and noisy and unreliable as the one my parents now owned, but even if that had not been so we would never have thought of making the two sets of relatives acquainted with each other. Everybody, and we ourselves, would have been in a hurry to get off, to leave behind the pockets of uproar about lost property or who had or had not met their relatives or boarded the bus.

By chance, years later, I saw her wedding picture. This was at a time when wedding pictures were still published in the newspapers, not just in small towns but in the city papers as well. I saw it in a Toronto paper I was looking through while I waited for a friend in a café on Bloor Street.

The wedding had taken place in Guelph. The groom was a native of Toronto and a graduate of Osgoode Hall. He was quite tall — or else Charlene had turned out to be quite short. She barely came up to his shoulder, even with her hair done up in the dense, polished helmet-style of the day. The hair made her face seem squashed and insignificant, but I got the impression her eyes were outlined heavily, Cleopatra fashion, her lips pale. This sounds grotesque, but it was certainly the look admired at the time. All that reminded me of her child-self was the little humorous bump of her chin.

She — the bride, it said — had graduated from St. Hilda's College, in Toronto.

So she must have been here in Toronto, going to St. Hilda's, while I was in the same city, going to University College. We had been walking around perhaps at the same time and on some of the same streets or paths on the campus. And never met. I did not think that she would have seen me and avoided speaking to me. I would not have avoided speaking to her. Of course I would have considered myself a more serious student, once I discovered she was going to St. Hilda's. My friends and I regarded St. Hilda's as a Ladies College.

Now I was a graduate student in anthropology. I had decided never to get married, though I did not rule out having lovers. I wore my hair long and straight — my friends and I were anticipating the style of the hippies. My memories of childhood were much more distant and faded and unimportant than they seem today.

I could have written to Charlene, in care of her parents, whose Guelph address had been published in the paper. But I didn't do so. I would have thought it the height of hypocrisy to congratulate any woman on the occasion of her marriage.

But she wrote to me, perhaps fifteen years later. She wrote in care of my publishers.

"My old pal Marlene," she wrote. "How excited and happy I was to see your name in *Maclean's* magazine. And how dazzled I am to think you have written a book. I have not picked it up yet because we have been away on holidays but I mean to do so — and read it too — as soon as I can. I was just going through the magazines that had accumulated in our absence and there I saw the striking picture of you and the interesting review. And I thought that I must write and congratulate you.

"Perhaps you are married but use your maiden name to write under? Perhaps you have a family? Do write and tell me all about yourself. Sadly, I am childless, but I keep busy with volunteer work, gardening and sailing with Kit (my husband). There always seems to be plenty to do. I am presently serving on the Library Board and will twist their arms if they have not already ordered your book.

"Congratulations again. I must say I was surprised but not entirely because I always suspected you might do something special."

I did not get in touch with her at that time either. There seemed to be no point to it. At first I took no notice of the word *special* right at the end, but it gave me a small jolt when I thought of it later. However, I told myself, and still believe, that she meant nothing by it.

The book that she referred to was one that had grown out of a thesis I had been discouraged from writing. I went ahead and wrote another thesis but went back to the earlier one as a sort of hobby project when I had time. I have collaborated on a couple of books since then, as was duly expected of me, but that book I did on my own is the only one that got me a small flurry of attention in the outside world (and needless to say some disapproval from colleagues). It is out of print now. It was called *Imbeciles and Idols* — a title I would never get away with today and that even then made my publishers nervous, though it was admitted to be catchy.

What I was trying to explore was the attitude of people in various cultures — one does not dare say the word *primitive* to describe such cultures — the attitude toward people who are mentally or physically unique. The words *deficient, handicapped, retarded,* being of course also consigned to the dustbin and probably for good reason — not simply because such words may indicate a superior attitude and habitual unkindness but because they are not truly descriptive. Those words push aside a good deal that is remarkable, even awesome — another word to go by the boards — or at any rate peculiarly powerful, in such people. And what was interesting was to discover a certain amount of veneration as well as persecution, and the ascribing — not entirely inaccurately — of quite a range of abilities, seen as sacred, magical, dangerous, or valuable. I did the best I could with historical as well as contemporary research and took into account poetry and fiction and of course religious custom. Naturally I was criticized in my profession for being too literary and for getting all my information out of books, but I could not run around the world then. I had not been able to get a grant.

Of course I could see a connection, a connection that I thought it just possible Charlene might get to see too. It's strange how distant and unimportant that seemed, only a starting point. As anything in childhood appeared to me then. Because of the journey I had made since, the achievement of adulthood. Safety.

Maiden name, Charlene had written. That was an expression I had not heard for quite a while. It is next door to *maiden lady,* which sounds so chaste and sad. And remarkably inappropriate in my case. Even when I looked at Charlene's wedding picture I was not a virgin — though I don't suppose she was either. Not that I have had a swarm of lovers — or would even want to call most of them *lovers.* Like most women in my age group who have not lived in a monogamous marriage, I know the number. Sixteen. I'm sure that for many younger women that total would have been reached before they were out of their twenties or possibly out of their teens. (When I got Charlene's letter, of course, the total would have been less. I cannot — this is true — I cannot be bothered getting that straight now.) Three of them were important and all three of those were in the chronological first half-dozen of the count. What I mean by "important" is that with those three — no, only two, the third meaning a great deal more to me than I to him — with those two, then, the times would come when you want to split open, surrender far more than your body, dump your whole life into one basket with his.

I kept myself from doing so, but just barely.

Not long ago I got another letter. This was forwarded from the college where I taught before I retired. I found it waiting when I returned from a trip to Patagonia. (I have become a hardy traveler.) It was over a month old.

A typed letter — a fact for which the writer immediately apologized.

"My handwriting is lamentable," he wrote, and went on to introduce himself as the husband of "your old childhood buddy, Charlene." He said that he was sorry, very sorry, to send me bad news. Charlene was in Princess Margaret Hospital in Toronto. Her cancer had begun in the lungs and spread to the liver. She had, regrettably, been a lifelong smoker. She had only a short time left to live. She had not spoken of me very often, but when she did, over the years, it was always with delight in my remarkable accomplishments. He knew how much she valued me and now at the end of her life she seemed very keen to see me. She had asked him to get hold of me.

Well she is probably dead by now, I thought.

But if she was — this is how I worked things out — if she was, I would run no risk in going to the hospital and inquiring. Then my conscience or whatever you wanted to call it would be clear. I could write him a note saying that unfortunately I had been away but had come as soon as I could.

No. Better not a note. He might show up in my life, thanking me. The word *buddy* made me uncomfortable.

So in a different way did *remarkable accomplishments.*

Princess Margaret Hospital is only a few blocks away from my apartment building. On a sunny spring day I walked over there. I don't know why I didn't just phone. Perhaps I wanted to think I'd made as much effort as I could.

At the main desk I discovered that Charlene was still alive. When asked if I wanted to see her I could hardly say no.

I went up in the elevator still thinking that I might be able to turn away, before I found the nurses' station on her floor. Or that I might make a simple U-turn, taking the next elevator down. The receptionist at the main desk downstairs would never notice my leaving. As a matter of fact she would not have noticed my leaving the moment she had turned her attention to the next person in line, and even if she had noticed, what would it have mattered?

I would have been ashamed, I suppose. Not ashamed at my lack of feeling so much as at my lack of fortitude.

I stopped at the nurses' station and was given the number of the room.

It was a private room, quite a small room, with no impressive apparatus or flowers or balloons. At first I could not see Charlene. A nurse was bending over the bed in which there seemed to be a mound of bedclothes but no visible person. The enlarged liver, I thought, and wished I had run while I could.

The nurse straightened up, turned, and smiled at me. She was a plump brown woman who spoke in a soft beguiling voice that might have meant she came from the West Indies.

"You are the Marlin," she said.

Something in the word seemed to delight her.

"She was so wanting for you to come. You can come closer."

I obeyed, and looked down at a bloated body and a sharp ruined face, a chicken's neck for which the hospital gown was a mile too wide. A frizz of hair — still brown — about a quarter of an inch long on her scalp. No sign of Charlene.

I had seen the faces of dying people before. The faces of my mother and father, even the face of the man I had been afraid to love. I was not surprised.

"She is sleeping now," said the nurse. "She was so hoping you would come."

"She's not unconscious?"

"No. But she sleeps."

Yes there was, I saw it now, there was a sign of Charlene. What was it? Maybe a twitch, that confident playful tucking away of a corner of her mouth.

The nurse was speaking to me in her soft happy voice. "I don't know if she would recognize you," she said. "But she hoped you would come. There is something for you."

"Will she wake up?"

A shrug. "We have to give her injections often for the pain."

She was opening the bedside table.

"Here. This. She told me to give it to you if it was too late for her. She did not want her husband to give it. Now you are here, she would be glad."

A sealed envelope with my name on it, printed in shaky capital letters.

"Not her husband," the nurse said, with a twinkle, then a broadening smile. Did she scent something illicit, a women's secret, an old love?

"Come back tomorrow," she said. "Who knows? I will tell her if it is possible."

I read the note as soon as I got down to the lobby. Charlene had managed to write in an almost normal script, not wildly as in the sprawling letters on the envelope. Of course she might have written the note first and put it in the envelope, then sealed the envelope and put it by, thinking she would get to hand it to me herself. Only later would she see a need to put my name on it.

Marlene, I am writing this in case I get too far gone to speak. Please do what I ask you. Please go to Guelph and go to the church and ask for Father Hofstrader. Church of Our Lady Immaculate. Must be personal they may open his mail. Father Hofstrader. This I cannot ask C and do not want him ever to know. Father H knows and I have asked him and he says it is possible to save me. Only I left so late. Marlene please do this bless you. Nothing about you.

C. That must be her husband. He doesn't know. Of course he doesn't.

Father Hofstrader.

Nothing about me.

I was free to crumple this up and throw it away once I got out into the street. And so I did, I threw the envelope away and let the wind sweep it into the gutter on University Avenue. Then I realized the note was not in the envelope, it was still in my pocket.

I would never go to the hospital again.

Kit was her husband's name. Now I remembered. They went sailing. Christoper. Kit.

When I got back to my apartment building I found myself taking the elevator down to the garage, not up to my apartment. Dressed just as I was, I got into my car and drove out onto the street, and began to head toward the Gardiner Expressway.

The Gardiner Expressway, Highway 427, Highway 401. It was rush hour now, a bad time to get out of the city. I hate this sort of driving, I don't do it often enough to be confident. There was under half a tank of gas, and what was more, I had to go to the bathroom. Around Milton, I thought, I could pull off the highway and fill up on gas and use the toilet and reconsider. At present I could do nothing but what I was doing, heading north, then heading west.

I didn't get off. I passed the Mississauga exit and the Milton exit. I saw a highway sign telling me how many kilometers to Guelph, and I translated that roughly into miles in my head, as I always have to do, and I figured the gas would hold out. The excuse I made to myself for not stopping was that the sun would be getting lower and more troublesome, now that we were leaving the faint haze that lies over the city even on the finest day.

At the first stop after I took the Guelph turnoff I got out and walked to the ladies' washroom with stiff trembling legs. Afterward I filled the tank with gas and asked, when I paid, for directions to the church. The directions were not very clear, but I was told that it was on a big hill and I could find it from anywhere in the heart of town.

Of course that was not true, though I could see it from almost anywhere. A collection of delicate spires rising from four fine towers. A beautiful building where I had expected only a grand one. It was grand too, of course, a grand dominating church for such a relatively small city.

Could that have been where Charlene was married?

No. Of course not. She had been sent to a United Church camp, and there were no Catholic girls at that camp though there was quite a variety of Protestants. And then there was the business about C not knowing.

She might have converted secretly. Since.

I found my way in time to the church parking lot, and sat there wondering what I should do. I was wearing slacks and a jacket. My idea of what was required in a Catholic church were so antiquated that I was not even sure if my outfit would be all right. I tried to recall visits to great churches in Europe. Something about the arms being covered? Head scarves, skirts?

What a bright high silence there was up on this hill. April, not a leaf out yet on the trees, but the sun after all was still well up in the sky. There was one low bank of snow as gray as the paving in the church lot.

The jacket I had on was too light for evening wear, or maybe it was colder here, the wind stronger, than in Toronto.

The building might well be locked, at this time, locked and empty.

The grand front doors appeared to be so. I did not even bother to climb the steps to try them, because I decided to follow a couple of old women — old like me — who had just come up the long flight from the street and who bypassed those steps entirely, heading around to an easier entrance at the side of the building.

There were more people inside, maybe two or three dozen people, but there wasn't a sense that they were gathered for a service. They were scattered here and there in the pews, some kneeling and some chatting. The women ahead of me dipped their hands in a marble font without looking at what they were doing and said hello — hardly lowering their voices — to a man who was setting out baskets on a table.

"It looks a lot warmer out than it is," said one of them, and the man said the wind would bite your nose off.

I recognized the confessionals. Like separate small cottages or large playhouses in a Gothic style, with a lot of dark wooden carving, dark brown curtains. Elsewhere all was glowing, dazzling. The high curved ceiling most celestially blue, the lower curves of the ceiling — those that joined the upright walls — decorated with holy images on gold-painted medallions. Stained-glass windows hit by the sun at this time of day were turned into columns of jewels. I made my way discreetly down one aisle, trying to get a look at the altar, but the chancel, being in the western wall, was too bright for me to look into. Above the windows, though, I saw that there were painted angels. Flocks of angels, all fresh and gauzy and pure as light.

It was a most insistent place but nobody seemed to be overwhelmed by all the insistence. The chatting ladies kept chatting softly but not in whispers. And other people, after some businesslike nodding and crossing, knelt down and went about their business.

As I ought to be going about mine. I looked around for a priest, but there was not one in sight. Priests as well as other people must have a working day. They must drive home and go into their living rooms or offices or dens and turn on the television and loosen their collars. Fetch a drink and wonder if they were going to get anything decent for supper. When they did come into the church they would come officially. In their vestments ready to perform some ceremony. Mass.

Or to hear confessions. But then you would never know when they were there. Didn't they enter and leave their grilled stalls by a private door?

I would have to ask somebody. The man who had distributed the baskets seemed to be here for reasons that were not purely private though he was apparently not an usher. Nobody needed an usher. People chose where they wanted to sit — or kneel — and sometimes decided to get up and choose another spot, perhaps being bothered by the glare of the jewel-inflaming sun. When I spoke to him I whispered, out of old habit in a church — and he had to ask me to speak again. Puzzled or embarrassed, he nodded in a wobbly way toward one of the confessionals. I had to become very specific and convincing.

"No, no. I just want to talk to a priest. I've been sent to talk to a priest. A priest called Father Hofstrader."

The basket man disappeared down the more distant side aisle and came back in a little while with a briskly moving stout young priest in ordinary black costume.

He motioned me into a room I had not noticed — not a room actually, we went through an archway, not a doorway — at the back of the church.

"Give us a chance to talk, in here," he said, and pulled out a chair for me.

"Father Hofstrader —"

"Oh no, I must tell you, I am not Father Hofstrader. Father Hofstrader is not here. He is on vacation."

For a moment I did not know how to proceed.

"I will do my best to help you."

"There is a woman," I said, "a woman who is dying in Princess Margaret Hospital in Toronto —"

"Yes, yes. We know of Princess Margaret Hospital."

"She asks me — I have a note from her here — she wants to see Father Hofstrader."

"Is she a member of this parish?"

"I don't know. I don't know if she is a Catholic or not. She is from here. From Guelph. She is a friend I have not seen for a long time."

"When did you talk with her?"

I had to explain that I hadn't talked with her, she had been asleep, but she had left the note for me.

"But you don't know if she is a Catholic?"

He had a cracked sore at the corner of his mouth. It must have been painful for him to talk.

"I think she is, but her husband isn't and he doesn't know she is. She doesn't want him to know."

I said this in the hope of making things clearer, even though I didn't know for sure if it was true. I had an idea that this priest might shortly lose interest altogether. "Father Hofstrader must have known all this," I said.

"You didn't speak with her?"

I said that she had been under medication but that this was not the case all the time and I was sure she would have periods of lucidity. This too I stressed because I thought it necessary.

"If she wishes to make a confession, you know, there are priests available at Princess Margaret's."

I could not think of what else to say. I got out the note, smoothed the paper, and handed it to him. I saw that the handwriting was not as good as I had thought. It was legible only in comparison to the letters on the envelope.

He made a troubled face.

"Who is this C?"

"Her husband." I was worried that he might ask for the husband's name, to get in touch with him, but instead he asked for Charlene's. This woman's name, he said.

"Charlene Sullivan." It was a wonder that I even remembered the surname. And I was reassured for a moment, because it was a name that sounded Catholic. Of course that meant that it was the husband who could be Catholic. But the priest might conclude that the husband had lapsed, and that would surely make Charlene's secrecy more understandable, her message more urgent.

"Why does she need Father Hofstrader?"

"I think perhaps it's something special."

"All confessions are special."

He made a move to get up, but I stayed where I was. He sat down again.

"Father Hofstrader is on vacation, but he is not out of town. I could phone and ask him about this. If you insist."

"Yes. Please."

"I do not like to bother him. He has not been well."

I said that if he was not well enough to drive himself to Toronto, I could drive him.

"We can take care of his transportation if necessary."

He looked around and did not see what he wanted, undipped a pen from his pocket, and then decided that the blank side of the note would do to write on.

"If you'll just make sure I've got the name. Charlotte —"

"Charlene."

Was I not tempted, during all this palaver? Not once? Not swayed by longing, by a magic-lantern show, the promise of pardon? No. Not really. It's not for me. What's done is done, what's done remains. Flocks of angels, tears of blood, notwithstanding.

I sat in the car without thinking to turn the motor on, though it was freezing cold by now. I didn't know what to do next. That is, I knew what I could do. Find my way to the highway and join the bright everlasting flow of cars toward Toronto. Or find a place to stay overnight, if I did not think I had the strength to drive. Most places would provide you with a toothbrush, or direct you to a machine where you could get one. I knew what was necessary and possible, but it was beyond my strength, for the moment, to do it.

The motorboats on the lake were supposed to stay a good distance out from the shore. And especially from our camping area, so that the waves they raised would not disturb our swimming. But on that last morning, that Sunday morning, a couple of them started a race and circled close in — not as close as the raft of course, but close enough to raise waves. The raft was tossed around, and Pauline's voice was lifted in a cry of reproach and dismay. The boats made far too much noise for their drivers to hear her, and they had already set a big wave rolling toward the shore, causing most of us in the shallows either to jump with it or be tumbled off our feet.

Charlene and I both lost our footing. We had our backs to the raft because we were watching Verna come toward us. We were standing in water about up to our armpits, and we seemed to be lifted and tossed at the same moment that we heard Pauline's cry. We may have cried out as many others did, first in fear and then in delight as we regained our footing and that wave washed on ahead of us. The waves that followed proved to be not as strong, so that we could hold ourselves against them.

At the moment we tumbled, Verna had pitched toward us. When we came up, with our faces streaming, arms flailing, she was spread out under the surface of the water. There was a tumult of screaming and shouting all around, and this increased as the lesser waves arrived and people who had somehow missed the first attack pretended to be knocked over by the second. Verna's head did not break the surface, though now she was not inert but turning in a leisurely way, light as a jellyfish in the water. Charlene and I had our hands on her, on her rubber cap.

This could have been an accident. As if we, in trying to get our balance, grabbed on to this nearby large rubbery object, hardly realizing what it was or what we were doing. I have thought it all out. I think we would have been forgiven. Young children. Terrified.

Is this in any way true? It is true in the sense that we did not decide anything, in the beginning. We did not look at each other and decide to do what we subsequently and consciously did. Consciously, because our eyes did meet as the head of Verna tried to rise up to the surface of the water. Her head was determined to rise, like a dumpling in a stew. The rest of her was making misguided feeble movements down in the water, but the head knew what it should do. We might have lost our grip on the rubber head, the rubber cap, were it not for the raised pattern that made it less slippery. I can recall the color perfectly, the pale insipid blue, but I never deciphered the pattern — a fish, a mermaid, a flower — whose ridges pushed into my palms.

Charlene and I kept our eyes on each other then, rather than looking down at what our hands were doing. Her eyes were wide and gleeful, as I suppose mine were too. I don't think we felt wicked, triumphing in our wickedness. More as if we were doing just what was — amazingly — demanded of us, as if this was the absolute high point, the culmination, in our lives, of our being ourselves.

The whole business probably took no more than two minutes. Three? Or a minute and a half?

It seems too much to say that the discouraging clouds cleared up just at that time, but at some point — perhaps at the trespass of the motorboats, or when Pauline screamed, or when the first wave hit, or when the rubber object under our palms ceased to have a will of its own — the sun burst out, and more parents popped up on the beach, and there were calls to all of us to stop horsing around and come out of the water. Swimming was over. Over for the summer, for those who lived out of reach of the lake or municipal swimming pools. Private pools were only in the movie magazines.

As I've said, my memory fails when it comes to parting from Charlene, getting into my parents' car. Because it didn't matter. At that age, things ended. You expected things to end.

I am sure we never said anything as banal, as insulting or unnecessary, as *Don't tell.*

I can imagine the unease starting, but not spreading quite so fast as it might have if there had not been competing dramas. A child has lost a sandal, one of the youngest children is screaming that she got sand in her eye from the waves. Almost certainly a child is throwing up because of the excitement in the water or the excitement of families arriving or the too-swift consumption of contraband candy. And the anxiety running through this, that someone is missing.

"Who?"

"One of the Specials."

"Oh drat. Wouldn't you know."

The woman in charge of the Specials running around, still in her flowered bathing suit, with the custard flesh wobbling on her thick arms and legs. Her voice wild and weepy.

Somebody go check in the woods, run up the trail, call her name.

"What is her name?"

"Verna."

"Wait."

"What?"

"Is that not something out there in the water?"

MIROSLAV PENKOV

Buying Lenin

FROM *The Southern Review*

WHEN GRANDPA LEARNED I WAS LEAVING for America to study, he wrote me a goodbye note. "You rotten capitalist pig," the note read. "Have a safe flight. Love, Grandpa." It was written on a creased red ballot from the 1991 elections, which was a cornerstone in Grandpa's Communist ballot collection, and it bore the signatures of everybody in the village of Leningrad.

I was touched to receive such an honor, so I sat down, took out a one-dollar bill, and wrote Grandpa the following reply: "You Communist dupe. Thanks for the letter. I'm leaving tomorrow, and when I get there I'll try to marry an American woman ASAP. I'll also try to have American children. Love, your grandson."

My senior year in high school, while most of my peers were busy drinking, smoking, having sex, playing dice, lying to their parents, hitchhiking to the sea, counterfeiting money, or making bombs for soccer games, I studied. English. I memorized words and grammar rules and practiced tongue twisters specifically designed for Eastern Europeans. *Remember the money,* I repeated over and over again — in the street, under the shower, even in my sleep. *Remember the money, remember the money, remember the money.* Phrases like this help you break your tongue. Develop an ear.

I lived alone in the apartment because by that time almost everybody I'd loved had died. First Grandma. Then my parents. Grandpa had moved to the village renamed Leningrad and stubbornly refused to come back and visit. I must have said some pretty bad things on a few occasions, especially when we had that big fight, and he was acting offended.

So I decided to seek my fortune elsewhere.

Early in the spring of 1999 I got admitted to the University of Arkansas and received a free ride — full scholarship, room and board, even a plane ticket. I called Grandpa.

"My grandson, a capitalist!" he said. "I can't believe you'll do this to me. Not when you know what I've been through."

What Grandpa had been through is basically this: The year was 1944. Grandpa was in his midtwenties. His face was tough but fair. His nose was sharp. His dark eyes glowed with the spark of something new, great, and profoundly world-changing. He was poor. "I," he often told me, "would eat bread with crab apples for breakfast. Bread with crab apples for lunch. And crab apples for dinner, because by dinnertime, the bread would be over."

That's why when the Communists came to his village in Bulgaria to steal food, Grandpa joined them. They had all run to the woods and made dugouts and lived in them for weeks on end — day and night, down there in the dugouts. Outside, the fascists sniffed for them, trying to hunt them down with their greyhounds, with their guns and bombs and missiles, these bastards, these czarist sons of bitches. "If you think a grave is too narrow," Grandpa told me on one occasion, "make yourself a dugout. No, no, make yourself a dugout and get fifteen more people to join you in it for a week. And get a couple pregnant women too. And a hungry goat. Then go around telling everybody a grave is the narrowest thing on earth."

"I never said a grave was the narrowest thing, Grandpa."

"But you were thinking it."

So finally, Grandpa got too hungry to stay in the dugout and decided to strap on a shotgun and go down to the village for food. When he arrived in the village, he found everything changed. A red flag was flapping from the church tower. The church had been shut down and turned into a meeting hall. All people walked free, and their dark eyes glowed with the spark of something new, great, and profoundly world-changing. Grandpa fell to his knees and wept and kissed the soil of the motherland. Immediately, he was assimilated by the Party. Immediately, he was given a high position in the local governing force. Immediately, he climbed up the ladder and moved to the city, where he became something-something of the something-something department. He got an apartment, married Grandma; a year later they had a baby boy.

"What so terrible have you been through?" I asked him one day over the phone, before I left for America. "You've had a good life."

"I hate the capitalists," he said. "I love Lenin."

"Do you love me?"

"You are my grandson."

"Then come to the city. Live with me in the apartment."

"I have things to do here," he said. "I have responsibilities."

"You have graves to clean."

"I can't come," he said. "You know I can't."

"I know. That's why I'm leaving."

I arrived in Arkansas on August 11, 1999. At the airport I was picked up by two young men and a girl, all in suits. They were from some sort of organization that cared for international students and had e-mailed me in advance to offer the pickup.

"Welcome to America," they said in one warm, friendly voice. They had good, honest faces. We shook hands. Then in the car they gave me a Bible.

"Do you know what this is?" the girl said, very slowly and very loudly.

"No," I said. She seemed genuinely pleased.

"These are the deeds of our Savior. The word of our Lord."

"Oh, Lenin's collected works," I said. "Which volume?"

When I was still a boy, I used to spend my summers at the village with my grandparents. In the winter they lived in the city, two blocks away from our apartment; but when the weather warmed, they always packed and left.

Sometimes when the moon was full, Grandpa would take me crawfish hunting. We spent most of the day in the yard, preparing the big bags, reinforcing their bottoms with tape, patching the holes from previous hunts at the river. Finally, when we were done, we sat on the porch and watched the sun dive behind the peaks of the Balkan range. Grandpa lit a cigarette, took out his pocketknife, and drew patterns along the bark of the chestnut sticks we had honed for catching the crawfish. We waited for the moon to rise, and sometimes Grandma sat by us and sang, or Grandpa told stories of the days he had been out in the woods, hiding in the dugouts with his Communist comrades.

When the moon was finally up, shining brightly, Grandpa would get to his feet and stretch.

"They are out on pasture," he would say. "Let's get them."

Grandma made sandwiches for the road and wrapped them in paper napkins that were always difficult to peel off completely. She wished us luck, and we left the house and walked out of the village, and then on the muddy path through the woods. Grandpa carried the bags and sticks and I followed. The moon lit our way; the wind was soft on our faces. Somewhere close by the river was booming.

We would step out of the woods, into the meadow, and with the night sky unfolding above us we would see them. The river and the crawfish. She was always dark and roaring, and they were always out on the grass, moving slowly with their pincers pinching blades of crowfoot.

We would sit on the grass, take out the sandwiches, and eat. In the sharp moonlight the wet bodies of the crawfish glistened like live coals, and the banks seemed covered with burning embers, little eyes that watched us through the dark. When we were done eating, the hunt began.

Grandpa would give me a stick and a bag. Hundreds of twitching crawfish at our feet: touch their pincers with the stick, poke them, and they pinch as hard as they can. I learned to lift them, then shake them off in the bag. One by one you collect.

"They are easy prey," Grandpa often remarked. "You catch one, but the others don't run away. The others don't even know you are there until you pick them up, and even then they still have no idea. Teaches us a lesson to apply to human nature, doesn't it?" I was too young to understand what that lesson was, so I listened and hunted.

One, two, three hours. The moon, tiring, swims toward the horizon. The east blazes red. And then the crawfish in perfect synchrony turn around and slowly, quietly, make for the river. She takes their bodies back, cold and harsh, and lulls them to their sleep as a new day ripens. We sit on the grass, the bags heavy with prey. I fall asleep on Grandpa's shoulder. He carries me home to the village. He lets the crawfish go.

In my dorm I called Grandpa. I couldn't connect for a long time, but then the line gave a crack and I heard his voice on the other side.

"Grandson?"

"I'm here."

"You are there." His voice was low and muted, and its echo made it seem like we were standing on the opposite ends of a tunnel.

"How do you feel?" he asked.

"I need to sleep. Did you get my goodbye card?"

"I fed it to the pigs. Pigs like American money."

The line cracked between us as if tossed by the wind.

"Grandpa, there is so much water between us. We are so far apart."

"We are," he said. "But blood, I hope, is thicker than the ocean."

When he was thirty and holding the position something-of-the-something, Grandpa met the woman of his heart. It was the classic Communist love story: They met at an evening gathering of the party. Grandma came in late, wet from the rain, took the only free seat, which was next to Grandpa, and fell asleep on his shoulder. Right there on the spot he hated her slack interest in party matters, and right there on the spot he fell in love with her scent, with her face, with her breath on his neck. After that they talked about pure ideals and the bright future, about the capitalist evil of the West, about the nurturing embrace of the Soviet Union, and most important, about Lenin. Grandpa found out that they shared the same passion, viewed the same things with gratitude and admiration, and so on the next morning he took Grandma to the Civil Office, where they got married.

Grandma died of breast cancer in 1989, only a month after Communism was abolished in Bulgaria. I was eight and I remember it all very clearly. We buried her in the village where she was from. We put the coffin in a cart and tied the cart to a tractor, and the tractor pulled the cart and the coffin and we walked behind it all. Grandpa was sitting inside, by the coffin, holding Grandma's dead hand. I don't think it actually rained that day, but in my memories I see rain and clouds and wind. It must have rained inside of me — that quiet, cold rain that falls when you lose someone close to your heart. It must have rained inside of Grandpa too, but he shed no tears. He just sat there in the cart, the rain of my memories falling on him, on his bald head, on the open coffin, on Grandma's closed eyes; the music flowing around them — deep, sad music of the oboe, the trumpet, the funeral drum. There is no priest at a Communist funeral, and there was no priest when we lay Grandma in her grave. Grandpa read from a book, volume twelve of Lenin's collected works, and his words rose to the sky, and the rain knocked them down to the ground like wet feathers and they flowed in muddy rivers, in roaring waterfalls from the edges of the grave.

"It's a good grave," Grandpa was saying when it was all over. "It's not as narrow as a dugout, which makes it good. Right? It's not too narrow, right? She'll be all right in it, right? She'll be all right. Certainly, she'll be all right."

After Grandma's funeral Grandpa refused to leave the village. In one year he had lost everything a man could lose: the woman of his heart, and the love of his life — the Communist Party.

"There is no life for me in the city," I remember him telling my dad. "I have no desire to serve these traitors. Let capitalism corrupt them all, these bastards, these murderers of innocent women."

Deep inside, Grandpa was convinced that it had been the fall of Communism that had killed Grandma.

"Her cancer was a consequence of the grave disappointments of her pure and idealistic heart," Grandpa would explain. "She could not watch her ideals being trampled on, and she did the only possible thing an honest woman like her could do — she died."

Grandpa bought a village house so he could be close to Grandma and every day at three o'clock in the afternoon he went to her grave, sat by the tombstone, opened volume twelve of Lenin's collected works, and read aloud. Summer or winter, he was there, reading — he never skipped a day — and it was there, at Grandma's grave, that the idea hit him.

"Nothing is lost," he told me and my parents one Saturday on which we'd come to visit him. "Communism may be dead all over this country, but ideals never die. I will bring it all here, to the village. I will build it all from scratch, so your Grandma's deepest wish can be fulfilled. Your Grandma would be proud of me."

On October 24, 1993, the great October village revolution took place, quietly, underground, without much ado. At that time, everybody who was sixty or younger had already left the village to live in the city, and so those who remained were people pure and strong of heart, in whom the idea was still alive, and whose dark eyes glowed with the spark of something great and profoundly world-changing. Officially the village was still part of Bulgaria, and it had a mayor who answered to the national government and so on and so forth; but secretly, underground, it was the new Communist village party that decided its fate. The name of the village was changed to Leningrad. Grandpa was unanimously elected secretary-general. Every evening there was a Party meeting in the old village hall, where the seat next to Grandpa was always left vacant, and water was sprinkled from a hose outside on the windows to create the illusion of rain.

"Communism blossoms better with moisture," Grandpa explained, when the other Party members questioned his decision to water; in fact, he was thinking of Grandma and the rain on their first meeting. And indeed, Communism in Leningrad blossomed.

Grandpa and the villagers decided to salvage every Communist artifact remaining in Bulgaria and bring them all to Leningrad: to the living museum of the Communist doctrine. Monuments, scarred deep by the red ideal, were being demolished all over the country. Statues erected decades ago, proudly reminding, glorifying, promising, were now taken down and melted for scrap. Poets who were once extolled now lay forgotten. Their paper bodies gathered dust. Their ink blood was washed away by rainwater.

In one of his letters, Grandpa told me the villagers had convinced a bunch of gypsies to do the salvaging for them. "Comrade Hassan, his wife, and their thirteen gypsy children, doubtlessly inspired by the bright Communist ideal and only mildly stimulated by the money and the two pigs we gave them, have promised to supply our village with the best of the best 'red' artifacts that could be found across our pitiful country. Today the comrade gypsies brought us their first gift: a monument of the Nameless Russian Soldier, liberator from the Turks, slightly deformed from the waist down and missing a shotgun, but otherwise in excellent condition. The monument now stands proud next to the statues of Alyosha, Seryoja, and the Nameless Maiden of Minsk."

Life in America was good. I went to class, studied, made new friends. I wrote letters to Grandpa or called him on the phone early in the morning in Bulgaria when I knew he would be awake, sitting in his chair, reading Lenin. Yet I started having bad dreams again.

I saw the car crash over and over in my head and woke up with a scream, covered in cold sweat. Then when I fell asleep again, Grandma would come and sit down on my bed and caress my forehead the way she had done when I had been sick with fever. "Your grandpa's dying," she warned me. "We are expecting him soon. And please, my dear, next time you talk to him, ask him to stop reading me Lenin at my grave."

Grandpa wanted to know more about the Americans. I told him he should read a book, then.

"I can't analyze people," I said. "I make wrong judgments."

"Why do you study psychology then?"

So I tried to explain what Americans were like. "They are different," I wrote in one of my letters. "They don't think of what they'll eat tomorrow, whether there will be food on the table. These," I wrote, "are solved problems for them. Like walking. Walking, we studied, is a solved problem. Evolution has taken care of it and it is no longer necessary for anyone to figure out how to walk. All it takes is a year for the brain to wire itself properly, and then boom! Off you go on your feet. People here have different problems. They worry about different things."

"What do you mean?" Grandpa asked on the phone, after he had read my letter.

"Take this girl I know," I said, "Samantha. She's been depressed for a month now. Her father gave her a BMW with a stick shift instead of automatic transmission. She cried. 'I can't drive it,' she said. 'It's awful. I want to die.'"

"It *is* awful," Grandpa said.

"But then there are other people with problems more similar to ours. My roommate's parents are getting divorced. They've been together for twenty years, and one morning they just decided they didn't want to wake up in the same bed anymore."

Grandpa coughed on the other side.

"Your parents died on this day," he said. "Seven years ago."

"I know," I said. "I have it marked on my calendar."

My parents died one week before I turned twelve. They were going to give me a bicycle as a present — I saw it hidden in the basement. A white BMX with a leather seat and dynamo-powered headlights.

Mom had already written the card and attached the envelope to the bike. "To our dearest boy," the card read. "When you fall and bruise your knees, think of us."

I remember the night they died as if it just happened. It was 2:30 in the morning when the phone rang. Dad picked it up and talked for a while. I woke up from his worried whispering, then drifted away, then woke up again. Mom was sitting by him on the sofa, holding his hand, and they were both washed in blue darkness, looking like two shadows of flesh.

"Thank you, doctor," Dad said at last. "We are on our way."

Mom came to my bed and sat down. I held my eyes closed, shivering with fear.

"*Mishe,*" she said, "little mouse, wake up."

"Is it Grandpa?" I asked. She leaned forward and kissed me on the forehead.

"He's had a stroke," she said, "but he has stabilized and they've taken him to the village hospital."

"Will he die?"

Dad came and gave me a kiss. His eyes glistened in the light from the streetlamps. He picked me up, wrapped me in my blanket, and carried me out the door. When we got on the highway it was four o'clock. One hour later they were dead.

All I remember is bright truck lights coming our way. The car spinning out of the road. The hit. Then the dark.

I woke up with cables on my chest.

"Mom?" I said. "Dad?"

"*Sinko,*" I heard. "My son, you woke up!"

Then Grandpa appeared from somewhere. He stood before me, crying.

"You woke up," he repeated, "you woke up."

Doctors came. And nurses. They were all excited. They were all very happy to see me awake.

"Grandpa, where is Mom?"

"*Sinko,*" he kept repeating, "you woke up!"

He took me to the graveyard a week later, to see the fresh grave. The earth was piled into a mound, dark and wet. My parents had been buried in the same grave, and next to them lay Grandma.

"Grandpa, you are lying," I said. I stared at my parents' names on the wooden crosses. "You're a liar."

He rested a hand on my shoulder.

"I'm glad you missed the funeral."

"Liar," I whispered. I kneeled and grabbed earth in my fist. I turned around and threw it at his face. Then I hugged him.

My sophomore year in college, during one of our long-distance phone calls, Grandpa asked me, "What do you know about eBay?"

"What?"

"eBay. Have you heard of it?"

"Yeah, I have. I mean, sure, but why?"

"Comrade Hassan has done research," Grandpa explained, "and found something interesting. It seems like someone is selling Lenin's body on eBay."

"Lenin on eBay." I let that soak in for a moment. "Grandpa, are you crazy?"

"That's irrelevant," he said. "The party needs your help now. We want you to help us bring Vladimir Ilyich to Leningrad."

"You are kidding me. You can't possibly . . ."

"The seller requires a credit card," Grandpa said. "Visa, MasterCard, or Discover. We have none of these in the village. That's why we need you. Do your research. Call me tomorrow."

I sat at my computer and opened the Internet browser. Then I closed it. Then I opened it again and browsed to eBay. I typed "Lenin" and hit the search spot: 430 items. Postcards, badges, T-shirts. Did Grandpa mean a bust? Or a hat? Or maybe a fake beard? And just when I was getting ready to close the window, I saw it: "CCCP Creator Lenin. Mint Condition. *Serious bidders only!*"

I followed the link and waited for the page to load. I read the content aloud: "You are bidding for the body of Vladimir Ilyich Lenin. The body is in excellent condition and comes with a refrigerating coffin that works on both American and European current. *Serious bidders only.* Pay immediately after purchase."

The item location was marked as Moscow. The shipment was worldwide. I checked the seller but found he had no previous feedback and no other auctions. Clearly this was a scam. I returned to the auction page and read it a few more times. No one had bid so far, and the starting price was set at $1.99 (reserve not met). I typed in a bid of $5 and hit the button to post it. The page disappeared, then a new page loaded. "Reserve met," the page read. "Congratulations, CommunistDupe_1944. You bought Lenin."

I called Grandpa on the following day.

"I wasted ten dollars for your stupid Lenin," I said. "I hope you're happy."

"Grandson!"

"Yes, I bought him. Five dollars for the body and five for shipping. I filled in your village address."

"We must build a mausoleum then!" Grandpa said. "We have no time. We must start building right away!"

"Grandpa, this is a scam. It is a joke. No one has the right to sell or buy Lenin."

"We must build."

"Do you even hear what I'm saying?"

"A mausoleum. On the square. And we must paint. Yes, paint the square red."

"Grandpa, stop it!"

He paused, then said, "Listen, Grandson. I'm tired of cleaning graves. I'm having terrible headaches lately. My right hand goes numb and just drops. I can feel pinches and needles in my leg. So, please, please, please," he said, "don't tell me to stop. I would like to think I could buy Lenin if I wanted, or build a mausoleum or a pyramid or even a sphinx."

"I'm sorry, Grandpa."

"Grandson," he said, "are you still angry with me? Do you still think it was my fault your parents died?"

I said it was his fault, on my sixteenth birthday when he gave me a bike as a present. We were in our apartment, celebrating. He had bought a cake and candles and balloons, and while I was unwrapping the gift he was singing and clapping his hands.

"It's a BMX," he said, and winked at me. "I used connections to get it."

Then I snapped.

"It's all your fault!" I shouted. "Dad was so worried about you and your stupid stroke that he crashed the car."

I knocked the cake to the floor. I got up and tore to pieces every picture of our happy family before the incident. I broke dishes and glasses.

"I wish *you* had died!" I shouted. "I wish you had died right there in your sleep."

"Sinko," he said.

"Don't call me *sinko*!" I shouted. "Your son is dead. They are both dead because of you."

On the following day Grandpa left the city. He went back to Leningrad, once more joined the local underground party, and resumed his daily visits to the graveyard with a volume of Lenin's works under his arm. I never heard him call me *sinko* again. For one year we did not speak. Then I phoned to tell him I was leaving for America.

"My grandson, a capitalist," he said. "After all I've been through."

Five months after we bought Lenin, during one of our conversations, Grandpa told me.

"He's here," he said. "The leader of nations came to Leningrad."

"You're funny, Grandpa."

"We received the body yesterday. A refrigerating coffin and everything. We are almost finished with the mausoleum, so in the meanwhile Lenin is staying at home. We put him in your room. Do you mind?"

"I mind that you are crazy."

"I thought so," Grandpa said.

"You need to see a doctor. Why don't you see a doctor?"

"What good will that do? The headache is always with me. The pinches in my hand. And I have bad dreams again — about the people in the dugout."

"What about them?"

"Well, do you remember how I lived in the dugout, with fifteen more people and two pregnant women and a hungry goat, and how when I was starving and desperate I found the courage finally to go down to the village?"

"Yes, I remember."

"Three years later I went back to that same place in the forest. To the dugout. I wanted to see it once again, now with my free eyes. I cleared the entrance, climbed down the ladder, and I saw them.

The fifteen men and the two women and the hungry goat. All dead."

"In the dugout?"

"In the dugout. No one told them the war was over. No one told them they could come out. They had not the courage to walk out themselves, and so they starved to death."

I sat in my chair, held the receiver, and thought of these men and women and the goat and how no one had told them they were free. I thought of Lenin, whom we had bought over the Internet and whose body was now being refrigerated in my room. And so I burst out laughing. And when I started laughing Grandpa started laughing, and we laughed for a long, very long time until our voices mixed along the wire and at the end sounded like one.

On the following day I called again, but no one picked up the phone. I called again a few hours later. And a few hours after that. No one answered. For two weeks I called every day. My hand was sore from gripping the receiver. I sat in my chair and listened to the silence at the other end of the line, interrupted regularly by the long, monotonous beeps. They sounded like a pulse in my head — a pulse very slow and tired, bidding me goodbye. I cried a lot. I paced the room, holding the receiver, calling. I knew no other numbers — just Grandpa's.

The other day, I got a letter in the mail. I did not open it for a very long time. I had no strength. I cried for two days and then finally made myself take out the letter.

"Dear Grandson," it said. "I am dead now. I instructed Comrade Penkov to send this in the mail the day my heart would stop beating. He is a good man. He would pay for the shipping expenses.

"Grandson, we've had a hard life, you and I. We grew old, not with years, but with deaths. You are now one death older. Carry this baggage with dignity, and don't let it break your back. Always remember that you've suffered a lot more than many, but that others have suffered even greater pains. Be thankful for what you have. For what you've seen and for what you've been spared from seeing.

"They are easy prey, the crawfish," Grandpa went on. "You catch one, but the others don't run away. The others don't even know you are there until you pick them up, and even then they still have no idea. All this teaches us a lesson about human nature, Grandson, a lesson you should remember: Not every stick that falls in your pincers is worth pinching. Sometimes pinching the wrong stick may even take you to your end. So think carefully, my dear one, which stick to pinch and which to miss. Fight only the fights that are worthy; let all others pass you. And even when the stick hits hard, learn not to pinch it back.

"My dear one, forgive me."

And at the end Grandpa had written just four words.

"*Sinko,* I love you."

KAREN RUSSELL

Vampires in the Lemon Grove

FROM *Zoetrope: All-Story*

IN OCTOBER, the men and women of Sorrento harvest the *primofiore,* or "first fruit," the most succulent lemons; in March, the yellow *bianchetti* ripen, followed in June by the green *verdelli.* In every season you can find me sitting at my bench, watching them fall. Only one or two lemons tumble from the branches each hour, but I've been sitting here so long, their falling seems contiguous, close as raindrops. My wife has no patience for this sort of meditation. "Jesus Christ, Clyde," she says. "You need a hobby."

Most people mistake me for a small, kindly Italian grandfather, a *nonno.* I have an old *nonno*'s coloring, the dark walnut stain peculiar to southern Italians, a tan that won't fade until I die (which I never will). I wear a neat periwinkle shirt, a canvas sunhat, black suspenders that sag at my chest. My loafers are battered but always polished. The few visitors to the lemon grove who notice me smile blankly into my raisin face and catch the whiff of some sort of tragedy; they whisper that I am a widower, or an old man who has survived his children. They never guess that I am a vampire.

Santa Francesca's Lemon Grove, where I spend my days and nights, was part of a Jesuit convent in the 1800s. Now it's privately owned by the Alberti family, the prices are excessive, and the locals know to buy their lemons elsewhere. In summers a teenage girl named Fila mans a wooden stall at the back of the grove. She's painfully thin, with heavy, black bangs. I can tell by the careful way she saves the best lemons for me, slyly kicking them under my bench, that she knows I am a monster. Sometimes she'll smile vacantly in my direction, but she never gives me any trouble. And because of her benevolent indifference to me, I feel a swell of love for the girl.

Fila makes the lemonade and monitors the hot dog machine, watching the meat rotate on wire spigots. I'm fascinated by this machine. The Italian name for it translates as "carousel of beef." Who would have guessed at such a device two hundred years ago? Back then we were all preoccupied with visions of apocalypse; Santa Francesca, the foundress of this very grove, gouged out her eyes while dictating premonitions of fire. What a shame, I often think, that she foresaw only the end times, never hot dogs.

A sign posted just outside the grove reads:

CIGARETTE PIE
HEAT DOGS
GRANITE DRINKS
SANTA FRANCESCA'S LIMONATA —
THE MOST REFRISHING DRANK ON THE PLENET!!

Every day, tourists from Wales and Germany and America are ferried over from cruise ships to the base of these cliffs. They ride the funicular up here to visit the grove, to eat "heat dogs" with speckly brown mustard and sip lemon ices. They snap photographs of the Alberti brothers, Benny and Luciano, teenage twins who cling to the trees' wooden supports and make a grudging show of harvesting lemons, who spear each other with trowels and refer to the tourist women as "vaginas" in Italian slang. "*Buona sera,* vaginas!" they cry from the trees. I think the tourists are getting stupider. None of them speak Italian anymore, and these new women seem deaf to aggression. Often I fantasize about flashing my fangs at the brothers, just to keep them in line.

As I said, the tourists usually ignore me; perhaps it's the dominoes. A few years back, I bought a battered red set from Benny, a prop piece, and this makes me invisible, sufficiently banal to be hidden in plain sight. I have no real interest in the game; I mostly stack the pieces into little houses and corrals.

At sunset, the tourists all around begin to shout. "Look! Up there!" It's time for the path of *I Pipistrelli Impazziti* — the descent of the bats.

They flow from cliffs that glow like pale chalk, expelled from caves seemingly in billions. Their drop is steep and vertical, a black hail. Sometimes a change in weather sucks a bat beyond the lemon trees and into the turquoise sea. It's three hundred feet to the lemon grove, six hundred feet to the churning foam of the Tyrrhenian. At the precipice, they soar upward and crash around the green tops of the trees.

"Oh!" the tourists shriek, delighted, ducking their heads.

Up close, the bats' spread wings are an alien membrane — fragile, like something internal flipped out. The waning sun washes their bodies a dusky red. They have wrinkled black faces, these bats, tiny, like gargoyles or angry grandfathers. They have teeth like mine.

Tonight, one of the tourists, a Texan lady with a big strawberry-red updo, has successfully captured a bat in her hair, simultaneously crying real tears and howling: "TAKE THE GODDAMN PICTURE, Sarah!"

I stare ahead at a fixed point above the trees and light a cigarette. My bent spine goes rigid. Mortal terror always trips some old wire that leaves me sad and irritable. It will be whole minutes now before everybody stops screaming.

The moon is a muted shade of orange. Twin discs of light burn in the sky and the sea. I scan the darker indents in the skyline, the cloudless spots that I know to be caves. I check my watch again. It's eight o'clock, and all the bats have disappeared into the interior branches. Where is Magreb? My fangs are throbbing, but I won't start without her.

I once pictured time as a black magnifying glass and myself as a microscopic, flightless insect trapped in that circle of night. But then Magreb came along, and eternity ceased to frighten me. Suddenly each moment followed its antecedent in a neat chain, moments we filled with each other.

I watch a single bat falling from the cliffs, dropping like a stone: headfirst, motionless, dizzying to witness.

Pull up.

I close my eyes. I press my palms flat against the picnic table and tense the muscles of my neck.

Pull UP. I tense up until my temples pulse, until little black and red stars flutter behind my eyelids.

"You can look now."

Magreb is sitting on the bench, blinking her bright pumpkin

eyes. "You weren't even *watching.* If you saw me coming down, you'd know you have nothing to worry about." I try to smile at her and find I can't. My own eyes feel like ice cubes.

"It's stupid to go so fast." I don't look at her. "That easterly could knock you over the rocks."

"Don't be ridiculous. I'm an excellent flier."

She's right. Magreb can shape-shift midair, much more smoothly than I ever could. Even back in the 1850s when I used to transmute into a bat two, three times a night, my metamorphosis was a shy, halting process.

"Look!" she says, triumphant, mocking. "You're still trembling!"

I look down at my hands, angry to realize it's true.

Magreb roots through the tall, black blades of grass. "It's late, Clyde; where's my lemon?"

I pluck a soft, round lemon from the grass, a summer moon, and hand it to her. The *verdelli* I have chosen is perfect, flawless. She looks at it with distaste and makes a big show of brushing off a marching ribbon of ants.

"A toast!" I say.

"A toast," Magreb replies, with the rote enthusiasm of a Christian saying grace. We lift the lemons and swing them to our faces. We plunge our fangs, piercing the skin, and emit a long, united hiss: *"Aaah!"*

Over the years, Magreb and I have tried everything — fangs in apples, fangs in rubber balls. We have lived everywhere: Tunis, Laos, Cincinnati, Salamanca. We spent our honeymoon hopping continents, hunting liquid chimeras: mint tea in Fez, coconut slurries in Oahu, jet black coffee in Bogotá, jackal's milk in Dakar, cherry Coke floats in rural Alabama, a thousand beverages that purported to have magical quenching properties. We went thirsty in every region of the globe before finding our oasis here, in the blue boot of Italy, at this dead nun's lemonade stand. It's only these lemons that give us any relief.

When we first landed in Sorrento I was skeptical. The pitcher of lemonade we ordered looked cloudy and adulterated. Sugar clumped at the bottom. I took a gulp, and a whole small lemon lodged in my mouth; there is no word sufficiently lovely for the first taste, the first feeling of my fangs in that lemon. It was bracingly sour, with a delicate hint of ocean salt. After an initial prickling — a sort of chemical effervescence along my gums — a soothing blankness traveled from the tip of each fang to my fevered brain. These lemons are a vampire's analgesic. If you have been thirsty for a long time, if you have been suffering, then the absence of those two feelings — however brief — becomes a kind of heaven. I breathed deeply through my nostrils. My throbbing fangs were still.

By daybreak, the numbness had begun to wear off. The lemons relieve our thirst without ending it, like a drink we can hold in our mouths but never swallow. Eventually the original hunger returns. I have tried to be very good, very correct and conscientious about not confusing this original hunger with the thing I feel for Magreb.

I can't joke about my early years on the blood, can't even think about them without guilt and acidic embarrassment. Unlike Magreb, who has never had a sip of the stuff, I listened to the village gossips and believed every rumor, internalized every report of corrupted bodies and boiled blood. Vampires were the favorite undead of the Enlightenment, and as a young boy I aped the diction and mannerisms I read about in books: Vlad the Impaler, Count Heinrich the Despoiler, Goethe's blood-sucking bride of Corinth. I eavesdropped on the terrified prayers of an old woman in a cemetery, begging God to protect her from . . . me. I felt a dislocation then, a spreading numbness, as if I were invisible or already dead. After that, I did only what the stories suggested, beginning with that old woman's blood. I slept in coffins, in black cedar boxes, and woke every night with a fierce headache. I was famished, perennially dizzy. I had unspeakable dreams about the sun.

In practice I was no suave viscount, just a teenager in a red velvet cape, awkward and voracious. I wanted to touch the edges of my life. The same instinct, I think, that inspires young mortals to flip tractors and enlist in foreign wars. One night I skulked into a late Mass with some vague plan to defeat eternity. At the back of the nave, I tossed my mousy curls, rolled my eyes heavenward, and then plunged my entire arm into the bronze pail of holy water. Death would be painful, probably, but I didn't care about pain. I wanted to overturn my sentence. It was working; I could feel the burn beginning to spread. Actually, it was more like an itch, but I was sure the burning would start any second. I slid into a pew, snug in my misery, and waited for my body to turn to ash.

By sunrise, I'd developed a rash between my eyebrows, a little late-flowering acne, but was otherwise fine, and I understood I truly was immortal. At that moment I yielded all discrimination; I bit anyone kind or slow enough to let me get close: men, women, even some older boys and girls. The littlest children I left alone, very proud at the time of this one scruple. I'd read stories about Hungarian *vampirs* who drank the blood of orphan girls and mentioned this to Magreb early on, hoping to impress her with my decency. Not *children*! she wept. She wept for a day and a half.

Our first date was in Cementerio de Colón, if I can call a chance meeting between headstones a date. I had been stalking her, following her swishing hips as she took a shortcut through the cemetery grass. She wore her hair in a low, snaky braid that was coming unraveled. When I was near enough to touch her trailing ribbon, she whipped around. "Are you following me?" she asked, annoyed, not scared. She regarded my face with the contempt of a woman confronting the town drunk. "Oh," she said, "your teeth . . ."

And then she grinned. Magreb was the first and only other vampire I'd ever met. We bared our fangs over a tombstone and recognized each other. There is a loneliness that must be particular to monsters, I think, the feeling that each is the only child of a species. And now that loneliness was over.

Our first date lasted all night. Magreb's talk seemed to lunge forward like a train without a conductor; I suspect even she didn't know what she was saying. I certainly wasn't paying attention, staring dopily at her fangs, and then I heard her ask: "So, when did you figure out that the blood does nothing?"

At the time of this conversation, I was edging on 130. I had never gone a day since early childhood without drinking several pints of blood. *The blood does nothing?* My forehead burned and burned.

"Didn't you think it suspicious that you had a heartbeat?" she asked me. "That you had a reflection in water?"

When I didn't answer, Magreb went on. "Every time I saw my own face in a mirror, I knew I wasn't any of those ridiculous things, a blood-sucker, a *sanguina*. You know?"

"Sure," I said, nodding. For me, mirrors had the opposite effect: I saw a mouth ringed in black blood. I saw the pale son of the villagers' fears.

Those initial days with Magreb nearly undid me. At first my euphoria was sharp and blinding, all my thoughts spooling into a single blue thread of relief — *The blood does nothing! I don't have to drink the blood!* — but when that subsided, I found I had nothing left. If we didn't have to drink the blood, then what on earth were these fangs for?

Sometimes I think she preferred me then: I was like her own child, raw and amazed. We smashed my coffin with an ax and spent the night at a hotel. I lay there wide-eyed in the big bed, my heart thudding like a fishtail against the floor of a boat.

"You're really sure?" I whispered to her. "I don't have to sleep in a coffin? I don't have to sleep through the day?" She had already drifted off.

A few months later, she suggested a picnic.

"But the sun."

Magreb shook her head. "You poor thing, believing all that garbage."

By this time we'd found a dirt cellar in which to live in Western Australia, where the sun burned through the clouds like dining lace. That sun ate lakes, rising out of dead volcanoes at dawn, triple the size of a harvest moon and skull-white, a grass-scorcher. Go ahead, try to walk into that sun when you've been told your bones are tinder.

I stared at the warped planks of the trapdoor above us, the copper ladder that led rung by rung to the bright world beyond. Time fell away from me and I was a child again, afraid, afraid. Magreb rested her hand on the small of my back. "You can do it," she said, nudging me gently. I took a deep breath and hunched my shoulders, my scalp grazing the cellar door, my hair soaked through with sweat. I focused my thoughts to still the tremors, lest my fangs slice the inside of my mouth, and turned my face away from Magreb.

"Go on."

I pushed up and felt the wood give way. Light exploded through the cellar. My pupils shrank to dots.

Outside, the whole world was on fire. Mute explosions rocked the scrubby forest, motes of light burning like silent rockets. The sun fell through the eucalyptus and Australian pines in bright red bars. I pulled myself out onto my belly, balled up in the soil, and screamed for mercy until I'd exhausted myself. Then I opened one watery eye and took a long look around. The sun wasn't fatal! It was just uncomfortable, making my eyes itch and water and inducing a sneezing attack.

After that, and for the whole of our next thirty years together, I watched the auroral colors and waited to feel anything but terror. Fingers of light spread across the gray sea toward me, and I couldn't see these colors as beautiful. The sky I lived under was a hideous, lethal mix of orange and pink, a physical deformity. By the 1950s we were living in a Cincinnati suburb; and as a day's first light hit the kitchen windows, I'd press my face against the linoleum and gibber my terror into the cracks.

"So-o," Magreb would say, "I can tell you're not a morning person." Then she'd sit on the porch swing and rock with me, patting my hand.

"What's wrong, Clyde?"

I shook my head. This was a new sadness, difficult to express. My bloodlust was undiminished but now the blood wouldn't fix it.

"It never fixed it," Magreb reminded me, and I wished she would please stop talking.

That cluster of years was a very confusing period. Mostly I felt grateful, above-ground feelings. I was in love. For a vampire, my life was very normal. Instead of stalking prostitutes, I went on long bicycle rides with Magreb. We visited botanical gardens and rowed in boats. In a short time, my face had gone from lithium white to the color of milky coffee. Yet sometimes, especially at high noon, I'd study Magreb's face with a hot, illogical hatred, each pore opening up to swallow me. *You've ruined my life,* I'd think. To correct for her power over my mind I tried to fantasize about mortal women, their wild eyes and bare swan necks; I couldn't do it, not anymore — an eternity of vague female smiles eclipsed by Magreb's tiny razor fangs. Two gray tabs against her lower lip.

But like I said, I was mostly happy. I was making a kind of progress.

One night, children wearing necklaces of garlic bulbs arrived giggling at our door. It was Halloween; they were vampire hunters. The smell of garlic blasted through the mail slot, along with their voices: "Trick or treat!" In the old days, I would have cowered from these children. I would have run downstairs to barricade myself in my coffin. But that night, I pulled on an undershirt and opened the door. I stood in a square of green light in my boxer shorts hefting a bag of Tootsie Roll Pops, a small victory over the old fear.

"Mister, you okay?"

I blinked down at a little blond child and then saw that my two hands were shaking violently, soundlessly, like old friends wishing not to burden me with their troubles. I dropped the candies into the children's bags, thinking: *You small mortals don't realize the power of your stories.*

We were downing strawberry velvet cocktails on the Seine when something inside me changed. Thirty years. Eleven thousand dawns. That's how long it took for me to believe the sun wouldn't kill me.

"Want to go see a museum or something? We're in Paris, after all."

"Okay."

We walked over a busy pedestrian bridge in a flood of light, and my heart was in my throat. Without any discussion, I understood that Magreb was my wife.

Because I love her, my hunger pangs gradually mellowed into a comfortable despair. Sometimes I think of us as two holes cleaved together, two twin hungers. Our bellies growl at each other like companionable dogs. I love the sound, assuring me we're equals in our thirst. We bump our fangs and feel like we're coming up against the same hard truth.

Human marriages amuse me: the brevity of the commitment and all the ceremony that surrounds it, the calla lilies, the veiled mother-in-laws like lilac spiders, the tears and earnest toasts. Till death do us part! Easy. These mortal couples need only keep each other in sight for fifty, sixty years.

Often I wonder to what extent a mortal's love grows from the bedrock of his or her foreknowledge of death, love coiling like a green stem out of that blankness in a way I'll never quite understand. And lately I've been having a terrible thought: *Our love affair will end before the world does.*

One day, without any preamble, Magreb flew up to the caves. She called over her furry, muscled shoulder that she just wanted to sleep for a while.

"What? Wait! What's wrong?"

I'd caught her midshift, halfway between a wife and a bat.

"Don't be so sensitive, Clyde! I'm just tired of this century, so very tired, maybe it's the heat? I think I need a little rest . . ."

I assumed this was an experiment, like my cape, an old habit to which she was returning; and from the clumsy, ambivalent way she crashed around on the wind I understood I was supposed to follow her. Well, too bad. Magreb likes to say she freed me, disabused me of the old stories; but I gave up more than I intended: I can't shudder myself out of this old man's body. I can't fly anymore.

Fila and I are alone. I press my dry lips together and shove dominoes around the table; they buckle like the cars of a tiny train.

"More lemonade, *nonno?*" She smiles. She leans from her waist and boldly touches my right fang, a thin string of hanging drool. "Looks like you're thirsty."

"Please." I gesture at the bench. "Have a seat."

Fila is seventeen now and has known about me for some time. She's toying with the idea of telling her boss, weighing the sentence within her like a bullet in a gun: *There is a vampire in our grove.*

"You don't believe me, signore Alberti?" she'll say, before taking him by the wrist and leading him to this bench, and I'll choose that moment to rise up and bite him in his hog-thick neck. "Right through his stupid tie!" she says with a grin.

But this is just idle fantasy, she assures me. Fila is content to let me alone. "You remind me of my *nonno,*" she says approvingly. "You look very Italian."

In fact, she wants to help me hide here. It gives her a warm feeling to do so, like helping her own fierce *nonno* do up the small buttons of his trousers, now too intricate a maneuver for his palsied hands. She worries about me too. And she should: lately I've gotten sloppy, incontinent about my secrets. I've stopped polishing my shoes; I let the tip of one fang hang over my pink lip. "You must be more careful," she reprimands. "There are tourists *everywhere.*"

I study her neck as she says this, her head rolling with the natural expressiveness of a girl. She checks to see if I am watching her collarbone, and I let her see that I am. I feel like a threat again.

Last night I went on a rampage. On my seventh lemon I found with a sort of drowsy despair that I couldn't stop. I crawled around on all fours, looking for the last *bianchetti*s in the dewy grass: soft with rot, mildewed, sun-shriveled, blackened. Lemon skin bulging with tiny cellophane-green worms. Dirt smells, rain smells, all swirled through with the tart sting of decay.

In the morning, Magreb steps around the wreckage and doesn't say a word.

"I came up with a new name," I say, hoping to distract her. "*Brandolino.* What do you think?"

I have spent the last several years trying to choose an Italian name, and every day that I remain Clyde feels like a defeat. Our names are relics of the places we've been. "Clyde" is a souvenir from the California Gold Rush. I was callow and blood-crazed back then, and I saw my echo in the freckly youths panning along the Sacramento River. I used the name as a kind of bait. It sounded innocuous, like someone a boy might get a malt beer with or follow into the woods.

Magreb chose her name in the Atlas Mountains for its etymology, the root word *ghuroob,* which means "to set" or "to be hidden." "That's what we're looking for," she tells me. "The setting place. Some final answer." She won't change her name until we find it.

She takes a lemon from her mouth, slides it down the length of her fangs, and places its shriveled core on the picnic table. When she finally speaks, her voice is so low, the words are almost unintelligible.

"The lemons aren't working, Clyde."

But the lemons have never worked. At best, they give us eight hours of peace. We aren't talking about the lemons.

"How long?"

"Longer than I've let on. I'm sorry."

"Well, maybe it's this crop. Those Alberti boys haven't been fertilizing properly, maybe the *primofiore* will turn out better."

Magreb fixes me with one fish-bright eye. "Clyde, I think it's time for us to go."

Wind blows the leaves apart. Lemons wink like a firmament of yellow stars, slowly ripening, and I can see the other, truer night behind them.

"Go where?" Our marriage, as I conceive it, is a commitment to starve together.

"We've been resting here for decades. I think it's time . . . what is that thing?"

I have been preparing a present for Magreb, for our anniversary, a "cave" of scavenged materials — newspaper and bottle glass and wooden beams from the lemon tree supports — so that she can sleep down here with me. I've smashed dozens of bottles of fruity beer to make stalactites. Looking at it now, though, I see the cave is very small. It looks like an umbrella mauled by a dog.

"That thing?" I say. "That's nothing. I think it's part of the hot dog machine."

"Jesus. Did it catch on fire?"

"Yes. The girl threw it out yesterday."

"Clyde." Magreb shakes her head. "We never meant to stay here forever, did we? That was never the plan."

"I didn't know we had a plan," I snap. "What if we've outlived our food supply? What if there's nothing left for us to find?"

"You don't really believe that."

"Why can't you just be grateful? Why can't you be happy and admit defeat? Look at what we've found here!" I grab a lemon and wave it in her face.

"Good night, Clyde."

I watch my wife fly up into the watery dawn, and again I feel the awful tension. In the flats of my feet, in my knobbed spine. Love has infected me with a muscular superstition that one body can do the work of another.

I consider taking the funicular, the ultimate degradation — worse than the dominoes, worse than an eternity of sucking cut lemons. All day I watch the cars ascend, and I'm reminded of those American fools who accompany their wives to the beach but refuse to wear bathing suits. I've seen them by the harbor, sulking in their trousers, panting through menthol cigarettes and pacing the dock while the women sea-bathe. They pretend they don't mind when sweat darkens the armpits of their suits. When their wives swim out and leave them. When their wives are just a splash in the distance.

Tickets for the funicular are twenty lire. I sit at the bench and count as the cars go by.

That evening, I take Magreb on a date. I haven't left the lemon grove in upwards of two years, and blood roars in my ears as I stand and clutch at her like an old man. We're going to the Thursday night show, an antique theater in a castle in the center of town. I want her to see that I'm happy to travel with her, so long as our destination is within walking distance.

A teenage usher in a vintage red jacket with puffed sleeves escorts us to our seats, his biceps manacled in clouds, threads loosening from the badge on his chest. I am jealous of the name there: GUGLIELMO.

The movie's title is already scrolling across the black screen: *Something Clandestine Is Happening in the Corn!*

Magreb snorts. "That's a pretty lousy name for a horror movie. It sounds like a student film."

"Here's your ticket," I say. "I didn't make the title up."

It's a vampire movie set in the Dust Bowl. Magreb expects a comedy, but the Dracula actor fills me with the sadness of an old photo album. An Okie has unwittingly fallen in love with the monster, whom she's mistaken for a rich European creditor eager to pay off the mortgage on her family's farm.

"That Okie," says Magreb, "is an idiot."

I turn my head miserably and there's Fila, sitting two rows in front of us with a greasy young man. Benny Alberti. Her white neck is bent to the left, Benny's lips affixed to it as she impassively sips a soda.

"Poor thing," Magreb whispers, indicating the pig-tailed actress. "She thinks he's going to save her."

Dracula shows his fangs, and the Okie flees through a cornfield. Cornstalks smack her face. "Help!" she screams to a sky full of crows. "He's not actually from Europe!"

There is no music, only the girl's breath and the *fwap-fwap-fwap* of the off-screen fan blades. Dracula's mouth hangs wide as a sewer grate. His cape is curiously still.

The movie picture is frozen. The *fwap*ing is emanating from the projection booth; it rises to a grinding *r-r-r,* followed by lyrical Italian cussing and silence and finally a tidal sigh. Magreb shifts in her seat.

"Let's wait," I say, seized with an empathy for these two still figures on the screen, mutely waiting for repair. "They'll fix it."

People begin to file out of the theater, first in twos and threes and then in droves.

"I'm tired, Clyde."

"Don't you want to know what happens?" My voice is more frantic than I intend it to be.

"I already know what happens."

"Don't you leave now, Magreb. I'm telling you, they're going to fix it. If you leave now, that's it for us, I'll never . . ."

Her voice is beautiful, like gravel underfoot: "I'm going to the caves."

I'm alone in the theater. When I turn to exit, the picture is still frozen, the Okie's blue dress floating over windless corn, Dracula's mouth a hole in his white greasepaint.

Outside I see Fila standing in a clot of her friends, lit by the marquee. These kids wear too much makeup, and clothes that move like colored oils. They all looked rained on. I scowl at them and they scowl back; and then Fila crosses to me.

"Hey, you." She grins, breathless, so very close to my face. "Are you stalking somebody?"

My throat tightens.

"Guys!" Her eyes gleam. "Guys, come over and meet the *vampire.*"

But the kids are gone.

"Well! Some friends," she says, then winks. "Leaving me alone, defenseless . . ."

"You want the old vampire to bite you, eh?" I hiss. "You want a story for your friends?"

Fila laughs. Her horror is a round, genuine thing, bouncing in both her black eyes. She smells like hard water and glycerin. The hum of her young life all around me makes it difficult to think. A bat filters my thoughts, opens its trembling lampshade wings.

Magreb. She'll want to hear about this. How ridiculous, at my age, to find myself down this alley with a young girl: Fila powdering her neck, doing her hair up with little temptress pins, yanking me behind this Dumpster. "Can you imagine," Magreb will laugh, "a teenager goading you to attack her! You're still a menace, Clyde."

I stare vacantly at a pale mole above the girl's collarbone. *Magreb,* I think again, and I smile; and the smile feels like a muzzle. It seems my hand has tightened on the girl's wrist, and I realize with surprise, as if from a great distance, that she is twisting away.

"Hey, *nonno,* come on now, what are you —"

The girl's head lolls against my shoulder like that of a sleepy child, then swings forward in a rag-doll circle. The starlight is white mercury compared to her blotted-out eyes. There's a dark stain on my periwinkle shirt, and one suspender has snapped. I sit Fila's body against the alley wall, watch it dim and stiffen. Spidery graffiti weaves over the brick behind her, and I scan for some answer contained there: GIOVANNA & FABIANO. VAFFANCULO! VAI IN CULO.

A scabby-furred creature, our only witness, arches its orange back against the Dumpster. If not for the lock I would ease the girl inside. I would climb in with her and let the red stench fill my nostrils, let the flies crawl into the red corners of my eyes. I am a monster again.

I ransack Fila's pockets and find the key to the funicular office, careful not to look at her face. Then I'm walking, running for the lemon grove. I jimmy my way into the control room and turn the silver key, relieved to hear the engine roar to life. Locked, locked, every car is locked, but then I find one with thick tape in *X*'s over a busted door. I dash after it and pull myself onto the cushion, quickly, because the cars are already moving. The box jounces and trembles. The chain pulls me into the heavens link by link.

My lips are soon chapped; I stare through a crack in the glass window. The box swings wildly in the wind. The sky is a deep blue vacuum. I can still smell the girl in the folds of my clothes.

The cave system is vaster than I expected; and with their grandfather faces tucked away, the bats are anonymous as stones. I walk beneath a chandelier of furry bodies, heartbeats wrapped in wings the color of rose petals or corn silk. Breath ripples through each of them, a tiny life in its translucent envelope.

"Magreb?"

Is she up here?

Has she left me?

(I will never find another vampire.)

I double back to the moonlit entrance, the funicular cars. When I find Magreb, I'll beg her to tell me what she dreams up here. I'll tell her my waking dreams in the lemon grove: the mortal men and women floating serenely by in balloons freighted with the ballast of their deaths. Millions of balloons ride over a wide ocean, lives darkening the sky. Death is a dense powder cinched inside tiny sandbags, and in the dream I am given to understand that instead of a sandbag I have Magreb.

I make the bats' descent in a cable car with no wings to spread, knocked around by the wind with a force that feels personal. I struggle to hold the door shut and look for the green speck of our grove.

The box is plunging now, far too quickly. It swings wide, and the igneous surface of the mountain fills the left window. The tufa shines like water, like a black, heat-bubbled river. For a disorienting moment I expect the rock to seep through the glass.

Each swing takes me higher than the last, a grinding pendulum that approaches a full revolution around the cable. I'm on my hands and knees on the car floor, seasick in the high air, pressing my face against the floor grate. I can see stars or boats burning there, and also a ribbon of white, a widening fissure. Air gushes through the cracks in the glass box.

What does Magreb see, if she can see? Is she waking from a nightmare to watch the line snap, the glass box plummet? From her inverted vantage, dangling from the roof of the cave, does the car seem to be sucked upward, rushing not toward the sea but to another sort of sky? To a black mouth open and foaming with stars?

I like to picture my wife like this: Magreb shuts her thin eyelids tighter. She digs her claws into the rock. Little clouds of dust rise around her toes as she swings upside-down. She feels something growing inside her, unstoppable as a dreadful suspicion. It is solid, this new thing, it is the opposite of hunger. She's emerging from a dream of distant thunder, rumbling and loose. Something has happened tonight that she thought impossible. In the morning, she will want to tell me about it.

GEORGE SAUNDERS

Puppy

FROM *The New Yorker*

TWICE ALREADY MARIE had pointed out the brilliance of the autumnal sun on the perfect field of corn, because the brilliance of the autumnal sun on the perfect field of corn put her in mind of a haunted house — not a haunted house she had ever actually seen but the mythical one that sometimes appeared in her mind (with adjacent graveyard and cat on a fence) whenever she saw the brilliance of the autumnal sun on the perfect etc. etc., and she wanted to make sure that, if the kids had a corresponding mythical haunted house that appeared in their minds whenever they saw the brilliance of the etc. etc., it would come up now, so that they could all experience it together, like friends, like college friends on a road trip, sans pot, ha ha ha!

But no. When she, a third time, said, "Wow, guys, check that out," Abbie said, "Okay, Mom, we get it, it's corn," and Josh said, "Not now, Mom, I'm Leavening my Loaves," which was fine with her; she had no problem with that, Noble Baker being preferable to Bra Stuffer, the game he'd asked for.

Well, who could say? Maybe they didn't even have any mythical vignettes in their heads. Or maybe the mythical vignettes they had in their heads were totally different from the ones she had in her head. Which was the beauty of it, because, after all, they were their own little people! You were just a caretaker. They didn't have to feel what *you* felt; they just had to be supported in feeling what *they* felt.

Still, wow, that cornfield was such a classic.

"Whenever I see a field like that, guys?" she said. "I somehow think of a haunted house!"

"Slicing Knife! Slicing Knife!" Josh shouted. "You nimrod machine! I chose that!"

Speaking of Halloween, she remembered last year, when their cornstalk column had tipped their shopping cart over. Gosh, how they'd laughed at that! Oh, family laughter was golden; she'd had none of that in her childhood, Dad being so dour and Mom so ashamed. If Mom and Dad's cart had tipped, Dad would have given the cart a despairing kick and Mom would have stridden purposefully away to reapply her lipstick, distancing herself from Dad, while she, Marie, would have nervously taken that horrid plastic army man she'd named Brady into her mouth.

Well, in this family, laughter was encouraged! Last night, when Josh had goosed her with his GameBoy, she'd shot a spray of toothpaste across the mirror and they'd all cracked up, rolling around on the floor with Goochie, and Josh had said, such nostalgia in his voice, "Mom, remember when Goochie was a puppy?" Which was when Abbie had burst into tears, because, being only five, she had no memory of Goochie as a puppy.

Hence this Family Mission. And as far as Robert? Oh, God bless Robert! There was a man. He would have no problem whatsoever with this Family Mission. She loved the way he had of saying "Ho HO!" whenever she brought home something new and unexpected.

"Ho HO!" Robert had said, coming home to find the iguana. "Ho HO!" he had said, coming home to find the ferret trying to get into the iguana cage. "We appear to be the happy operators of a menagerie!"

She loved him for his playfulness — you could bring home a hippo you'd put on a credit card (both the ferret and the iguana had gone on credit cards) and he'd just say "Ho HO!" and ask what the creature ate and what hours it slept and what the heck they were going to name the little bugger.

In the back seat, Josh made the *git-git-git* sound he always made when his Baker was in Baking Mode, trying to get his Loaves into the oven while fighting off various Hungry Denizens, such as a Fox with a distended stomach; such as a fey Robin that would improbably carry the Loaf away, speared on its beak, whenever it had succeeded in dropping a Clonking Rock on your Baker — all of which Marie had learned over the summer by studying the Noble Baker manual while Josh was asleep.

And it had helped, it really had. Josh was less withdrawn lately, and when she came up behind him now while he was playing and said, like, "Wow, honey, I didn't know you could do Pumpernickel," or "Sweetie, try Serrated Blade, it cuts quicker. Try it while doing Latch the Window," he would reach back with his noncontrolling hand and swat at her affectionately, and yesterday they'd shared a good laugh when he'd accidentally knocked off her glasses.

So her mother could go right ahead and claim that she was spoiling the kids. These were not spoiled kids. These were *well-loved* kids. At least she'd never left one of them standing in a blizzard for two hours after a junior-high dance. At least she'd never drunkenly snapped at one of them, "I hardly consider you college material." At least she'd never locked one of them in a closet (a closet!) while entertaining a literal ditchdigger in the parlor.

Oh, God, what a beautiful world! The autumn colors, that glinting river, that lead-colored cloud pointing down like a rounded arrow at that half-remodeled McDonald's standing above I-90 like a castle.

This time would be different, she was sure of it. The kids would care for this pet themselves, since a puppy wasn't scaly and didn't bite. ("Ho HO!" Robert had said the first time the iguana bit him. "I see you have an opinion on the matter!")

Thank you, Lord, she thought, as the Lexus flew through the cornfield. You have given me so much: struggles and the strength to overcome them; grace, and new chances every day to spread that grace around. And in her mind she sang out, as she sometimes did when feeling that the world was good and she had at last found her place in it, "Ho HO, ho HO!"

Callie pulled back the blind.

Yes. Awesome. It was still solved so *perfect.*

There was plenty for him to do back there. A yard could be a whole world, like her yard when she was a kid had been a whole world. From the three holes in her wood fence she'd been able to see Exxon (Hole One) and Accident Corner (Hole Two), and Hole Three was actually two holes that if you lined them up right, your eyes would do this weird crossing thing and you could play Oh My God I Am So High by staggering away with your eyes crossed, going "Peace, man, peace."

When Bo got older, it would be different. Then he'd need his freedom. But now he just needed not to get killed. Once they found him way over on Testament. And that was across I-90. How had he crossed I-90? She knew how. Darted. That's how he crossed streets. Once a total stranger called them from Hightown Plaza. Even Dr. Brile had said it: "Callie, this boy is going to end up dead if you don't get this under control. Is he taking the medication?"

Well, sometimes he was and sometimes he wasn't. The meds made him grind his teeth and his fist would suddenly pound down. He'd broken plates that way, and once a glass tabletop and got four stitches in his wrist.

Today he didn't need the medication because he was safe in the yard, because she'd fixed it so *perfect.* He was out there practicing pitching by filling his Yankees helmet with pebbles and winging them at the tree.

He looked up and saw her and did the thing where he blew a kiss.

Sweet little man.

Now all she had to worry about was the pup. She hoped the lady who'd called would actually show up. It was a nice pup. White, with brown around one eye. Cute. If the lady showed up, she'd definitely want it. And if she took it, Jimmy was off the hook. He'd hated doing it that time with the kittens. But if no one took the pup, he'd do it. He'd have to. Because his feeling was, when you said you were going to do a thing and didn't do it, that was how kids got into drugs. Plus, he'd been raised on a farm, or near a farm anyways, and anybody raised on a farm knew that you had to do what you had to do in terms of sick animals or extra animals — the pup being not sick, just extra.

That time with the kittens, Jessi and Mollie had called him a murderer, getting Bo all worked up, and Jimmy had yelled, "Look, you kids, I was raised on a farm and you got to do what you got to do!" Then he'd cried in bed, saying how the kittens had mewed in the bag all the way to the pond, and how he wished he'd never been raised on a farm, and she'd almost said, "You mean near a farm" (his dad had run a car wash outside Cortland), but sometimes when she got too smart-assed he would do this hard pinching thing on her arm while waltzing her around the bedroom, as if the place where he was pinching were like her handle, going, "I'm not sure I totally heard what you just said to me."

So, that time after the kittens, she'd only said, "Oh, honey, you did what you had to do."

And he'd said, "I guess I did, but it's sure not easy raising kids the right way."

And then, because she hadn't made his life harder by being a smart-ass, they had lain there making plans, like why not sell this place and move to Arizona and buy a car wash, why not buy the kids "Hooked on Phonics," why not plant tomatoes, and then they'd got to wrestling around and (she had no idea why she remembered this) he had done this thing of, while holding her close, bursting this sudden laugh/despair snort into her hair, like a sneeze, or like he was about to start crying.

Which had made her feel special, him trusting her with that.

So what she would love, for tonight? Was getting the pup sold, putting the kids to bed early, and then, Jimmy seeing her as all organized in terms of the pup, they could mess around and afterward lie there making plans, and he could do that laugh/snort thing in her hair again.

Why that laugh/snort meant so much to her she had no freaking idea. It was just one of the weird things about the Wonder That Was Her, ha ha ha.

Outside, Bo hopped to his feet, suddenly curious, because (here we go) the lady who'd called had just pulled up?

Yep, and in a nice car too, which meant too bad she'd put "Cheap" in the ad.

Abbie squealed, "I love it, Mommy, I want it!" as the puppy looked up dimly from its shoebox and the lady of the house went trudging away and one-two-three-four plucked up four *dog turds* from the rug.

Well, wow, what a super field trip for the kids, Marie thought, ha ha (the filth, the mildew smell, the dry aquarium holding the single encyclopedia volume, the pasta pot on the bookshelf with an inflatable candy cane inexplicably sticking out of it), and although some might have been disgusted (by the spare tire *on the dining-room table,* by the way the glum mother dog, the presumed in-house pooper, was dragging its rear over the pile of clothing in the corner, in a sitting position, splay-legged, a moronic look of pleasure on her face), Marie realized (resisting the urge to rush to the sink and wash her hands, in part because the sink had *a basketball in it*) that what this really was was deeply sad.

Please do not touch anything, please do not touch, she said to Josh and

Abbie, but just in her head, wanting to give the children a chance to observe her being democratic and accepting, and afterward they could all wash up at the half-remodeled McDonald's, as long as they just please please kept their hands out of their mouths, and God forbid they should rub their eyes.

The phone rang, and the lady of the house plodded into the kitchen, placing the daintily held, paper-towel-wrapped turds *on the counter.*

"Mommy, I want it," Abbie said.

"I will definitely walk him like twice a day," Josh said.

"Don't say 'like,'" Marie said.

"I will definitely walk him twice a day," Josh said.

Okay, then, all right, they would adopt a white-trash dog. Ha ha. They could name it Zeke, buy it a little corncob pipe and a straw hat. She imagined the puppy, having crapped on the rug, looking up at her, going, *Cain't hep it.* But no. Had she come from a perfect place? Everything was transmutable. She imagined the puppy grown up, entertaining some friends, speaking to them in a British accent: *My family of origin was, um, rather not, shall we say, of the most respectable . . .*

Ha ha, wow, the mind was amazing, always cranking out these —

Marie stepped to the window and, anthropologically pulling the blind aside, was shocked, so shocked that she dropped the blind and shook her head, as if trying to wake herself, shocked to see a young boy, just a few years younger than Josh, harnessed and chained to a tree, via some sort of doohickey by which — she pulled the blind back again, sure she could not have seen what she thought she had —

When the boy ran, the chain spooled out. He was running now, looking back at her, showing off. When he reached the end of the chain, it jerked and he dropped as if shot.

He rose to a sitting position, railed against the chain, whipped it back and forth, crawled to a bowl of water, and, lifting it to his lips, took a drink: a drink *from a dog's bowl.*

Josh joined her at the window. She let him look. He should know that the world was not all lessons and iguanas and Nintendo. It was also this muddy simple boy tethered like an animal.

She remembered coming out of the closet to find her mother's scattered lingerie and the ditchdigger's metal hanger full of orange flags. She remembered waiting outside the junior high in the bitter cold, the snow falling harder, as she counted over and over to two hundred, promising herself each time that when she reached two hundred she would begin the long walk back —

God, she would have killed for just one righteous adult to confront her mother, shake her, and say, "You idiot, this is your child, your child you're —"

"So what were you guys thinking of naming him?" the woman said, coming out of the kitchen.

The cruelty and ignorance just radiated from her fat face, with its little smear of lipstick.

"I'm afraid we won't be taking him after all," Marie said coldly.

Such an uproar from Abbie! But Josh — she would have to praise him later, maybe buy him the Italian Loaves Expansion Pak — hissed something to Abbie, and then they were moving out through the trashed kitchen (past some kind of *crankshaft* on a cookie sheet, past a partial red pepper afloat *in a can of green paint*) while the lady of the house scuttled after them, saying, wait, wait, they could have it for free, please take it — she really wanted them to have it.

No, Marie said, it would not be possible for them to take it at this time, her feeling being that one really shouldn't possess something if one wasn't up to properly caring for it.

"Oh," the woman said, slumping in the doorway, the scrambling pup on one shoulder.

Out in the Lexus, Abbie began to cry softly, saying, "Really, that was the perfect pup for me."

And it was a nice pup, but Marie was not going to contribute to a situation like this in even the smallest way.

Simply was not going to do it.

The boy came to the fence. If only she could have said to him, with a single look, *Life will not necessarily always be like this. Your life could suddenly blossom into something wonderful. It can happen. It happened to me.*

But secret looks, looks that conveyed a world of meaning with their subtle blah blah blah — that was all bullshit. What was not bullshit was a call to Child Welfare, where she knew Linda Berling, a very no-nonsense lady who would snatch this poor kid away so fast it would make that fat mother's thick head spin.

*

Callie shouted, "Bo, back in a sec!" and, swiping the corn out of the way with her non-pup arm, walked until there was nothing but corn and sky.

It was so small, it didn't move when she set it down, just sniffed and tumped over.

Well, what did it matter, drowned in a bag or starved in the corn? This way Jimmy wouldn't have to do it. He had enough to worry about. The boy she'd first met with hair to his waist was now this old man shrunk with worry. As far as the money, she had sixty hidden away. She'd give him twenty of that and go, "The people who bought the pup were super-nice."

Don't look back, don't look back, she said in her head as she raced away through the corn.

Then she was walking along Teallback Road like a sportwalker, like some lady who walked every night to get slim, except that she was nowhere near slim, she knew that, and she also knew that when sportwalking you did not wear jeans and unlaced hiking boots. Ha ha! She wasn't stupid. She just made bad choices. She remembered Sister Carol saying, "Callie, you are bright enough but you incline toward that which does not benefit you." *Yep, well, Sister, you got that right,* she said to the nun in her mind. But what the hell. What the heck. When things got easier moneywise, she'd get some decent tennis shoes and start walking and get slim. And start night school. Slimmer. Maybe medical technology. She was never going to be really slim. But Jimmy liked her the way she was, and she liked him the way he was, which maybe that's what love was, liking someone how he was and doing things to help him get even better.

Like right now she was helping Jimmy by making his life easier by killing something so he — no. All she was doing was walking, walking away from —

Pushing the words *killing puppy* out of her head, she put in her head the words *beautiful sunny day wow I'm loving this beautiful sunny day so much* —

What had she just said? That had been good. *Love was liking someone how he was and doing things to help him get better.*

Like Bo wasn't perfect, but she loved him how he was and tried to help him get better. If they could keep him safe, maybe he'd mellow out as he got older. If he mellowed out, maybe he could someday have a family. Like there he was now in the yard, sitting quietly, looking at flowers. Tapping with his bat, happy enough. He looked up, waved the bat at her, gave her that smile. Yesterday he'd been stuck in the house, all miserable. He'd ended the day screaming in bed, so frustrated. Today he was looking at flowers. Who was it that thought up that idea, the idea that had made today better than yesterday? Who loved him enough to think that up? Who loved him more than anyone else in the world loved him?

Her.

She did.

CHRISTINE SNEED

Quality of Life

FROM *New England Review*

MR. FULGER CALLED WHEN he wanted to see her and she obliged. For a while it was all very matter-of-fact, like a visit to the library, the reasons for going unequivocal. Regret rarely played a part. And there was little premeditation, as far as she could tell. Mr. Fulger, when not with her, resided on a plane that did not intersect her own, and after her initial period of infatuation had worn off, she had ceased to hope they might meet by chance. She had tried for a few weeks to find where he lived and worked, but he had remained unreachable, her attempts at tracing him fruitless, and soon she began to feel ridiculous for having spent the effort searching for him — in their tremendous haystack of a city, he was smaller than a needle. In any case, she did not know what she had expected — certainly not a marriage proposal, nor more permanent terms for their involvement. It seemed to her that primarily she had wanted acknowledgment of his steadfast desire for her, however infrequently this desire was manifested. At times she saw him twice a week; others, twice a month. Even when she was dating another man — a man closer to her age who sought her out in earnest, publicly and otherwise — she answered Mr. Fulger's phone calls with a yes that triggered the naming of a meeting place, almost always a restaurant or hotel close to the center of the city, rarely the same one.

Mr. Fulger may not have been his real name. She had found only two in the phone book and neither, when she had called them, had turned out to be him. One had died very recently; the dead man's brother had answered her call, informing her tonelessly that there would not be a funeral service but donations could be sent to a Vietnam veterans' charity. The other had spoken in a high-pitched voice that had possibly been female. "No," this person replied when she asked to speak with Mr. Fulger, explaining that he was a tall man with salt-and-pepper hair. "I'm not the one you're looking for," replied the unpleasant voice. "Wrong number, miss."

After a while it became evident that Mr. Fulger traveled frequently overseas, and at times he had gifts for her that were not extravagant, though it was clear they had been chosen with care. One evening he had given her a necklace with a heavy tiger's-eye pendant; another night, a book from the Louvre. He knew that she could draw; she had once shown him a charcoal sketch of a mournful-looking elephant. She had meant it to be funny, but he had admired the drawing and asked to see others. Aside from her sister and a few close friends, he was the first person who had shown more than a solicitous interest in her talent. He told her that he might want to buy some of her work, and when he saw how this surprised her, he suggested almost harshly that she take herself more seriously. She did not tell him that hers was a family long-distrustful of artists, having been burdened with a legacy of schizophrenia on one side and depression on the other. Her accountant father and real-estate agent mother had objected strenuously to her choice to study graphic design in college, their tacit worry being that if she met with failure, she would end up in an institution as her great-grandfather and his brother had, or else do herself in as had two poet aunts years before, darkly inspired by Sylvia Plath and Anne Sexton. Whenever she heard these melodramatic stories told and retold by various family members over the years, Lyndsey remained dismissive, though in her private heart she wondered if theirs truly was a family more fragile than most.

She had met Mr. Fulger at a concert hall where she bartended during intermission, not long before she found a better job with a firm that designed theater programs. He had given her a tip much larger than the cost of his drink. He had also left his phone number, which had turned out to be an answering service. She had called him two weeks after meeting him, leaving her name and number, the concert hall's name as a reference. He had called back in less than three hours, inviting her to meet him for dinner that evening at an Italian restaurant on the top floor of a famously tall building.

"An old story," Mr. Fulger had said, sipping his wine. "The decrepit and shiftless enraptured by youthful beauty."

"You're hardly decrepit," she said, barely suppressing a nervous laugh.

He smiled. "But perhaps I'm shiftless."

"I wouldn't know about that."

"And that is my good fortune."

"I know nothing about you at all." She felt a shiver climb her spine. His dark eyes unnerved her; he was grander, his manner more daunting, than on the night they had met.

He nodded, not replying. She fidgeted with her napkin, not looking at him for several seconds. When she met his gaze again, his expression was mild, as if he were patiently listening to someone tell a dull joke.

Unable to match his silences during the hour and a half that they dined, she talked on and on about herself. He was possibly older than she had initially thought, somewhere in his late fifties instead of his late forties. She did not want to think that he might already have reached sixty. She was twenty-six. Her maternal grandfather was sixty-eight. Mr. Fulger seemed nothing like her grandfather, but she still did not want to imagine him her grandfather's peer.

She felt that in a way, however, she deserved what she got; if she were allowing herself to call strange men, the circumstances of their meeting would presumably be strange as well. This tendency to court real danger was new, something she would have to monitor.

The first night he did not suggest that they go to a hotel. He had instead taken her for a drink in a cavernous, smoky bar where a brass trio improvised discordant, rambling songs that would have impressed one of her former boyfriends, an unsuccessful pianist who violently detested his job as a receptionist at a popular radio station.

"Why do you live in this city?" Mr. Fulger asked.

She smiled, inexplicably embarrassed. "I went to college here. It's not a bad place to be."

"Will you stay forever?"

"Forever? I doubt it."

"Why stay at all if you know eventually you'll leave?"

"I wouldn't know where else to go right now."

"But at some point you'll meet someone who will."

Her face colored. "I don't know. Maybe."

"Of course, Lyndsey, of course." He smiled, swirling the red wine in his glass. "We often rely on others to make our most important decisions. There's no reason to be ashamed of this."

"But I don't think I've done that." She realized it might be a lie, though at that moment she did not want him to know it.

When they left the bar, he hailed two taxis, pressing money for her fare into her hand and brushing her cheek with his lips. She tried to refuse the money, but he turned abruptly away, disappearing into his taxi. He had given her too much, fifty dollars for a twelve-dollar fare.

It would become his habit to give her money, and after a month and a half of seeing him, she would stop trying to return it. His money, indisputably, made her life more easeful. Also, the promise of his spontaneous reappearance enriched it, the phone call that arrived like a herald of what one day her life might be, though not necessarily with him: no more tiny apartments, nor the hopscotch from one debt payment to the next, nor the envy she often felt for those who wore impeccable clothes. In the end, the invincible protection of a powerful man's money and esteem, perhaps also his love. It would have been very easy for her to do much worse.

Mr. Fulger, whose first name was Reginald, though Lyndsey rarely used it, had a small chicken-pox scar below his right eye that she found fascinating in its allusion to his unknowable childhood. There was another scar on his chest, in the cleft between his pectorals. It looked as if he had been shot — the flesh puckered in a starlike pattern — but he had smiled with amusement when she had asked if a bullet might have made the scar. A bullet so close to his heart that hadn't killed him? No, no. He had burned himself many years ago, falling asleep with a cigarette in his hand, the pain of the fire against his bare chest causing a frenzied awakening. "I was out of my head, as I have rarely been in my life," he said. "It's never an ideal situation. A person who can avoid such situations is the one whom other people naturally flock to. And then, of course, all manner of deceit and handshakes follow."

Once she had said, "Why do you give me money? You don't have to."

He had not liked the question. "It's my desire to do so" was his curt reply.

Their affair seemed as if it would go on indefinitely, until one of them died or was otherwise spirited away. Never did he fail to take her to bed after the first night he had invited her to a hotel, asking first if she wanted a view of the park, which she had, its lights distantly reassuring, as if to say she was incapable of making terrible choices and suffering their consequences. When she closed her eyes and felt her body's warmth blend with his, there was the scent of cinnamon and then of smoke, a smell she could not detect on him at any other time.

From the start it took her breath away — in part out of shame, in part astonishing pleasure. He was far from youthful, his body trim but slackening, his chest and stomach inspiring a twinge of sadness since it was clear that they had once been very firm and strong. How many women, she wanted to ask. How many have there been? It thrilled her to think that perhaps he had slept with a hundred or more. In sixty years, a hundred was not so many — if he had started young, that was only two or three a year. And not particularly unnatural since in all things, except for sexual intimacy, variety was a virtue in human enterprise — experience, the sampling of the unknown, was a state of grace and laudable industry.

She told no one of her involvement with Mr. Fulger. For long weeks she wouldn't see him and when at last he called, she was sometimes tempted to refuse his invitation, to say that she had other plans, which at times she did. The one night she had done this, however, he had not called again for twenty-three days. She had known him for several months and was seeing someone else she liked more than usual, but they did not yet have an understanding. Like Mr. Fulger, the new lover called her when he wanted to; he did not appear to feel beholden to her in any way.

In her head a running tally of the amount of money he had given her sometimes arrived without warning. After eleven months: $3,268, not including dinners, gifts, or hotel rooms. Because of him, she had been able to pay off one of her credit cards, and fly in her mother and sister for a long weekend, taking them to two plays. They had asked how she could afford it. A scratch-off lottery ticket, she had explained. Beginner's luck, since she had never before spent money on such a foolish thing.

When Mr. Fulger called during their visit, she had made an excuse to her mother and sister. "A sick friend. I'll be gone for three hours, maybe four. I'm sorry about this."

Late that evening, on her way out of the hotel room, Mr. Fulger had given her an inordinately thick envelope. She saw in the cab that he had filled it with singles and five-dollar bills. She felt the chilly heat of acute embarrassment, as if she were checking a payphone for stray nickels, passersby laughing at her petty avarice.

And when she returned to her apartment with whisker burn, her sister noticed. "A sick friend," she said knowingly. "I wish I had a sick friend."

"I'd like you to move out of this city," said Mr. Fulger after a year of amorous meetings. "I'll make the arrangements. You could be closer to your family if you'd like."

She stared at him. "I don't want to move."

"I know someone who could give you a much better job if you allow me to make the plans for your relocation. I don't see what you have to lose." He regarded her. "Unless there's someone here you'd miss too much?"

"Most of my friends are here."

"You'd make new ones." He paused. "You've said yourself that eventually you'll move away. There's no reason it couldn't be next month."

She shook her head. "No, thanks. Are you trying to get rid of me?"

"Of course not. I'd see you just as often."

"I don't want to move right now."

He sighed. "Think about it for a little while. Your salary would double."

She gazed at him in surprise. "What would I be doing?"

"The same thing you do here."

"I don't know if I should believe you."

"You can. Truthfully, you can. I'd arrange for a contract from your new employer."

"My God," she said, her stomach sickened.

He smiled. "It's not a bad suggestion, is it? Few would say you're making a foolish move."

"I haven't made up my mind yet."

"I'll check with you in the morning then."

No one else she knew lived like this. She was half enamored and half appalled with a man she knew nothing about, other than the intimacies of his body, his style of lovemaking, a few other superficial details. She knew his voice well enough to recognize it the moment he spoke a syllable into the phone; she knew some of the foods he favored (salmon over beef tenderloin, quail over chicken). She had never seen him drive, did not know if he could. She thought it odd that he carried no keys. All that he removed from his pockets before taking off his tailored slacks were a billfold with only two credit cards; a money clip with several crisp bills; a few coins; a linen handkerchief, usually pale blue. His address was never on any of the items he carried; she had checked several times, risking this indecency while he used the bathroom. The only time she had ever seen him angry was on a night when a young thief had tried to steal her small beaded purse from the back of her chair in a quiet, exclusive restaurant. Mr. Fulger had risen from the table, motioned to the maitre d', and the thief was then stopped at the door with Lyndsey's purse hidden under his overcoat.

"You might know the expression, 'If thy hand offends, cut it off,'" said Mr. Fulger, fuming at the craven, inappropriately handsome thief outside the restaurant while they waited with a security guard for the police.

She had wanted to leave, feeling the thief's fear and humiliation almost as her own, but Mr. Fulger had made her stay with him until the police arrived. "They'll need your testimony," he insisted, looking from her to the thief. "I'm sure this isn't his first offense. He knew what he was doing. But obviously so did I."

Certain words she did not allow herself to consider — concubine, whore, slut. Early on she had come to think of the money she took from him as a gift. If he had been her father, sending her money once a month because he worried about her well-being, few would have faulted her for keeping it. Mr. Fulger as well appeared to worry about her well-being. His money was meant to make her happy and on its face there could be nothing wrong with this. He insisted; he was forceful, persuasive, right about so many of the observations he made while in her company. She would have continued to see him even if he stopped paying her. At least, she considered this to be true since she could not imagine not seeing him. The sex was satisfying, often thrilling. The money was simply something extra. Many would have said, once their moralizing had been proven specious, that she was very lucky.

The new job was far away, on the coast most distant from the city where she currently lived. Instead of theater programs, she would be designing print ads for feature films. Her parents would be only a three-hour drive away if she agreed to accept Mr. Fulger's offer. The night of the offer she didn't sleep. She regarded the contents of her studio apartment, the new sofa, the sleek Chinese screen, the walnut hat stand that was purely ornamental. She sat in the window seat, looking down at the cars streaming toward and away from the city's center. She had grown to adore her small place, unsure if she could leave it so hastily, despite the promise of a doubled salary. She knew that Mr. Fulger had not lied to her; his offer, indisputably, was valid. But she did not know that she would accept it until he called her in the morning, at precisely eight o'clock. It seemed wrong to her, but she could not decide why. A terrifying thought arrived — perhaps this was the first stage of madness.

Though she also knew that always trying to be logical was equally mad. If a spectacular chance came along, it would be foolish not to take it.

"You should put in your notice today. The new office will expect you to be moved in and ready to start with them in four weeks."

She felt panic rise up, her heart stammering. "You said a month."

"Give or take a few days. Four weeks is hardly less than a month."

"I suppose you're right," she said, defeated. "But it's so soon."

"Maybe, but not unmanageable. You'll be fine."

After she hung up, she sat on her bed and sobbed. It was all so ridiculous. She had been handed an enviable new job and was now mourning her good fortune. She had previously thought herself pragmatic, prone to displays of cool appraisal, bracing practicality, sometimes at the expense of those who deserved better from her.

The man she was seeing still had not declared himself to her, but when she told him the following evening that she would be moving across the country, he said that he did not want her to go.

"Is there any way that you could stay a little longer, maybe a few more months?" he asked.

She shook her head, wanting to explain but unable to do it. He trusted her, even though they had never declared anything to each other.

"I could fly out there to visit, I suppose," he said.

"Of course," she said. "That'd be nice."

"You never told me that you were looking for another job."

"I wasn't," she said. "It came out of nowhere."

"Are you sure it's what you want?" he murmured.

"I think it is," she said, smiling wanly.

Her family was happy for her, pleased that she was moving closer to where she had grown up after so many years in a city they considered dangerous, a place also prone to abominable weather for half the year, if not more. The new job sounded interesting, and surely at some point she might even meet a few movie stars? (Even so, they did not want her to be seduced by the glamour and reckless lifestyle of these actors — she should have a good time but keep her wits about her!)

Lyndsey did not know who Mr. Fulger knew at the firm that had hired her. She risked a few awkward inquiries shortly after she started but was rewarded with blank stares. No one had heard of anyone named Mr. Fulger. Was she sure it wasn't Fellsted? Or Fulstein? She tried again, using only his first name. No. No Reginald. Only a Ronald. A Gerald too.

Mr. Fulger kept his word; he began calling not long after she had settled in, arranging to take her out to new restaurants and chic hotels that had been built into verdant mountainsides.

"We could go to my new place instead sometime," she said during their third meeting in the new city. "It's more spacious than my old apartment."

"I'm sure it is," he said. "But it's your refuge, not mine."

"I wouldn't mind sharing."

He shook his head. "I prefer hotels."

"Why?"

He gazed at her, his face more tired than usual. "The possibilities."

She was unhappy with his reply, with her new job, with her loneliness. "Where is your wife?"

Surprise briefly transformed his features. "I've told you that I'm divorced."

She looked at him, doubtful.

"It's of no consequence, Lyndsey."

"So I'm the only one?"

He took a long time to reply. "In a way, yes."

"Why did you make me move?"

"I didn't make you do anything. You chose to move."

"You basically forced me."

He shook his head, his expression tolerant. "The position opened and I knew it'd be a good match for you. You couldn't disagree."

"I don't like it."

"Not yet."

"I want to go back."

He sighed. "You've been here for four weeks. Hardly more than a blink of an eye when measured against your entire life."

Her other lover soon flew out to see her, his delight with her new situation causing her to question her displeasure. "You've got it made," he said. "I'd move here tomorrow if I could find a setup like this one."

"Maybe you could. I could ask around."

"We'll see," he said. "I'll do a little research first."

But after he left, she did not hear from him for several days, and he admitted when they spoke that he had not started looking for something closer to her. Mr. Fulger was also curiously silent. A month passed, then another. Perhaps he had seen her with her lover during his visit and had felt jealous, angered to find her enjoying herself with a much younger man. Countless times she had wondered if she had ever passed by a store or an apartment building where Mr. Fulger might have stood looking out at her. It had always seemed possible that he might spy on her or else hire someone to do it for him, but of course she had never caught him or noticed anyone following her.

She began to wake in the middle of the night, feeling keenly the absurdity of their relationship. It could not continue. When at last he called after ten weeks of silence, she told him that she wanted everything between them to stop.

"No," he said simply.

"Why not?" she said.

"Because this requires almost nothing of you. I've never been stingy, you'd have to agree."

"But I don't want to do it anymore. It's become too upsetting."

"You're being foolish," he said, naming a hotel, giving her an address. "Come out tonight and I know you'll feel better."

In their room, he had two dozen pink roses waiting for her. He spent time on her body, more than usual. She started to cry, her face buried in his shoulder.

"Do you want more money?" he asked, drawing away. "Would that make it easier?"

She shook her head, covering herself with the sheets. "I have more than enough now."

"I doubt that," he murmured.

"We have to stop this before I go crazy."

He sat up, his face hardened with displeasure. His thick, graying hair stood up on one side of his head, giving him a comical air in spite of the scowl. She wiped roughly at her wet cheeks, hoping her mascara hadn't run.

"Quality of life has greatly improved for you since we've met," he said.

"I don't know if I agree."

He regarded her. "Don't be melodramatic."

"Why can't I ever call you? Why did you wait more than two months to call me?"

"I was away on an extended business trip."

"Doing what?"

He hesitated. "I have never understood why people feel the need to know everything about each other. What would it change if I told you how I spend my time when I'm not with you?"

"I wouldn't feel so much like I'm sleeping with a stranger."

He shook his head. "It's clear that you have no trouble enjoying it."

"I'm going to say no the next time you call."

His expression was noncommittal. "We shall see."

"What do you do for a living?"

He sighed. "I sell clothing. I own several factories. Some in Asia, some in Eastern Europe. That's all."

"Couldn't I travel with you sometime?"

He gave her an unreadable look. "I don't think so, Lyndsey. That wouldn't work very well. You wouldn't enjoy yourself anyway. I'm always in meetings."

*

After a time, things again became routine, her former life and her regret at its loss receding — she went to work, she had dinner on occasion with a few people who were now her friends, she saw other friends from high school who lived in the city or occasionally visited it. Her lover on the opposite coast began to see someone else. She met a man who worked for a movie studio for whom she designed posters. Mr. Fulger called every two or three weeks, their lovemaking remained predictably, perversely satisfying. After ten months, the man from the movie studio asked her to marry him. She said yes and told Mr. Fulger that she would have to stop seeing him because of her engagement.

Again he said no.

She felt more desperate than she ever had with him. "It has to stop," she said. "I could pay you back everything you've given me."

"No. I'm not interested in a refund."

"I want to marry this man."

"Fine. I won't stop you, but you and I will still be seeing each other after your marriage. That's all I require."

"Please find someone else."

He shook his head. "You suit me perfectly. It wouldn't be as pleasurable with someone else."

She left him that night thinking that she would have to move, request an unlisted phone number, dye her hair, change jobs, attempt everything to get away from him. She would ask her fiancé if they could move far away and find new jobs; she would say she was tired of the traffic, the unhealthy air. They would do better to move up the coast, maybe work from home if possible.

But when she began to explain to him why she wanted to make these changes, her fiancé suspected the story wasn't complete and connived the truth from her. When he learned that she had continued to sleep with Mr. Fulger during their courtship, he broke off their engagement, explaining that it might be old-fashioned in their permissive times to be upset about such a thing, but he couldn't help his innate squeamishness when it came to infidelity. He marveled as well over her ability to be so calmly deceitful during their courtship. Had she loved him at all?

"He is simply one man among the many thousands more you'll meet," said Mr. Fulger upon learning of the broken engagement.

"And I won't live forever. Or perhaps the next man you fall for won't mind me so much."

She made plans to leave the city, to move north to another state. Nothing else seemed possible — this, she recognized dimly, was hysteria. When the contents of her apartment were packed in boxes and ready to go on the moving truck, profound despair seized her. The moving men were sent away. She tossed one box from her second story window, narrowly missing a woman who walked by with a bag of groceries. "I should call the police," yelled the woman, staring up at Lyndsey from the sidewalk in fear and amazement, half of her groceries now spilled on the ground next to the ruined box of cooking pots.

"It was an accident," cried Lyndsey, trembling with horror. "I'm so sorry."

"You could have killed me," yelled the woman, angrier now. "What's your fucking problem?"

He did not understand why she remained so unhappy. She was not poor, or dying prematurely from some vicious illness, or imprisoned on wrongful charges, or grievously disabled, or the wife of an abusive husband in a place where religion made divorce impossible. Why was she wasting time feeling so sorry for herself? She had so much freedom, was accountable to him for so little, only a few hours a month, and it wasn't like he did anything but spoil her.

He had a point, of course. His logic, though it troubled her more than she could say, remained unassailable. She would not be released, even if she threatened to harm one or both of them, even if what he did to her became rape. What was so terrible about her situation, he wanted to know. She remained young and beautiful; she had a good job, a nice home, friends, a loving family. Obviously there were much worse things to lament if she would spend a moment or two considering the range of horrors just outside her usual frame of reference. She could of course be happy again. In the frankest analysis, this would remain, as always, her choice.

BRADFORD TICE

Missionaries

FROM *The Atlantic*

JOSEPH WATCHED AS Case began to undress on the bluff overlooking the rock quarry. Case removed his shirt, then his shoes and socks. He planted his feet on the weathered rock at the edge and leaned over to peer into the water below. The sun was directly overhead, and a breeze riffled through the sycamores lining the old factory road. Case's chest was a white-marble tone, and the line on his arms where his tan began made him look like a painting someone had only half finished. He removed his watch and tossed it onto the pile. It landed with a click, striking the plastic LDS tag upon which his name was spelled out in white letters. Joseph sat behind him in the dirt of the road, next to two bikes and a parked van, studying Case's outline against the blue sky.

"Not only does the Mormon Church offer salvation," Case was saying, "but in addition to your salvation package, you receive a principality in the kingdom of God." He smiled over his shoulder, then pulled his belt out of its loops and tossed it onto the pile. "Which sure beats the living arrangements you have now, Claude."

Claude was sitting on the bumper of the van, its back doors thrown open to reveal a stained mattress and sheets, across which were scattered several water-stained romance novels. His face was framed by wiry gray hair that extended down his jaw and collected under his chin, and he was trying to roll a joint on the frayed knee of his corduroys. The reek of mildew and sweat coming from the van was overpowering, and Joseph, who was sitting in front of Claude, wondered how long he could hold his breath.

"Don't get me wrong," Case continued. "You've got a nice thing going here, living in your van. No neighbors to bother you, only one key to worry about, nice view. But it's not what God's got planned for you, Claude. Elder Joseph, what does God have planned for Claude here?"

Case turned to Joseph, who'd just picked a dandelion from the grass and was holding it against his nose to combat the odor. Joseph didn't answer immediately, and Case gave him a look and coaxed him with his hands. "He has a condo set aside for you in heaven, Claude," Joseph finally answered.

"That's right, Claude. Have you ever been inside a condo?" Claude looked at Case as if he was crazy. Case just smiled and scratched at the hair under his arms.

Case and Joseph, both nineteen, their birthdays within a month of each other, had arrived a little over an hour earlier, walking their bikes down the stretch of railroad bisecting Ijams Nature Center until they found the overgrown access road that led to an abandoned marble plant and the adjacent quarry. Case had learned about the place from a college student at the fort, where he and Joseph had been handing out tracts. They'd found Claude's van parked beneath the kudzu-choked mill, nearly fifty feet above the water in the quarry.

Claude was stretched across the mattress in the back of his van, reading a romance novel called *Gentle Rogue*. The cover depicted a man and a woman, scantily clad, swooning across the rigging of a ship. Joseph was wary of the old man, but Case saw only opportunity.

"Morning," Case had called, with genuine enthusiasm.

Claude dropped the paperback onto his chest, looking at the two over the spine with obvious distrust. "The quarry's over there, if that's what you came for," he mumbled.

"Well, we did come for a swim, but that's not all," Case said. "We're here to help you, sir."

It amazed Joseph how effortlessly Case was able to sell the Church. He envied Case's confidence, his ability to grab people. Case had been out in the field for nearly a year now, and by the time Joseph arrived three months ago, Case had already baptized fifteen converts, which put him well on his way to becoming district leader in the Knoxville branch. Case believed what Elder Robert back at mission headquarters had told him the day he arrived: "As long as the convert puts out his cigarette on the way down to the water, he is worthy."

Case shielded his eyes against the sun and turned toward the quarry. The water was a grayish blue, which reminded Joseph of the Great Salt Lake. He pictured his mother standing ankle-deep in it, head haloed by brine flies, talking about the wonders of God. "A sea in the middle of the waste," she'd said. "That's what you have to be in this life, Joseph. Balm in the desert."

"Hey, Claude. You ever jump from here?" Case ran a hand through his hair, cleared his throat, and spat off the side of the rock. Joseph noticed that the skin along Case's midriff had pimpled.

Claude ignored Case, concentrating on his efforts with the joint. Joseph rose to his feet and edged out toward the quarry. He put his hand on Case's shoulder. "I don't think you should be jumping into there," he said. "It's against the rules to swim, you know. Plus, no telling what's down there."

Case grunted and shook off Joseph's hand. "You're such a lamb, Joseph. Christ, my mother has more backbone than you."

Joseph lowered his eyes and shrugged. He never liked it when Case swore. "I'm just saying you're an idiot, that's all."

"Won't deny that." Case undid the button on his slacks and dropped them, and his briefs, to his ankles. He pulled his feet out, then kicked both garments over with the others. One of the first things Case had done upon arriving in Knoxville was replace his temple garment with Fruit of the Loom underwear. Joseph thought of this as Case turned to him and grinned. For the past few months Joseph hadn't been able to look at Case without being reminded of what wasn't under the other boy's clothes.

Case looked over his shoulder at Claude, and Joseph followed his gaze, trying not to let his eyes rest too long on Case's naked body. Claude had finished rolling the joint and was passing it in and out of his lips. Case yelled, "You know God doesn't like you to do drugs to combat loneliness."

A smile wavered at the corner of Claude's lips. "You want to hit it?" he asked.

"Well, it seems like the only Christian thing to do." Case walked over, light-stepping over the gravel and the broken glass. As he approached, Claude moved around to the front of the van.

"Where you going, Claude? Ow, shoot!" Case raised his foot, regarded it for a second, and extracted a thorn from his heel.

"Need a light," Claude yelled from the front of the van. A few seconds later he came back, lighting the joint with the van's cigarette lighter.

"You're a sad man, Claude. It's divine intervention we came when we did. Isn't it, Joseph?" Case kept his back to Joseph as he took a hit.

"Yeah, Case." Joseph noticed the muscles of Case's back tense, and he wondered if Case could feel him watching. Case passed the joint back to Claude, and the old man extended it toward Joseph, who shook his head and focused on a puddle filled with water and gasoline in the road beside the van, around which hovered tiny violet butterflies.

"You'll have to forgive Joseph. He lacks social grace." Case looked over his shoulder, blowing smoke into the air and beckoning Joseph with his finger.

Joseph hesitated. Then he walked over, took the joint from Claude's hand, and brought it to his lips. He tried to inhale as little as possible. The wind picked up, and the rusted girders of the mill groaned audibly under their cover of vines. Case shivered and wrapped his arms around his chest.

"You going to walk around naked all day?" Claude asked. "You haven't exactly walked into Eden."

"Does it bother you, Claude?"

"Not really. You're not going to tell me about how man was made in the image of God and we shouldn't be afraid of our nakedness, are you?"

Case smirked and shook his head. "No, I can see you're the kind of man who doesn't appreciate a lot of smoke and mirrors. Let's face it, Claude. You're hellbound, and I doubt anything can save you."

"At least you're honest."

"I try, Claude. Now." Case slammed the palm of his hand against Joseph's chest. "Let's do this."

"Do what?" Joseph asked, rubbing his chest.

"Strip." Case began pulling at Joseph's shirt.

Joseph watched as one button snapped off and went sailing into the grass. He pulled away and stood staring at Case.

"Come on, Joe. We're a team. We're going to the river together."

"It's not a river, it's —"

"Whatever. You know I wouldn't make you do anything I wouldn't do." Case extended his arm. His palm looked soft to Joseph, like an infant's. "I'll even hold your hand."

Joseph felt the blood rise in his neck. "I don't need to hold your hand."

Claude began to giggle, which set the van bouncing. Joseph noticed that his teeth were broken and jagged.

"Don't do it, boy," Claude said. "Your friend's crazy."

"All right," Case said. "Let's go take a leap."

Joseph straightened his shoulders, but as they approached the cliff, he felt his stomach kink. As he inched up to the edge and peeked over, Case came up behind him and swatted the back of his pants. Joseph jumped and clutched Case's arm.

"Don't worry," Case said. "I was just going to suggest you take those off. You don't want to walk around wet, do you?"

Joseph let go of Case and began to remove his shirt and pants. Case picked up several rocks from the cliff and spun them into the air above the quarry. He turned to look at Joseph, flipping a flat stone over on his palm as he spoke. "You keeping your temple garment on?"

"It'll dry."

Case shrugged and hurled the stone away. "Suit yourself. You first."

"Why do I have to go first?"

"Because I said so." Case turned and walked a few paces behind Joseph. "I'll be right after you."

Joseph heard Claude yell from across the road, "Belly flop, boys."

A dull ringing started in Joseph's ear, and it seemed to him that the rest of the world got strangely quiet, that even the insects stopped whatever rituals they were engaged in. It was as if the world had turned to watch him, wondering what he intended to do next. He wondered briefly if God were watching and thought about Salt Lake and his parents. "Never be led from the path," his father had always said. "Even angels have been known to trip." Joseph decided he couldn't do it, the very thought of the fall made his guts churn. But a moment later the weight of Case's body slammed into his back, sending them both over the edge of the bluff.

He surfaced a second later, gasping for air. Case emerged a

few feet away from him and howled, the sound echoing around the walls of the quarry. The burning sensation in Joseph's side became a searing pain, and he began thrashing. Case swam over and snaked an arm under Joseph's, holding him above the water. "Sorry, man. I just thought you needed some inspiration up there."

Joseph tried to catch his breath. "You kay, Joe?" Case patted Joseph's chest and held him up so that they were both afloat.

"I can't breathe," Joseph said.

Case pulled Joseph toward him. "Just keep trying," he said. "It'll get easier." Joseph allowed his back to relax against the firm surface of Case's chest, their legs entangled under the water. "You did good, Joe. I'm proud of you. We should call it a day after this. To celebrate."

"What are we celebrating?" Joseph said, wheezing and coughing.

"Well, obviously somebody up there loves us."

Joseph lay sprawled on the bed with an ice pack pressed against the side of his chest. The swelling had gone down, but a dark purple bruise ran from under his right arm to below his waist. He winced as he tried to move, shifting his weight on the mound of pillows under him. He eyed Case, who was on the other side of the room crouched in front of the open door of the refrigerator. He emerged with a tub of butter and a butter knife and came and stood by the bed. "Here, put some butter on the bruise," he said. "It'll help reduce the swelling."

"What?" Joseph looked at Case dubiously.

"Trust me. It works."

Joseph took the tub and knife from Case. He opened the lid and smeared the butter gingerly on his discolored skin. He cringed at the cold.

Case and Joseph's studio apartment was in the partitioned attic of an old Victorian on Fifth Street. In the three months they'd lived there, clumps of dust had curled into the corners of the linoleum floors. The ceiling sloped at odd angles, and at night the wind whimpered around the eaves, sometimes keeping Joseph awake.

Joseph studied the few stars he could see through the window. He usually tried not to think about his parents until after Case had drifted off into sleep. He was an only child, and his mother hadn't wanted him to go on the mission. His father, however, insisted it would be a growing experience and would get him out of an awkward phase. Joseph stared at the butter smeared down his side. Some of it was still curled from where the knife had cut it. He thought about the Family Home Evenings he'd spent with his parents. He could hear his father's slow baritone relating the story of Daniel in the lions' den. Afterward, he'd sat between his father's legs and watched as he carved sleeping lions from bars of Dial soap. He'd loved the way the soap curled around the edge of his father's pocketknife, as if the world were bending to his will.

He blinked and tried to turn his head without moving his lower body. "Case, what did you do with your parents on Family Home Evenings?"

Case snorted. "My mother would turn off the TV and make me and my sisters read the Book of Mormon. God, Mondays were frigging boring."

"What about your dad?"

Case ran a finger through the mess on Joseph's chest and put his finger in his mouth. "Did I ever tell you my dad is a physicist?" he asked. "He took me to his research facility once for Family Day, when I was ten. He worked with supercolliders at Stanford. We went in 1993, just a few years before someone in his department won the Nobel Prize for discovering the tau lepton, or something like that. That's what my dad does. He uses these machines to throw particles and atoms at each other to try and see what they're made of."

"Sounds interesting."

"That kind of stuff always excited my dad. He'd come home talking about how he hurled a helium atom at a whatever particle and something remarkable happened. It was all Greek to me, and that's all he could talk about. Quarks, mesons, dark matter — scientist stuff. It was like some secret code. How's your side feeling?"

"I can't feel the lower half of my body. Or the upper half."

Case laughed. "Me either." He took a swat at the dust clots on the floor. "So what does your father do for a living, Joe?"

"He sells insurance for an indemnity company."

"That sounds really ordinary."

"Sorry."

Case nudged Joseph's shoulder. "Scoot over. And give me a pillow. We've got an early day tomorrow." He carried the tub of butter and the knife back to the refrigerator.

"Where are we going?" Joseph asked, sliding toward the wall.

"North Knoxville. Mechanicsville. Elder Robert says the families out that way are lower-income. Poor people are more pliable."

Case pulled his undershirt over his head and jerked down his pants. He dropped both on the floor and switched off the overhead light. Once his eyes had adjusted to the dark, Joseph looked at Case, who was lying on his back with his arms behind his pillow, staring at the ceiling. His shoulder seemed to radiate heat.

"Hey, Case," Joseph said.

"What?"

"How come you never call your parents on our P days?"

Case sighed. "I don't have anything in particular to tell them. Once I make district leader, I'll call home to let them know. Shouldn't be too much longer. I've brought in more baptisms than anyone else. My dad made AP of the San Francisco mission when he was out in the field, before he went off to college."

They stopped talking, and Joseph listened as a listless summer rain passed over the roof, the drops pattering against the window above them.

The next morning, the rain had passed to the east, and the wet lawns grew steamy as Case and Joseph pedaled into North Knoxville. Joseph's clothes clung to his body, and sweat ran down his forehead into his eyes. Each revolution of the pedals hurt his side. He tried to ignore the pain, keeping his eyes on Case's back ahead of him. As they headed into Mechanicsville, Joseph saw that most of the houses they passed were white or sickly green clapboard and leaning at precarious angles, seemingly held up by telephone lines. Some were boarded up and wrapped in yellow police tape.

Case had ripped a street map out of the phone book. They would start on the east end and work their way west, ending up at the edge of the industrial park. Case leaned into a curve and came to a stop in front of a house nearly swallowed by dogwoods. Panting, Joseph came to rest beside him. Case propped his bike against a low wrought-iron fence and slung his backpack off his shoulder. He unzipped the side pouch and took out a tattered copy of the Book of Mormon. "Let me do the talking while we're here," he said. He looked at Joseph, who nodded.

Case's hair was wet on the sides and clung to his face. He

swabbed his forehead with the sleeve of his shirt. "All right, then. Let's do this."

Joseph leaned his bike against Case's and followed after him. Old tires lined the walkway, and from their centers swelled fistfuls of geraniums, marigolds, and some flowers he didn't recognize. Their scent hovered around him like the perfume his mother wore on Sundays when she attended chapel.

Case stood holding the screen door open against his hip and knocked loudly, breaking the quietness of the morning. Joseph felt the muscles of his neck tense. This was the part of the job he hated — standing at a door unsure what lay behind it. "Do you think anyone's home?" he asked, just as the door swung open to the end of a chain. The face of the elderly black woman framed by the door seemed surprised it didn't open all the way.

"Hello, ma'am. My name is Case Riseler, and I was wondering if I might have a moment of your time today."

"I don't have any money to give you," said the woman. She was wearing a blue bathrobe with two huge pockets on the sides, and her gray hair was cut close to her head.

"We're not looking for money, ma'am. We'd like to talk to you about the Church of Latter-Day Saints. It'll take no more than fifteen minutes of your time." Case took half a step closer to the threshold and smiled. Somehow he made it seem as if he'd already been invited in. Or at least it seemed that way to Joseph.

The woman hesitated and looked behind her into the house.

She mumbled softly, "The house isn't really clean. And I don't have much time for religion anymore."

"That's all right, ma'am. We're not here to pressure you. But could we at least step inside for a moment? Maybe cool down a bit? Plus, Elder Joseph here needs to use your restroom, if you don't mind. Isn't that right, Elder Joseph?"

"Yes, ma'am," Joseph said. "I need to use your restroom."

The woman stared hard at them for a moment. "You don't look old enough to be elders." The two boys didn't respond. "House is a mess," she said again.

"It'll just take a moment. Scout's honor." Case held up two fingers and put his other hand over his heart.

The old woman began to fish inside the pockets of her robe, then stopped and stared at the two boys. Joseph wondered if she remembered what she was doing. Then she reached up, unlatched the chain, and swung open the door. "All right. But just for a minute."

The interior of the house was dark. Rays of light stole in through the curtained windows, highlighting the dust. The place smelled of polyester. Behind the woman was what at one time might have been a living room. Joseph could make out a couch and table on the far wall, but the couch was covered with heaps of clothes, newspapers, and assorted gimcracks. Every available inch of the table was covered with curios — porcelain clowns and angels, boys with straw hats and fishing poles, animal figurines. The old woman turned and hobbled through the snarl, down a path that angled to the right into an equally overrun kitchen. Case turned and whispered to Joseph. "Jesus Christ, this woman's a loon. Look at this place."

Joseph nodded and fell into step behind Case as they trailed the woman into the kitchen. She seated herself at the kitchen table, upon which rested a tower of salt and pepper shakers, stacked plastic cups, and canned food. Lines of ants stalked across the yellowed linoleum floor, which sagged in several places. Case took a seat beside the woman at the table, balancing the Book of Mormon on his thigh. He smiled and looked around. "Seems cozy. Joseph, why don't you go find the restroom, while me and Mrs. — I'm sorry, I didn't catch your name."

"Ida Marsh," the old woman answered.

"Ida. That's lovely. Where's your bathroom?"

Ida raised a gnarled finger and pointed to a door at the back of the kitchen next to the stove. "Through there and to the left. Down at the end of the hall."

Case looked at Joseph. "You heard the woman, Joseph. In the back there." He made a scooting motion with his hands.

As Joseph headed into the dim hallway, he heard Case start his spiel. "Ida, have you ever wondered what God has planned for you . . ." He found the bathroom at the end of the hallway. In the corners of the room, dust-colored mushrooms had sprung up in clusters between the tiles. He stood in front of the mirror and thought about Ida in the kitchen with Case. Then he thought about his own mother, dusting her collection of cut-crystal angels in the living room, where the light from the windows could catch them.

He wondered if she could ever end up like Ida — alone, with the house slowly filling in around her. The possibility felt very real. He pictured his mother's wrist as she went to open a door, her veins visible under her skin, as if they were wrapped in the thin pages of a Bible. He waited a few more minutes, then headed back toward the kitchen.

"I don't have any way to get down to the mission," Ida was saying.

"That's all right," Case said. "We can send an elder down here to pick you up and take you to the church to be baptized."

"They'd do that for me?"

She said it without emotion, yet the tone of her voice put Joseph at the edge of tears — he felt just as he had on the tarmac of the airport in Salt Lake City when his mother pressed a silver dollar and a gilt-edged copy of the Book of Mormon into his hand. The book was to keep him on the path. The dollar was for luck, she started to say; his father finished explaining when it was clear she could not. He'd spent it accidentally at an airport kiosk when the plane touched down in Knoxville, on a magazine and a bag of saltwater taffy. He'd reached into his pocket and pulled out all the bills and change he could grasp. When the cashier lifted the coin from the counter, he was too embarrassed to ask for it back. He told himself it didn't matter. Yet he could still hear the weight of that coin as it was dropped into the coin drawer among its lesser brothers.

"Of course," Case said. "I'd see to it myself."

Ida's hands picked at the threads of her robe. She appeared to be weighing her options. "Well, maybe I should start back to church. Once Stuart gets back from the war, he'll want to go."

"Who's Stuart?" Case asked, swiping at the grime that had appeared on his pant leg.

"He's my son. He's over in Vietnam right now."

Case glanced up at Joseph, who was standing behind Ida. He rolled his eyes and grinned.

"Maybe Stuart could be a deacon in the church when he gets back," Ida said.

Case turned toward her. "Maybe."

"Case, we should probably tell Ida how some Mormons feel about blacks in the priesthood," Joseph said. "I think she should know."

Ida turned and looked at him as if she didn't understand what he was saying. Case glared and made a cutting gesture with his hands.

"I mean, the Church officially allowed blacks into the priesthood in 1978, but still . . ." Joseph's voice trailed off, and he dropped his eyes.

Ida turned back to Case. "What's he saying?" She shuffled her feet.

"Don't pay any attention to him," Case said. "He's talking about the Mormon Church, not the Church of Latter-Day Saints. So if I send a car around on Thursday, will you be here?"

She looked at the corner of the room and grunted. Then she nodded slowly. "I'll be here."

Case stood up. "All right, then. We'll send a car around on Thursday. We'll let ourselves out, if you don't mind."

Case motioned with his book for Joseph to follow. As they crossed the yard, he said, "What was that all about? Why did you tell her about the blacks-in-the-priesthood thing?"

Joseph kicked at the head of a marigold. "I don't know. I felt sorry for her."

"Jesus Christ, Joe. It's not like we were robbing her." Case pointed at Joseph's face. "You just thank God she was soft in the head, because if you'd ruined that conversion, I would have skinned your scrawny hide."

"Don't you feel bad at all?" Joseph asked.

"Why should I, Joe? Grow a frigging backbone. We're here to do a job. We're here to bring people to the Lord."

It's like a game to you, Joseph thought. It doesn't mean anything.

"Don't you want to make AP?" Case said, as if he'd heard Joseph's thought. "Don't you want to make our parents proud? That's what we're here to do, Joe."

Everything felt off-kilter to Joseph. Who did Case think he was, bartering with salvation as if it were currency? "This just isn't what I thought I'd be doing here."

Case sighed and shook his head. When he spoke, his voice was quiet but hard. "If there was one thing I learned from my father, it's that the way to make it is by force of will. It's what people respond to. Otherwise, you end up a statistic, like Ida there." He pointed toward the house.

Joseph didn't say anything, and Case stepped toward him until he was uncomfortably close. "Listen to me, Joe. The ends always justify the means." He stared hard into Joseph's face and then punched him on the arm. "Come on, don't look like that. We got a lot more houses to get through. I promise we'll do whatever you want tomorrow. Just you and me. But right now, I need you to focus."

Joseph sat on the carpeted floor of the girl's living room, picking at the matted spots around him. A chronicle of accidents, he thought, his eyes following the lines of the stains, wondering if he could determine where they came from. He was seated Indian-style in front of a blue La-Z-Boy. Case and the girl were seated on the couch. Joseph thought she was a little older than they were, but not by much. She was what Case called a goth kid, dressed all in black, with scuffed combat boots peeking out from under the hem of the layered, gauzy skirts of her dress. She was wearing thick coats of lipstick and eyeliner, and the purple-black color made her look bruised. She and Case were smoking cigarettes, flicking their ashes into the ashtray between them. Case was selling salvation. The girl was listening with a strange expression, a half-smirk. She picked at the fabric of her skirts.

"So do you live here alone?" Case asked. He had his arm slung over the back of the couch.

"Just me," she answered, smoke streaming from her nostrils.

A stereo on a low table was playing a CD of some band Joseph wasn't familiar with — a soft, brooding music that he didn't particularly like. Several shelves of books lined the walls, and he tried to focus on the titles. The only ones he could see clearly were a collection of Lovecraft stories and Jack London's *The Call of the Wild.*

"So you guys are Mormons?" the girl asked. "How many wives do you all get?" She looked at Case from under her eyelids.

"Most Mormons don't follow the polygamy thing anymore," he said. "It's only the really devout and unconventional sects." He scratched at his hairless cheek, looking bored. It was the same routine he used with all younger people, pretending that he wasn't really that interested in what he was doing, that he was cool with just hanging out.

"That's unfortunate. Polygamy was the one thing that made you guys interesting."

Case gave the girl a mock-hurt look. "You don't find me interesting?"

"I haven't decided yet."

Joseph was growing restless. He didn't like being in the girl's house. It smelled of stale incense. Candles were tiered throughout the room, the wax puddled around their bases in stiff globs. "It's getting dark, Case. Shouldn't we be going?"

Case turned toward Joseph, but his expression was vacant. Joseph began to feel that he could be heard only vaguely and not seen at all.

"I can take you back to your apartment," the girl said. "I'm still waiting to see if you can convert me, though."

"So what's it going to take?" Case asked.

The girl smiled, and her teeth flashed in the half-light. She flicked her cigarette over the ashtray, and a stray fleck of ash landed on her lap. Case leaned forward and pinched it from the fabric. "Thank you," she said.

"Don't mention it."

"You're getting warmer."

Case's eyebrows darted up. "What do you mean?"

"Never mind. So how did you two get placed together?" She turned toward Joseph as if to include him in the conversation, but he ignored her.

"Luck of the draw. I'd say it was a pretty good match, though. We get along really well. Isn't that right, Elder Joe?"

Joseph nodded, but kept his eyes down. "We get along okay."

The girl snickered and tucked a strand of hair behind her ear. "Why do you call each other 'Elder'?"

"It's an address of respect."

"Should I call you 'Elder'?" She stubbed out her cigarette.

"You can call me whatever you want. Speaking of which, I never got your name."

"Margo."

"Nice to meet you, Margo. So what's it going to take to get you into the Church?"

"I have reservations," she said, a smile playing across her lips. "I'm not a stranger to sin. Impure thoughts and all that."

Joseph suddenly realized that his lungs felt swollen, and he wondered if he'd injured himself seriously when he fell into the quarry.

"Well, we all have those," Case said. "Nothing to be ashamed of. I don't think God splits hairs over salvation."

Joseph could see Case's erection press against his pants, and he felt himself stiffen. He pulled at the legs of his slacks and hoped no one would notice.

"That's good to know," she said, then paused a moment. "Do you want to come to the bedroom with me?"

Case smiled and stubbed out his cigarette. He stood up quickly. "Yeah, let's go." Then he looked down at Joseph. "You can find something to do, can't you, Joe?"

"My side's really starting to hurt again," Joseph said, but Case's attention was focused on the front of Margo's dress, on the dark velvet pulled snug around her small breasts.

"I have some Advil and other stuff in the cabinet above the stove," Margo said. "You're welcome to it. We won't be long." She rested her hand briefly on Joseph's head and walked slowly toward the kitchen, looking back at Case as she entered the short hallway that led to the bedroom.

Case squatted beside Joseph, who leaned forward and crossed his arms over his lap, afraid Case would notice his erection. "I owe you one for this, Joe," Case said. "Anything you want. I swear."

Joseph watched as Case followed Margo into the bedroom in back. He heard the squeak of the door. For a few moments, he remained seated, listening to the faint hum that seemed to come from the walls. He rose to his feet and tiptoed to the kitchen and stood in the center of it for a moment, not knowing what to do next. The silence was choking. Then he turned and headed down the hallway toward the sliver of light seeping from a crack in the bedroom door.

He pressed his eye to the crack and saw Case sitting at the edge of the bed, Margo standing in front of him. Case had stripped to his underwear and was slowly unzipping the back of Margo's dress. It slid off her body and crumpled onto the floor. Case reached for the clasp of her bra, and she pulled the straps from her shoulders. Case bit his lower lip as he hooked his fingers under the elastic band of Margo's panties and pulled.

Joseph stood watching Case's hands move up and down the girl's belly and between her breasts. He thought about all the doors he and Case had passed through over the past few months, and of what Case had told him about the kind of force he needed to be in the world. Joseph reached for the doorknob, but his hand paused above it. He knew if he went any further he would set something off, some part of himself he didn't wish to recognize. Case pressed his lips against the white of Margo's stomach, and Joseph heard a sigh escape her lips. She tangled her fingers into Case's hair.

Joseph forced himself to turn away. He pressed a hand against his bruise as if he were trying to contain it, the throb of the thing. His loneliness at that instant made him gasp. The weight of everything was immense. He pictured his mother and father, growing accustomed to his absence. Somehow everything they'd given him wasn't enough for this mission.

His back to the door, he decided then that he was going to be different. He was going to be what Case wanted — a force to be reckoned with. With his faith, he would be unstoppable, blessed, a god on this earth, and the world would bend to him. He would take all the Claudes and Idas and Margos and shelter them from lions. Cleanse them of their sins and fears. Then Case would have no choice but to recognize his greatness.

Walking to the end of the hallway by the kitchen, he seated himself against the wall. He sat there quietly, waiting for Case to emerge.

MARK WISNIEWSKI

Straightaway

FROM *The Antioch Review*

NINE TIMES OUT OF TEN it's a woman who calls Bark to answer his ad in the Westchester *Pennysaver,* and sometimes when we pull up to her yard in his pickup, she's outside waiting for us. Sometimes she even has something inside for us to eat, which, besides needing money, is why James and I never ask Bark if he wants our help: we just get in his truck and hope he lets us go.

On the Saturday morning he drives us past Poughkeepsie, though, no one's waiting outside. Maybe this has to do with the five hundred dollars this woman offered: she doesn't feel the need to be friendly beyond that. Or maybe she's with the junk that needs to be hauled. Anyway, Bark pulls off the country road into her driveway, which drops through her uncut lawn toward her shabby yellow house, and we all get out, Bark headed to knock on her front door.

Hey, I hear from the left-hand side of the house, and I turn but see no one. Down here, the voice calls, and there, crouched near an open crawlspace hole, is a woman about as dark as me, maybe five years older.

Over here, Bark, I shout, and Bark makes his way down the porch, then over to her, James and I lagging behind to let her know he's boss.

I took care of the rest myself, she says, and Bark kneels beside her, then pokes his head and a good half of him into the crawlspace. He stays in there for a while, making sure, I figure, that we can do what needs doing. Then he's back out, and he stands, slapping dirt off his knees.

Just that oil drum? he says.

Yeah, she says.

I thought you said there was a bunch of stuff, he says.

No, she says. Just that.

What's in it? he asks.

I have no idea, she says, but she's scratching her arm and keeps scratching it: if she's not flat-out lying, she's more than a little nervous.

Because the thing is, Bark says. I can't just take a drum like that to a dump without them asking what's inside.

Then don't take it to a dump, she says. Just, you know, get rid of it.

Bark grabs his unshaven jaw, considering. Probably he's stumped by why a sister is living this far upstate; plus it doesn't make much sense that *any* woman living in a house this shabby could have five hundred dollars, let alone give it to us to haul off a drum with nothing bad in it. It crosses my mind this woman loves some guy who's given her five hundred to get rid of the drum, some dude, maybe a white one, that she loves and cheated with — and that inside the drum is this man's wife. But all kinds of things are crossing my mind, including how I could use five hundred dollars divided by three.

How 'bout a thousand? the woman says.

Here's where all of us, including her, gaze off at her uncut lawn, the dandelions and weeds in it, some of them pretty enough to call flowers. We gaze our separate ways for a long time, letting whatever truth of what's going on sink into us while we play as if it isn't, and I feel my guts work their way higher toward my lungs, threatening to stay there if Bark agrees. But there's a lot I could do with my share of a thousand, especially since I'm used to walking away from these jobs with fifty at most. I could eat more than apples and white bread and ham. I could start saving for a truck of my own — to haul things for pay myself.

Then, to the woman, Bark says, In cash?

As soon as that drum's in your truck, she says.

Bark glances at James, who nods.

Tre? Bark asks me, and I know he's working me over with his eyes, using them to try to convince me in their I-don't-care-either-way manner, but what I'm watching is the women's feet, which are the tiniest bit pigeon-toed. They are also perfectly still, which could mean she's no longer nervous, but my eyes, I know, are avoiding her fingers and arms. Still, the sight of those pigeon-toed feet coax me to trust her: I could stay loyal to a woman who stands like that.

Why not? I answer. I haven't, I tell myself, actually said yes, but when I look up, James is following Bark into the crawlspace, the woman checking me out.

Sure appreciate it, she says, in the flat way of someone who could do two men on the same day yet allow none of it to show on her face, but now she's scratching her collarbone — over and over she's scratching it, without one bug bite on her. There's death in that drum, I think, but with her pigeon-toed feet aimed at me, I fall even more in love.

Then she walks off, toward a stream behind her house, and it hits me that if I want my share of the thousand, I should get my ass in that crawlspace, since the actual removal of the drum might take but five minutes — and the last thing I need is Bark and James saying I don't deserve a cent. Then I realize that if I don't take a cent, I might not be guilty of any crime that's going on here, but thoughts like that help only if you can afford a lawyer who cares more than a public defender, plus I need to be in Bark's truck to get home, and even before I'm done thinking all this I'm on my hands and knees, my head brushing morning glory vines, then on its way through the square opening in the woman's cracked foundation.

It's quieter in there, and it stinks. James and Bark are on their bellies, snaking their way over damp dirt and rocks toward the drum, which lies on its side in the far corner. With the thousand in mind, I work myself toward them, trying to get a hand on the drum when they do, but Bark yells, We got it, Tre.

What are you saying? I ask.

I'm saying this is a two-man job, so back off.

You trying to cut me out of my share.

No. It's just there ain't enough room for all three of us if we want to get this thing past us.

So what do you want me to do?

Bark humps up his backside, reaches into a front pocket, pulls out his keys, tosses them toward me. Pull the truck down the driveway, he says. His hands dig dirt away from the drum. As close to the house as you can, he says.

Bark, I say. You know I can't drive.

Sure you can, he says. Just start it, put it in gear, and steer it so you don't hit nothing.

Okay, I say, though Bark's confidence in me has taken away the little I have in myself. I used to have confidence — gold confidence — but the older I get, I have less. Still, I back myself out of the crawlspace, pretend the woman isn't watching as I jog up the driveway to Bark's truck, hop inside it, start it, put it in drive, and let it roll down there. Steering is easier than I thought, but when I put on the brake, I about fly through the windshield. The woman, still near the stream, has her arms folded now, checking me out like she recognizes me from when we were in grammar school together, which, who knows, maybe we were. There's that kind of thing between us, that half-knowledge about each other we'd ruin with conversation, and I want to make love to her bad.

Now Bark and James are yanking the drum top-first through the hole in her foundation: the drum is too wide to roll out. They struggle like hungry playground kids; whatever's in that thing is dumb-heavy. Wind blows past my face, the woman now picking a weed's yellow flower from between pebbles beside the stream. It's her husband in the drum, I think. She got carried away in an argument over nothing and the thousand is all they ever saved.

Tre, Bark calls to me. Gonna help us or not?

I nod, toss him his keys, which he catches like it's the old days. I walk toward him and James, and all three of us roll the drum to the driveway, flattening a strip of knee-high grass, acting like we haul mystery drums every day. When it's time to get it onto the bed, we all take extra care to hold the top of it closed as we heave it up and lower it. Dead weight, I think. If this isn't a corpse, she would have said so.

Bark slams closed the tailgate, works his toolbox and scrap wood to make sure the drum won't move. No way are we taking it to the dumps we sometimes hit, even the unguarded one that isn't supposed to be a dump. The woman has her back to us, facing the stream. I'll never see her again, but I need to. Finally she walks toward the crawlspace hole, hooks its screen window back onto it, and heads into the house. While she's inside, James flicks a horsefly off his neck. She returns and walks toward us with her lips pursed; she's even finer-looking with sunshine on her face. She gives Bark a handful of cash folded in half. He counts it, mostly twenties, then nods, slips it into his shirt pocket, and says, Anything else?

Nope, she says.

Any ideas about where we should take it? he says.

That's your business, she says. Anyone asks me, I never seen that drum in my life.

Right, Bark says, and I can tell by how he gets inside his truck — without shaking her hand, which he usually does with people we take junk from — that he wishes we could just roll the drum back down the lawn and give back the cash. But he starts the engine, lets it eat gas while me and James get in beside him, me in the middle. And after we back up and ease out onto the road, I notice the woman's gone — inside her house, I guess.

We're headed away from the city, I realize after Bark stops accelerating. North, it seems. Farther upstate. Two miles an hour under the speed limit, none of us making a sound. The radio's off. I think to ask Bark where we're going, but it's like the three of us have made a side deal not to talk.

And if anyone's going to break that deal, I'm guessing, it'll be James, but James doesn't say jack, and neither do Bark and I the whole time we cruise over tar-striped highways zigzagging us toward tree-covered hills. I imagine it'll take hours to reach those trees, and maybe it does, but when we're finally alongside their shadows, I don't want to stop. Behind us in the bed is, as far as I know, only one shovel, and damned if I'll be the one to use it. We pass a farmhouse, a line of crammed-together mailboxes, a boarded-up gas station where a rusted sign reminds us of when unleaded was $1.74. Bark is scanning the bushy fields on either side of us, trying, I can tell by his grimace, to be more smart than scared.

We pass a state park with no one in the guard station. Then Bark is speeding down a straightaway. There's no one around us, from what I can tell, but no place for the drum. Then Bark brakes and pulls over. There's a hill to our right, but it's a football field away. How 'bout here? he asks.

Where, James says.

Yeah, I say. Where.

Right next to the road.

Are you high? I say.

Got any better ideas? Bark says.

Someplace more hidden, I say. I mean, with trees.

You're high, he says. The last thing we need is someone up here seeing three brothers walking out of some woods. They'll follow the truck. They'll read my license plate. We get out now — without any cars passing us — and roll it out quick and take off, there's no way anyone can trace anything to us.

Then let's do it, James says. Fast, he says, and he's out his door, and Bark is out his, and again I tell myself I'm with them anyway, so I might as well make sure I get paid. James can't lower the tailgate, so Bark slaps away his hand and lowers it himself, and they roll out the drum, and I do what I can to help, though all I manage is to get my hands on the thing two seconds before they drop it on the weedy emergency lane. I try to roll it into red bushes twenty feet from the gravel, but Bark is running back inside the truck, then James too, and the drum feels heavier than it was and a rock is in the way — and behind me on the highway, a car is coming. I think to run, then undo my fly as if I'm about to piss, using this as an excuse to turn my face as the car passes, honking its horn.

It doesn't stop, though. It's two dressed-up white women, speeding to wherever. When I get back in the truck, Bark says, What you do that for?

To take their eyes off the drum, I say.

That was *stupid,* James says.

I don't think so, I say.

He might be right, Bark tells James, and Bark waits until the car, shrinking ahead of us down that straightaway, is out of sight. Then he glances behind us, U-turns, and takes off in the direction we came from, and now, with the drum gone, James starts talking as if he has to make up for everything we all three didn't say since we left the woman's house, asking why we did it, asking why *he* did it, saying we should have thought it over, should have discussed it in the privacy we had to ourselves in the crawlspace — one of us, he says, should have put a foot down to keep all of us from losing our heads. We could have said no! he shouts. We could have said no at *any* time. We were greedy. We did it for bad money. Money that big is always evil. Then he goes on about how he hates being poor, hates the *forever* of it — it's like we were all born into these rubber bags we can't punch our way out of. There's no *light* in his life, he says. Not even in summer. Never was. He never should have hung around us, even in high school. He should have listened to his mother when, after we won state, she said we were bad influences, God rest her soul.

But that's as close as he gets to talking about the death in the drum, and his carefulness about that promises me there was death in there hands down, even though I've been waiting for him to zip it so I could say that, for all we know, we just dumped off a crammed bunch of laundry that got moldy after the stream rose and flooded the woman's house. There's a million other things besides a person that could be in a drum was what I convinced myself while James went off like that, but now that he's done, that million feels like a million too many.

Then a word of my own won't leave my mind: fingerprints. Bark turns on the radio and presses SCAN, but it keeps coming back to this station that plays lite songs for white folks. He lets it play, though, and the news comes on, and I listen expecting the dude to report a dead body found in a drum even though I know that's impossible so soon. After the news ends, Bark snaps off the radio, and I imagine he's thinking the same thing I am: for the rest of our lives, we won't but will want to hear any news on any radio or watch it on TV.

And I don't need to ask him if this thought's on his mind right now, because a glance from him, as we roll toward the city, tells me. That's how it was in both our championship seasons: all he and I needed was eye contact to know if I should lob the ball down to him or fake away and come back with a bounce-pass or pull up with a jumper he was getting set to rebound. We'd never say a word, never even nod. We were tight like that, and now we're still that tight, but I don't like where our tightness has taken us. James never had that unspoken vibe with us; in fact, he was always yakking at us and everyone on the court, refs included, even at the families in the stands. I used to think this was because he had the least talent of our starting five, but anyway since then he's used talk as a weapon in just about every situation he finds himself in: keeping the threat of it to himself at times, letting the world have it when he's backed into a corner. In a way it was good he talked so much when we played ball — it hid that eye contact Bark and I used — but now he just sits. And what makes me worry even more is that it's

Bark who finally speaks up, and, worse, what he says is: I say we go to Mississippi.

Mississippi, I say.

Ditch the truck in Virginia or something, take a bus the rest of the way, start all over down there.

Hang on, man, I say. For one thing, where would we stay?

We'll rent. Like we do now.

With a thousand dollars?

It's not like anything's keeping us in New York, he says. None of us has a woman, none of us has a job other than to haul junk. Maybe this never crossed your mind, Tre, but you can haul junk for cash just about anywhere.

But we'll go through the thousand like that, James says with a snap of his fingers. We got gas to buy, bus tickets, food — and you don't just walk into a new town and start *living,* in an apartment and all, without a good pile of cash.

True, Bark says.

Maybe ten miles pass while the three of us sit like strangers on an F-train. Then, just by Bark's suddenly stiff posture, I know what he's got in mind. He's not just heading to the city; he's heading to Belmont Park, to try to bet our thousand into more.

Bark, tell me we're not going to Belmont, I say.

Why not? he says, and I expect James to start lecturing, but he doesn't.

Well, *I'm* not going, I say.

Where you gonna go? Bark says. Back to that stinkin' apartment to wait for the cops?

They ain't gonna find me.

Well, they ain't gonna find *me,* Bark says. Because I'll be in Mississippi. With a helluva lot more cash than I have now.

You're saying I don't get my share if I don't go to the track? I ask.

No, Bark says. You'll get yours.

But it hits me he's already planning to take a chunk from my third for gas and wear-and-tear on his truck, which he does now and then — and which is fair, even though it seems unfair because he does it only when he wants cash to bet on horses. So now I'm looking at $300, maybe even only $275, and as many groceries as $275 might buy me, it feels like it's already nothing no matter whose pocket it winds up in, or where. Plus if Bark does leave for

Mississippi, James and I will need to make up for his share of the rent in the apartment — and damned if I'll live with some stranger.

And what if he wins? I think. Bark usually doesn't win, but, almost always, he comes close. His problem isn't that he doesn't know horses; fact is, in just about every race I've seen when I've gone to the track with him, he pretty much knows which horse will finish first. His problem is he lives for the big payoff, so he bets trifectas — which means he has to pick first, second, and third in the exact order — and it's usually third place, or sometimes only the exactness, that gets him.

I'll take you home, Tre, he says now. But on the way there, just hear out my plan.

He turns on the radio, turns it off.

We don't bet every race, he says. We bet one. And before we do, we study all the races to see which one's best.

For the thousand, I say.

Right, he says.

We put it *all* on one race? James says.

Bark nods. You guys are the ones saying we need more cash to move. *You* got any ideas about how we can make a pile in a hurry? I mean, legally?

Here's where I most wish James would go off on another yakking streak — about all sorts of money-making ideas that never entered my mind — but again he keeps still. And all I can think about when it comes to big, fast money is what would have happened if I hadn't messed up my knee in the semifinals the first year we won state. Yeah, we won state anyway, and yeah, everyone on the team propped me over their heads as we left the court, and, yeah, the ligament healed in time for us to win state again our senior year, but everyone who scouted us that year saw my ugly-ass knee brace, saw how I'd lost a half a second off my first step to the hoop, and even though I'd compensated my senior year by improving my jumper and passing game, everyone knew my burst of speed was why I'd gotten thirty-four letters of interest from pro and college scouts my junior year — and that, for all the points and assists I'd racked up, my best bursts of speed were behind me.

So we sit like that, all three of us, I imagine, remembering those days, as Bark takes us farther down toward the city, then pulls left onto the Sprain Brook, then exits onto the Cross County Parkway.

The greens of the trees and bushes and fields around us are too soon replaced by faster traffic and concrete, reminding us we live in the Bronx. And it's not Mississippi or the death in the drum or the hope of winning a pile of cash that changes my mind about whether I'll go along with Bark's plan; it's this appearance of the Bronx that does it. That feeling of being squeezed in. That feeling of knowing you are one of thousands, if not millions, of brothers caged into a future in which you will finally do something no-holds-barred-stupid. There's that stretch of moments, after we pay the toll for the Throg's Neck Bridge and stay just under the limit while we rise, when you see the blue water and yachts on either side and think the good life could happen to at least a few people who live where you do, but then the water is behind us and a Mercedes cuts us off as we signal to make the Hutch, and then there's the construction and the slow-downs, and you sit, itching to move forward, knowing that Belmont is, after all, a park with burgers and picnic tables and tents that sell beer. Fuck it, you think. We're almost there.

And then we are there, on Belmont's grounds, me and Bark and James, both of them, in hazier sunshine than we came from, looking older than I thought we were. Bark buys a program, the thousand again dented as it was to pay our parking and entry fees, and sits on a painted-green bench near where they bring the horses to saddle and pet them before they bust ass out on the track. They already ran the first two races, he says, a little pissed, and he slouches and studies away while James and I sit on either side of him like we're shielding his head from the thoughts of the white chumps walking past — whose clothes say they know far less about horses than they should. All we need, I think, is for Bark to find that one, best race. And to concentrate enough to pick the three horses in the right order. The death in the drum means pressure, I know, but Bark, I remember, played his best under pressure. In fact, *lack* of pressure was why he never made the pros or a college team either: in the high school games we knew we'd win, which was most of them, he could never get himself to try all that hard, and, if you believed our coach, word got out he was lazy. But in those few big games, the major-pressure ones, he always showed up to leave sweat on the court, and even if his shot was off or he dragged down fast breaks from being out of shape, he did the kinds of things that make championships, like elbowing the wind out of the other team's star when the refs weren't looking, or giving a soft high-five just before I'd toe the line for a free throw.

Now he's walking us to another green bench — beside the homestretch of the track. Again James and I sit up against his shoulders. He's flipping pages in his program, back and forth from Race 4 to Race 6. He's got it down to those two, he's told me without even clearing his throat. I want Race 4 so we'll know sooner if we've won or not, but I don't want to mess with what all those numbers are teaching him. He holds Race 6 closer to his face. He sighs. I look off around us.

We'll do it in the fourth, he says.

You know which horses? James asks.

The three-horse for sure. And the one. It's just a matter of whether we go with the four, seven, or nine after that.

That don't exactly sound solid, James says.

Just being straight with you, Bark says. What's left of the races today are hard as shit to pick.

Can we just go with the three and one to finish first and second? I ask.

That would be an exacta, Bark says. And *everyone's* gonna box the three-one exacta. Which means it'll hardly pay.

We can't take the three and the one with all three of those other ones you like? I ask. I mean, in trifectas?

That would be three different bets, Bark says. Meaning we'd bet only three-hundred-some on each. Which again means a lower payoff.

But we'd be more likely to win.

Bark returns to studying, but I'd guess he's also considering what I've said. Then I'm sure he's trying to figure how much each of those three trifectas could pay, but then I'm not sure of anything.

How much do we need? he asks.

Who knows? James says. But you'd have to think five or six grand would be cool.

And here's where I both believe we'll win but also wish we wouldn't. I wish we could just get in the truck and go home. I want to start the day over. I want to go back in time even before that, and meet the pigeon-toed woman before whatever happened in her life that forced her to call Bark. I want to make love to her back then, night after night, so often and well, the drum will stay empty.

But it's not back then. It's today, and now Race 3 is running, without Bark betting a penny on it, which reminds me we're here for serious business despite the white college boys beside us drinking beer, all of them hooting as the six-horse pulls ahead.

Bark looks up as the six wins easily. He glances at the odds board and says, Twenty-five to one. He hunches over to reread the program.

You know what? James says.

Shut up, I say. Let the man think.

You're right, James says.

Seagulls almost land on the lawn inside the track, then swoop off. They're headed north, toward the drum. That six-horse was headed north, toward the drum. Wind blows past the three of us: north, toward the drum.

The more I look at this, Bark says, the more I can see *any* horse finishing up with the one and the three. And the way the crooks here fix these races, any horse could *beat* the one and the three.

So what do we do? I ask.

Key the one and the three with every other horse in the race.

Which means what? James asks.

Which means if the one and the three finish first, second, or third, we collect.

Sounds good, James says.

But they both have to finish in the top three.

Sounds tough, I say.

It's as easy as I can make it, Bark says.

How much would we win? I ask.

Bark shrugs. Anywhere from double our money to a ton.

But like you say, what good is double our money?

Tre, Bark says. We gotta leave here with *something.*

Which tells me that, today, he's lost faith in horses. If it were yesterday, or any day before we moved that drum, he'd have enough faith for the three of us. But it's today. It doesn't matter that he's got more cash in his pocket than he's ever had at the track: today is today is today.

We all three sit. The horses walk onto the track, a jockey on each. Then Bark stands and says, Let's do it, and James and I follow him under the grandstand to the betting windows, where we wait in a short but slow line. Finally Bark leans in close to our teller, an old white lady. He talks so quietly, she needs to lean too, and then he pulls out the cash and hands it over for a ticket he reads even after his feet begin to shuffle off.

Gentlemen! the teller shouts. Your change? She's holding three twenties, and James jogs back to her, takes them, gives one apiece to me and Bark, then stuffs the third in his pocket, and as we walk back out toward the homestretch, it hits me I might have done something for a twenty I'd never do again for all the money in the world.

Bark veers left, toward the bench near the homestretch. Shouldn't we watch by the finish line? James asks, but Bark keeps on. James stands still, knees locked, yakking about how what we'd see from that bench won't matter, about how he wants to eyewitness the very end, about how, if all of us shout enough near the finish line, we could affect whether we win or lose.

Go ahead and shout, Bark says. I'm gonna watch from here.

James huffs off, leaving me to decide who to watch with. I don't follow him since the last thing I need is the sound of his voice. I don't sit beside Bark since I'm pissed he's a reason I went upstate. I stand where I am, partway between Bark and the finish line: in front of the odds board beyond the dirt where they'll run. It all of a sudden doesn't mean shit that the three of us won state twice together, lived together ever since, might end up together in Mississippi for the rest of our lives: we're all strung out along that wire fence like cousins who never met, each of us as alone as the old drunk beside me, all of us as stuck inside ourselves as whoever's rotting in that drum.

And we stay like that until the horses are in the gate. I glance over at Bark, who nods. Then I see that the horses are running, already on their way down the backstretch. Because of their distance I can't tell if we're winning, and then, because of the odds board, I can't see them at all. I hear names being called, but to us it's all about the one and three. Then I see every horse out there bunched into a pack, and as they reach the far turn, what looks like a three is in second. Then they're in their best full sprints toward and past Bark. Then they're passing me, getting whipped, with the three for sure in front. But the rest of them are gaining — or maybe they're not. The three might be fading, and a woman in the grandstand screams, and then I watch the rear ends of ten horses, and I haven't seen the one at all.

James is still beside the finish line, pointing but not yelling. Bark, with his arms at his sides, leans back against his bench. Then both of them are walking toward me, as if I'm in charge.

Well? Bark asks James.

I couldn't tell, James says. They were all bunched together.

Bark shrugs, his eyes aimed at the odds board, on the three boxes beside WIN, PLACE, and SHOW. A lit-up ten is in the WIN box, the other two boxes unlit.

We were right to key them with every other horse, Bark says. *Nobody* would have guessed the ten.

Which means a big payoff? I ask.

Bark nods. If we win.

Then, in the place-box, I see the lit-up number one. Here we go, James says, and the whole board goes dark, blinks twice, then lights up. The ten is still up over the one, the show-box still empty.

The three was toward the front, I say. Wasn't it?

It was when they passed me, Bark says. And it was *supposed* to stay up there.

He won't look at James, so I do.

Well, James? I say. Did the three hold on?

It might have, he says. But I'm telling you, man: from where I was standing, I really couldn't see.

Sonofabitch, Bark says, and I look at the board, where a clear-as-dawn number is now in the show-box: three.

It's not official, Bark says. And when it is, pretend it isn't. The last thing we need is someone following us out to the parking lot.

Let's get in line, I say. Let's get our cash and get out of here.

Just chill, Bark says, but then he's heading back under the grandstand, and James and I follow.

The three held on, James says, and he grabs my wrist.

Yeah, I say. We did it.

TOBIAS WOLFF

Bible

FROM *The Atlantic*

IT WAS DARK when Maureen left the Hundred Club. She stopped just outside the door, a little thrown by the sudden cold, the change from daylight to night. A gusting breeze chilled her face. Lights burned over the storefronts, gleaming in patches of ice along the sidewalk. She reached in her pockets for her gloves, then hopelessly searched her purse. She'd left them in the club. If she went back for them, she knew she'd end up staying — and so much for all her good intentions. Theresa or one of the others would pick up the gloves and bring them to school on Monday. Still, she stood there. Someone came out the door behind her, and Maureen heard music, and voices raised over the music. Then the door swung shut, and she tightened her scarf and turned down the sidewalk toward the lot where she'd left her car.

She had gone almost a block when she realized that she was walking in the wrong direction. Easy mistake — the lot where she and the others usually parked had been full. She headed back, crossing the street to avoid the club. Her fingers had gone stiff. She put her hands in her coat pockets, but then yanked them out when her right foot took a skid on the ice. After that she kept them poised at her sides.

Head bent, she shuffled in tender steps from one safe spot to the next — for all the world like her own worn-out, balding, arthritic mother. Maureen allowed herself this thought in self-mockery, to make herself feel young, but it did not have this effect. The lot was farther than she'd been aware of as she strolled to the club with Molly and Jane and Evan, laughing at Evan's story about his manic

Swedish girlfriend. She'd had an awful day at school and was happy to let the week go, to lose herself in jokes and gossip and feel the pale late sunshine almost warm on her face. Now her face was numb, and she was tense with the care of simply walking.

She passed a hunched, foot-stamping crowd waiting to get into Harrigan's, where she herself had once gone to hear the local bands. It had been called Far Horizon then. Or Lost Horizon. *Lost* Horizon, it was.

She scanned the faces as she walked by, helplessly on the watch for her daughter. She hadn't seen her in almost two years now, since Grace walked away from a full scholarship at Ithaca College to come back and live with one of Maureen's fellow English teachers from Saint Ignatius. It turned out they'd been going at it since Grace's senior year at SI — and him a married man with a young daughter. Maureen had always tried to see Grace's willfulness as backbone, but this she could not accept. She had said some unforgivable things, according to Grace. Since when, Maureen wanted to know, had a few home truths become unforgivable?

She was still trying to bring Grace around when Father Crespi got wind of the whole business and fired the teacher. Maureen had not been Father Crespi's source, but Grace wouldn't believe it. She declared things at an end between them, and so far she had kept that vow, though she dumped the luckless fool within a few weeks of his leaving his wife.

Grace was still close to Maureen's mother. From her, Maureen had learned that Grace was doing temp work and keeping house with another man. Maureen couldn't get her mother to say more — she'd given her word! But the old bird clearly enjoyed not saying more, being in the know, being part of Maureen's punishment for driving Grace away, as she judged the matter.

Maureen crossed the street again and turned into the parking lot — an unpaved corner tract surrounded by a chainlink fence. The attendant's shack was dark. She picked her way over ridges of frozen mud toward her car. Last summer's special-offer paint job was already dull, bleached out by road salt. Through a scrim of dried slush on the window, Maureen could see the stack of student blue books on the passenger seat — a weekend's worth of grading. She fished the keys from her purse, but her hand was dead with cold and she fumbled them when she tried to unlock the door.

They hit the ground with a merry tinkle. She flexed her fingers and bent down for the keys. As she pushed herself back up, a pain shot through her bad knee. "Goddammit!" she said.

"Don't curse!" The voice came from behind Maureen, a man's voice, but high, almost shrill.

She closed her eyes.

He said something she couldn't make out; he had some sort of accent. He said it again, then added, "Now!"

"What?"

"The *keys.* Give them to me."

Maureen held the keys out behind her, eyes pressed shut. She had just one thought: Do not see him. The keys were taken from her hand, and she heard the door being unlocked.

"Open it," the man said. "Open the door. Yes, now get in."

"Just take it," Maureen said. "Please."

"*Please,* you will get *in.* Please." He took her arm and half pushed, half lifted her into the car and slammed the door shut. She sat behind the steering wheel with her head bent, eyes closed, hands folded over her purse. The passenger door opened. "Compositions," the man muttered.

"Exams," she said, and cringed at her stupidity in correcting him.

Maureen heard the blue books thud onto the floor in back. Then he was on the seat beside her. He sat there a moment, breathing quick shallow breaths. "Open your eyes. Open! Yes, now drive." He jingled the keys.

Looking straight ahead over the wheel, she said, "I don't think I can."

She sensed a movement toward her and flinched. He jingled the keys beside her ear and dropped them in her lap. "Drive."

Maureen had once taken a class in self-defense. That was five years ago, after her marriage ended and left her alone with a teenage daughter — as if the dangers were outside somewhere and not already in the house, between them. She'd forgotten all the fancy moves, but not her determination to fight, for Grace or for herself — to go on the attack, kick the bastard in the balls, scream and kick and hit and bite, fight to the very death. She hadn't forgotten any of this, even now, watching herself do nothing. She was aware of what she was failing to do — was unable to do — and the shock of understanding that she could not depend on herself produced a sense of resignation, an empty echoing calm. With steady hands she started the car and pulled out of the lot and turned left as the man directed, away from the lights of the commercial zone, toward the river.

"Not so slow," he said.

She sped up.

"Slower!"

She slowed down.

"You are trying to be arrested," he said.

"No."

He made a mirthless laughing sound. "Do I look like a fool?"

"No . . . I don't know. I haven't seen you."

"I am not a fool. Turn right."

They were on Frontage Road now, heading upriver. The night was clear, and the almost-full moon hung just above the old tanneries on the far bank. The moon made a broad silver path on the smooth water in the middle of the river, glimmered dully on the slabs of ice jammed up along the sides. The moonlight on Maureen's bare hands turned them ghostly white on the steering wheel. They looked cold; they *were* cold. She felt chilled through. She turned up the heater, and within moments the car was filled with the man's smell — ripe, loamy, not unpleasant.

"You were using alcohol," the man said.

She waited for him to say more. His knees were angled toward her, pressed together against the console. "A little," she said.

He was silent. His breathing slowed, deepened, and Maureen felt obscurely grateful for this. She could feel him watching her.

"Over seventy dollars is in my purse," she said. "Please just take it."

"Seventy dollars? That is your offer?" He laughed the unreal laugh.

"I can get more," she said. Her voice was small and flat — not her voice at all. She hesitated, then said, "We'll have to go to an ATM."

"This is not about money. Drive. Please."

And so she did. This was something she could do, drive a car on Frontage Road, as she'd done for almost thirty years now. She drove past the Toll House Inn, past the bankrupt development with its unfinished, skeletal houses open to the weather, past the road to the bridge that would take her home, past the burned-out house with the trailer beside it, on past the brickworks and the quarry and a line of dairy farms and the farm her grandparents had worked as tenants to escape the tannery, where, after several years of learning the hard way, the owner sold out and a new owner found more experienced hands and sent them packing, back across the river. When she was young, Maureen and her sisters had picked strawberries with their mother on different farms, and Maureen had marveled at how her mother could chat with a woman in the next row or just look dully into the distance while her fingers briskly ransacked the plants for ripe berries, as if possessed of their own eyes and purpose. At the end of a day she'd look over Maureen's card (punched for a fraction of the flats she herself had picked), then hand it back and say, "At least that mouth of yours works."

Maureen drove on past the harshly lit 7-Eleven and the Christmas tree farm and the old ferry pier where she and Francis, her ex-husband, then a sweet, shy boy, had parked after high school dances to drink and make out; on through pale fields and brief stands of bare black trees that in summer made a green roof overhead. She knew every rise and turn, and the car took them easily, and Maureen surrendered to the comfort of her mastery of the road. The silent man beside her seemed to feel it too; it seemed to be holding him in a trance.

Then he shifted, leaned forward. "Turn right up there," he said in a low voice. "On that road, you see? That one up there, after the sign."

Maureen made the turn almost languidly. The side road was unplowed, covered with crusty snow that scraped against the undercarriage of the car. She hit a deep dip; the front end clanged, the wheels spun wild for a moment, then they caught and the car shot forward again, headlights jumping giddily. The road bent once and ended in a clearing surrounded by tall pines.

"You drive too fast," the man said.

She waited, engine running, hands still on the wheel, headlights ablaze on a Park Service sign picturing animals and plants to be seen hereabouts. The peaked roof over the sign wore a hat of snow. It came to Maureen that she'd been to this place before — a trailhead, unfamiliar at first in its winter bleakness. She had come here with Grace's scout troop to hike up to the palisades overlooking the river. The trail was historic, a route of attack for some battle in the Revolutionary War.

The man sniffed, sniffed again. "Beer," he said.

"I was having a drink with friends."

"*A drink.* You stink of it. The great lady teacher!"

That he knew she was a teacher, that he knew anything about her, snapped the almost serene numbness that had overtaken Maureen. She thought of his seeing the essays. That could explain his knowledge of her work, but not his tone — the personal scorn and triumph in his discovery of her weakness, as he clearly saw it.

A small dull pain pulsed behind her eyes, all that was left of the drink she'd had. The heat blowing in the car was making her contacts dry and scratchy. She reached over to turn it down, but he seized her wrist and pulled it back. His fingers were thin and damp. He turned the heat up again. "Leave it like this — warm," he said, and dropped her hand.

She almost looked at him then, but stopped herself. "Please," she said. "What do you want?"

"This is not about sex," he said. "That is what you are thinking, of course. That is the American answer to everything."

Maureen looked ahead and said nothing. She could see the lights of cars on Frontage Road flickering between the tree trunks. She wasn't very far from the road, but the idea of running for it appeared to her a demeaning absurdity, herself flailing through the drifts like some weeping, dopey, sacrificial extra in a horror movie.

"You know nothing about our life," he said. "Who we are. What we have had to do in this country. I was a doctor! But okay, so they won't let me be a doctor here. I give that up. I give up the old life so my family will have this new life. My son will be a doctor, not me! Okay, I accept, that's how it is."

"Where are you from?" Maureen asked, and then said, "Never mind," hoping he wouldn't answer. It seemed to her that the loamy smell was stronger, more sour. She kept her eyes on the Park Service sign in the headlights, but she was aware of the man's knees knocking rapidly and soundlessly together.

"*Never mind,*" he said. "Yes, that is exactly your way of thinking. That is exactly how the great lady teacher destroys a family. Without a thought. Never mind!"

"But I don't know your family." She waited. "I don't know what you're talking about."

"No, you don't know what I'm talking about. You have already forgotten. Never mind!"

"You have the wrong person," Maureen said.

"Have you told a lie, lady teacher?"

"Please. You must have the wrong person. What you're saying — none of it makes sense." And because this was certainly true, because nothing he'd said had anything to do with her, Maureen felt compelled — as prelude to a serious sorting-out of this whole mess — to turn and look at him. He was leaning back into the corner, hunched into a puffy coat of the vivid orange color worn by highway crews. In the reflected glare of the headlights, his dark eyes had a blurred, liquid brightness. Above the straight line of his eyebrows the bald dome of his head gleamed dully. He wore a short beard. A few thin patches of it grew high on his cheeks, to just below his eyes.

"I have the right person," he said. "Now you will please answer me."

She was confused; she shook her head as if to clear it.

"No?" he said. "The great lady teacher has never told a lie?"

"What are you talking about? What lie?"

A sudden glint of teeth behind the beard. "You tell me."

"Any lie? Ever?"

"Ever. Any lie or cheat."

"This is ridiculous. Of course I have. Who hasn't, for God's sake?"

He rocked forward and jabbed his head at her. "Don't curse! No more cursing!"

Maureen could see his face clearly now, the full, finely molded, almost feminine lips, the long thin nose, the dark unexpected freckles across the bridge of his nose and under his eyes, vanishing into the beard. She turned away and leaned her throbbing head against the steering wheel.

"You can lie and cheat," he said. "That's okay, no problem. Who hasn't? Never mind! But for others — poof! No faults allowed!"

"This is crazy," she murmured.

"No, Mrs. Casey. What is crazy is to destroy a good boy's life for nothing."

Her breath caught. She raised her head and looked at him.

"Hassan makes one mistake — one mistake — and you destroy him," he said. "Understand this, most esteemed lady teacher, I will not allow it."

"Hassan? Hassan is your son?"

He leaned back again, lips pursed, cheeks working out and back, out and back like a fish's.

Hassan. She liked him, too much. He was tall and graceful and broodingly, soulfully handsome. Not very bright, Hassan, and bone idle, but with a sudden offhand charm that amused her and had distracted her from dealing firmly with him, as he well knew. He'd been getting away with murder all year, fudging on his homework, handing in essays he obviously hadn't written, and Maureen had done nothing but warn him. She hated calling people on their offenses; her own raised voice and shaking hands, her heart pumping out righteousness, all the rituals of grievance and reproach were distasteful to her, and had always held her back, up to a point. Beyond that point she did not spare the lash. But she was slow to get there. Her sisters had pushed her around, she'd spoiled her daughter. Her husband's gambling had brought them to the point of ruin before her cowardice became too shameful to bear and she began to challenge his excuses and evasions, and finally faced him down — "ran him off," as Grace liked to say when she wanted to cut deep.

A similar self-disgust had caught up with Maureen this morning. After months of letting Hassan slide, she'd seen him blatantly cheating during an exam, and she'd blown — really blown, surprising even herself. She'd pulled him out of class and told him in some detail how little she thought of him, then sent him home with a promise — shouted at his back — to report his cheating to Father Crespi, who would certainly expel him. Hassan had turned then and said, evenly, "Stupid cow." And now, remembering that betrayal, the advantage he'd taken, his insulting confidence that he could cheat in front of her with impunity, she felt her fingers tighten on the steering wheel and she stared fixedly in front of her, seeing nothing.

"Hassan!" she said.

"I will not allow it," he repeated.

"Hassan has been cheating all year," she said. "I warned him. This was the last straw."

"*Warnings.* You should give him help, not warnings. It's hard for Hassan. He wasn't born here, his English is not good."

"Hassan's English is fine. He's lazy and dishonest, that's his problem. He'd rather cheat than do the work."

"Hassan is going to be a doctor."

"Sure."

"He will be a doctor! He will. And you won't stop him — you, a drunken woman."

"Oh," she said. "Of course. Of course. *Women.* All our fault, right? Bunch of stupid cows messing things up for the bulls."

"No! I bow before woman. Woman is the hand, the heart, the soul of her home, set there by God himself. All comes from her. All is owed to her."

"Now you're quoting," Maureen said. "Who's your source?"

"The *home,*" he said. "Not the army. Not the surgery. Not the judge's chair, giving laws. Not the discotheque."

"Who's your source?" Maureen repeated. "God, is it?"

The man drew back. "Have some care," he said. "God is not mocked."

Maureen rubbed her scratchy eyes and one of her contacts drifted out of focus. She blinked furiously until it slipped back into place. "I'm turning the heat off," she said.

"No. Leave it warm."

But she turned it off anyway, and he made no move to stop her. He looked wary, watching her from his place against the door; he looked cornered, as if *she* had seized *him* and forced him to this lonely place. The car engine was doing something strange, surging, then almost dying, then surging again. The noise of the blower had masked it. Piece of shit. Another paycheck down the drain.

"Okay, doctor," she said. "You've got your parent-teacher conference. What do you want?"

"You will not report Hassan to Mr. Crespi."

"Father Crespi, you mean."

"I call no man father but one."

"Wonderful. So you choose a school called Saint Ignatius."

"I understand. This would not happen if Hassan were Catholic."

"Oh, *please.* Hassan can't speak English, Hassan needs help, Hassan isn't Catholic. Jesus! *I'm* not even Catholic."

He made his laughing sound. "So you choose a school called Saint Ignatius. With your Jesus on the cross behind your desk — I have seen it myself at the open house. I was there! I was there. But no, she is not Catholic, not Mrs. Maureen Casey."

Even with the heat off, the air in the car was stale and close. Maureen opened her window halfway and leaned back, bathing her face in the cold draft of air. "That's right," she said. "I've had it with clueless men passing on orders from God."

"Without God, there is no foundation," he said. "Without God, we stand on nothing."

"Anyway, you're too late. I've already reported him."

"You have not. Mr. Crespi is out of town until Monday."

"Father Crespi. Well, I'm impressed. At least *you've* done your homework."

"Hassan is going to be a doctor," he said, rubbing his hands together, gazing down at them as if expecting some visible result.

"Look at me. *Look at me.* Now listen." She held the man's liquid eyes, held the moment, not at all displeased that what she was about to say, though true, would give him pain. "Hassan is not going to be a doctor," she said. "Wait — just listen. Honestly, now, can you picture Hassan in medical school? Even supposing he could get in? Even supposing he can get through college at all? Think about it — Hassan in medical school. What an idea! You could make a comedy — *Hassan Goes to Medical School.* No. Hassan will not be a doctor. And you know it. You have always known it." She gave that thought some room to breathe. Then she said, "So it doesn't really matter if I report him or not, does it?"

Still she held his eyes. His lips were working, he seemed about to say something, but no sound emerged.

She said, "So. Let's say I don't play along. Let's say I'm going to report him, which I am. What are you going to do about it? I mean, what were you thinking tonight?"

He looked away, back down at his hands.

"You followed me from school, right? You waited for me. You had this spot picked out. What were you going to do if I didn't play along?"

He shook his head.

"Well, what? Kill me?"

He didn't answer.

"You were going to kill me? Too much! Have you got a gun?"

"No! I own no guns."

"A knife?"

"No."

"What, then?"

Head bent, he resumed rubbing his hands together as if over a fire.

"Stop that. What, then?"

He took a deep breath. "Please," he said.

"Strangle me? With those? Stop that!" She reached over and seized his wrists. They were thin, bony. "Hey," she said, then again, "Hey!" When at last he raised his eyes to her, she lifted his hands and pressed the palms to her neck. They were cold, colder than the air on her face. She dropped her own hands. "Go on," she said.

She felt his fingers icy against her neck. His eyes, dark and sad, searched hers.

"Go on," she said, softly.

The engine surged, and he blinked as if in surprise and pulled his hands away. He rested them in his lap, looked at them unhappily, then put them between his knees.

"No?" she said.

"Mrs. Casey . . ."

She waited, but that was all he said. "Tell me something," she said. "What did your wife think of this brainstorm? Did you tell her?"

"My wife is dead."

"I didn't know that."

He shrugged.

"I'm sorry."

"Mrs. Casey . . ."

Again she waited, then said, "What?"

"The window? It is very cold."

Maureen had a mind to say no to him, let him freeze, but she was getting pretty numb herself. She rolled the window up.

"And please? The heater?"

Maureen drove back down Frontage Road. He kept his face to the other window, his back to her. Now and then she saw his shoulders moving but he didn't make a sound. She had planned to put him out by the turnoff for her bridge, let him find his own way from there, but as she approached the exit she couldn't help asking where he'd left his car. He said it was in the same lot where she'd parked hers. Ah, yes. That made sense. She drove on.

They didn't speak again until she had stopped just up from the parking lot, under a streetlight, in plain view of the drunks walking past. Even here, cocooned in the car, engine surging, Maureen could feel the heavy bass thump of the music coming from Harrigan's.

"Hassan will be dismissed from school?" he asked.

"Probably. He's spoiled, it'll do him good in the long run. You're the one I haven't made up my mind about. You're the one on the hot seat. Do you understand?"

He bowed his head.

"I don't think you do. Forget the prison time you're looking at — you haven't even said you're sorry. I said it, about your wife, which makes me the only one who's used that word tonight. Which strikes me as pretty damned ridiculous, given the circumstances."

"But I am. I am sorry."

"Yeah — we'll see. One thing, though. Suppose I'd promised not to report Hassan. Whatever made you think I'd keep my word?"

He reached into the breast pocket of his coat and took out a white book and laid it on the dashboard. Maureen picked it up. It was a Bible, a girl's Bible bound in imitation leather with gilt lettering on the cover, the pages edged in gilt. "You would swear," he said. "Like in court, to the judge."

Maureen opened it, riffled the thin, filmy pages. "Where did you get this?"

"Goodwill."

"My dear," she said. "You really thought you could save him."

He pushed the door open. "I am sorry, Mrs. Casey."

"Here." Maureen held out the Bible, but he put up the palms of his hands and backed out of the car. She watched him make his way down the street, a short man, hatless, his bright, puffy coat billowing with the gusts. She saw him turn into the parking lot but forgot to observe his leaving, as she'd intended, because she got caught up leafing through the Bible. Her father had given her one just like it after her confirmation; she still kept it on her bedside table.

This Bible had belonged to Clara Gutierrez. Below her name, someone had written an inscription in Spanish; Maureen couldn't make it out in the dim light, only the day, large and underlined — *Pascua 1980*. Where was she now, this Clara? What had become of her, this ardent, hopeful girl in her white dress, surrounded by her family, godparents, friends, that her Bible should end up in a Goodwill bin? Even if she no longer read it, or believed it, she wouldn't have thrown it away, would she? Had something happened? Ah, girl, where were you?

Contributors' Notes

100 Other Distinguished Stories of 2007

Editorial Addresses

Contributors' Notes

T. C. Boyle is the author of twenty-one books of fiction, including *The Women, Talk Talk, Tooth and Claw,* and the forthcoming collection *Wild Child and Other Stories.* He is a graduate of the Iowa Writers' Workshop and a member of the English Department at USC. His novels and story collections have received a number of awards, including the PEN/Faulkner Award for *World's End,* the Prix Médicis Étranger for *The Tortilla Curtain,* and the PEN/Malamud Award for short fiction. His website is tcboyle.com.

▪ Like most of us, I suppose, I am utterly bewildered by the speed with which our habits change as a result of the imposition of one technology or another (remember when people shouting to themselves on the street were considered lunatics but are now merely a pedestrian feature of our cell-phone-obsessed lives?). In many of my stories and novels I've tried to address how these changes affect us, especially in light of the fact that we are and will always remain animals bound by the natural controls that restrict all life forms. I explored ecological mismanagement, for example, in stories like "Hopes Rise" and "Top of the Food Chain," wondered what it might mean to have alarms on our cars and houses in "Peace of Mind" or indulge in video voyeurism in "Peep Hall," or, at greater length, what the effects of species extinction and global warming might come to be in my novel *A Friend of the Earth.*

"Admiral," with its exploration of how the cloning of animals might affect us, is another of these forays into the terra incognita of technological change. Yes, you can have your beloved dog or cat cloned, and why not? I'd like to clone my beloved dog or cat, and, for that matter, my beloved wife, children, and my beloved self. But at what cost? And yes, yes, I know: we are returning here to the ethos of Mary Shelley's *Frankenstein* and the overwrought horror films of the past — *"But you're mad!"* — to examine the consequences of messing with Mother Nature. I ask you, though: has Mother Nature ever been so thoroughly and relentlessly messed with as She has been today?

KEVIN BROCKMEIER is the author of the novels *The Brief History of the Dead* and *The Truth About Celia,* the story collections *Things That Fall from the Sky* and *The View from the Seventh Layer,* and the children's novels *City of Names* and *Grooves: A Kind of Mystery.* His stories have appeared in magazines such as *The New Yorker, Georgia Review, McSweeney's, Zoetrope,* and *Oxford American,* as well as in *The Best American Short Stories* and the *O. Henry Prize Stories* anthologies. Recently he was awarded a Guggenheim fellowship and named one of *Granta* magazine's Best Young American Novelists. He lives in Little Rock, Arkansas, where he was raised.

▪ In my midtwenties, I became oddly sensitive to noise. I resented the cars that drove by my apartment with their stereos thumping and the hum my refrigerator made releasing its heat. I felt plagued by the police helicopter that made its rounds over my roof every night when I was trying to fall asleep. I remember wishing that I could harness the momentary quiet that sometimes came over a room at parties and apply it where it was really needed — to the many engines of the world.

"The Year of Silence" began with that notion and with a certain narrative architecture I had been wanting to attempt, in which something was bit by bit taken away from a community and then bit by bit returned to it. I was interested in both the mechanism by which the city achieved and later dismantled its silence and also by the effect it had on the lives of the people who lived there, so I tried to balance my attention between the two. It wasn't until I finished the last page that I realized I had been building the narrative in small discrete chunks of incident. I decided that it would work best if I presented it that way, and that was when I divided the story into the short numbered sections in which it now appears.

Though I was not deliberately working in any particular tradition when I wrote it, I think now that it must have been influenced by James Salter's "Akhnilo," a story I have long admired, in which a man awakens to the noise of insects and, in that "infinite sea of cries," gradually discerns four words "from an order vaster and more dense than our own."

Here is a key to the Morse code.

A .-	H	O ---	U ..-
B -...	I ..	P .--.	V ...-
C -.-.	J .---	Q --.-	W .--
D -..	K -.-	R .-.	X -..-
E .	L .-..	S ...	Y -.--
F ..-.	M --	T -	Z --..
G --.	N -.		

KAREN BROWN's first collection of short stories, *Pins and Needles*, was the recipient of AWP's Grace Paley Prize for Short Fiction and published in 2007 by the University of Massachusetts Press. Her work has appeared in *O. Henry Prize Stories 2006*, and in journals that include *Georgia Review, Epoch, Tampa Review*, and *Crazyhorse*. She studied creative writing at Cornell University, and the University of South Florida in Tampa, where she is currently working on a novel.

▪ I spent a year in Ithaca, New York, in a farmhouse with a small stream that ran through the basement. The memory of snow-swept roads and rattling windowpanes surfaced, and I decided to set a story there. I came across an old *Ithaca Journal* and found two things: a brief article about the apprehension of a man who'd become known as the Collegetown Creeper, and another piece about a homeless encampment. The absence of any real detail made it easy for me to create my own version of both the man and the place.

KATIE CHASE was born in 1980 and raised in a suburb of Detroit. She received her B.A. from the University of Michigan and her M.F.A. from the University of Iowa, where she was a Teaching-Writing Fellow and a Provost's Postgraduate Writing Fellow. "Man and Wife" is her first published story.

▪ This is the last story I wrote before coming to graduate school and the first one I workshopped there. It hasn't changed greatly from its original form. I had been reading a lot of Edith Wharton and "envying" the very concrete conflicts her society provided for female characters, so I decided to create some constraints for mine. I liked the idea of evoking the contemporary and familiar and disturbing it with a tradition typically outside it. Of course, child, and arranged, marriage still occurs today, but I wanted to bring the practice closer to home. A seriously off-kilter version of the setting of my own childhood seemed the right place to start. The fun in writing this came from seeing mentions of Diet Coke and *Jeopardy!* become discomforting, while the strange and even condemnable went unquestioned. But in the end the story was to me more about having to grow up — whatever that may mean in any society — and how that might be negotiated by someone like my character Mary Ellen. I owe many thanks to *Missouri Review* for supporting this story.

DANIELLE EVANS has published fiction in *The Paris Review, Phoebe, Black Renaissance Noire*, and *The L Magazine*. She received an M.F.A. in fiction from the Iowa Writers' Workshop and was a fellow at the Wisconsin Institute for Creative Writing. Her first short story collection is forthcoming from Riverhead, and she is currently at work on a novel.

▪ "Virgins" owes a debt of gratitude to whoever was in charge of the music playlist at my gym a few years ago. Somewhere between "No Time" and "California Love," I was acutely reminded of a summer afternoon years earlier. I found myself thinking about the relationship between music and memory, the way that in the space of one song, I could be transported from an Iowa winter to an East Coast summer. I was also thinking about the mix of performative bravado and raw (though sometimes equally staged) vulnerability that's so much a part of both adolescence and celebrity, and by the end of my hour on the elliptical, Erica had presented herself with such force and clarity that I had to go home and start writing. The first draft came very easily, as did the first set of revisions — I was preparing for a reading, and in hearing the story out loud over and over again, caught most of what sounded unnatural to my ear. I wanted Erica to be sharp, but on her own terms. I wanted her language to remain hers, and the narration to respect her intelligence. I'd read a lot of stories in which women or girls are taken advantage of, or make questionable decisions about sex, and I found myself resisting the lack of agency on the part of women in many such stories, the unwillingness of some stories to recognize any internal logic at work. I wanted a narrator who could make calculated bad decisions, who could be sympathetic without being pathetic, who could know what was going on and still end up in a sad situation, but not so sad that she became flatly tragic. I wanted to explore the possibilities of a character who sees what's coming and heads toward it anyway.

I thought the first version of the story did well by Erica and Jasmine, but I worried that Michael became a bit of an afterthought in what was ultimately a story about the girls' friendship in the face of that moment when sex becomes a part of everything. My first set of structural revisions tried to establish that it was a story about three friends, rather than two, and that Michael was as much an important part of (and product of) the world of the story as were Erica and Jasmine. When I was satisfied with it, the story went out into the world, where it got a careful and intuitive edit from Radhika Jones and others at *The Paris Review.* I am both thrilled and amazed by the reception "Virgins" has gotten.

Born in New York and raised in Honolulu, ALLEGRA GOODMAN is the author of the novels *Intuition, Paradise Park,* and *Kaaterskill Falls,* which was a finalist for the National Book Award. She has written two collections of shorts stories: *The Family Markowitz* and *Total Immersion.* Her fiction has appeared in *The New Yorker, Ploughshares,* and *Commentary.* Her essays and reviews have appeared in *The American Scholar, The New York Times Book Review*, and *The New Republic.* She is the recipient of a Whiting Writer's Award, the *Salon* Award for Fiction, and a fellowship at the Radcliffe Institute for Advanced Study. Her new novel, *The Other Side of the Island,* has just been published.

▪ In my experience one story often begets another. First I wrote a story about the human resources director of an Internet start-up called ISIS. "Long Distance Client," which was published in *The New Yorker,* is the tale of a middle-aged man named Mel Millstein who finds himself in the company of programmers young enough to be his children. Discombobulated in every way, Mel throws his back out. He lies in pain in the company hammock, where he stares up at a pair of "tall, lanky programmers. From this angle, their arms looked extraordinarily long. He could see the stubble under their chins. Orion wore his blond hair in a ponytail. Jake's mop fell into his eyes. The two of them seemed to play all day and work all night. They were like wild horses."

When I find a rich subject, I keep working. I wanted to say more about ISIS and decided to explore the point of view of one of the young programmers Mel finds so mysterious. "Closely Held" is Orion's story. Together, "Long Distance Client" and "Closely Held" led me to the novel I am currently writing — a book that weaves all the characters I have mentioned into a much larger tapestry.

A. M. HOMES is the author of the novels *This Book Will Save Your Life, Music for Torching, The End of Alice, In a Country of Mothers,* and *Jack,* along with the short story collections *Things You Should Know* and *The Safety of Objects* and the memoir *The Mistress's Daughter.* Her work has been translated into eighteen languages and appears frequently in *Granta, McSweeney's, The New Yorker,* and *Zoetrope.* She is a contributing editor to *Vanity Fair, Bomb,* and *Blind Spot.* She has been the recipient of numerous awards including fellowships from the John Simon Guggenheim Foundation, the National Endowment for the Arts, NYFA, and the Cullman Center for Scholars and Writers at the New York Public Library. Born in Washington, D.C., she now lives in New York City.

▪ I started working on this story when Zadie Smith asked me to contribute a piece to *The Book of Other People,* an anthology she was working on as a benefit for 826 New York, an organization that helps students with their writing skills. The mandate was Make Somebody Up, and so I started thinking about "strong" characters, and these two complex, angry brothers came to mind. The problem was I didn't finish in time for Zadie's collection, and then a month or so later, William Boyd said *Granta* wanted something for their Special 100th Issue and I first gave them several other things, all the while still hammering away at this story. The truth is I'm still not finished — as soon as I started making the notes for Zadie, I e-mailed her, saying, "I think I have a problem; it's not a story, but a novel." That said, it's so dark, as I keep working I find myself looking for cracks of light, moments of lightness, and I'm finding none — which is really hard if I think about how it takes me years to write a novel. Stay tuned — who knows what it will become.

NICOLE KRAUSS is the author of the novels *Man Walks into a Room* and *The History of Love,* which received many awards, including France's Prix du Meilleur Livre Étranger. Her fiction has been published in *The New Yorker, Harper's,* and *Esquire,* and in 2007 she was selected as one of *Granta*'s Best of Young American Novelists. She was born in New York City in 1974 and now lives in Brooklyn. Her books have been translated into more than thirty languages.

▪ Two things led me down the path to this story. I set part of my second novel, *The History of Love,* in Valparaiso, Chile. I wanted a place far away, and for a New Yorker Chile is just about the end of the earth. I didn't spend very much time researching the city, or Chile in general; for me it was just an evocative name for a place in my imagination.

After I finished the novel, I found myself reading a book that detailed some of the atrocities committed under the regime of General Pinochet. When I finished that book, I began another on the same subject, and then another after that. The hope and energy that led to the election of Dr. Allende in 1970, and the horrors of the seventeen years that followed the military coup in 1973, became something of an obsession for me, although the things I read often made it difficult for me to sleep.

The second thing is that every writer spends a lot of time staring at her desk. You get to know it as well as your spouse's face; maybe better. I inherited the desk I write at from the prior owner of my house, who had it designed to his esoteric specifications. It is a monumental piece of furniture, far bulkier than any I would have chosen for myself, with cabinetry made from three species of trees extending up the wall. I use it mostly because I have no idea how to dismantle it and get it down the stairs, and because I don't think anyone else would want it, which seems to me sad as well as a waste. Before moving out, the prior owner's wife had a handyman dislodge a long rectangular painted panel that had been set into the shelves. It left a gaping hole in the woodwork, centered above my head, that I have never known how to resolve or fix. It is an ugly hole, and at first it seemed necessary to do something about it, but with time I have come to reconcile myself to it, or at least to the idea that the hole and the desk are part of a burden.

JONATHAN LETHEM has written seven novels, including *Girl in Landscape* and *Motherless Brooklyn,* which won the 1999 National Book Critics Circle Award and has been translated into twenty languages. His stories and essays have been collected in *The Wall of the Sky, The Wall of the Eye, Men and*

Cartoons, and *The Disappointment Artist.* In 2005 he was named a MacArthur Fellow. He lives in Brooklyn and Maine.

▪ How embarrassing to be caught dreaming about literary greatness. Of course, that's what every writer's always caught at because it's what we're all so often doing, though it takes another writer to know it (or at least nonwriters are too kind to mention it, or to let us see it in their eyes). That's why we all find one another so embarrassing. So, sure, I was thinking about X, and Y too. No, not him, or him, I've met those folks, and dealt with my sycophantic urges rather decorously in each case, thank you. X and Y are two I haven't met, so my reverential projections aren't tempered by prosaic episodes (grinding panel talk, green-room halitosis, blurb request, etc.). And of course I was recalling a time in life (long ago, I stress) when every passion got confusingly sexualized. Even out-of-print editions maundering on bookstore shelves sometimes appeared humpable, just because.

And then again, I came at this from the obverse angle too. Any wish to appear admirably modest aside, I've been unnervingly adored at least once or twice. I'm guess I'm sort of stranded in the long middle between the narrator and the King, so I can do the *Ah, Humanity!* thing in both directions here. I may seem to be skewering these characters, but really I'm bilaterally (sym)pathetic.

One last note, a curiosity: I visited Hastings-on-Hudson by way of Google Maps' satellite view, so the post office is on the right street, but the interior décor is completely fictional (and for the hotel and its street I reverted to my usual nonsense). A first time for everything.

REBECCA MAKKAI has published stories in *Threepenny Review, Iowa Review, Shenandoah,* and *Sewanee Review.* She is at work on a novel and on a collection of stories linked by the themes of music and war. She is twenty-nine and lives near Chicago with her husband and baby.

▪ My original title for this story was "First Generation," and I'd say that concept is still at its heart: the strange vantage point of the child born safe in America to immigrant parents, trying to comprehend the horrific journey of which America is (or was supposed to be) the happy ending.

My own father escaped Hungary following the failed 1956 revolution, and as I was growing up in the 1980s a fairly constant stream of Hungarian and Romanian refugees flowed through our house, occasionally living in our basement. My father's typical welcome tour included the Sears Tower, the Lake Michigan beach, and the produce section of the Jewel grocery store.

Radelescu is a fabrication, but he was inspired by György Cziffra, a Hungarian pianist who was jailed by the Communists in the 1950s. According to legend, Cziffra drew a keyboard in charcoal on the wall of his cell in order to practice, and when he was released three years later was able to play as well as ever. The Iaşi pogrom was real. Iaşi (pronounced *yäsh*) is a beautiful university town on the eastern edge of Romania, and until the 1940s it was a Yiddish cultural center. Two thousand Jews died in the 1941 pogrom itself, and twelve thousand more in its aftermath. The "death trains" Aaron references were not headed for concentration camps, but rather drove slowly back and forth over the countryside in the heat for days until nearly all the passengers were dead. I've never been to Iaşi, any more than Aaron has. I think I'd like to go.

STEVEN MILLHAUSER is the author of eleven works of fiction, including *Edwin Mullhouse, Martin Dressler,* and *Dangerous Laughter* (2008). He was born in Brooklyn, grew up in Connecticut, and now lives in Saratoga Springs, New York.

▪ While reading a biography of Thomas Edison, I began to realize that he had neglected to imagine certain inventions. Between the phonograph (sense of hearing) and the kinetoscope (sense of sight), shouldn't he have invented a machine dedicated to the sense of taste? Another devoted to the sense of smell? Still another to the sense of touch? This idle thought, of no particular interest in itself, was the impulse that led, several years later, to "The Wizard of West Orange."

DANIYAL MUEENUDDIN is a graduate of Dartmouth College, Yale Law School, and the M.F.A. program at the University of Arizona. For a number of years he practiced law in New York City. During 2007 he held a residency at the Fine Arts Work Center in Provincetown, Massachusetts. Currently he is based in Pakistan. His stories have appeared in *The New Yorker* and in *Zoetrope. In Other Rooms, Other Wonders,* his debut collection of linked stories, will be published by Norton in spring 2009.

▪ Several years ago over a cup of tea I first heard the tale told in "Nawabdin Electrician," from the incomparably salty mouth of — Nawabdin Electrician, now aged, but during my childhood the most colorful though certainly not the most crooked employee on my father's farm in South Punjab. Yes, a robber put six bullets in him, and yes, he survived.

Nawab and I have, as they say, a lot of history. For example: Arriving in my early twenties to take over the management of my father's farm, bearing in hand my fresh-minted Dartmouth degree in English literature, hopelessly without a clue, I hit on the idea of building a fish farm on a piece of waste land. I hired bulldozers, drilled a tube well, managed to get electric lines pushed forward to run the pumps, etc. From the first day old Nawab showed tremendous enthusiasm, abandoning all other duties. Finally, the ponds stood brimming with water, surrounded by strong geometrical dikes, tube wells pumping, the whole thing breathing enterprise and money. Tribesmen from along the Indus delivered thirty thousand seedling fry in steel drums. Now, who to run this project? Who but Nawabdin, expert in tube wells, rapidly becoming expert in the nurture of carp.

We poured the fry into turbid water the color of liquid chocolate, and never saw them again — but Nawab assured me they were growing apace. Finally, the day of the long anticipated harvest arrived. Fishers came from the river, armed with nets, girded up their loincloths, said a brief prayer, and stepped into the waist-high water, one at each end, a couple of them in the middle, and boys coming from the opposite shore to drive the fish forward. They made a pass, emerged from the water, dragging the net. Out came one flailing turtle, several sticks and stones, and fourteen kilos of enormous carp, meaning about seven of the creatures, each the size of a two-year-old baby. Puzzled, we cast again, then again. There just weren't any fish. Nawab paced the sidelines, waving his arms, shouting imprecations to call down the heavens: He would get to the bottom of this, heads would roll!

Only years later did I learn how he did it. Every few nights Nawab removed the screen blocking the watercourse leading into the pond. The fish swam upstream into the current, he closed the screen again behind them, drained the watercourse, picked up the fish, put them in burlap sacks, and headed to market. He'd been doing it steadily and thoroughly for the past year, the good citizens of nearby Khanpur relishing a steady diet of fresh fish.

So there it is. A story glosses a story.

ALICE MUNRO grew up in Wingham, Ontario, and attended the University of Western Ontario. She has published eleven new collections of stories — *Dance of the Happy Shades; Something I've Been Meaning to Tell You; The Beggar Maid; The Moons of Jupiter; The Progress of Love; Friend of My Youth; Open Secrets; The Love of a Good Woman; Hateship, Friendship, Courtship, Loveship, Marriage; Runaway; The View from Castle Rock,* and a volume of *Selected Stories* — as well as a novel, *Lives of Girls and Women.* During her distinguished career she has been the recipient of many awards and prizes, including three of Canada's Governor General's Literary Awards and two of its Giller Prizes, the Rea Award for the Short Story, the Lannan Literary Award, England's W. H. Smith Book Award, the U.S. National Book Critics Circle Award, and the Edward MacDowell Medal in literature. Her stories have appeared in *The New Yorker, The Atlantic, The Paris Review,* and other publications, and her collections have been translated into thirteen languages.

Alice Munro divides her time between Clinton, Ontario, near Lake Huron, and Comox, British Columbia.

▪ This is a very specific story about an almost playful, ruthless, irresistible crime committed by children, and what they do about it as a moral sense develops and they have to carry it through life.

MIROSLAV PENKOV was born and raised in Bulgaria. In 2001, at the age of eighteen, he arrived in America to study. He is currently pursuing an M.F.A. in creative writing at the University of Arkansas, where he was a Walton Fellow in Fiction. His stories have appeared in *Blackbird* and twice in *Southern Review.* He is the recipient the 2007 Eudora Welty Prize in Fiction.

▪ Factually this story is not biographical. Like the narrator, I arrived in America after finishing high school, but all similarities end there. My grandfathers were in fact hurt by the Communist regime, and let's face it — the narrator losing his parents is just a cheap writer's trick. All emotions, though, I drew from my own life.

I spent the summer of 2005 back home, in Bulgaria. My parents have an apartment in the outskirts of Sofia, in one of those neighborhoods you might see in movies like *Moscow Doesn't Believe in Tears* or documentaries about the ghost towns around Chernobyl. I was walking down the street, looking at the long, tall, gray apartment buildings, and they seemed awfully ugly to me. I knew that one of my grandfathers had spent a portion of his life building just such buildings and it occurred to me that he must have looked upon them with different eyes. Surely he had seen promise and beauty in the creations of his own hands.

The first line of the story came to me then, verbatim, as it is now. Wouldn't it be funny, I thought, to write about the two ends of the chain — an old man painfully obsessed with his ideals and his past, and his grandson fighting to escape this same past and these same ideals? I knew that grandfather and grandson would come together in the end and that a strange, absurd cause would unite them. Wouldn't it be funny, I wondered, if someone tried to sell Lenin's body on eBay, and if someone else could buy that body? What an awful capitalist thing to do.

I wrote a version of the story in two days and thought — that was that. I had not bothered to fulfill my initial idea, and now this was the story of an old Communist fanatic, whom I, as a writer, had failed to take seriously. I had left him a character in a twelve-page story.

I presented the story in my first M.F.A. workshop, and most of my friends liked it fine. At the back of her copy Ellen Gilchrist, who then led the workshop, had written only "Send it out for publication."

A week after that, a visiting writer I admire greatly came to our program.

He liked the opening paragraph but said the story ought to be about the grandson. He said the story, in its present form, was a political allegory no one would read. The characters, he said, came from a world where people worry if there will be food on the table. In America, he said, people worried about new cars. It's never too late, he told me, to go back to your undergraduate psychology major and get a master's.

Instead, I expanded the story, put much more of the grandson in, and thought — that was that. My workshop hated the new version.

They said the grandfather had lost much of his charm and eccentricity. I rewrote again. I was, as Americans might say, frustrated. I printed all scenes on separate pages and spread the pages across the floor, and rearranged, and rearranged, and in the end felt like a fool. I let a month go by, then sat down and wrote two more scenes. Hunting for crawfish, which I knew my great-grandfather had loved to do, and the final letter. It is a preachy letter, sentimental, as workshop folk might say. But as I wrote it, I wept. I was the grandson, away, facing death, alone. It is an awful thing to weep along with the characters you write. It is a terrifying blessing.

I thank my friends for their advice, Bret Lott for publishing the story, and Donna Perreault for her thoughtful edits. I thank the editors of this series for choosing my work. I thank you for reading it.

KAREN RUSSELL's first collection of short stories, *St. Lucy's Home for Girls Raised by Wolves,* was named a Best Book of 2006 by the *Chicago Tribune,* the *San Francisco Chronicle,* and the *Los Angeles Times;* in 2007 she was featured in *Granta*'s Best of Young American Novelists. She lives in New York City, where she is working on another story collection and a novel about a family of alligator wrestlers, *Swamplandia!*

▪ My sister and brother and I took the train to Sorrento, a trip that was in large part motivated by my brother's desire for booze with vitamin C, limoncello. Lemon trees grew in zagging lines along the cliff sides, and I could see the sea crashing below them as we toured the groves. Unfortunately, my sister has no recollection of any of this — the famous lemons of Sorrento had caused her eyes to swell into tiny moons. She had terrible allergies to the whole town. Then my brother announced that his shoes were filling up with blood. So, that's where the story was born — at this picnic bench in a Sorrento lemon grove, where we paused so that my brother could examine the spot where his pinky toes had burst through his Converse All-Stars.

While we were sitting there, I began to imagine a tiny old guy — not playing, exactly, but sort of presiding over a domino set. He was keeping some diurnal vigil here, very dapper in his green cap and vest, waiting for dusk. A vampire, I realized. "What if you had a vampire who sucks on lemons?" I asked my siblings. "You know, like a gag, so that he doesn't have to drink human blood?"

Which in an alternate universe would make a great SNL sketch, I think — Will Ferrell's fangs in a big foam lemon or something.

But the vision of that old man was never just a joke to me; there was some darker stripe inside it that I had to figure out.

GEORGE SAUNDERS, a 2006 MacArthur Fellow, is the author of six books, including the short story collections *CivilWarLand in Bad Decline, Pastoralia,* and *In Persuasion Nation* and, most recently, the essay collection *The Braindead Megaphone.* He teaches at Syracuse University.

▪ This story was started so long ago that its origins are a little hazy. I seem to remember driving with my wife and our then very young daughters, past a ranch house in Central New York after a long day at a lake, and looking over and seeing — surprise, surprise — a little boy tied up and harnessed in the backyard, kind of racing around like a maniac, his "lead" playing out behind him. And I thought, as I guess anybody would: Jeez, what the hell?

CHRISTINE SNEED lives in Evanston, Illinois, and teaches writing classes at DePaul University and Loyola University in Chicago. Her stories and poems have appeared in *New England Review, Massachusetts Review, Other Voices, South Dakota Review, Pleiades, Greensboro Review,* and several other journals. She studied French language and literature at Georgetown University and creative writing and a little more French at Indiana University.

▪ I wrote this story in the early fall of 2003, a few weeks after I had left my office job of five years at the School of the Art Institute of Chicago to teach part-time at DePaul and Loyola. While teaching four writing classes, I was working on a novel that rapidly became something I wasn't sure I was interested in, let alone understood. Grading eighty-five student essays nearly every week might have had something to do with this. When I started "Quality of Life," I immediately felt more relaxed and relieved to be working on a piece with an end that did not seem such a faraway, chimerical thing.

Initially I thought Mr. Fulger and Lyndsey would have a strictly sexual, possibly idyllic, relationship, but then the story turned into a rumination on power, madness, and the abdication of what little control one has over one's life.

Maybe it's a given that we often permit others to make our most important decisions for us, whether it be following forceful advice or simply doing what's expected — for example, taking the unwanted job transfer or going through with a marriage that we're sure is doomed — but it's no less true. I guess I was thinking about the fact there's so often a close-your-eyes-and-hope-for-the-best quality to our lives, and in view of the current state of the world, I find this to be a scary prospect. But, as happens to Lyndsey, we often don't know how to extricate ourselves from the entanglements we've more or less willed ourselves into.

A most heartfelt thanks to Stephen Donadio and Carolyn Kuebler at the *New England Review* for taking a chance on this story, for editing it so scrupulously, and for being such generous advocates for literary fiction.

BRADFORD TICE received his master's in creative writing from the University of Colorado, and is now at work on his Ph.D. at the University of Tennessee. His poetry and fiction have appeared or are forthcoming in such periodicals as *The Atlantic, North American Review, The American Scholar, Alaska Quarterly Review, Mississippi Review, Crab Orchard Review,* and the anthology *This New Breed: Gents, Bad Boys, and Barbarians 2* (Windstorm Creative, 2003).

▪ In early 2001, when I was finishing up my undergraduate studies in Knoxville, I began noticing Mormon missionaries, always in pairs, riding their bikes around my neighborhood. As children, my brothers and I were under strict orders from my mother to never answer the door whenever we saw one of these individuals approaching, and I'm somewhat ashamed to say that many's the occasion I've dove behind the couch and pretended, while the lights blazed and the TV blared, to not be at home. Years later, watching those satcheled kids pedal through suburbia, it struck me what an exacting, terrifying, and often thankless task that must be, going door to door. I began to wonder what kind of person would measure up to that kind of charge. It was then that I had the idea of writing a story about two missionaries, but as often happens, it wasn't until two years later that this idea came back around, knocking at my door.

When I went to write "Missionaries," I remember wanting the fact that these two boys were Mormon to be secondary to what I saw as the real tension. One of the cheerless realities of organized religion, in my secular opinion, is that often its spokespersons, the advocates of faith, end up seeming like used-car salesmen, while the truly devout go voiceless. My assumption here may indeed be flawed, but I guess that's where the characters of Case and Joseph came from. I wanted to see what would happen if two young men of faith, both given this monumental mission, set their sights on two very different goals.

MARK WISNIEWSKI is the author of the novel *Confessions of a Polish Used-Car Salesman,* the collection of short fiction *All Weekend with the Lights On,* the book of narrative poems *One of Us One Night,* and the book *Writing and*

Revising Your Fiction. Awarded two Regents' Fellowships in Creative Writing by the University of California at Davis, he won a 2006 Isherwood Foundation Fellowship in Fiction, the 2006 Tobias Wolff Award, the TIL Kay Cattarulla Award for Best Short Story for 2006, and the 2007 Gival Press Short Story Award. More than one hundred of his short stories have appeared in magazines such as *Southern Review, Virginia Quarterly Review, New England Review, TriQuarterly, American Short Fiction, Georgia Review, The Sun,* and *Yale Review,* and about as many poems of his are published or forthcoming in venues including *Poetry, New York Quarterly,* and *Poetry International.*

▪ For the good part of a warm Sunday afternoon, I bemoaned the future of the short story, and then my wife suggested I spend the next hour on two pages about three guys who needed to get to work. The result was two pages about three guys who were unemployed, and regardless of how hard I tried, no substantive plot suggested itself.

But a few years later, after devoting maybe too much time to writing poetry, I came upon the two pages and wondered what would happen if the three guys were asked by the mob to dispose of a corpse. A visible corpse and an actual mobster soon proved over the top — thus the forty-gallon drum and the reticent woman.

Why I chose a black male narrator likely had to do with how, as a young adjunct professor on both coasts and in numerous towns between, I grew bothered by the tendency of reading lists and curricula to neglect the interests of black male students, several of whom would seek refuge with me in whichever godforsaken office I'd been assigned. We would talk and listen and laugh. Sometimes our discussions involved their thwarted basketball careers, and in those days my first novel was still unpublished, and I remember thinking, as we'd sit in those offices, that no matter what we accomplished — as either athletes or writers — we faced futures of possible voicelessness. In any case the more I drafted and revised "Straightaway," the more these students' stories became one I needed to tell.

Tobias Wolff's books include the memoirs *This Boy's Life* and *In Pharaoh's Army: Memories of the Lost War;* the short novel *The Barracks Thief;* three collections of short stories, *In the Garden of the North American Martyrs, Back in the World,* and *The Night in Question;* and, most recently, the novel *Old School.* His fourth collection, *Our Story Begins: New and Selected Stories,* appeared in April 2008. He has also edited several anthologies, among them *The Best American Short Stories 1994, A Doctor's Visit: The Short Stories of Anton Chekhov,* and *The Vintage Book of Contemporary American Short Stories.* His work is translated widely and has received numerous awards, including the PEN/Faulkner Award, the *Los Angeles Times* Book Prize, both the PEN/

Malamud Award for Short Fiction and the Rea Award for Excellence in the Short Story, and the Academy Award in Literature from the American Academy of Arts and Letters. He is the Ward W. and Priscilla B. Woods Professor of English at Stanford.

▪ Many years ago I taught English in a Catholic high school in San Francisco. The dominant culture of the school was Irish American, but other of our students came from all over the world and you had to be blind not to see the difficulty they had in making themselves a place in this strange, sometimes unwelcoming terrain, and the anxiety of their parents that they do better than well, that they shine most brilliantly and win every prize this new land could offer — no matter what the nature, and limits, of their personal interests and gifts. This experience of cultural collision and frustration gave me something of the social context and atmosphere of the story. At its heart, though, it grew out of a parent's recognition of the love and hope we all have for our children, and the extremes to which that fierce care can drive us.

100 Other Distinguished Stories of 2007

ACIMAN, ANDRÉ
Monsieur Kalishnikov. *Paris Review,* vol. 49, no. 181.

ALARCÓN, DANIEL
A Circus at the Center of the World. *Virginia Quarterly Review,* vol. 83, no. 1.

ALMOND, STEVE
Nixon Swims. *Subtropics,* no. 3.

APPEL, JACOB M.
Creve Coeur. *Missouri Review,* vol. 30, no. 1.

BARRY, REBECCA
Not Much Is New Here. *West Branch,* no. 60.

BARTH, JOHN
The End. *Mississippi Review,* vol. 35, no. 3.

BAUSCH, RICHARD
Sixty-five Million Years. *Narrative Magazine.*

BAXTER, CHARLES
Ghosts. *Ploughshares,* vol. 33, no. 1.

BEACH-FERRARA, JASMINE
Safe Enough. *American Short Fiction,* vol. 10, issue 39.

BEATTIE, ANN
Girls in Bad Weather. *McSweeney's,* no. 23.

BEATTIE, ANN
Moni Wayside Blue. *Tin House,* vol. 8, no. 4.

BENDER, KAREN E.
Candidate. *Ecotone,* vol. 2, no. 2.

BENEDICT, PINCKNEY
Bridge of Sighs. *Zoetrope: All-Story,* vol. 11, no. 2.

BHASKAR, SITA
Swayamvaram. *Crab Orchard Review,* vol. 12, no. 2.

BLACK, ALETHEA
That of Which We Cannot Speak. *Antioch Review,* vol. 65, no. 3.

BOSWELL, ROBERT
No River Wide. *Southern Review,* vol. 43, no. 2.

BOYLE, T. CORAGHESSAN
Sin Dolor. *The New Yorker,* October 15, 2007.

BUNN, AUSTIN
The End of the Age Is Upon Us. *American Short Fiction,* vol. 10, no. 37.

CAIN, SHANNON
Cultivation. *Tin House,* vol. 9, no. 2.

CARRILLO, H. G.
Co-Sleeper. *Kenyon Review,* vol. 30, no. 1.

CHAPPELL, FRED
Tradition. *Shenandoah,* vol. 57, no. 2.

COOPER, T.
Swimming. *The New Yorker,* August 20, 2007.

CUMMINGS, JOHN MICHAEL
Marshmallow People. *Kenyon Review,* vol. 30, no. 1.

DEMARINIS, RICK
Odessa. *Antioch Review,* vol. 65, no. 1.

DINH, VIET
Substitutes. *Five Points,* vol. 11, no. 3.

DOLLEMAN, RUSTY
September, 1981. *Iowa Review,* vol. 37, no. 1.

DRISCOLL, JACK
Wonder. *Southern Review,* vol. 43, no. 4.

DYBEK, STUART
If I Vanished. *The New Yorker,* July 9 & 16, 2007.

EGAN, JENNIFER
Found Objects. *The New Yorker,* December 10, 2007.

FERRIS, JOSHUA
Uncertainty. *Tin House,* vol. 9, no. 2.

FINCKE, GARY
Isn't She Something. *Sonora Review,* no. 51.

FINN, PATRICK MICHAEL
In What She Has Done, and in What She Has Failed to Do. *TriQuarterly,* no. 129.

FURMAN, LAURA
Here It Was, November. *Subtropics,* no. 3.

GILBRETH, JILL
When the Stars Begin to Fall. *Ploughshares,* vol. 33, nos. 2 & 3.

GORDON, MARY
Dilly. *Daedalus,* Fall 2007.

GRATTAN, THOMAS
I Am a Souvenir. *Colorado Review,* vol. 24, no. 3.

GREENFIELD, KARL TARO
Silver. *Paris Review,* 180.

GREER, ANDREW SEAN
Darkness. *Zoetrope: All-Story,* vol. 11, no. 2.

GREWAL-KOK, RAV
The Disappearance of Harbhajan Singh. *Santa Monica Review,* vol. 19, no. 2.

GRUNEBAUM, JASON
Maria Ximenes da Costa de Carvalho Perreira. *One Story,* no. 92.

HARDING, PAUL
Miss Hale. *Harvard Review,* no. 33.

HORROCKS, CAITLIN
Going to Estonia. *Tin House,* vol. 9, no. 2.

JAMES, TANIA
Aerogrammes. *One Story,* no. 88.

JENSEN, BEVERLY
Gone. *New England Review,* vol. 28, no. 2.

JOHNSTON, TIM
Lucky Gorseman. *Colorado Review,* vol. 34, no. 2.

JULY, MIRANDA
Roy Spivey. *The New Yorker,* June 11 & 18, 2007.

KADISH, RACHEL
Love Story. *New England Review,* vol. 28, no. 3.

KAMLANI, BEENA
Zanzibar. *Virginia Quarterly Review,* vol. 83, no. 3.

KEMPER, MARJORIE
Specific Gravity. *The Atlantic* fiction issue.

KIM, DAVID HOON
Sweetheart Sorrow. *The New Yorker,* June 11 & 18, 2007.

KING, STEPHEN
Ayana. *Paris Review,* no. 182.
KRASIKOV, SANA
Maia in Yonkers. *The Atlantic* fiction issue.

LEE, DON
UFOs. *Kenyon Review,* vol. 30, no. 1.
LYNCH, THOMAS
Block Island. *Southern Review,* vol. 43, no. 3.

MATHEWS, BRENDAN
Airborne. *Epoch,* vol. 56, no. 1.
MATHEWS, BRENDAN
Dunn & Sons. *Virginia Quarterly Review,* vol. 83, no. 3.
MATTISON, ALICE
Brooklyn Circle. *The New Yorker,* November 12, 2007.
MCAULIFFE, SHENA
Anatomy of the Eye. *Black Warrior Review,* vol. 34, no. 1.
MCCORKLE, JILL
Midnight Clear. *Southern Review,* vol. 43, no. 1.
MCNALLY, JOHN
I See Johnny. *Virginia Quarterly Review,* vol. 83, no. 3.
MCNETT, MOLLY
Quiché Lessons. *Missouri Review,* vol. 30, no. 2.
MEANS, DAVID
Facts Toward Understanding the Spontaneous Human Combustion of Errol McGee. *Zoetrope: All-Story,* vol. 11, no. 2.
MILLER, MARY
Leak. *The Oxford American,* no. 59.
MILLHAUSER, STEVEN
A Report on Our Recent Troubles. *Harper's Magazine,* November 2007.
MOUNTFORD, PETER
Horizon. *Michigan Quarterly Review,* vol. 46, no. 4.
MUNRO, ALICE
Fiction. *Harper's,* August 2007.
MURPHY, YANNICK
Pan, Pan, Pan. *Conjunctions,* no. 49.
MYKA, LENORE
King of the Gypsies. *Massachusetts Review,* vol. 48, no. 4.

NELSON, ANTONYA
Falsetto. *Glimmer Train,* no. 64.
NELSON, ANTONYA
Nothing Right. *Tin House,* vol. 8, no. 4.

PEARLMAN, EDITH
Hat Trick. *Cincinnati Review,* vol. 4, no. 2.
PERCY, BENJAMIN
In the Rough. *Antioch Review,* vol. 65, no. 3.
PERCY, BENJAMIN
Someone Is Going to Have to Pay for This. *Paris Review,* no. 180.
PITTARD, HANNAH
Hunger and Night and the Stars. *Mississippi Review,* vol. 35, no. 3.
POMERANTZ, SHARON
The Virgin of Upper Broadway. *Prairie Schooner,* vol. 81, no. 1.
PROBST, MARK
Daytrip. *Yale Review,* vol. 95, no. 4.

REICH, TOVA
Plot. *Conjunctions,* no. 48.

SCHWARTZ, STEVEN
Galisteo Street. *Prairie Schooner,* vol. 81, no. 3.
SEAY, MARTIN
Grand Tour. *Gettysburg Review,* vol. 20, no. 2.
SHEPARD, JIM
Courtesy for Beginners. *A Public Space,* no. 4.
SHEPARD, JIM
Pleasure Boating in Lituya Bay. *Ploughshares,* vol. 33, no. 1.

SHEPARD, JIM
The Zero Meter Diving Team. *Bomb,* no. 101.

SILVER, MARISA
The Visitor. *The New Yorker,* December 3, 2007.

SMITH, CHARLIE
Albermarle. *Southern Review,* vol. 43, no. 1.

SOROS, ERIN
Surge. *Iowa Review,* vol. 37, no. 3.

SPECHT, MARY HELEN
House of Guns. *Florida Review,* vol. 32, no. 1.

STANSEL, IAN
All We Have. *Antioch Review,* vol. 65, no. 3.

THEROUX, PAUL
Mr. Bones. *The New Yorker,* September 17, 2007.

THON, MELANIE RAE
A Song Unbroken. *Conjunctions,* no. 49.

TOWER, WELLS
Retreat. *McSweeney's,* no. 23.

TROY, JUDY
Harold Carlisle. *Kenyon Review,* vol. 29, no. 2.

TROY, JUDY
The Order of Things. *Epoch,* vol. 56, no. 1.

UPDIKE, JOHN
The Apparition. *The Atlantic* fiction issue.

WALBERT, KATE
Playdate. *The New Yorker,* March 26, 2007.

WALLACE, DAVID FOSTER
Good People. *The New Yorker,* February 5, 2007.

WATERS, DON
The Bulls at San Luis. storyquarterly.com

WILBUR, ELLEN
Evelyn. *Yale Review,* vol. 95, no. 3.

WILDER, APRIL
The Butcher Shop. *McSweeney's,* no. 23.

YOON, PAUL
And We Will Be Here. *Ploughshares,* vol. 33, nos. 2 & 3.

Editorial Addresses of American and Canadian Magazines Publishing Short Stories

African American Review
St. Louis University
Humanities 317
3800 Lindell Boulevard
St. Louis, MO 63108-2007
$40, Joycelyn Moody

Agni Magazine
Boston University Writing Program
Boston University
236 Bay State Road
Boston, MA 02115
$17, Sven Birkerts

Alaska Quarterly Review
University of Alaska, Anchorage
3211 Providence Drive
Anchorage, AK 99508
$10, Ronald Spatz

Alfred Hitchcock Mystery Magazine
Dell Magazines/Themysteryplace.com
475 Park Avenue South, 11th floor
New York, NY 10016
$34.97, Cathleen Jordan

Alimentum
P.O. Box 776
New York, NY 10163
$18, Paulette Licitra

Alligator Juniper
Prescott College
220 Grove Avenue
Prescott, AZ 86301
$7.50, Miles Waggener

American Letters and Commentary
850 Park Avenue, Suite 5B
New York, NY 10021
$8, Anna Rabinowitz

American Literary Review
University of North Texas
P.O. Box 311307
Denton, TX 76203-1307
$10, John Tait

American Short Fiction
P.O. Box 301209
Austin, TX 78703
$30, The Editors

Another Chicago Magazine
Left Field Press
3709 North Kenmore
Chicago, IL 60613
$8, Sharon Solwitz

Antioch Review
Antioch University
150 East South College Street

Yellow Springs, OH 45387
$35, Robert S. Fogerty

Apalachee Review
P.O. Box 10469
Tallahassee, FL 32302
$15, group

Arkansas Review
Department of English and Philosophy
P.O. Box 1890
Arkansas State University
State University, AR 72467
$20, Tom Williams

Ascent
English Department
Concordia College
901 Eighth Street
Moorhead, MN 56562
$12, W. Scott Olsen

The Atlantic
The Watergate
600 NH Avenue NW
Washington, DC 20037
$14.95, C. Michael Curtis

Backwards City Review
P.O. Box 41317
Greensboro, NC 27404
$10, Gerry Canavan

Ballyhoo Stories
P.O. Box 170
Prince St. Station
New York, NY 10012
$8, Josh Mandlebaum

Baltimore Review
P.O. Box 36418
Towson, MD 21286
$15, Barbara Westwood Diehl

Bayou
Department of English
University of New Orleans
2000 Lakeshore Drive
New Orleans, LA 70148
$10, Joanna Leake

Bellevue Literary Review
Department of Medicine
New York University School of Medicine
550 First Avenue
New York, NY 10016
$12, Danielle Ofri

Bellingham Review
MS-9053
Western Washington University
Bellingham, WA 98225
$14, Brenda Miller

Bellowing Ark
P.O. Box 55564
Shoreline, WA 98155
$18, Robert Ward

Blackbird
Department of English
Virginia Commonwealth University
P.O. Box 843082
Richmond, VA 23284–3082
Anna Journey

Black Warrior Review
P.O. Box 862936
Tuscaloosa, AL 35486–0027
$14, Laura Hendrix

Blue Mesa Review
Department of English
University of New Mexico
Albuquerque, NM 87131
Julie Shigekuni

Bomb
New Art Publications
594 Broadway, 10th Floor
New York, NY 10012
$18, Betsy Sussler

Boston Review
35 Medford Street, Suite 302
Somerville, MA 02143
$25, Joshua Cohen, Deborah Chasman

Boulevard
PMB 325
6614 Clayton Road

Richmond Heights, MO 63117
$15, Richard Burgin

Brain, Child: The Magazine for Thinking Mothers
P.O. Box 714
Lexington, VA 24450–0714
$18, Jennifer Niesslein, Stephanie Wilkinson

Briar Cliff Review
3303 Rebecca Street
P.O. Box 2100
Sioux City, IA 51104–2100
$10, Tricia Currans-Sheehan

Callaloo
Department of English
Texas A&M University
4227 TAMU
College Station, TX 77843–4227
$40, Charles H. Rowell

Calyx
P.O. Box B
Corvallis, OR 97339
$19.50, Margarita Donnelly and collective

Carolina Quarterly
Greenlaw Hall CB 3520
University of North Carolina
Chapel Hill, NC 27599–3520
$12, Amy Weldon

The Chariton Review
Brigham Young University
Jim Barnes, Cora McKown

Chattahoochee Review
Georgia Perimeter College
2101 Womack Road
Dunwoody, GA 30338–4497
$16, Lawrence Hetrick

Chelsea
P.O. Box 773
Cooper Station
New York, NY 10276
$13, Alfredo de Palchi

Chicago Quarterly Review
517 Sherman Avenue
Evanston, IL 60202
$10, S. Afzal Haider, Jane Lawrence, Lisa McKenzie

Chicago Review
5801 South Kenwood
University of Chicago
Chicago, IL 60637
$18, Erik Steinhoff

Cimarron Review
205 Morrill Hall
Oklahoma State University
Stillwater, OK 74078–0135
$24, E. P. Walkiewicz

Cincinnati Review
Department of English
McMicken Hall, Room 369
P.O. Box 210069
Cincinnati, OH 45221
$12, Brock Clarke

Colorado Review
Department of English
Colorado State University
Fort Collins, CO 80523
$24, Stephanie G'Schwind

Commentary
editorial@commentarymagazine.com
Neal Kozody

Confrontation
English Department
C. W. Post College of Long Island University
Greenvale, NY 11548
$10, Martin Tucker

Conjunctions
21 East 10th Street, Suite 3E
New York, NY 10003
$18, Bradford Morrow

Connecticut Review
English Department
Southern Connecticut State University
501 Crescent Street

New Haven, CT 06515
John Briggs

Crab Orchard Review
Department of English
Southern Illinois University at Carbondale
Carbondale, IL 62901
$15, Carolyn Alessio

Crazyhorse
Department of English
College of Charleston
66 George Street
Charleston, SC 29424
$15, Carol Ann Davis

Crucible
Barton College
P.O. Box 5000
Wilson, NC 27893-7000
Terrence L. Grimes

Daedalus
136 Irving Street, Suite 100
Cambridge, MA 02138
$33, James Miller

Denver Quarterly
University of Denver
Denver, CO 80208
$20, Bin Ramke

Descant
P.O. Box 314
Station P
Toronto, Ontario M5S 2S8
$25, Karen Mulhallen

Descant
TCU
Box 297270
Fort Worth, TX 76129
$12, Lynn Risser, David Kuhne

Ecotone
Department of Creative Writing
University of North Carolina, Wilmington
601 South College Road
Wilmington, NC 28403
$18, David Gessner

Epiphany
71 Bedford Street
New York, NY 10014
$10, Willard Cook

Epoch
251 Goldwin Smith Hall
Cornell University
Ithaca, NY 14853-3201
$11, Michael Koch

Esquire
300 West 57th Street, 21st Floor
New York, NY 10019
$17.94, Fiction Editor

Event
Douglas College
P.O. Box 2503
New Westminster
British Columbia V3L 5B2
$22, Cathy Stonehouse

Fairy Tale Review
University of Alabama
English Department
Box 780224
Tuscaloosa, AL 35487
$12, Kate Bernheimer

Fantasy and Science Fiction
P.O. Box 3447
Hoboken, NJ 07030
$44.89, Gordon Van Gelder

Fiction
Department of English
The City College of New York
Convent Avenue at 138th Street
New York, NY 10031
$10, Mark Jay Mirsky

Fiction International
Department of English and Comparative Literature
San Diego State University
San Diego, CA 92182
$12, Harold Jaffe

Fiddlehead
UNB P.O. Box 4400
Fredericton
New Brunswick E3B 5A3
$20, Mark Anthony Jarman

Five Points
Georgia State University
Department of English
University Plaza
Atlanta, GA 30303–3083
$20, David Bottoms

The Florida Review
Department of English
University of Hawaii at Manoa
1733 Donagho Road
Honolulu, HI 96822
$10, Chris Kelsey

Fugue
Department of English
Brink Hall 200
University of Idaho
Moscow, ID 83844–1102
$14, Ben George, Jeff P. Jones

Georgia Review
University of Georgia
Athens, GA 30602
$24, T. R. Hummer

Gettysburg Review
Gettysburg College
Gettysburg, PA 17325–1491
$24, Peter Stitt

Glimmer Train Stories
1211 NW Glisan Street, Suite 207
Portland, OR 97209
$36, Susan Burmeister-Brown, Linda Swanson-Davies

Grain
Box 67
Saskatoon, Saskatchewan S4P 3B4
$26.95, Kent Bruyneel

Granta
1755 Broadway, 5th Floor
New York, NY 10019–3780
$39.95, Ian Jack

Green Mountains Review
Box A58
Johnson State College
Johnson, VT 05656
$15, Jack Pulaski

Greensboro Review
3302 Hall for Humanities
and Research Administration
University of North Carolina
Greensboro, NC 27412
$10, Jim Clark

Gulf Coast
Department of English
University of Houston
4800 Calhoun Road
Houston, TX 77204–3012
$14, Mark Doty

Gulf Stream
English Department
Florida International University
Biscayne Bay Campus
3000 NE 151st Street
North Miami, FL 33181
$15, John Dufresne, Cindy Chinelly

Hanging Loose
231 Wyckoff Street
Brooklyn, NY 11217
$17.50, group

Harper's Magazine
666 Broadway
New York, NY 10012
$16, Ben Metcalf

Harpur Palate
Department of English
Binghamton University
P.O. Box 6000
Binghamton, NY 13902
$16, Letitia Moffitt, Doris Umbers

Harvard Review
Poetry Room
Harvard College Library

Cambridge, MA 02138
$16, Christina Thompson

Hayden's Ferry Review
Box 871502
Arizona State University
Tempe, AZ 85287–1502
$14, Christopher Becker, Eric Day

Hobart
P.O. Box 1658
Ann Arbor, MI 48103
Aaron Burch

Hudson Review
684 Park Avenue
New York, NY 10021
$24, Paula Deitz

Hyphen
P.O. Box 192002
San Francisco, CA 94119
$18, Melissa Hung

Idaho Review
Boise State University
1910 University Drive
Boise, ID 83725
$9.95, Mitch Wieland

Image
Center for Religious Humanism
3307 Third Avenue West
Seattle, WA 98119
$36, Gregory Wolfe

Indiana Review
Ballantine Hall 465
1020 East Kirkwood Avenue
Bloomington, IN 47405–7103
$14, Esther Lee

Iowa Review
Department of English
University of Iowa
308 EPB
Iowa City, IA 52242
$20, David Hamilton

Iris
University of Virginia Women's Center
P.O. Box 800588
Charlottesville, VA 22908
$9, Gina Welch

Iron Horse Literary Review
Department of English
Texas Tech University
Box 43091
Lubbock, TX 79409–3091
$12, Leslie Jill Patterson

Italian Americana
University of Rhode Island
Providence Campus
80 Washington Street
Providence, RI 02903
$20, Carol Bonomo Albright

Jabberwock Review
Department of English
Drawer E
Mississippi State University
Mississippi State, MS 39762
$12, Joy Murphy

Jewish Currents
45 East 33rd Street
New York, NY 10016–5335
$20, editorial board

The Journal
Department of English
Ohio State University
164 West Seventeenth Avenue
Columbus, OH 43210
$12, Kathy Fagan, Michelle Herman

Kalliope
Florida Community College
3939 Roosevelt Boulevard
Jacksonville, FL 32205
$12.50, Mary Sue Koeppel

Kenyon Review
Kenyon College
Gambier, OH 43022
$30, David H. Lynn

Lady Churchill's Rosebud Wristlet
Small Beer Press
176 Prospect Avenue

Northampton, MA 01060
$20, Kelly Link

Lake Effect
Penn State Erie
5091 Station Road
Erie, PA 16563–1501
$6, George Looney

The Literary Review
Fairleigh Dickinson University
285 Madison Avenue
Madison, NJ 07940
$18, René Steinke

Louisiana Literature
LSU 10792
Southeastern Louisiana University
Hammond, LA 70402
$12, Jack B. Bedell

Louisville Review
Spalding University
851 South Fourth Street
Louisville, KY 40203
$14, Sena Jeter Naslund

Madison Review
University of Wisconsin
Department of English
H. C. White Hall
600 North Park Street
Madison, WI 53706
$12, Abram Foley, Laura Weingarten

Mānoa
English Department
University of Hawaii
Honolulu, HI 96822
$22, Frank Stewart

Massachusetts Review
South College
Box 37140
University of Massachusetts
Amherst, MA 01003
$22, David Lenson, Ellen Dore Watson

McSweeney's
826 Valencia Street
San Francisco, CA 94110
$36, Dave Eggers

Memorious: A Forum for
New Verse and Poetics
Memorious.org
Rebecca Morgan Frank

Meridian
Department of English
P.O. Box 400145
University of Virginia
Charlottesville, VA 22904–4145
$10, Caitlin Johnson

Michigan Quarterly Review
3574 Rackham Building
915 East Washington Street
University of Michigan
Ann Arbor, MI 48109
$25, Laurence Goldstein

Mid-American Review
Department of English
Bowling Green State University
Bowling Green, OH 43403
$12, Michael Czyzniejewski

Minnesota Review
Department of English
Carnegie Mellon University
Pittsburgh, PA 15213
$30, Jeffrey Williams

Mississippi Review
University of Southern Mississippi
Southern Station, Box 5144
Hattiesburg, MS 39406–5144
$15, Frederick Barthelme

Missouri Review
1507 Hillcrest Hall
University of Missouri
Columbia, MO 65211
$22, Speer Morgan

Ms.
433 South Beverly Drive
Beverly Hills, CA 90212
$45, Amy Bloom

n + 1
Park West Finance Station
P.O. Box 20688
New York, NY 10025
$16, Allison Lorentzen

Narrative Magazine
narrativemagzine.com
The Editors

Natural Bridge
Department of English
University of Missouri, St. Louis
8001 Natural Bridge Road
St. Louis, MO 63121–4499
$15, Jason Rizos

New Delta Review
English Department
15 Allen Hall
Louisiana State University
Baton Rouge, LA 70803–5001
$30, Shane Noecker

New England Review
Middlebury College
Middlebury, VT 05753
$25, Stephen Donadio

New Letters
University of Missouri
5100 Rockhill Road
Kansas City, MO 64110
$22, Robert Stewart

New Ohio Review
English Department
360 Ellis Hall
Ohio University
Athens, OH 45701
$20, John Bullock

New Orleans Review
P.O. Box 195
Loyola University
New Orleans, LA 70118
$12, Christopher Chambers

New Orphic Review
706 Mill Street
Nelson, British Columbia V1L 4S5
$25, Ernest Hekkanen

New Quarterly
English Language Proficiency
Programme
Saint Jerome's University
200 University Avenue West
Waterloo, Ontario N2L 3G3
$36, Kim Jernigan

New Renaissance
16 Heath Road
Arlington, MA 02474
$38, Louse T. Reynolds

News from the Republic of Letters
P.O. Box 247
BU Station
Boston, MA 02215
$9.95, Keith Botsford

The New Yorker
4 Times Square
New York, NY 10036
$46, Deborah Treisman

New York Stories
English Department
LaGuardia Community College
31–10 Thomson Avenue
Long Island City, NY 11101
$13.40, Daniel Caplice Lynch

Nimrod International Journal
Arts and Humanities Council of Tulsa
600 South College Avenue
Tulsa, OK 74104
$17.50, Francine Ringold

Ninth Letter
Department of English
University of Illinois
608 South Wright Street
Urbana, IL 61801
$19.95, Jodee Rubins

Noon
1324 Lexington Avenue
PMB 298

New York, NY 10128
$9, Diane Williams

North American Review
University of Northern Iowa
1222 West 27th Street
Cedar Falls, IA 50614
$22, Grant Tracey

North Carolina Literary Review
Department of English
2201 Bate Building
East Carolina University
Greenville, NC 27858–4353
$20, Margaret Bauer

North Dakota Quarterly
University of North Dakota
P.O. Box 8237
Grand Forks, ND 58202
$25, Robert Lewis

Northwest Review
1286 University of Oregon
Eugene, OR 97403
$22, John Witte

Notre Dame Review
840 Flanner Hall
Department of English
356 O'Shag
University of Notre Dame
Notre Dame, IN 46556–5639
$15, John Matthias, William O'Rourke

One Story
425 Third Street, No. 2
Brooklyn, NY 11215
$21, Maribeth Batcha, Hannah Tinti

Ontario Review
9 Honey Brook Drive
Princeton, NJ 08540
$16, Raymond J. Smith

Open City
225 Lafayette Street, Suite 1114
New York, NY 10012
$32, Thomas Beller, Joanna Yas

Opium
Opiummagazine.com
1272 Page Street
San Francisco, CA 94117
Todd Zuniga

Other Voices
University of Illinois at Chicago
Department of English, M/C 162
601 South Morgan Street
Chicago, IL 60607–7120
$24, Gina Frangello

Oxford American
201 Donaghey Avenue, Main 107
Conway, AR 72035
$29.95, Marc Smirnoff

Pak N Treger
National Yiddish Book Center
Harry and Jeanette Weinberg Bldg.
1021 West Street
Amherst, MA 01002
$36, Aaron Lansky

Paper Street
Paper Street Press
P.O. Box 14786
Pittsburgh, PA 15234
Dory Adams

Paris Review
62 White Street
New York, NY 10013
$34, Philip Gourevitch

Parting Gifts
3413 Wilshire Drive
Greensboro, NC 27408–2923
Robert Bixby

Passages North
English Department
Northern Michigan University
1401 Presque Isle Avenue
Marquette, MI 49007–5363
$10, Katie Hanson

Pearl
3030 East Second Street

Long Beach, CA 90803
$18, group

Phantasmagoria
English Department
Century Community and Technical College
3300 Century Avenue North
White Bear Lake, MN 55110
$15, Abigail Allen

Phoebe
George Mason University
MSN 2D6
4400 University Drive
Fairfax, VA 22030–4444
$12, Lisa Ampleman

The Pinch
Department of English
University of Memphis
Memphis, TN 38152
$12, Kristen Iverson

Playboy
680 North Lake Shore Drive
Chicago, IL 60611
$12, Amy Grace Lloyd

Pleiades
Department of English and Philosophy
Central Missouri State University
P.O. Box 800
Warrensburg, MO 64093
$12, Susan Steinberg

Ploughshares
Emerson College
120 Boylston Street
Boston, MA 02116
$22, Fiction Editor

Poem Memoir Story
Department of English
University of Alabama at Birmingham
217 Humanities Building
900 South 13th Street
Birmingham, AL 35294–1260
$7, Linda Frost

Porcupine
P.O. Box 259
Cedarburg, WI 53012
$15.95, editorial group

Post Road
P.O. Box 400951
Cambridge, MA 02420
$18, Mary Cotton

Potomac Review
Montgomery College
51 Mannakee Street
Rockville, MD 20850
$20, Eli Flam

Prairie Fire
423–100 Arthur Street
Winnipeg, Manitoba R3B 1H3
$25, Andris Taskans

Prairie Schooner
201 Andrews Hall
University of Nebraska
Lincoln, NE 68588–0334
$26, Hilda Raz

Prism International
Department of Creative Writing
University of British Columbia
Buchanan E-462
Vancouver, British Columbia V6T 1W5
$22, Catharine Chen

A Public Space
323 Dean Street
Brooklyn, NY 11217
Brigid Hughes

Puerto del Sol
MSCC 3E
New Mexico State University
P.O. Box 30001
Las Cruces, NM 88003
$10, Kevin McIlvoy

Quarterly West
2055 South Central Campus Drive
Department of English/LNCO 3500
University of Utah

Salt Lake City, UT 84112
$14, Mike White, Paul Ketzle

Redivider
Emerson College
120 Boylston Street
Boston, MA 02116
$10, Chip Cheek

Red Rock Review
English Department, J2A
Community College of Southern Nevada
3200 East Cheyenne Avenue
North Las Vegas, NV 89030
$9.50, Richard Logsdon

Red Wheelbarrow
De Anza College
21250 Stevens Creek Boulevard
Cupertino, CA 95014–5702
$5, Randolph Splitter

River Oak Review
River Oak Arts
P.O. Box 3127
Oak Park, IL 60303
$12, Mary Lee MacDonald

River Styx
3547 Olive Street, Suite 107
St. Louis, MO 63103–1014
$20, Richard Newman

Roanoke Review
221 College Lane
Salem, VA 24153
$13, Paul Hanstedt

Rock & Sling
P.O. Box 30865
Spokane, WA 99223
Susan Cowger

Room Magazine
P.O. Box 46160
Station D
Vancouver, British Columbia V6J 5G5
$25, Patricia Robitaille

Rosebud
P.O. Box 459
Cambridge, WI 53523
$18, Roderick Clark

Ruminate
140 North Roosevelt Avenue
Fort Collins, CO 80521
$28, Brianna Van Dyke

Salamander
Suffolk University
English Department
41 Temple Street
Boston, MA 02114
$23, Jennifer Barber

Salmagundi
Skidmore College
Saratoga Springs, NY 12866
$20, Robert Boyers

Salt Flats Annual
P.O. Box 2381
Layton, UT 84041
$10, Dana Layton Sides

Santa Monica Review
1900 Pico Boulevard
Santa Monica, CA 90405
$12, Andrew Tonkovich

Sewanee Review
University of the South
Sewanee, TN 37375–4009
$24, George Core

Shenandoah
Mattingly House
2 Lee Avenue
Washington and Lee University
Lexington, VA 24450–0303
$22, R. T. Smith, Lynn Leech

Small Spiral Notebook
172 Fifth Avenue, Suite 104
Brooklyn, NY 11217
$12, Felicia Sullivan

Sonora Review
Department of English
University of Arizona

Tucson, AZ 85721
$12, David James Poissant, Mark Polansak

South Dakota Review
University of South Dakota
P.O. Box 111 University Exchange
Vermilion, SD 57069
$15, Brian Bedard

Southeast Review
Department of English
Florida State University
Tallahassee, FL 32306
$10, Tony R. Morris

Southern Humanities Review
9088 Haley Center
Auburn University
Auburn, AL 36849
$15, Dan R. Latimer, Virginia M. Kouidis

Southern Indiana Review
College of Liberal Arts
University of Southern Indiana
8600 University Boulevard
Evansville, IN 62026
$20, Matthew Graham

Southern Review
43 Allen Hall
Louisiana State University
Baton Rouge, LA 70803
$25, Bret Lott

Southwest Review
Southern Methodist University
P.O. Box 4374
Dallas, TX 75275
$24, Willard Spiegelman

Sou'Wester
Department of English
Box 1438
Southern Illinois University
Edwardsville, IL 62026
Allison Frank

StoryQuarterly
431 Sheridan Road
Kenilworth, IL 60043–1220
$12, M.M.M. Hayes

StorySouth
898 Chelsea Avenue
Bexley, OH 43209
Jason Sanford

Subtropics
Department of English
University of Florida
P.O. Box 112075
Gainesville, FL 32611–2075
David Leavitt

The Sun
107 North Roberson Street
Chapel Hill, NC 27516
$34, Sy Safransky

Swink
244 Fifth Avenue, No. 2722
New York, NY 10001
$16, Leelila Strogov

Sycamore Review
Department of English
500 Oval Drive
Purdue University
West Lafayette, IN 47907
$12, Sean M. Conrey

Tampa Review
University of Tampa
401 West Kennedy Boulevard
Tampa, FL 33606–1490
$15, Richard Mathews

Third Coast
Department of English
Western Michigan University
Kalamazoo, MI 49008–5092
$11, Glenn Deutsch

Threepenny Review
P.O. Box 9131
Berkeley, CA 94709
$16, Wendy Lesser

Timber Creek Review
8969 UNCG Station

Greensboro, NC 27413
$15, John Freiermuth

Tin House
P.O. Box 10500
Portland, OR 97296–0500
$39.80, Rob Spillman

Transition
69 Dunster Street
Harvard University
Cambridge, MA 02138
$28, Kwame Anthony Appiah, Henry Louis Gates Jr., Michael Vazquez

TriQuarterly
629 Noyes Street
Evanston, IL 60208
$24, Susan Firestone Hahn

Upstreet
P.O. Box 105
Richmond, MA 01254
$10, Vivian Dorsel

Virginia Quarterly Review
One West Range
P.O. Box 400223
Charlottesville, VA 22903
$18, Ted Genoways

War, Literature, and the Arts
Department of English and Fine Arts
2354 Fairchild Drive, Suite 6D45
USAF Academy, CO 80840–6242
$10, Donald Anderson

Water-Stone Review
Graduate School of Liberal Studies
Hamline University MS-A1730
1536 Hewitt Avenue
Saint Paul, MN 55104
$15, Mary F. Rockcastle

Weber Studies
Weber State University
1214 University Circle
Ogden, UT 84408–1214
$20, Brad Roghaar

West Branch
Bucknell Hall
Bucknell University
Lewisburg, PA 17837
$10, Paula Closson Buck

Western Humanities Review
University of Utah
255 South Central Campus Drive
Room 3500
Salt Lake City, UT 84112
$16, Barry Weller

Willow Springs
Eastern Washington University
705 West First Avenue
Spokane, WA 99201
$13, Samuel Ligon

Yale Review
P.O. Box 208243
New Haven, CT 06520–8243
$27, J. D. McClatchy

Zoetrope
The Sentinel Building
916 Kearney Street
San Francisco, CA 94133
$19.95, Michael Ray

Zyzzyva
P.O. Box 590069
San Francisco, CA 94109
$28, Howard Junker

THE BEST AMERICAN SERIES®

THE BEST AMERICAN SHORT STORIES® 2008
Salman Rushdie, editor, Heidi Pitlor, series editor

ISBN: 978-0-618-78876-7 $28.00 CL
ISBN: 978-0-618-78877-4 $14.00 PA

THE BEST AMERICAN NONREQUIRED READING™ 2008
Edited by Dave Eggers, introduction by Judy Blume

ISBN: 978-0-618-90282-8 $28.00 CL
ISBN: 978-0-618-90283-5 $14.00 PA

THE BEST AMERICAN COMICS™ 2008
Lynda Barry, editor, Jessica Abel and Matt Madden, series editors

ISBN: 978-0-618-98976-8 $22.00 POB

THE BEST AMERICAN ESSAYS® 2008
Adam Gopnik, editor, Robert Atwan, series editor

ISBN: 978-0-618-98331-5 $28.00 CL
ISBN: 978-0-618-98322-3 $14.00 PA

THE BEST AMERICAN MYSTERY STORIES™ 2008
George Pelecanos, editor, Otto Penzler, series editor

ISBN: 978-0-618-81266-0 $28.00 CL
ISBN: 978-0-618-81267-7 $14.00 PA

THE BEST AMERICAN SPORTS WRITING™ 2008
William Nack, editor, Glenn Stout, series editor

ISBN: 978-0-618-75117-4 $28.00 CL
ISBN: 978-0-618-75118-1 $14.00 PA

THE BEST AMERICAN TRAVEL WRITING™ 2008
Anthony Bourdain, editor, Jason Wilson, series editor

ISBN: 978-0-618-85863-7 $28.00 CL
ISBN: 978-0-618-85864-4 $14.00 PA

THE BEST AMERICAN SCIENCE AND NATURE WRITING™ 2008
Jerome Groopman, editor, Tim Folger, series editor

ISBN: 978-0-618-83446-4 $28.00 CL
ISBN: 978-0-618-83447-1 $14.00 PA

THE BEST AMERICAN SPIRITUAL WRITING™ 2008
Edited by Philip Zaleski, introduction by Jimmy Carter

ISBN: 978-0-618-83374-0 $28.00 CL
ISBN: 978-0-618-83375-7 $14.00 PA